BLUE ICE

by
Karin Richardson

A Deer Creek Mystery

BLUE ICE is also available as a Kindle edition from
Amazon.com

10 9 8 7 6 5 4 3 2 1

ISBN 978-1-57550-059-1

Printed in the United States of America
Cover Art by Johanna M. Bolton

*BLUE ICE is a work of fiction. All the characters
and events portrayed in this book are fictional, and
any resemblance to real people and incidents is
purely coincidental.*

Win this beautiful aquamarine necklace!

The author is offering a beautiful emerald-cut aquamarine necklace set in sterling silver to one of her readers. The winner will be chosen by raffle from among the readers who leave a review on Amazon. The raffle will be held after the sale of the 100th copy of *BLUE ICE* or November 14th, 2016, whichever comes first. The winner will be announced on the Facebook page: Deer Creek Mystery Series by Karin Richardson.

The necklace in the book has an interesting story. Oh, yes, it's an actual necklace! Originally it was a ring and the author said that she used to play with it when she was a small child. "I thought it was just a pretty piece of costume jewelry! One of my relatives wore the ring when she came over from Sweden as a young bride," Richardson said. "Later my mother had the ring made into the necklace that was the inspiration for this book."

Write a review in Amazon, and you could end up wearing this gorgeous aquamarine set in sterling silver!

(The photo is of the actual necklace that will be awarded in the raffle.)

I want to dedicate the first book
of my new series
to my grandmother,

Ruth Ann Lilgestrom Kraft

for being a kind, loving, and strong role model
in my life.

I would also like to thank my husband, Kerry,
and our son, Alex
for always being there for me.

Lastly, a shout out to Glenn for helping with
the book, and to Don Kafrissen for opening
new doors in my life, and to Johanna Bolton for
making the book happen.

Chapter 1

"Ruth Ann, pick up…hurry!"

"Please, Ruth Ann, I don't have much time left…I need to hear your voice."

"This may be my last seconds and I need to tell you that you and the girls have been the most important part of my life and I love you all more than I can ever say."

"You need to know there are 2 gunmen on the plane and they're desperately trying to get into the cockpit. They have the 2 flight attendants held with guns to their heads and threatening to shoot them and all of us if they don't get in."

Deep breaths were heard through the phone line.

"I may lose you any second with this airline phone but…

"Oh no! They got into the cockpit … wait … yes…"

Loud bangs were heard through the phone line.

"They're taking the plane down, Ruth Ann … I'm so sorry to leave you, but always remember I love…"

Phone line went dead.

I woke in a sweat. It's been a long time since I've had that nightmare and I thought it wouldn't happen again. It's been about twenty years since that horrific night when my husband's plane crashed and left me and my two ten-year-old twin daughters behind. I'll never forgive myself for not being home that night to comfort my husband in his last moments.

There was no particular reason for the dream to occur that night. It was actually my favorite time of year, right before the winter ski season begins and the tourists flood into my small, quiet Colorado town. Halloween was only two weeks away and there was already quite a chill in the air.

I moved to Deer Creek about twenty years ago after losing my husband in that horrible airplane accident. At the time of the accident we were living near Los Angeles with our twins, Nancy and Lynne. I had just gone back to work as a research assistant in an antique auction house. It was time to go back to work since the twins were older and kept themselves busy with school and activities.

Our small town is at the base of Deer Creek Mountain in western Colorado near Grand Junction. It's a massive mountain that isn't listed in the travel books. In fact, outside of Grand Junction we're quite isolated, surrounded only by mountains and numerous creeks. I liked it that way, except during ski season. All the people from the popular ski resorts who didn't want to spend their life's fortune came to Deer Creek Run, the only ski resort in town. That is, if they ever heard of it. But once they did, they were sure to return.

Henry Hamilton, our town mayor, wanted to keep it that way. He liked our town to be clean and virtually free of crime by controlling the number of inhabitants. I personally thought we could use another resort just for jobs and keeping costs in check.

I never planned on being a widow in my early thirties. It was so horrific that I packed up the twins and moved. I didn't have much family except a sister, Irene, had who moved to a small Colorado town with her husband a few years back. They never had any children but stayed very involved with kids since Irene was a schoolteacher in town and her husband worked for a toy distributor in Grand Junction. They didn't want to live in a large town and by sheer dumb luck came upon Deer Creek one day while exploring the area. That was all it took, the town just stuck out to them and they moved there immediately.

After talking with Irene about my predicament living in Los Angeles, she suggested I bring the girls out to them for a visit. I figured it was worth the visit. I never imagined we'd permanently move there, but just like my sister, I fell in love with the town.

Fast forward twenty years and we're still here. It was exactly what the girls and I needed. The town hasn't changed much since we've been here. Surrounding the town was a creek that was used for fishing, swimming and small boating. It was your basic small town except for the ski resort run by Richard and Carol Dickson. That was the breadwinner of our town. If the resort didn't do well financially, nothing else did either.

We had two seasons here for the tourists, winter ski season and summer hiking and fishing season. If there was a mild winter our town suffered and jobs were lost. However, we've been lucky for the last ten years or so and have had tons of snow.

The resort is the largest building in town. It was designed to look like an enormous log cabin. The Dickson family has owned this resort for many generations. I believe Richard's great-great grandfather built the place and over the years the family has added to the structure and renovated numerous times. It really is a beautiful resort and even the local residents stay there once in a while for a treat.

There are only three eating-places in town. One is in the resort, which is known for their elegant cuisine. The other is in the lower level of the resort and serves burgers, pizza, and ice cream. The third restaurant is a family owned café, Deer Creek Café, run by Wilma Pennington. She's run that café as long as I've been living here. Wilma is the town gossip. If you want to know anything about anyone just go and eat at the café. But plan on spending double the amount of time you intended because Wilma will never stop talking.

The layout of Deer Creek is one long Main Street with the ski resort smack dab in the middle. Main Street is only about a mile or so long and is full of shops and businesses. The resort takes up most of it. On one end of the street is the café. Going up the street from the café is a small grocery store, a bakery, a hardware store, a gas station, then you run into the entrance to the resort. On the other side of the resort are the more practical businesses such as the Town Hall, which houses the post office, the police department and jail, judges and lawyers' offices, a bank, and medical offices for a doctor and a vet, and lastly a real estate office.

Down the street a bit past the businesses are the schools. A kiddy care facility and library are also located there because it is the only area large enough for a sports field.

 Just behind Main Street is a small hospital. Grand Junction was used for serious medical issues, but since we are a ski resort town, the mayor felt it was best to have a small functioning hospital in town.

Most of the houses and apartments are scattered behind the

businesses on Main Street. The large ski mountain and surrounding creeks don't leave a large amount of space, but there were still quite a few houses built in the area.

I neglected to mention my business. I opened a business about a year ago, after many years of volunteering and working at the schools as a substitute teacher. I was fortunate that I didn't have to work, because my husband's life insurance provided for us. I never spent any of the money unless it was absolutely necessary. I can only think of two times before opening the store that I used the money. The first was to purchase a house here in town. The second time was to pay for both my daughters' college education.

Lynne and Nancy went together to the University of Denver. Lynne studied food science and nutrition while Nancy went into education. Lynne opened the local bakery here and I blame her for the ten extra pounds I can never lose. Nancy became a schoolteacher locally and teaches American history for high school students. I feel blessed that they came back to our small town to work and be close to their mom.

Back to my business. I mentioned earlier that I worked for an antique auction house back in Los Angeles. I loved doing the research and learning about a piece's history. So I decided to open an antique store named Ruth Ann's. Ruth Ann's is named after the owner, me! I was able to obtain an open space between the hardware store and the gas station that used to be a small parking lot. I purchased the lot and had a two story Victorian house built. I don't live in the house, but thought it would be appropriate to have an antique business in a Victorian building.

It was quite an expensive undertaking due to our remote location, and materials had to be hauled in from Grand Junction. It took a year to build and furnish, but the outcome was marvelous. From my lucrative business earnings so far, it appears most tourists love to browse in an antique store. Much of the inventory in my store came from the locals and the rest I purchased online through my contacts back in LA. It's amazing how much knowledge I've gained from using a computer. If I don't recognize an item I just research it online and get my price. I haven't come across an item I couldn't price until recently. This is where my story really begins.

As I mentioned in the beginning of this tale, it was mid-October and getting into the winter ski season. The summer tourists were gone and the town was gearing up for a busy winter. My store was also getting quite full of items for sale. The ski season isn't the only thing that spurs my business. Christmas is right around the corner, and unique and odd gifts are my specialty, so I enjoy having a full store.

My daughter Lynne's business was only a couple doors down from me and even though I wouldn't trade being so close for anything, I wish it wasn't a bakery she ran. Daily I'm there trying her new baked goods. I pride myself in the fact that I exercise daily, however, it doesn't counteract the sweets I consume daily. My weaknesses for food consist of sweets and pizza. Give me a cold piece (or two) of pizza for breakfast and I'm a happy camper.

Getting back on track, the bakery, named Sinful Sweets, is close and I'm always walking up and down our street to walk off whatever I just consumed at Lynne's place. It was during one of these walks on a Friday afternoon around 5 pm when my life took a wild turn. I was doing my version of speed walking in walking shoes, skirt and blouse since I was also working that day. I had just finished a new brownie my daughter created with caramel and three different chocolates mixed in. I must tell you that one of my favorite things in life is to eat brownie dough. Lynne's aware of this and saved me scoopfuls of her dough. Besides eating the dough, I also had to try the baked version of her brownie, too. So let's just say I was feeling a bit sick to my stomach (regular event after leaving her store) and needed to walk and digest all the chocolate.

I figured if I walked to the end of Main Street and back a few times it would equal about two to three miles. Not too bad, but not near enough to walk off what I ate. As I passed the resort I saw Carol, the owner, pulling into the entrance. Carol stopped, rolled down her window and asked laughing, "What did you eat today, Ruth Ann?"

"Very funny Carol," I said with a smile on my face. "It was brownies. Or should I say brownie dough and cooked ooey gooey caramel brownies."

"That sounds wonderful!" Carol said, licking her lips wishing she had a taste. "Maybe she can send a batch to the resort."

"I think Lynne was really happy with them. She mentioned that she was going to add them to the menu. She can warm them up so the caramel oozes out and she thinks it's a good winter comfort item." I added, "I believe she's right... after devouring quite a few of them."

"Well, have her come see me with a few samples. That sounds like a perfect item for the ice cream shop. Who doesn't like brownies topped with ice cream?"

"Thanks Carol, I'll pop in and tell her on my way back down the street. I know she appreciates all the business you give her.

Carol said, "I should be the one to thank her, she's a terrific baker and we hike up the price so it has been quite profitable for us, too!" Carol rolled up her window and waved good-bye.

I continued down the street and passed the offices of A & A Roberts Law Offices, and was about to pass by the bank. It should be closed by now since it was after 5 pm and Doug, the president of the bank, always ran a tight ship and locked the doors promptly at 5 pm, especially on Fridays. Doug usually went to the resort for their Friday Fish Fry. It was all you can eat for $14.95 and that was a bargain considering Doug was a large man with a big appetite. Lucy, his secretary, sometimes stayed later to organize herself for the next work day. She had a key and could let herself out the back entrance which led to a long alley that all the businesses up and down Main Street shared. The alley only broke off for the resort since it took up much more depth than the rest of the stores along the street. I loved having the alley behind my antique store. It was the only entrance I utilized, plus my products were all delivered back there.

I was approaching the bank looking inside the large front window. The bank itself was small, no bigger than Lynne's bakery and the front was mostly windows. Personally, I think that's strange because anyone could break through a window and rob the bank. However, if someone wanted in badly enough they would find a way no matter what the building looked like. We live in such a small town if anybody broke a window that size people would come running.

As I was staring through the windows of the bank I was suddenly distracted by a loud *bang*. It sounded like a mini explosion. Loud enough to startle me but not knock me over. I stopped and tried to figure out where the sound came from when I spotted a dim light coming from inside the bank. From my knowledge of the bank, the light came from Doug's office in the back of the bank. That was strange since I knew it was late and Doug was surely gone. Lucy wasn't even allowed in his office once he left the bank. Suddenly, I saw movement near his door and wondered if Lucy was actually still in there and knew what caused the noise.

I wasn't sure what to do when all of a sudden a blurred image dressed in black from their pants to a black hooded sweatshirt ran toward the back exit. This was the door that opened to the alley. For one split second our eyes met and I dropped to my knees hoping that he or she didn't see me. As I stayed hunched down near the ground, my site line was blocked by the brick below the windows.

I waited only a second or two then slowly peered over the edge of the window to peek inside. My only thought was that whoever was inside the bank was up to no good and if they identified me I could be in serious danger. My eyes were squeezed shut as I kneeled and grabbed the edge of the window, but then I slowly opened them and looked inside. It appeared to be quiet, no sign of movement.

What now? My instincts should've been to call the police from my cell phone, but my feet didn't listen to my head. I ran around the side of the building knowing the alley was in the back. I wanted to see if there was any sign of who had been there and what direction they might have gone. As I reached the entrance to the alley I slowed my pace. I didn't want to rush in until I knew it was safe.

I leaned up against the building and looked around the corner toward the back door. There was no one in sight that I could see so far, but I did notice the back door of the bank stood ajar. I ran toward the door thinking that if someone was there they sure weren't going to hang around after they robbed the bank. I knew not to touch the door handle of the steel back door, so I took my coat sleeve and pushed the door open enough so I could see inside.

The back room was dark and the only light spilling in was from the street lamp in the alley. I couldn't see anything so I carefully and very quietly walked inside the back door of the bank. I entered a small lunchroom. There were a few long tables set up and I could see two vending machines and a large refrigerator. One of the vending machines was lit up and sold beverages and the other machine looked to be full of snacks. The room was dark except for the vending machines and an emergency light above the back door. I had never been in this part of the bank before. I assumed it was just for the employees. At this point I knew I should call the police, but I was so full of adrenaline I chose to take a quick peek first and then call.

As I left the break room through a swinging door, I entered the main heart of the bank. There were teller stations and several glassed in offices. The president's office was the largest one at the back of the bank. This is where I could still see a dim light glowing. I tip toed over toward the door, but before I reached the office I tripped over a large object on the floor. I couldn't see much of anything so I pulled out my cell phone and turned on the flashlight app. As I aimed my phone toward the floor I realized I tripped over a large briefcase. I didn't want to touch it in case the police would want to dust for fingerprints. But I did notice the initials, DMA imprinted on the front in large gold letters. It had to be Doug's since his name was Doug Albertson. I had no idea what the M stood for, but that was irrelevant at the moment.

I stepped over the briefcase and stood at the door to Doug's office. Before looking in I quietly asked, "Is, anyone in there, Doug?"

There was no answer so I decided to enter and noticed Doug's desk loaded with papers. The chair was swiveled around so the back faced me. Outside of the small desk lamp that was on I couldn't see anything out of the ordinary. My heart rate finally slowed to a normal pace and my head told me to go back to the alley and call John Wilkinson, the Police Chief and explain what happened.

I turned to leave the office when I heard a slight squeak from the desk chair. My heart skipped a beat then started racing again. I couldn't move. My eyes were fixed on Doug's chair when I noticed the chair move just ever so slightly. I jumped and tried to run but my feet took me in the wrong direction. I ended up standing next to Doug's desk.

What I saw at that moment I'll never forget. In the chair was Doug Albertson, the bank president, tied up in ropes with a large cloth stuffed in his mouth. I noticed he wasn't conscious and it terrified me to think that he could be dead. I put my finger on his wrist and felt for a pulse.

"Thank God," I whispered. "There's a pulse, slow, but still a pulse," I said out loud to myself.

"Doug, Doug, can you hear me?" I frantically called as I took ahold of his shoulders and gave a little shake, and then pulled the gag out of his mouth. No response. I shook him again, and as I did I noticed there was blood all over my hands. I screamed so loud it must have forced Doug to open his eyes!

"Doug, can you hear me? You're bleeding from your head." Nothing, just his open eyes staring back at me.

"I need to call the police and get you help, hold on, please Doug!" I wiped my hands on my coat and pulled out my cell phone from my pocket and dialed 9-1-1.

Delores, the police department's secretary picked up the call, "Please state your emergency," she requested.

"Delores, it's Ruth Ann. I'm at the bank and Doug's been hurt. It looks like a break in and they tied him up. Someone must've bashed him over the head because there's blood all over his clothes."

"Ruth Ann?" she asked calmly.

"Delores, please, send an ambulance right away!"

"Wait, Ruth Ann, are you telling me you were at the bank during the break in?" Then she added, "Is Doug alive?"

"Yes, he has a weak pulse, but it's there. He also popped his eyes open for a few seconds but he can't respond to me."

"Ruth Ann, I put in the request for police and an ambulance. Are you safe, can you hang in there until they arrive?"

"Yes, it's all clear, I saw someone in here as I was walking past the bank and then heard a loud noise, like an explosion. I looked inside the bank and saw a figure running out the back of the bank into the alley."

"Did he see you?" Delores asked, worried.

"I think so. For a split second our eyes met as I looked in, and as he or she was running out of Doug's office." I added, "I'm not sure if they really saw me, but by the time I got around to the back I noticed no one was around and the back door to the bank was partially opened."

"Ruth Ann, you should've called the police immediately and never ran to the back. You could've been hurt or worse if they caught you!"

"I know Delores, but it all happened so fast and I just reacted." I added, "I'm sure I'll hear all that and more from Chief John. It was stupid; I just couldn't seem to help myself."

"Well, at least you're safe and that's what's important. And that Doug's still alive, too." Delores added, "But I wonder why this happened, do you think it was a burglary?"

"Nothing seems to be amiss from what I can tell. I only looked around in Doug's office but it seems everything's in place. I haven't walked around the bank's lobby area so maybe they did rob the bank and then noticed Doug was here in his office so they tied him up and gagged him. Then they smashed his head with something to knock him out."

Delores said, "The police are just pulling up now, so don't be alarmed when they enter the bank. I'll hang up when I hear them in the background. Take care of yourself Ruth Ann, and don't leave anything out when telling John."

"Ok, thanks Delores, you talked me through this and my nerves are a little better. Doug's still unconscious, but I just checked and he still has a pulse. Thank God for that." All of a sudden there was a loud crash as two policemen and Chief John kicked in the front door and rushed into the bank.

"Bye, Ruth Ann. Let me know how it goes," Delores said, disconnecting the line.

I rushed over to the chief and asked, "Where's the ambulance? We need to get Doug to the hospital right away!"

"Where is he?" Chief John asked.

"He's in his office in his chair. Hurry, I think he's lost a lot of blood."

Chief John ordered his officers to go to the office but he didn't move. John turned back to me, "What on earth happened here, Ruth Ann? Why are you covered in blood?"

"It's a long story and I promise I'll tell you everything after we get Doug medical attention!" I answered rather curtly, sensing his accusatory look. "But I'll tell you I had nothing to do with any of this."

"I'm sure you didn't. I didn't mean to sound like I was blaming you. You could never hurt anyone, Ruth Ann."

"Look, John, I was just walking by the bank when I heard a

bang and saw a figure dressed in black running out the back door toward the alley." I looked at John's reaction for a moment but since he didn't interrupt me I continued, "I made a quick decision and ran to the alley to see if I could see the person…"

John looked stunned and asked, "You did what?"

"I know. I should've immediately called you, but I didn't have any time to think so I just reacted. I knew something was terribly wrong and had to see if I could help. I'm fine, nobody was there by the time I got to the alley."

"Ok, Ruth Ann. I get why you did it even though it was completely wrong and you could've gotten yourself killed." He took a deep breath to regain his composure. "However, when you got to the alley you should have called 9-1-1, not entered the bank. What were you thinking?"

I was becoming exasperated with the chief and repeated myself, "I told you I wasn't thinking, I just reacted. I saw the back door was partially opened and I knew the figure was gone so I truly believed I was safe. I needed to see if anyone from the bank was hurt so I very carefully entered and looked around. I touched nothing as I looked around until I found Doug in his office. I only touched him to see if he had a pulse. That was how I got blood on myself."

The chief shook his head and said, "Ruth Ann, I know you believe what you did was right, but promise me you'll never do that again!" Then he added, "Not that something like this would ever happen again."

"Ok, I get it John, just go to Doug and see if he's conscious yet," I begged, and finally John ran into Doug's office.

I heard the sirens for the ambulance closing in and I rushed into the office when Chief John yelled, "Stop, Ruth Ann!"

I froze just as I had one foot in Doug's office. "I just want you to know the ambulance is here."

"Oh, thanks, I just can't risk any more contamination in this area so please go and direct the paramedics," John stated.

I turned and ran to the front entrance of the bank. The paramedics were pulling a gurney out the back of the ambulance when I called out to them, "He's in here, go to the back of the bank and you'll see the office and police. Please hurry, the president of the bank has been seriously injured."

I must mention that the paramedics are part of our town's local fire department. The hospital is not equipped to handle major injuries so I wondered if they would fly him to Grand Junction Memorial after they examined him. I followed the paramedics to just outside Doug's office and looked on as they pulled him off the chair onto the floor. The police were blocking most of my view, but I did hear them radio his vitals to the local hospital. They were moving so quickly that before I knew it Doug was on the gurney, wrapped up, and strapped in as they rushed him out to the waiting ambulance.

I was going to follow them to the hospital when Chief John stopped me. "Ruth Ann, we're not done here. You need to go with Dave to the station and give a complete statement."

"But John, I need to see how Doug's doing; can't this possibly wait till later?" I pleaded. "I already told you most of what happened. Please can I go to the hospital?"

"I'm sorry but you need to go with Dave now while it's all fresh in your mind," Chief John ordered.

Dave walked over to me and put his hand on my arm to lead me away. I wasn't too happy as I shrugged his hand away. Chief John saw me do this and told his man, "Just leave her be, she'll follow you." Dave nodded and started to walk toward the front entrance.

"Please Ruth Ann, I have to follow police policies. I don't want anything to mess up my investigation. Just go with Dave, he'll drive you home afterward and you can drive over to the hospital then. It'll probably take Doc Albert a while to examine him and make his assessment anyway."

"Oh all right, I'll go. Not because I won't remember what happened, but you're probably right about Doc Albert needing time with Doug." I turned and followed Dave out of the bank and into his police car.

Policeman Dave was new to the department and quite young and a little too ambitious in my opinion. He's known around town as the Rule Enforcer and he just confirmed that by turning on the lights and siren with me in the back seat. I looked like the town criminal and I wasn't happy at all.

"Was that necessary, Dave?" I asked. "I'm not under arrest so why the lights and siren?"

"Just following the rules, ma'am," he replied.

Ma'am, I thought to myself, really? "Fine, let's just get this over with so I can leave and go to the hospital."

He led me into the police station and I passed by Delores, the secretary and manager of the station. Her eyes popped wide open as she watched me being led to Dave's desk. I sat down on the chair next to the desk and he asked, "Can I get you some coffee or water, ma'am?"

"No, thank you," I snapped.

Dave pulled out a pad of paper and a small device to record our conversation. I put a note in the back of my mind to tell the chief what I thought about this policy!

First, Dave asked why I was at the bank. I explained I was just walking by and he looked at me with a quizzical stare. "Why would you be walking over here on the business side of town? The bank was already closed."

"Let's just get this straight, Dave," I said sarcastically. "I was at my daughter's bakery and ate a little too many sweets so I laced up my walking shoes and started down the street." I added, "If you continue with this line of questioning as if I'm guilty of anything outside of being at the wrong place at the wrong time then you better hire me a lawyer!"

That did it. He rolled his head from side to side as if to stretch and took a deep breath and said, "I'm sorry. You're not a suspect; I'm just used to dealing with criminals and their interrogations. I promise I'll tone it down. So can we go on?"

I nodded and began to retrace my steps. He wrote fast and looked up when I was done and asked, "Is that everything you can remember?"

"I believe so, yes," I answered.

"So let me go through some of the information you gave me, step by step." He looked up from his pad of paper and added, "If that's alright with you?"

"Of course," I answered in a much cheerier tone.

He smiled at me, acknowledging that he was handling his questioning with more grace. "So, did you hear the loud bang before you reached the bank or after?"

"Right in front of the bank window," I answered.

"Ok, after the loud bang you said you dropped down to the

ground and then slowly peeked up over the edge so you could look in the window, correct?"

"Yes, that's what I did," I replied.

"That was when you saw a figure dressed in black toward the back of the bank running to the back exit, correct?" Dave asked.

"Yes, wait no! I dropped to the ground after I saw the figure dressed in black," I answered.

"What kind of black clothes was the person wearing? Was it black pants or jeans and a black shirt or jacket?" he questioned.

"I don't know for sure," I answered, trying to envision that scene again. "Wait, I don't know what kind of pants, but he was wearing a black hoodie sweatshirt with the hood pulled over his head."

"That's good, see you remember more details as you go over and over it," he said, smiling. "Why do you say he was wearing a black hoodie," Dave inquired.

"Because the size and shape, I guess," I answered.

"Keep going, explain," Dave said.

"Well, he seemed stocky, like over 200 pounds and when he looked at me," I was immediately interrupted.

"What did you just say?" Dave asked.

"I said, when our eyes met for a brief second, I could swear that it was a man," Even I was stunned when those words left my lips. "Oh my God, I forgot about that moment. I'm sorry, Dave, I didn't even remember that happened until now."

"That, Mrs. Conroy, is why we have you make your statement as close to the crime as possible," Dave said smugly. "That's great, let's keep going."

"Ok, but now I think you know it all. Am I in danger if he recognized me?" I asked tentatively.

"You never can be sure, but can you tell me what color eyes he had?" Dave questioned.

"No. He was pretty far away and it was dark. All I know was that when I looked in he was on his way out of the office and he looked out at the window at the exact time I was looking in. I couldn't tell you what color anything was except for the black clothing." I added, "I'm sorry, that doesn't help you very much. Hey, maybe he didn't really see me but just paused to look outside to make sure no one was in front of the bank. I was on my knees just peering in."

"That's a possibility, ma'am," Dave said, writing all this down.

"I feel better actually. Maybe the person didn't see me at all," I said.

"I'll go over all this with the chief and see what he thinks about it. Can we move forward to you going into the office?" Dave asked.

"Yes, what more can I tell you about that?"

"When you walked into the office you said nothing was out of order?" Dave asked.

"Yes," I answered.

"But how would you know? Do you frequent Mr. Albertson's office?" Dave asked quizzically.

"Not too often, but we're friends so whenever I do my banking I stop in and talk with Doug. We go back a number of years," I replied.

"Ok, so when you were about to leave you mentioned that a noise caught your attention and you turned back and walked over to the desk, is that correct?"

"Yes, I was about to leave thinking no one was in his office when I heard a squeak, like from a chair. So I walked over and that was when I discovered Doug unconscious in his desk chair," I stated.

"Then what did you do, again?" he asked.

"I rushed up to him to see if he had a pulse," I stopped and blurted out, "No wait, I called his name out first and then took his pulse."

"So he didn't reply when you called out his name?" Dave asked.

"No, there was no reply until after I checked his pulse. I screamed because of all the blood, and his eyes popped wide open," I stopped and added, "Uh oh, I did it again didn't I?" I asked Dave.

"Go on please," Dave said.

"I forgot to mention that after I found his pulse I backed away and looked down at my blood covered hands. And when I looked up I was shocked to find his eyes were open. I tried to get a response from him but there was none. It was then I noticed the blood all over his neck and shirt. I looked at the back of his head and noticed that was where the blood was coming from."

"Very good, see the more you go over this, the more comes out," Dave said proudly. "What did you see on his head, a gash or a bump?"

"I didn't look long enough," I said. "That was when I called the police."

"Ok, that's really good, thanks," Dave replied.

"Are we almost finished here?" I inquired. "I would really like to get over to the hospital."

"Yes," Dave answered, finishing up writing in his notepad. He snapped the lid shut and looked up at me. "I'll drive you home, it's getting late."

"That's ok, I can walk. I only live about four blocks from here."

"No, the chief would have my head if I let anything happen to you. You two seem pretty friendly with each other," Dave said, smirking

"We go way back, too," I answered quickly to satisfy his curiosity about our relationship. "Wait, what do you mean not let anything happen to me? Am I in danger?"

"Oh, no that's not what I meant," Dave replied in a hurry. "It's just that it's dark out and I'm sure you're in a hurry to get home so you can drive over to the hospital."

"Good answer, Dave!" I said smiling. "Ok, you can drive me because I'm in a hurry, not because I'm afraid."

Dave stood up, grabbed his keys and led me to his car. It only took about two minutes to drive me home but he was right, it was quicker. I was about to exit his car when he advised, "Be cautious of your surroundings just in case, ma'am."

I didn't want to further our conversation so I said, "I will, thank you," and exited the car. I hurried to the front door of my house and noticed that Dave waited until I was safely inside. Hmmm, I thought, maybe I should be more careful just in case the bank criminal spotted me. I hurried inside and threw my purse on the bench right inside my foyer. I ran down the hall to the right to my bedroom and bathroom. All I wanted to do was wash my hands thoroughly. The blood had been wiped off but I still felt dirty and needed my own soap to feel truly clean. After making sure there were no signs of blood, I went into my closet and pulled out a sweater and pants. I headed toward the kitchen and grabbed a bottle of water and an apple from the refrigerator. I was hungry but not for sweets or junk. I rushed back to the front door, grabbed my purse and headed back to the kitchen and out the door to the garage. All I wanted to do was to get over to the hospital to check on Doug.

I was about to step into the garage when my cell phone rang. "Not now," I said out loud. I let it ring and figured when I was waiting around at the hospital I'll call whoever it was back.

Thinking about what the young policeman, Dave, said, I decided to go back into the house and turn on a few lights so it appeared the house was occupied. Just in case, I said to myself. I hurried from room to room turning on lights in two bedrooms, the great room and kitchen area. Feeling more comfortable, I went out into the garage and hopped in my car.

Chapter 2

I learned pretty quickly that one needed a sturdy SUV to get around our mountainous area. So I purchased my first SUV twenty years ago and have been driving one since. My newest truck was only a year old and bright yellow. It may sound like a strange color to buy, but white, gold, and silver just blended into the surroundings, so I knew either cherry red or yellow would be best. Driving around in a bright yellow SUV definitely stuck out in the snow. But what I didn't consider was that it made me a target, too.

I zoomed down a couple side streets that led to Main and drove to the end of the street near the schools. Just before the school lot was a side street that wound around behind the medical offices and Andy and Arthur's law practice. About a quarter mile down the street I entered the small parking lot for the hospital. I parked my car and ran into the front entrance.

The lobby of the hospital was a small white, sterile room with a desk straight ahead of the front doors. There were small seating arrangements spread throughout the room for patients and visitors to gather and wait. I headed straight for the desk where Claire Owens, the hospital's receptionist sat. She was reading a book as I hurried over to her.

"Claire," I said, trying to get her attention. "Did you see where they took Doug? He was brought in here over an hour ago I think?"

"Yes, he's here with Doc Albert. Why don't you sit down and as soon as the Doc's done I'll have him come talk with you."

"But do you know his condition? He must still be alive if Doc Albert is still with him, that's a relief," I said, taking a deep breath.

"Oh dear, Ruth Ann, I have no idea what condition he's in. He looked pretty bad when they rolled him in here. The paramedics had Doc meet them at the front door. I think it was pretty bad."

"Thanks a lot, Claire," I said sarcastically. I watched Claire as she adjusted her "nurse's hat" that she wore to look more official. Everyone knew Claire had zero nurse's training. She was just the receptionist, and informed people where to go. I could tell my temper was making her nervous so I said, "I'm sorry, I'm just so worried about Doug."

Claire smiled and said, "I'm sure he's okay, just give Doc a little more time. If he's not out soon I'll go look for Shirley."

"Thanks, Claire." Shirley was Doc Albert's nurse and had been with him for as long as I knew. She was extremely protective of Doc and everyone knew not to cross her or she would hold a grudge forever. I decided to sit down on one of the chairs closest to Claire's desk and wait. Shirley and I got along fine, but if I got too pushy with her she might not tell me anything. I had a feeling Shirley was right alongside Doc Albert because rumor had it that Shirley had a bit of a crush on Doug. They both were single and widowed, but I didn't think Doug had any interest in Shirley. The reason I knew is because Doug's been after me for a number of years and has told me many times that I'm the only one he's wanted to date since his wife passed away.

However, time passed and I kept Doug hanging too long so maybe he has turned to Shirley. I haven't dated much since I've been widowed myself, but I have enjoyed many male friendships. The other friendship I have is with Chief John. We've gone to several town functions and have enjoyed each other's companionship. Chief John has never married so I'm aware that he would like to get married one day, but I'm not there, yet.

As I sat waiting for news, I pondered my two, let's call them, relationships. Chief John and Doug, the bank president. How strange it is giving a statement to John about Doug being attacked. They were both aware that each of them had feelings for me. It's funny at my age, two men fighting for my attention! I smiled as I thought about this and when I looked up I saw Shirley standing right smack in front of me.

"Shirley," I called out as I popped up out of my chair, "How's Doug? Please tell me he's doing okay?"

Shirley looked at me for a moment before snapping, "He's

alive if that's what you want to know." She looked as if I was the person responsible for putting Doug in the hospital.

"What on earth is your problem, Shirley? You look like you're ticked off at me! I didn't do anything but find Doug and save his life!" I barked. "Well, I personally didn't save his life but I found him and called for help."

Shirley relaxed a little, but not much. She wasn't exactly fond of me anyway; jealous would be the word. "He's still with Doc Albert, but I thought I'd come out and tell you he's still hanging in there. Claire informed me you were here waiting for word on his condition."

"Thanks, Shirley," I said, trying to diffuse her attitude toward me. "Can't you tell me anything else?"

"He's stable for the moment, thanks to Doc, but it was touch and go when he arrived. Doug lost a lot of blood thanks to the head bashing he received." Shirley's face turned a deep shade of red and added, "Who would ever commit such a violent crime?"

"I don't know, Shirley, but we'll catch whoever did this!" I proclaimed.

"And how do you know that? The burglar probably is out of state by now!" Shirley remarked sarcastically.

"C'mon Shirley, we're on the same side with this one. Please try to be civil to me. I know you don't like me very much anyway."

"Ruth Ann! Why would you think I didn't like you?" Shirley answered, appearing totally shocked.

"Seriously? Shirley, you know Doug has been a close friend for years and I'm aware that you would like a closer relationship with Doug. Maybe become more than just friends, eh?" I asked.

"This isn't the time to discuss any of this!" she snapped. "I need to get back to Doc. I only came out to tell you he was still alive and being treated. I'll come out when I have more information for you." Shirley said, turning and going back through the double doors that led into the hospital rooms.

She didn't even give me a second to say thanks. But I sure got my answer about how she feels about dating Doug. Her glare spoke a thousand words.

I walked over to the desk where Claire was sitting reading her book.

"Well that went well, didn't it?" Claire said smiling. "I told you Shirley would get all bent out of shape being interrupted. I went back there after I noticed you were still sitting here and asked about Doug's condition. I mentioned you were out here waiting." Claire put her book down and added, "She immediately snapped at me and told me that she would come out when she was ready."

"Well, she sure takes her job seriously, I guess," I said.

"No, the minute she heard you were here all concerned she turned a bit hostile," Claire said. "She really doesn't like you very much does she?"

"I don't think so. She claims she doesn't have an issue with me but her attitude tells a different story."

Claire laughed a little and said, "It's all about Doug. She wants him and she knows he only has eyes for you. She tries and tries to be all sweet and nice to him but he just doesn't respond romantically to her."

"Oh! Please Claire, Doug and I are just friends," I exclaimed.

"Maybe on your side, but everyone knows he would give just about anything to date you," she stated emphatically.

"Hmmm, He's so sweet and I just haven't seriously thought about him that way. Maybe it's time I rethink things and give him a chance." I added, "I hope I get the chance, that is."

Claire stood up and walked around to the front of the desk where I was standing and put her arms around me in a tight hug and said, "Ruth Ann, he will make it! Doc Albert's the best and he won't let anything happen to Doug."

"Thanks, Claire, I needed that." I gently backed away from her and wiped a tear from the corner of my eye. I was surprised at my reaction. I guess I'm ready to move on more than I thought. But was Doug the one or John?

I walked back to my chair and sat down. I pulled out my phone and checked my messages. I had missed 31 texts? Wow, I don't think I know 31 people here in town I said to myself jokingly. Well it wasn't 31 people. The texts were all from Lynne, who knew I went for a walk and never went back to her bakery or my store.

I quickly dialed her cell number. There was no answer so I decided to text her briefly and tell her what happened. While I was texting a rather long message, my phone rang.

"Hello," I answered.

"Ruth Ann, it's John. Are you still at the hospital?" The chief inquired.

"Yes John, I'm still waiting. Doc's working on Doug and I have no information except for that he's still alive."

"Wow, that's all you've got?" he asked, surprised.

"Yes, Shirley came out and that's all she said. You know Shirley and how seriously she takes her job as Doc's nurse."

"Ah, Shirley," John said. "She has a personal stake in this one, too."

"Yes, I'm aware that she has feelings for Doug and for all I know they could be dating," I stated.

"Dating, huh?" John asked. "Interesting don't you think?"

"Why so interesting? Doug's single and so is Shirley, I assume. They're free to date anyone they like!" I snapped.

"Of course they are, Ruth Ann. I wasn't being snarky, just thought it funny that she's all protective of Doug."

"Wait a minute," I quickly said. "Do you think Shirley had something to do with Doug's accident?"

"What, no, I mean jealousy can make people kill you know," John replied.

"Ok John, let me get this straight. You're saying that Shirley dressed herself all in black and broke into the bank and bashed Doug's head in because she was jealous that he has feelings for me? What a crazy, insane, out of the ballpark idea!"

"Not so unheard of Ruth Ann," John said. "I admit it's not a very solid theory and maybe she didn't even have to break in. Maybe she was already visiting Doug and excused herself to the bathroom. When the bank was officially closed and all the employees had left she came out of the bathroom dressed in black and took her anger out on Doug."

"Wow, I have no response to that, John," I cried out. "That's impossible!"

"Impossible or improbable?" he asked. "I'll call Doc Albert directly and see if I can speak with him about Doug's condition. If I hear anything more I'll call you right away."

"Thanks, John, it's getting pretty late and after my interrogation with Dave I feel a tiny bit unsafe going home alone," I stated.

"What did Dave say to you?" John asked curiously. "He's still a rookie, and I've told him hundreds of times to not scare people!"

"He got better as the interview progressed, but he did mention I could be in danger by whoever tried to kill Doug."

"I'll just have to have a little chat with him, but in the meantime, stay put and I'll come by in a little while and follow you home. How does that sound?" John asked.

"I don't want to put you out, John. I'm sure I'm ok." I thought about it for a second longer and said, "Why don't I just call you when I leave here and when I get home. Then you'll know I'm all right. If I don't answer, then check it out."

"Sounds like a plan. I'll let you know if I learn anything from Doc. Talk to you soon," John replied and hung up the phone.

I pulled up my text to Lynne, finished it and pushed send. It was pretty late but I didn't think she would mind receiving a text. She may not even see it until the morning. Her bakery starts early in the morning, so I'm pretty sure she already went to sleep.

I had just about had it with the waiting when Doc Albert pushed through the doors into the waiting area. He walked straight over to me, "Hi Ruth Ann, Shirley told me you were still here." He pulled off his gloves and tossed them into the garbage next to Claire's desk and sat down next to me. He was a tall, lean man in his late fifties. He was also single, never married I believe. Rumor has it that he had a very serious relationship and when she jilted him at the altar, he swore he'd never go through that again. Kind of sad, he would've made very good-looking children with his dark hair and baby blue eyes. His hair was graying at the temples and that made him appear very distinguished.

At the moment his blue eyes were ringed by redness. I think Doug had him scrambling to save his life and it took quite a toll on Albert. Doug and Albert were also good friends. Maybe Doc never asked me out on a date because he thought it would offend Doug; or maybe he just wasn't interested.

"He's still hanging in there. I can't be gone long. I knew you were out here and wanted to let you know how he's doing. I'll be staying with him overnight to make sure he remains stable. I would normally call and have him transported to Grand Junction Memorial, but I didn't think he would survive the trip." Doc was about to continue when I interrupted him.

"Are you saying he's that bad that he could die overnight?"

"I can't lie to you Ruth Ann, he's in bad shape. He lost a lot of blood and the severe blow created a lot of swelling around his brain. If we move him in the slightest, he could die." Doc lowered his head and rubbed the back of his neck with his hand. "I'm sorry to be so blunt, this has been very difficult working on my close friend. Especially how it happened, why would anyone try and kill him? Just to rob the bank, really?" Doc asked, exasperated.

Doc kept going, "I had a call from the chief and I told him what I just told you." He turned his face and looked directly into my brown eyes and asked, "Is it true that you were the one who rushed into the bank and found Doug?"

"Uh, I guess that is true," I replied.

"What do you mean by you guess so? John said you were the one who called and saved his life. I owe you for that, if Doug would've been left any longer he wouldn't be in the room behind those doors still alive."

"Ya, but if he doesn't survive then I did no good," I said, thinking about the danger I put myself into by running inside a bank where there was a burglary in progress.

"Yes, you gave him a chance Ruth Ann. That says it all. I understand you might've seen who did this to him. That was pretty risky don't you think? Rushing in with a criminal still there?" Doc asked.

"I didn't just rush in, Albert. I ran around to the back alley and made sure the coast was clear before I went inside. That's when I found Doug in his office. It was horrible, all the blood and Doug non-responsive."

"That had to be horrible, Ruth Ann," Doc said, patting me on my shoulder affectionately. "I'm not so sure I would be so brave!"

"I didn't think, I just reacted," I answered pensively. "If I took time to actually realize what was happening I'm not so sure myself if I would've rushed in there either."

"No matter, you did and you should be proud of yourself. You've given Doug a fighting chance and I'm going to stay positive," Doc stated emphatically. "You can send positive vibes through these walls, too," he said smiling.

"I will," I said. "You should go be with him. If there's any change will you let me know?"

"Of course, but you should go home. I'll call you with any changes. He's stable right now so go home and get some sleep,"

Doc said, standing up and heading for Claire's desk. "Claire, you go home, too. In fact, to be safe you should both leave together. I would feel better, with some lunatic running around, if you both were not out there alone."

"Sounds good, but if there's any change will you please remember to call me?" I asked.

"Of course, let's hope he stays quiet and tomorrow I'll assess whether he should recover here or go to Memorial," Doc said, taking off into the patient rooms.

The hospital isn't large. It's just a single story building with only twenty patient rooms. If there was ever a time they were swamped and needed more rooms, patients were shipped to Memorial Hospital in Grand Junction. Most patients came from ski or snowmobile accidents in the winter, and heat stroke and hiking accidents in the summer. There were local patients as well, but we rarely filled all the rooms at one time.

I asked Claire as we walked out to our cars, "How many patients are registered at the hospital right now?"

"Thank God it's really slow right now. In a couple weeks all the skiers will be here and it will fill up. Now I think only Doug and Roger Connors is here."

"What's Roger in here for? Did something happen at his hardware store"? I inquired.

"No, Ricky's running it for him while he has his tonsils removed."

"What? His tonsils? Isn't he kind of old to be having that kind of surgery," I asked.

"No, it's not common, but he's had so many cases of tonsillitis his tonsils were basically falling out by themselves," she said laughing. "He's only here a day or two, then going home."

"That's good. Then Doc Albert can give his full concentration to Doug."

"Exactly," Claire said, arriving at her car. Mine was just a row over, so I bade her goodnight and hurried over to my car.

I opened the door and made sure my car was empty. I think I've become a bit paranoid knowing there is someone out there who was capable of killing. I was about to leave when I remembered to call John to tell him I was on my way home. I was so caught up in my conversation with Albert and Claire that I almost forgot.

I pulled my cell phone out of my purse and dialed John's personal phone number. I figured he'd be at home now since it was just after midnight. He answered immediately and I said, "It's just Ruth Ann, I feel horrible calling so late, I hope I didn't wake you up?"

"Hi Ruth Ann, and no I'm not even at home. I'm still at the station working on Doug's case," John said.

"Really?" I asked. "What could you be doing at midnight, did something turn up?" I was really hoping they caught whoever did this and I could rest easy and go back to not being paranoid.

"Nothing new Ruth Ann, sorry to say. I'm going over everyone's statements and trying to make sense of it," he said. "Are you tired? How about meeting me at the station and having a cup of tea or coffee here. I'd like to talk with you about this case if that's ok with you."

"No, I'm not tired. I'm all riled up and don't think I would sleep very well anyway. Doc Albert said Doug's touch and go and there's a chance he might not survive the night."

"I'm aware of that, Doc told me that too. So are you up to coming here?" he asked again. "I would suggest your place but I don't want any nosy neighbors reading something into my car being there at this time of night."

"Hey, that's a great idea!" I exclaimed. "Why don't you come by my place and I'll fix us something to eat. I'm starving and knowing you, I'm sure you haven't eaten either. We can talk while I cook."

"What about the gossip mills? Everyone knows my car, it's a police car," the chief said laughing. "Or let them all just wonder what's going on. That sounds better, we can become the scandal in Deer Creek!"

"Very funny, John," I said sarcastically. "I doubt anyone would notice now. Who would be awake?"

"Sounds like a plan. I'll be there in ten minutes," the chief said, hanging up.

I rushed home and pulled into the garage. Once my car was off, I shut the garage door and made sure no one entered while it was closing. Chief or not I'm still playing it safe. I walked in my house through the inside garage door and was happy I had turned on lights. Everything appeared in order so I hurried over to the refrigerator to see what I could come up with. Lynne was the baker, but I had a flare for plain old comfort food.

I only had a few minutes before John would be here and I wanted to have a plan before he arrived. I found some leftover boneless chicken in the refrigerator and some shredded cheese and tortillas. That was perfect. I would make chicken enchiladas and I'll even make the salsa. I pulled all the ingredients out when I saw the headlights in my front room window.

He walked up to the front door and I was there waiting for him. "C'mon in John. I found something to make and it should only take about thirty minutes from start to finish. Is that ok?" We headed to the back of the house and into the kitchen.

"Sounds perfect! My stomach's growling I'm so hungry," he said, rubbing his belly. "What can I do to help?"

"Nothing, just sit on a stool at the island and tell me everything," I said, turning to the sink and rinsing the tomatoes for the salsa.

"Now Ruth Ann, you know I can't divulge everything. It's a police matter and you're not an employee of the department. I'll go over what I can, is that good enough for you?" he asked, sitting down on the stool and propping his elbows on the counter.

"We'll see about that," I said, putting all my ingredients together and wrapping up the filled tortillas. I placed the enchiladas in the oven and went over to the island. "About twenty minutes in the oven and it'll be ready. Let's talk about who made statements while I make the salsa," I said, pulling out a very large, very sharp slicing knife.

"Ok, that I can do," he said, watching me chop. "There's you, obviously, and Lucy, his secretary, and Tom the guard, and the tellers, Sue and Christie."

"Hey, that brings up a good question, where was Tom? He's the guard, why wasn't he still in the bank?" I inquired.

"He had an appointment with Arthur Roberts so Doug gave him permission to leave early," John answered, grabbing a chip and dipping into the salsa I just finished.

"Why was he seeing a lawyer?" I asked, hoping John would say more, but feeling I was about to be shut down.

"He and Delores are getting a divorce," he replied, realizing he should've kept his mouth shut on this bit of information. "Uh, I'm not supposed to tell anyone that." He tapped his head with his hand and added, "Please Ruth Ann, it's not public knowledge yet. I know because Delores is my secretary and she has confided in me. So when Tom said he had an appointment, I knew it was the truth."

"Wow, divorce? That's so sad. I wish they could work it out. They always seemed so happy. Maybe not being able to have kids played a role in them separating. They went through years of fertility treatments. That has to take a toll on a marriage."

"I don't know about that, but Delores cries and cries to me in my office some days and I can't break her confidence and say too much more. I just wish she would confide in another woman and not me. I'm a guy, not a counselor," he said, munching loudly on another chip.

"You could always suggest me next time she's upset. I could listen and try to help her," I said.

"Thanks, maybe I'll suggest that next time. But before that, mum's the word, deal?"

"Fine, I won't say anything to anyone," I retorted. The oven timer beeped and I pulled out the enchiladas. We ate in silence until our plates were cleaned.

"Wow, I was hungrier than I thought," I said. "I shouldn't eat that much this late and try to sleep."

"I knew I was starving and could eat a ton," John said, stuffing one last chip into the salsa. I stood up and put the plates into the dishwasher and walked over to the island and sat on the stool next to him.

"We haven't really talked about anything except Tom's problems. What do you say we get back to who you think tried to kill Doug?" I asked, watching John look at me like I was crazy.

"No, no," he started saying. "We aren't talking about that. I just wanted to vent a little. Maybe starvation was making my thinking irrational. Now that I'm satisfied I think it would be a mistake bringing you into this investigation."

"C'mon John, I can be an objective party in your investigation. Give you a more personal viewpoint," I said. I really wanted to get in on this, I don't know why exactly, but I felt I had to help.

"You can't be objective and give a personal view, Ruth Ann," he remarked.

"You know what I mean. I can be someone outside of the police department who personally knows Doug and the people he's been involved with. That's if the injury against him was personal and not just some random burglar."

"Well, I can tell you this much, I'm no closer to solving this than I was when you called from the crime scene," John snapped.

"So you've got nothing?" I asked. "No fingerprints or pictures from the surveillance cameras?"

"Nope," he answered. "The person was wearing gloves and the camera came out blank."

"How can the camera not catch anything?" I asked.

"Because the camera wasn't functioning. Tom told me it had been broken for months and they just hadn't replaced it." John shook his head; "Tom said they figured nothing ever happened in the bank so they didn't think it was urgent."

"Seriously?" I questioned.

"Yes, can you believe that? I've never heard of a bank that didn't have surveillance. The only witness we have is you, Ruth Ann."

"*Me?*" I asked, stunned.

"Yes, that's why we have to make sure that you remember every detail of what you saw," John stated. "You need to close your eyes and imagine you're back in front of the bank and looking inside and seeing the person. Can you do that for me?"

"Of course, but I don't know how much good it'll do. It was so fast and I only saw the person for a split second." I added, "A second too long for me, knowing he or she might've seen me."

"Can you try this experiment for me?" John asked. "Close your eyes." I closed them. "Now, put yourself back on the ground at the bank. You heard the bang and went to the ground and when you started to look into the window…" John nudged me so I would take over the scene.

"Ok, I'm looking inside and this person was dressed in black from head to toe. I noticed the figure dart away from Doug's office and head toward the back. He stopped and looked toward the front window." I hesitated a moment, "That's when I felt our eyes meet for a second, then he turned and ran out." I opened my eyes suddenly and blurted, "Wait!"

"What, did you remember something, Ruth Ann?" John asked

hopefully.

"Yes!" I exclaimed. "I saw something shimmer, like glass or something in his hand. He must've been holding something that caused the light."

"Excellent, Ruth Ann, keep going," John said, excited.

"John, I think he was holding a piece of jewelry if you ask me," I said, looking up at John who was wide-eyed and smiling.

"Why do you say jewelry?" he asked curiously.

"Just the way it shone. He must've been wearing very dark gloves and if I know my gemstones at all I would swear it was a diamond or something close to one." I was so excited I jumped up and put my arms around John's neck to hug him.

"I'm proud of you, Ruth Ann," he said, hugging me back. "I told you this could work. We don't have solid proof of what you're saying, but at least it's a start in the right direction. We need a motive for this brutal crime and stealing a piece of valuable jewelry might just be the answer."

I was proud of myself. I can't believe I would've forgotten something so critical. John really was right in having me do this whole "close my eyes and put myself back at the scene" technique.

"I'm going to question Tom and the tellers first thing in the morning to see if they're aware of any jewelry stored at the bank that could cause someone to rob the bank and almost kill Doug." John stood up and added, "Thanks a lot, I'm going to let you get some sleep and I'll let you know what turns up regarding this."

"Wait, John, what about Doug?" I asked. "If you hear anything, please call me right away."

"You do the same. Doc may call you before me, so can you remember to call me?" John asked as we walked to the front door.

"Agreed," I answered, reaching for another hug. "I really appreciate you coming here tonight. I was so wound up after today I didn't think I could ever sleep."

"Try and get some rest. I feel better knowing you're safe at home. We'll get to the bottom of this." John turned to leave, "Please don't open your door to anyone without looking through your peephole. I'm just being cautious, I don't believe you're at any risk, whoever did this is probably far away by now."

"I sure hope you're right, John," I said. "If this person knew who I was, that makes me a target."

"Not if they think you don't know who they are," John answered.

"As long as they do think that," I replied. "I refuse to be afraid of whoever hurt Doug, that's just not me!" I stated. I cannot let myself get all wound up over something I can't change. I saw this person, and I can't take that back. So just move on, let Doug get better and catch whoever committed this crime. I gave John a quick peck on the cheek, and he walked down to his car.

"Oh, Ruth Ann," he called out. "Thanks for feeding me, too."

I nodded and closed the door. I bolted the door and watched John drive off through my front room window. I closed all blinds and curtains that looked outside and headed to bed. It really had been a long day.

Chapter 3

I never thought I would sleep a wink, but the next thing I knew the phone was ringing. I sat up and grabbed my cell phone from the nightstand next to my bed. It was six in the morning and I had only been asleep a few hours. Who could be calling at this time, Lynne or Nancy? Nancy wouldn't call me so early but Lynne would. She was already at her bakery preparing for the day.

"Hello?" I asked.

"Ruth Ann?" The caller on the other end inquired. "Is that you?"

"Yes," I replied. "Albert, is that you? Oh my gosh, what's happened with Doug?" I jumped out of bed and almost fell over the bat I put on the floor for security.

"Are you alright?" Doc Albert asked.

"Yes, I'm fine, clumsy, but fine. How is Doug? Please tell me you don't have bad news," I begged.

"No, actually I have some good news. He woke up just a little while ago and," I didn't let Albert finish when I interrupted and said, "He's awake? I'll be right over!"

"Ruth Ann, listen," he began. "He was only awake for a short time. He's unconscious again. I just thought I'd tell you that it's a good sign; he was able to speak briefly."

"He spoke?" I asked. "What did he say, Albert?"

"Let me begin by saying I called Chief John first since this is an ongoing investigation."

"Albert, what did Doug say?" I begged.

"He said two words, '*Ruth Ann danger*'," Albert responded.

"What?" I gasped. "He said I was in danger?"

"I don't know Ruth Ann, he just said your name followed by one word, danger." Albert continued, "I felt it was my duty to call the chief first and he told me it was ok to call you and let you know Doug was awake briefly. He told me to tell you that he was coming to your house right away and that you should only answer the door to him."

"When did you speak with John?" I asked. "I just woke up when you called me and John isn't here."

"I spoke with him right before I called you, so you might want to get yourself ready because he should be there any minute," Doc said. "I will let you know if Doug wakes up again."

I hung up the phone and ran to the bathroom to clean up and get dressed. I was just finishing when I heard a loud knock at my front door. I ran over to the living room window and peered through an opening in the curtain. I saw John's police car in the street. I took a deep breath and opened the front door.

"Can I come in, Ruth Ann? I hope Doc called you and informed you that I was on my way over," John said gloomily.

"Yes, come in John," I said holding the door for him. "You look horrible."

"Geez thanks. I didn't get much sleep, maybe an hour or so. I kept going over in my head what you and the bank employees said. I had just settled down when Doc Albert called and told me about Doug."

"So I heard," I added.

"He told you what Doug said I guess. Don't get scared, we don't even know whether what Doug said is true or even makes any sense. He was awake only a second or two."

"John, I'm not a child. I can figure out that my name followed by danger can't be good," I said. "I'm not afraid, we need to get more out of Doug, that's all."

"Doc thinks he'll start coming around more. It was a good sign that he woke up at all. I get the impression that his chances of staying in a coma were pretty high."

"Really? I didn't know that. I knew it was touch and go and he may not have survived the night, but I never heard Doc use the word, coma." I continued, "So Doc thinks he's back in a coma? "

"That's what he said, Doug was in a coma, but he woke up within 24 hours so Doc thinks Doug will continue improving. The bad news is that until Doug wakes up and starts communicating, Doc won't know if there's any permanent damage."

"Like what?" I asked.

"Brain damage were the words he used, Ruth Ann," John said

quietly.

"I don't believe it," I exclaimed. "I know that if Doug was able to say my name that his mind was fine. He just needs a little more time."

"I hope so, but in the meantime, you're not to be alone or go anywhere alone," John said. "I'm assigning Dave to you. He'll follow you wherever you go, and I'll assign Dave and Lou to take turns outside your home when you're here."

"What!" I cried out, "That's crazy. I'll be fine on my own."

"Look Ruth Ann, Doug's words implied an explicit threat toward you.. He's the only one who knows exactly what happened at the bank. Until I get more information out of Doug, you'll follow my orders. Is that clear?" John demanded. He looked into my eyes and softened his approach. "I don't want anything to happen to you. You know I have strong feelings for you and I would never forgive myself if something bad happened to you."

I smiled back at him and said, "I understand, John, but is all this really necessary? I can be careful and if anything out of the ordinary occurs, I'll contact you immediately."

"No, not going to happen," John said. He saw the anger building up in me again and added, "Look, why don't I just have the boys follow you around for a day or so and see if Doug wakes up and talks. I won't have them get too close or bother you, just watch you from a distance."

"Well, maybe for a day or two, but Doug should be awake by then and he'll identify who did this to him, and then you can arrest them," I said. "Case closed."

"Oh my God," John said out of nowhere, as he rushed to pull out his phone and contact the police office. "Get a man over to the hospital immediately to stand guard at Doug Albertson's door." He slammed the phone shut and said, "I'm too personally involved in this, Ruth Ann. I was so worried about that threat to you that I neglected to cover Doug."

"What on earth are you talking about?" I asked.

"Think about it Ruth Ann, if Doug wakes up and the person who almost killed him discovers this, Doug could be in serious danger. Plus, he's in such a weakened state that he couldn't fight back."

"I never thought about that either, " I said.

"But it's my job, Ruth Ann. My feelings for you interfered with my professional duties as the chief."

"Stop it, John," I said. "It was one oversight and I'm positive you'll never let that happen again."

"Hopefully you're correct," he said resignedly. "There's no one else who wants to find this creep more than me. I'll protect you and Doug, even if I have to keep the three of us in the same room until I do."

"Let's not get too carried away, John," I said smiling. "Between your men and the staff at the hospital we'll be safe."

"That reminds me," John said, pulling out his phone again. "Shirley, hi it's Chief John." Shirley spoke in the background. "Tell Doc and the staff that Doug is not allowed any visitors. I'm posting a man outside his door and no one is allowed past without my permission." He hung up with Shirley and we walked back into my kitchen.

"Hungry?" I asked. "It's only been about five hours since we last ate, but I could whip up a couple eggs for you if you'd like?"

"That would be great, thanks," John replied. "I could use a little fuel since I'm running on so little sleep."

I fed John and drank a cup of coffee myself to wake up. He suggested we both head over to the hospital to check on any updates with Doc Albert. I asked if I could take my own car and I was promptly told, "No." We drove over to the hospital and went inside. Claire was back behind the welcome desk and I wondered if she always worked 18-hour days. It was a little before seven in the morning, and she left the hospital with me late last night.

"Hi Claire," I said walking up to her desk. "Do you ever get to sleep in?"

"Oh, sure I do. Just thought with Doug here and a criminal on the loose I'd come in extra early today."

Chief John quickly responded, "That's very smart of you, Claire. Just in case any strange or suspicious person came in you would be the first person to greet them."

Claire sat up a little straighter, acknowledging that she took this assignment seriously. "That's right! I see everyone first, and if anyone looks funny, I'll call the police immediately."

"Sounds great, Claire," John answered. "Is Doc in the back? Can we go in and talk with him, and check on Doug?

Claire looked at me and said, "I'm not sure I can let the both of you back. John, you're here on official business, but, I'm sorry Ruth Ann, I don't know if you're allowed back there yet." She saw the disappointment on my face and perked up, "But let me check with Doc and see. Hold on one second." Claire picked up the phone on her desk and unfortunately got Shirley, his stiff, obedient nurse instead of Doc Albert. I knew Doc would let me back, but I'm positive Shirley wouldn't.

"Ok, thanks, Shirley," Claire spoke and hung up. She looked at John and told him to go back and told me to stay with her. I knew that would happen, but one way or another I planned on getting past those double doors and Shirley to get to Doug's room.

"Look, Ruth Ann," John started. "Let me go back and see what's happening with Doug and talk with Doc. I'm positive he'll allow you back, especially if you're with me." He turned and went through the swinging double doors and into the inner part of the hospital.

"Sorry, Ruth Ann, you know Shirley," Claire said. "She can be quite the stick in the mud."

"It's not your fault Claire," I said. "Doc or John will come get me soon. Have you heard any more about Doug's condition?"

"No, just that he spoke a couple words," she started to say and added, "but I don't even know what he said. I guess he went right back to being unconscious."

"Yes, that's what I heard too," I replied. I didn't want to give away that I knew the words Doug spoke. I wasn't sure who was privy to that information.

It didn't take long before Doc Albert pushed through the doors and grabbed my arm. He didn't say a word, just gently led me back through the doors down the hall to the last room on the right. I knew why Doug would be in there. First, the obvious reason was that there was a cop standing outside the door. Second, Doc Albert's office was located close to his room. He passed by the cop who nodded to let us enter. I walked in and what I found shocked me more than I could say.

John was standing next to the hospital bed. Doug was in the bed, but what shocked me the most was Doug, sitting up and smiling as I entered the room.

"What, how?" I couldn't get any other words out of my mouth.

John came next to me and put his arm around my shoulders and said, "It's okay, Ruth Ann. Doug's awake and doing better than any of us ever expected."

"But I thought you were still unconscious Doug?" my question directed at the patient. "I thought you only spoke a couple words and passed out again."

Doug looked at John and asked, "Can I answer that or should I leave that to you?"

John answered for Doug and said, "That was true, Ruth Ann, but over the last couple hours I guess Doug woke up and started talking. Doc thought it best to tell only me at first. When I walked back here I was as shocked as you are now. But I think this is a great idea to keep the public unaware of Doug's condition for a while. It'll keep him safe."

Doug looked over at me, "Ruth Ann, I feel pretty good considering. I was just explaining what I remembered to John when you came in. Quite the story, huh?"

"I'm so confused I don't know what to say, but give me time, I'm sure I'll be able to in a minute," I replied.

John took over the conversation, "Ok, Doug and Ruth Ann, whatever is talked about in this room stays with the people in this room only, got it?" He looked at Doc Albert and added, "That goes for you too, Doc, ok?"

We all nodded, but Doug's nod caused him quite a bit of pain. "Oh, I almost forgot about how much my head hurts. But I want to figure all this out, I'm a little fuzzy still but pieces are coming back to me."

"Ruth Ann, I should ask you to leave at this point, but I won't. I trust I can keep your word on this one. No talking to anyone outside this room. Not even your sister, Irene, Lynne or Nancy?" He gave me such an accusatory glance that I took offense.

"John, if you're implying that I'll gossip, I'm truly disappointed in you. I would never do anything to put Doug, or myself for that matter, in jeopardy."

"Sorry, I didn't mean to imply anything, it's just this could be very dangerous and the more people who know, the more lives we could endanger," John stated.

"Whoa," Doug held up his hand and stopped the chief. "What happened to me? And why is Ruth Ann in danger?"

Doc Albert chimed in and said, "Ok, John, we don't want to excite Doug. He just woke up from a serious injury to his head." John nodded and Doc turned to Doug, "And you have to remain quiet and calm. Just answer his questions. If you show any signs of discomfort or exhaustion I'm kicking everyone out for a while." Doc added, "Do we all understand what I'm saying?" He looked from the chief to me, and we both nodded. "Good, go on John."

"Ok," John began to explain. "Doug, Ruth Ann is the one who found you at the bank right after you were assaulted."

"What?" Doug said loudly, then noticed Doc's glare and nodded gently, knowing that he needed to calm down. "Why were you at the bank anyway?" he asked, looking directly at me.

"I wasn't exactly at the bank, I was just walking by and noticed a strange movement inside."

John interrupted and said, "Let me do the questioning please before we get stopped by Doc."

Doc smiled and John continued, "Let's go back to the beginning Doug. You were at the bank and it was closing time. Tom was gone and the tellers had also left the bank, is that correct?" Doug nodded. "So you stayed past closing time and were working in your office. Doug nodded. "What were you working on?"

"That I can't quite remember yet," Doug answered, disappointed.

"It'll come back, just relax and answer what you can," Doc Albert replied. Doug was ok with that.

Chief John asked, "So you don't remember why you were staying late at the bank, correct?" Doug carefully nodded. "Do you remember hearing any noise or voices in the bank after the staff had left?"

"No," Doug replied.

"Do you remember hearing any loud noise like a small explosion?" John inquired.

Doug became irritated and blurted out, "Explosion? No one said anything about an explosion!" Doc went to his side and checked his vitals and reprimanded Doug. "Ok, Doc, I promise I'll tone it down. But someone better explain to me about this explosion. Was the bank robbed?"

"That's what we're trying to find out," John said to him. "The safe is intact so don't worry about money or items in there being stolen. I can't figure out what loud noise Ruth Ann claimed she heard."

"I did hear it, John," I said, a little miffed. "Why else would I have dropped to my knees right in front of the bank?"

"True," John answered. "But are you sure the noise came from inside the bank? Maybe two things happened at the same time."

"What are you implying?" I asked curiously.

"Well, maybe at the same time you heard the loud bang you also caught a glimpse of what was happening in the bank. It's quite a coincidence, but it could've happened." John looked over at me and waited for my response.

"Humph, that could've happened, but seems too much a coincidence." I tried to think back to that exact moment and said, "You know, when I heard the bang my first reaction was to look behind me, not directly into the bank."

"Why would you say that?" John asked.

"Because at first I didn't know where the noise was coming from. It was pretty loud and I remember turning my head around then dropping to my knees. It all happened so fast I don't have any explanation, but that's when I peered over the edge of the outside window and looked inside the bank. I saw the black hooded figure and," I stopped and looked at John and asked, "do I go on with my account?"

Doug looked from me to John and asked, "Why wouldn't you? Is there something you don't want me to know yet?"

Doc squeezed Doug's shoulder and reminded him, "Stay calm". Doug agreed and let John continue.

"Ok, Ruth Ann, let me take it from there. I'm confident that I know what happened from there." I reluctantly agreed and let him tell the story.

"So, after Ruth Ann saw a figure in the bank she ended up in your office." John chose to skip how I entered the bank and the fact that the criminal saw me. But I digress and let John continue. "She discovered you unconscious at your desk and called 911. We showed up and you were transported here. You received quite a blow to your head, I would guess from a bat or other instrument we have not located so far."

Doug was silent for a minute or so. My guess would be he was trying to digest all the information. If Doug's mind worked the same as mine, he wouldn't accept that explanation so easily. "Wait a minute, John, you left a lot out of that story. Such as why and how did Ruth Ann get into the bank? Who is this black hooded figure and did Ruth Ann run into him? AHA! That's why she's in danger isn't it?" Doug exclaimed. "She saw who it was, or maybe he saw her and you haven't captured him and he could go after Ruth Ann, too."

"Yes, Doug," John replied as calmly as possible, hoping that Doug remained calm too. "Ruth Ann and the perp saw each other for just a split second from a distance. Ruth Ann was on her knees and peeking in the window when he glanced out at her. That was the only contact she had with him or her. By the time Ruth Ann ran around to the back and entered through your alley door, he or she was gone."

Doug looked at me and asked, "You ran around the building? What, were you hoping to run into this person?" He waited for me to answer, but before I could he said, "That is the dumbest thing you could've done, Ruth Ann! I'm sorry to sound so cruel, but you could've been shot or worse."

"Ok," Doc Albert interrupted. "I think that is enough for now. Let Doug rest and maybe he can talk with you both later."

"No," Doug blurted out. "I will not be able to settle down at all, Doc, unless we get through this. I don't understand why I was attacked if nothing was stolen."

John started talking before Doc could shut him down, "I agree, but let's take it down a notch and stay calm, can you do that Doug? Or Doc will have me thrown outta here."

"Fine, but Ruth Ann, you know better to run right into a fire don't you?" Doug asked me directly. "I didn't realize you were such a risk taker."

I was the one getting irritated now. "I've said several times that I didn't think, I reacted. I saw someone hooded and in dark clothing run out of the bank. There was a small light in your office so I thought you or Lucy were in danger. When I got around to the back my intention was to call 911 not actually enter inside the bank."

"Then why did you?" Doug questioned.

"Because I saw the coast was clear and the back door was ajar. I went over and looked in and didn't see anyone, so I entered.

From there, yes, I wasn't thinking clearly or very intelligently. I made my way to your office and there you were."

"I'll stop coming down so hard on you, for now, but please don't ever put yourself into a position like this again, please," Doug begged of me.

"I never put myself into anything, Doug, it just happened, very fast," I answered. I turned to John, "Hey, did you ever ask Doug if he knew about any large piece of jewelry, like a diamond, that was in his possession?"

"That's right!" the chief exclaimed. "I forgot to mention that."

"What are you talking about?" Doug asked. "Something about a diamond. Did you see one, Ruth Ann?"

"I saw something like a diamond or object that would shimmer like one in the criminal's hand as he was running toward the back door."

Frustrated, Doug tapped his head. "There has to be something in my head that knows about this. It sounds so familiar; I just can't place it yet."

"Ok, that's it," Doc said, pushing John and me toward the door. "Let him rest. You can come back in a few hours. If he's still improving, I'll let you ask him some more questions." Doc led us into the hall and said, "Maybe, if you give him some time, he'll remember this diamond or whatever it is on his own."

"Good call, Doc," John said as we walked back into the lobby of the hospital. "Remember, no talking about any of this. In fact, as far as anybody knows, Doug is still unconscious." John glanced over at Claire and whispered, "Not even to hospital staff'.

I nodded as I saw Claire waving me over to her. "You and John have been gone quite a long time. Doug must be doing better?" Claire inquired.

"As long as he's stable, he's doing better than last night," John answered for me from a distance. He was whispering with Doc Albert and I really wish I could hear what they were talking about instead of lying to Claire. I wasn't comfortable telling Claire that Doug was still unconscious.

"C'mon Ruth Ann, what's going on?" Claire asked suspiciously. "You, Chief John, and Doc Albert were in there a long time. And what's with the cop posted outside his door?"

"Well you know as much as I do about that. He was attacked in his own bank and they haven't caught the guy. They don't want to take any chances with Doug in case this person sneaks in and tries to finish him off," I said. "But with you manning the desk, that won't happen."

"Very true," Claire said proudly. I knew that would get her off topic. I praised her ability to guard the hospital against a potential criminal. "Nobody, and I mean nobody, will be get by me!" Claire declared.

"Exactly," I replied. "I'm going to grab John and get out of here. I'll be back later to see if there's been any change in Doug's condition." Before she could say more I turned and headed toward John just as Doc Albert went back into the treatment area of the hospital.

"Let's get going, John," I said, tugging at his arm. "Claire's asking too many questions." John discretely looked in her direction and took my hand and we walked out to the parking lot. "Why don't we grab a bite to eat before I drop you off? I've got to get over to the station and do some work."

"Sounds good to me, I'm hungry again. I just drank some coffee earlier while you ate the eggs. It was too early and I just wasn't hungry then. Now I'm starving," I said. "Afterwards, can you drop me off at my store? I need to check on the shop. I left yesterday without going through the register and checking my messages. It's not open today since it's Saturday so I can do some catching up."

"I don't know if you should be alone in there," John said. "What about that assistant of yours, what's her name?"

"Meme," I answered. "I'll give her a call and see if she'll spare a few hours. It's her day off, but she needs money so I'm sure she'll come in unless she already has plans." I pulled out my cell while we were on the way over to the Café to grab a bite to eat. Meme was only twenty-three, but she was very mature for her age. She already had a two-year-old toddler at home and she was single. She went away to college in Utah and ended up getting pregnant unexpectedly. She finished her degree in business though, despite being pregnant. I couldn't hold that against her because she worked so hard to finish her schooling. Like me, she looked for a small, far away town where she can escape her past and raise her baby.

Meme jumped at the chance to come into the shop and asked if she could bring Elijah. I didn't think it would matter since it was Saturday, but a toddler could do a lot of damage in a store like mine. But, I didn't have any choice. If I didn't say yes, John would stop me from going into the store. Knowing him, he would make me sit at the station the entire time he worked.

"Ok, John, Meme's coming in one hour and I even told her she could bring Elijah."

"You must be desperate to go to work, letting a toddler in your antique store. Couldn't he do a lot of damage in there with all your breakables?"

"Probably, but Meme will keep a close eye on him. Hopefully he'll nap while we're there," I said, just as John pulled into the Café.

We walked toward the door and I glanced down the street at my daughter's bakery, Sinful Sweets. I told myself that when I got to my shop I would either call or pop over to see her and fill her in on everything that's happened over the past twenty-four hours. I can't believe it's only been one day.

We walked into the café and didn't realize it was lunchtime. The place was packed. Everyone by now had heard about Doug's attack and the minute we walked through the door, all eyes were on us. The first to greet us was Wilma, the owner of the café.

"You sure you two want to be here now?" she asked curiously. "You won't be able to eat a bite in here. Everyone is going to bother you."

John, realizing this might've been a mistake, said, "Can't go back now. Might as well sit down and see if we can hold them off."

"Good luck," Wilma said, taking us to a table that was at the back of the café. "I hope this will help being back here. At least you're in a corner and they can't surround you!" she said laughing. "And I won't even ask how Doug's doing because you probably won't tell me. I figure if he weren't alive we would've heard that by now, too. All I ask is that if we're unsafe here in town, that you tell me that much."

Chief John patted Wilma on the back as he took his chair and said, "If there's any danger I wouldn't be sitting here about to eat some lunch."

"Good point," she said, handing us menus and walking away.

"I did good, didn't I?" I said, opening the menu. "I didn't say a word."

John smiled, "First test for you. Many more to come I'm sure". We both ordered chicken soup and triple cheese grilled cheeses. I was in need of comfort food and I suspect John was, too. We ate quickly and we were surprised that no one confronted us. They all stared and whispered, but nobody came over to the table. I was happy because we knew everyone in there, and it's really hard not say anything without looking like a liar.

We finished our meal and left the café. John drove down the alley and pulled his car right up to my back door of the store. Meme's car was already there so he let me go alone. "Now, Ruth Ann, I'm trusting you can stay away from any trouble or people prying information from you. I'll pick you up in three hours and we'll go back to see Doug. Hopefully by then he'll have thought about the diamond or whatever object it was that someone might've wanted to steal."

"They did steal it," I corrected him. "I would think a huge diamond would've been found when your guys searched the bank."

"Yes, that's what I meant," John amended and pulled away.

Free, I thought to myself, for now at least. I put my key in the back door and walked into the delivery room. The delivery room was specifically designed so that when trucks or customers needed to pick up or drop off an item they wouldn't have to go through the front entrance of my store.

Meme was in there steaming red velvet curtains that I had purchased on the Internet. They were from an estate in Virginia dating back to the mid 1800's. I thought they were quite a steal and knew they would sell here if I marketed them just right.

"Hi, Ruth Ann," Meme said. "These curtains are beautiful, almost like new."

"They are gorgeous and I know just the person I need to call to come in and look at them," I answered, walking over to Elijah who was busy in his pack n' play.

"Mrs. Hamilton, right?" Meme asked. "The Mayor's wife would love these in her house or should I say mansion."

"Exactly. Henry will pay anything to keep her happy," I chuckled. "He's got to keep up with her lifestyle if he wants to stay married to her."

"That's so true. He married someone thirty years younger than him so he better be doing something right." Meme laughed and added, "Everyone knows she only married him because he's the Mayor and he inherited a ton of money. I don't think she married him for his looks!"

"Now Meme, he's not too bad for a sixty-year-old. Just a little round in the middle and a little less hair than he used to have," I joked.

"A little less? He's totally bald!" Meme exclaimed.

I walked through the swinging door that led into the main area of the store. I loved this room. It was large with high ceilings and filled with items from the past. Some items had stories that I loved to hear over and over and some things were of unknown origin. Even so, I had documented the source and value of most of the unknown items. The second floor of my store held large furniture items such as dressers, beds, couches, tables and chairs. When a customer walked into the front door they could choose to browse the first floor or go up the extra wide staircase that I had built in the middle of the room to the open showroom filled with furniture. There were crystal chandeliers at the door entrance and at the top of the stairs, and throughout the room were miscellaneous chandeliers made of brass and silver. I didn't have one light that was modern or contemporary. The ambiance had to be Victorian and I sold only items recalling that period in time.

As I walked toward the grand staircase to head upstairs, it dawned on me that the Mayor, Henry Hamilton, could easily be a person who owned a large gemstone such as a diamond. He not only makes pretty good money as Mayor, but he also comes from old money. I'll mention my hunch to John when he picks me up.

I surveyed the store to make sure it was set up for opening on Monday morning and went into the back room to talk to Meme. I wanted to go over some new display ideas with her and give her extra decision-making power. "Meme, with the holidays coming up I think we should decorate the store with an old fashioned Christmas theme. What do you think?"

Meme put the steamer down and smiled, "That's a great idea. We could highlight all the objects we need to sell with a holiday theme. Like taking those brass candlesticks we've had for months and put them upstairs on the mahogany dining room table with deep red candles and a little Christmas greenery around them. It'll make people imagine how they could use them in their own home. What do you think?"

"That's a terrific idea. We have so many items like those candlesticks that we need to sell to make place for new items," I said, pleased with Meme's excitement. I knew Meme had great ideas and it was time I let her become an assistant manager. I could afford to give her a raise and I'm sure she could use the money. It'll be my Christmas gift to promote her and raise her salary.

"Great, I'll take inventory and see what else we need to push." She stopped, looked at me with a touch of fear in her eyes and said, "That's if it's ok with you of course."

"Of course it is. Feel free to market any item that's been in this store longer than a month. Just keep me posted on what you're working on." Meme smiled and went back to steaming. I walked into my office just off the delivery room. It was a comfortable room with a large antique writing desk and chair. I didn't want to have an office the size of a cubby hole, so when the store was built I made sure to create a good sized office. I kept all the store's paperwork in one of the two file cabinets behind my desk and even had an elliptical in the corner facing a television mounted on the wall. It was a comfortable room with a round table and four chairs, and even a loveseat covered in deep red and green flowers.

I sat down at my desk and attacked a pile of papers. The three hours John gave me flew by. Nothing out of the ordinary transpired during those hours and when John showed up in my office I was disappointed. I needed more time. But then again, it was time to get back to the hospital to see Doug. Plus, it gave me a chance to talk with John about the Mayor on the way over. "Hi John," I called, putting my papers in a neat pile on my desk. "I'm just finishing and we can head out. Let me get Meme out of here and I'll lock up." John left the office and when I found him he was holding Elijah and playing with a small rubber baseball. "No throwing that in here, John," I said. They were in the main storeroom on the first floor. "The breakables in here won't hold up if that ball hits them."

"We're just holding the ball, Ruth Ann, not throwing. That's for outside play, right Elijah?" John said, smiling and playing with the toddler.

"Ok, Meme, let's lock up and I'll see you on Monday morning," I said, leading the group toward the delivery room. "Thanks for your help today, I can always count on you."

Meme took Elijah from John and bundled him up and headed out the back door. John and I followed and soon we were on our way back to the hospital. "Oh, no," I blurted. "I completely forgot to call Lynne or Nancy."

"Have they tried to contact you?" John asked.

"Yesterday I got lots of texts from Lynne. All I did was reply that I was really busy and I would get back to her later."

"Well then don't worry. Maybe it's a good thing you aren't talking to them," John said. "We don't want anything to slip, right Ruth Ann?"

"Oh, I see what you mean. You're worried I'm going to blab to them about Doug."

"Exactly," he proclaimed with a smirk on his face.

"Gee, thanks for the vote of confidence, John," I said. "And for your information, I wasn't going to say anything to them. In fact, I wonder why they haven't asked me about Doug. By now I'm sure they heard about what happened to him."

"But they don't know *YOU* were involved," John added.

"True, that part of the story we've kept pretty quiet," I said. "Oh, I wanted to bring up a theory to you. You know that mysterious diamond?" John nodded curiously. "Who do you know of in this town that would or could actually own a large piece of jewelry?"

"What are you getting at?"

"If you really think, I bet you'll come to the same conclusion I did," I said. "We don't have that many wealthy, and I mean seriously wealthy, residents in Deer Creek."

John was silent for just a minute when he blurted out, "Mayor Henry Hamilton and his wife!"

"Exactly," I agreed. "Maybe Doug was holding a valuable piece of jewelry for the Mayor, and for some reason it wasn't in the vault at the time of the theft."

"Humph, not a bad theory. I'll check it out."

Chapter 4

We pulled into the hospital and went inside and Claire wasn't anywhere to be seen. I looked at my watch and saw it was close to five in the evening. Maybe she left for the day; it was a long day for her yesterday.

John looked unhappy and said, "Nobody's at the desk! Anyone could get into the patient area."

"Claire can't work twenty-four hours a day, John," I said.

"Claire's the only person who man's the desk? Maybe they should hire another person," he said, pushing through the double doors into the hallway. He stormed down the hall and went straight up to one of his men standing guard at Doug's door. They talked back and forth quietly for a moment and then he waved for me to come up to them.

"No one has been in this room except for Doc and Shirley," he said. "He told me it's been very quiet the last few hours."

Doc heard our voices and came out of his office. "Yes, it's been very quiet here since you've left. Exactly as it should be for a patient with a severe head injury."

"Doc, you told us we could come back. Is it ok to go in?" John asked.

Doc peeked inside the room and found Doug awake holding the TV remote flipping through channels. "Yes, but I'll be right here in my office and if I hear any raised voices, the interview will be over."

"Got it, Doc," John said. I followed John and we walked over to Doug's bed. "Hey, how ya feeling? You look much better."

John was being kind. Doug looked beat up. His face was bruising from being hit on the head and he had large, dark circles under his eyes as if he hadn't slept. I wondered if Doug knew more about this gem than he'd revealed or maybe he just couldn't remember anything at all yet, and it was driving him crazy. How thrilling, a mystery would sure add some excitement to my life.

Doug responded, "Doing better, a bit sore in the head, but better than it could've been I guess."

"Great, great," John said, ignoring Doug's obvious symptoms of fatigue and discomfort. "Anything jog your memory since we've been gone?" John went straight to the point. He didn't want to waste any time.

"Um, not much," Doug answered, looking away from John. "I'm still a little fuzzy." What was strange was Doug wasn't looking at me either. He was staring out the window, avoiding the two of us.

I quickly asked, "What's up, Doug? You didn't look at John when he asked you a question and you haven't looked at me since I walked into the room." I didn't wait for his answer and added, "Seems to me like something has either happened or you remember something that you don't want to disclose."

John, startled, said, "Gee Ruth Ann, I thought you would be the kind, caring one, but you just went for the jugular!"

Doug looked down at the remote he was holding and said, "Ruth Ann, can I talk to John privately for a moment?"

I was surprised at his request but felt I should comply. "Fine," I said, walking out the door and leaving the two of them alone. I wasn't that naïve though; I stayed right next to his door hoping I could catch some of their conversation. The cop outside his door noticed what I was doing but chose to ignore it.

Their conversation started out with their normal voices but then I heard nothing. I was so disappointed that I went over to Doc Albert's office and sat down on a chair in front of his desk. Doc looked up from his papers and said, "What's up, Ruth Ann?"

"I've been kicked out," I said sullenly. "Doug asked to talk to John alone."

"Ah, well maybe he had some official business to discuss. I'm sure it's nothing against you."

"I know that, I just want to hear what he has to say. He looked funny in there."

Doc asked, "What do you mean by funny?"

"He wouldn't look at John or me when we talked and did you notice how big the circles under his eyes are? He looks exhausted, and I don't mean from the last twenty-four hours, but maybe for some time."

Doc pulled his glasses off his face and said, "Yes, I noticed. The reason why it's more noticeable now is that his color is off from the head trauma and the dark circles seem to stick out. I would say there's more to Doug's problems than the crime that just happened."

"I agree, Doc," I said. "But what could it be?"

"I have no idea," Doc replied. "I haven't talked personally with Doug in ages. With our schedules we don't see each other often." He looked closely at me and said, "But you see Doug a lot, don't you?"

"I have, yes," I replied. "But come to think of it the last couple weeks I really haven't talked to him. Usually Doug calls and visits me at my store, but he hasn't done that in a while. Almost," I began, but hesitated a second, "Almost like he's been avoiding me, how strange."

"Well, now you may be getting somewhere. Maybe you should tell John this information. It could be connected with what happened to him yesterday."

Doc left me standing at his now empty desk, wondering if there really was more to this story. I was so deep in thought I didn't even notice John when he came and stood next to me. "Uh, Ruth Ann?" he asked. "Do I even want to know what's going on in that head of yours?"

"Oh, sorry, John," I said, coming back to reality. "No, I was just thinking about something Doc said to me."

"What would that be?" he asked curiously. "Or is it private?"

"Private?" I questioned. "No, not at all. We both noticed Doug acting strangely, didn't you?"

John didn't answer right away but looked around and finally, after what seemed like forever, said, "Doug did recall more, Ruth Ann." he looked me straight in the eyes, "I'll tell you some of it because it does concern you, but I can't discuss everything. Some is police business and I can't talk to you about it."

"Wait, John," I started. "Are you telling me I'm involved but you can't tell me?"

"Not everything." He took my arm and led me out to a chair in the waiting area. John took the seat next to mine and took my hand.

"Okay, now you're scaring me," I said, becoming quite worried. "Tell me this much, does this have to do with Doug's first words saying I was in danger?"

"Let me tell you what I can," he began, ignoring my question. "Doug does remember what he was working on in his office before he was attacked. You were correct that there was a large gem being held in the bank. What I can't tell you is how Doug took possession of the gem until I get solid proof."

"Ah ha! It was a diamond," I interrupted.

"No, not a diamond. It's actually a rare aquamarine with a carat weight of almost 13, originating in Sweden."

"It's not even a diamond?" I asked disappointed. "How much could an aquamarine cost? Not near the value of a diamond or even an emerald or ruby."

"Sorry to burst your knowledge of rare gems, Ruth Ann. This one is worth a hefty sum and Doug was holding it for someone."

"Who?" I asked.

"That I can't tell you until I verify all the facts of its origin and to whom it actually belongs," John stated. "Until then, I'm keeping quiet."

"Well, it doesn't really matter anyway right now does it?" I asked.

"Why not?"

"Because it's gone, stolen, vanished!" I replied.

"Well, yes I'm aware of that fact. However, I plan on recovering the stone," he replied. "And I still have to verify all the facts leading up to the robbery. At least we have more to go on now. We know it was a robbery and why Doug was attacked."

"Somebody really wanted that gem," I said. "How would anyone know about it if it's such a secret?"

"Well, word must've gotten out that the bank received it and that Doug would be the only one with access to it besides the real owner."

"True, but how did they know Doug had it in his office at that exact time?" I asked. "And wouldn't something of that value be in the vault?"

"Yes it was in the vault. That's why Doug looks so bad. He knew he shouldn't have taken it out of the vault, but he did. Doug was very stressed out over the whole thing and that's why he waited until the bank was closed for the day before he retrieved it from the vault. The question is how did the robber know he had it out at that exact time?"

"Somebody must have alerted them. Maybe that someone is an employee of the bank, or just coincidentally the robber was at the bank," I added.

"Probably the first theory would be more likely. But I did question all the employees and I would bet my badge none of them were involved. Maybe someone else was at the bank watching Doug's moves or knew more about the gem." John rubbed his head out of frustration, "That's what I have to find out next. Who tipped this criminal off that Doug had the gem out in the open in his office?"

"Well maybe you should ask the employees some different questions, like was anyone in the bank toward the end of the day that appeared suspicious? Or how about, was anyone in the bank frequently doing petty business or loitering?"

"Good questions, Ruth Ann," John said. "I may just do that." He stood up and was about to walk back to Doug's room when I stopped him.

"Hold on John," I said. "You never said why I'm at risk."

John rolled his head to stretch his neck and came back to me and stood over my chair. "I can only tell you for the time being that you do have a connection. You're not in any danger unless the robber saw you and knows how you're connected. I realize how confusing this all sounds. Just give me until tomorrow so I can check on a few facts. When I know for sure, I'll tell you everything."

"What am I supposed to do until tomorrow?" I asked. "You tell me I could be in danger but not to worry?"

"Let's go back into Doug's room. We'll talk with him more, but he knows he can't tell you much at this time. I'll drive you to your daughter's house, and why don't you stay with her tonight?"

"I haven't told Lynne or Nancy anything about this!" I exclaimed. "And I don't want to until I know more and I'm not putting them in any danger."

"Ok, give me a minute to come up with a solution," he said. "You could always stay at my place unless you're concerned with the gossip that might ensue if anyone sees you."

"Really?" I snapped. "I'm in my fifties, I think I'm allowed if I chose to."

John smiled and said, "Well, I'm kind of liking this solution, what do you say?"

I was a trifle upset at the situation and the inconvenience it was causing. I just wanted to go home and put my feet up and watch a good comedy, alone. I guessed that wasn't going to happen so I agreed to stay at John's place, but on his couch. He lived in a one-bedroom condo in a gated community. It was a pleasant area with a pool, tennis courts, and clubhouse. I had attended many parties there and knew quite a lot of people who live there. My only saving grace for tonight was that it was dark outside and nobody would notice me going in. Now, leaving tomorrow morning may be a different story.

"Ok, I'll stay on your couch for the night."

"Great, let's finish up with Doug and I'll drive you back to your place so you can pack a bag. I do need to pop in at the station, but that shouldn't take long. I just want to give this information to the guys so they can do some checking. Who knows, maybe I'll find out what I need and you can hear it all later tonight."

"That would be great, but I'm beat. Probably will doze off pretty quick," I said. I didn't want John to think this was a romantic night ahead. We did go out on occasion and I knew he would like more, but it wasn't the time for it now.

We went back into Doug's room, and I noticed he looked a little less stressed. He still couldn't look at me directly, but I figured tomorrow I would be able to clear up all this nonsense. We might not catch the criminal, but at least I'd understand what it's all about and why I'm involved. I couldn't imagine how I would be involved, unless it had to do with my business.

We finished going to my house and the police department pretty quickly. We were just pulling into John's spot in the garage. I didn't see anyone, but that didn't matter. It was still a respectable hour for me to visit and we headed into his condo. It was a typical single male residence. A kitchen table and chairs, a couch and recliner, and a couple tables were the only furnishings in the living area. I sat down on the recliner and put my feet up. It felt great; it had been a very long day.

"John, I know you can't tell me much, but I had a thought," I said. "I've been racking my brain trying to figure out how I could be involved, and then I realized it must be about my business, isn't it?" I waited for a look or response, but I didn't get one. He was rustling through the refrigerator and grabbed two bottles of beer.

He walked over to me and handed me one, "Thanks, I think I'll take this," I said, grabbing the beer and taking a large swig. It wasn't my first choice as a drink, but the cold beverage went down with ease. "So are you going to answer my question?"

"No," John stated, and finished his beer in no time at all. He went and took another one out and looked at me, "No thanks, I'm not done with this one."

We sat in silence for a while before I asked him again, "I'm not asking for any specific information, John. I just thought that if this gem involved me it had to be with my store. I don't own a valuable piece like that or know anyone who does."

"I know, Ruth Ann, just give it a rest until tomorrow. I'm sure we'll have some answers."

I normally would have kept bugging him, but I was so tired all I wanted to do was close my eyes. John insisted I take his bed and he would bunk on the couch. I didn't argue because I didn't want to sleep on the couch anyway.

I put my head down on the pillow I brought with me and fell asleep immediately. The next thing I knew it was morning and John was standing over me with a hot cup of tea. "Good morning," he said as I sat up and grabbed the steaming cup of tea.

"Oh this is perfect, my favorite," I said, smiling as I sipped the tea. "What time is it?"

"It's after nine in the morning, you slept in. I've already been up, exercised, and showered. Now I'm starving. I can whip up eggs or I have some bran cereal, your choice."

"You have bran cereal?" I asked, shocked. "Do you have milk to go with the cereal?"

"Of course, I put it in my coffee," he said, holding out his cup to show me.

I asked him to leave so I could clean up and get dressed. We both had a bowl of bran and some OJ and I asked him if he was going to church this morning.

"No, I think I'll go into the department. I need to find out if any information came in while I was gone. Do you want to go?"

I normally would head out to the Congregational Church and listen to Pastor Tom's sermon. It was a small, white steeple church, and if you weren't Catholic you went there. Most people in town went to church. It wasn't necessarily for the religious reasons, but for the social. Many town events were held at the church or through a committee within one of the churches.

"It'll look suspicious if I don't go, and I'm already late. I'll have to attend the eleven a.m. service so I better get going. I didn't bring church clothes with me, so can you drop me off at my house on your way to work?" I asked.

"I don't know," he said thinking. "You really shouldn't be alone at home."

"It'll just be for me to change clothes and go. This is ridiculous. I'm not going to walk around in fear, John." I stood up from the kitchen table and gathered my belongings. "Let's get going, please."

I didn't leave him much of a choice. We drove over to my house and John walked me inside and thoroughly checked over every inch of the house. "Seems like there's been no intrusions so I'll trust that you'll be on guard, and after church you will drive over to the station. Do I have your word?"

"Yes," I said smiling. Won this round, I told myself. Now I hope I really am safe. I hurried out of my house and drove to church. Most people in town knew Doug had been attacked and in the hospital. I'm sure the gossip mill had already spread the news that I had spent a lot of time at the hospital, so I better be ready for questions. I'd have to stick to one story and make sure I don't slip up. The two people I'm worried about the most are my daughters. I have ignored them for two days now and I'm sure they'll attack me the minute they see me. Especially since I usually sit with them at church every Sunday.

I walked in the front doors of the church and it was about ten minutes before eleven. I went in like it was any other Sunday, as normal as could be. Even though it was far from normal. Lynne spotted me immediately and glared. I walked to the pew where she was sitting and sat down. "Good morning sweetheart, how's your weekend been?"

The glare continued, and she shook her head and said, "My

weekend? I sent you so many texts I thought my phone would explode!" She turned beet red and quietly said, "Why didn't you answer or return my calls?"

"I'm sorry dear, I was really busy with Doug's accident and all. I've been at the hospital most of the time. Ask Claire, she saw me there and then Meme," I said as fast as I could spit out.

"Meme?" Lynne asked. "Meme was at the hospital?"

"No, no, I was at the shop yesterday and Meme came in with little Elijah. I was running behind with the holidays coming up and we spent time there."

Her gaze returned back to normal and she said, "Oh, I guess that makes sense." Phew, I thought, I think I handled that well. "How's Doug? I heard there was a robbery at the bank and all the money was taken out of the vault. Doug got hit with a bat trying to fend off the criminals."

Really, gossip does spread around here and boy how it changes from the truth! "No, not exactly, dear," I said. "I don't have many of the details because it's an ongoing investigation and John won't talk. All I know is that there was a robbery, but Doug was in his office and the robber found him in there and did hit him with some blunt object. He suffered a serious head injury and is unconscious in the hospital."

"He's unconscious?" Lynne exclaimed. "That can't be good."

I realized I just lied to my own flesh and blood. I forgot to ask John if we were still saying Doug was unconscious or not. If he suspects anyone in town I would guess we would have to keep saying that for Doug's safety. I know my daughter would never say anything, but I had to stick to one story I'll make it up to her somehow.

"No, he's in pretty serious condition," I said. "I've been just sitting around the hospital mostly talking to Claire."

"You should've called me. I could've sat with you to pass the time."

"I didn't want to bother you. Saturdays are busy days for you at your bakery and there was no reason for you to close shop to just sit with your mother," I said, feeling guilty that my daughter felt bad for me and that I just lied to her.

Church started and Lynne and I sat in silence until the service was over. I knew others would come up and ask a lot of questions, so I had to keep the same story. Doug was seriously hurt after a robbery and remains unconscious at the hospital.

Nancy never made it to church that morning. Lynne told me she had too many reports to read this weekend for her history class over at the high school. Good, I thought, at least I only lied to one daughter for now.

We left church so fast Lynne had to jog to keep up with me. I didn't want to talk to too many people so I went as fast as I could. "Slow down, mom," Lynne said, huffing and puffing. "What's the rush?"

"I promised John I would stop by the station right after church and then we're driving over to the hospital. I don't want to keep him waiting too long," I replied.

"So," Lynne said looking at me with a smile. "Who are you wanting to see, Doug or John?" I knew what she was getting at and I wasn't in the mood for teasing.

"You know Doug is seriously injured. I'm not even thinking about either relationship right now. All I care about is that they catch the criminal and Doug fully recovers."

Lynne's smile faded quickly, "I'm sorry, that was insensitive of me. I know you're worried about Doug."

"I'll drop by your shop tomorrow morning before I open my store and I'll explain all I know about Doug's case. Right now, I don't know much," I said, getting into my car and waving good-bye to Lynne.

I hurried over to the station. I was really hoping John had discovered the information he needed so that he could fill me in on what Doug confided yesterday. I pulled into the station's parking lot and ran into Delores, the station's secretary. I couldn't say anything to her about my knowledge of her and Tom's pending separation. John would tell me nothing if I couldn't keep that quiet.

"Hi Ruth Ann," Delores said as we walked in together. "What are you doing here?"

"Oh, going to see John, we're heading over to see how Doug's doing," I replied. I didn't know how much Delores knew and she is John's secretary.

We entered the station and Delores headed for her desk and I headed into John's office. It was a small station with an open area for Delores' desk at the front and several desks behind her. There were only a couple of offices, and one of them was John's. Toward the back of the room was a secure area where they held prisoners temporarily until they were either released or transferred to a larger prison. John was sitting behind his desk talking with one of his men, Lou. Quickly spotting my sudden appearance, they both stopped talking.

"Hi, Ruth Ann," Lou said. "Just get back from church?"

I nodded and sat down in a chair that was facing his desk. "Yes, it was a nice service, not too long."

Dan took his leave and John closed a folder on his desk. "So, I take it nothing out of the ordinary happened?"

"Nope, I sat with Lynne and I'm not too thrilled with myself about lying to her about Doug. I said he was still unconscious and we don't know why he was attacked."

"Did you mention your part in the occurrence?" John asked.

"No I didn't," I said. "I hate lying to my own daughter and as soon as you give me some valid information I'll tell her everything."

"Of course you will, I wouldn't expect you not to," he replied.

"Well. Was that folder you closed up about Doug's case?"

"Yes, it is," he said. "Now I can now tell you more about what Doug said yesterday. Have you checked with the hospital since I left you earlier?"

"Didn't have time. You gave me strict orders to go straight from church to your office, and here I am."

"That's good of you. I did talk with Doc about thirty minutes ago and told him we would be coming by shortly, so why don't we head over there together now?'

"You just told me you were going to fill me in on everything, what's the deal?" I questioned.

"I am, but it's best that Doug tell his story again and I'll fill in with the missing information. That way we all hear it together and can ask questions at that time."

I agreed, and within a few minutes John and I drove over to the hospital in the police car. Doc Albert was there to greet us and brought us immediately back to Doug's room. He didn't stay, just gave Doug a quick check and headed back out into the hall. There was still a cop posted outside Doug's room. John eyed him and the cop closed the door.

"Hi, Doug," I said, "You're looking much better."

"I feel a lot better. My head doesn't feel like it's going to explode, and I'm told we all get to talk about what happened."

John answered for me, "Yes we do, so let's get at it." He waited for Doug to begin.

"It was late Friday afternoon and I told the staff they could all leave exactly at five. It was a slow afternoon so they had finished most of their work. Tom wasn't in and I locked the doors myself. I waited a few minutes then went into the vault and pulled out the piece of jewelry we talked about. A 12.82 carat, rare Swedish Aquamarine necklace."

John stopped him, "Ok, this is where I start cutting in. The stone does have the proper papers and it actually did come from Sweden, back in the late 1800's. I'm told it arrived in the United States in 1882." He nodded for Doug to continue.

"Wait," I said, "I have a question. Who brought this stone to the U.S. and how did it get to your bank?"

"I'm getting there," Doug said. "Let me run down the events, then I'll give you those details, okay?" I nodded. "So, I brought the necklace to my office and turned on my desk lamp. I turned the inside bank lights off so everyone knew the bank was officially closed. I had received the necklace earlier that week and had a strange feeling it was going to cause trouble."

Chief John interrupted Doug. "Really? Why would you think that?"

"Because of the strange way it came into my possession." He looked to see if we would interrupt but we didn't. "I'll explain that in a moment. I took the necklace out of its black velvet pouch and set it on my desk. There was a small piece of paper in the pouch and I pulled that out and read it."

This is where John cut in, "That piece of paper is valid, Doug." He turned to me and said, "This is more information we had to prove was accurate, Ruth Ann. Doug will tell you what the note said."

"Yes, yes, I will in due time," Doug said. "I was trying to figure out how to handle the necklace, and the situation, when I heard a noise outside of my office. I looked up and didn't see anything out of the normal and figured the noise came from outside. You see, I had earphones on listening to some calming music. I wasn't very smart, I'm aware of that. I should've realized the noise was much louder than I thought since I was plugged in. I went back to examining the piece when all of a sudden a man dressed in black ran in holding a long object and just swung at my head. That's it, that's all I can remember."

"But," I said, "there has to be more."

"Well, those are the events, Ruth Ann," John said. "Now Doug will tell you about the necklace, note, and the stress it put on him."

"Stress?" I asked. "Why would a necklace cause stress? It sounds like whoever owns it would be lucky."

"Yes, that's the problem, Ruth Ann," John said. "The necklace is yours."

"What!" I yelled. "Sorry, Doug, didn't mean to scream. What on earth do you mean the necklace is mine?"

John remained quiet so Doug could explain. "It's true, Ruth Ann. The rightful owner of the piece is you." He hesitated a moment thinking I would question him but I let him explain. "A few days ago, Christie came into my office and handed me a box. She said when she went to lunch and came back this box was sitting on top of her desk. It was a plain, brown mailing box, bigger than was necessary to hold the pouch. There was no return mailing address, but the postage read shipped from Stockholm, Sweden. Are you following me so far?"

"Yes, I still don't understand how it's mine, but go on," I said.

"The box was to be sent to my bank, in care of myself. I have no idea why or how they knew of our bank or me. I opened the box, not thinking anything strange and I discovered this black pouch surrounded by packing popcorn."

John interrupted with his facts, "The box was thoroughly checked and it did come from Stockholm and it arrived in the United States about two weeks ago. So it took quite a while to arrive at the bank here in town."

"Okay, thanks John," Doug said. "Inside the black pouch was this beautiful blue stone on a silver or white gold chain. I had no idea of the importance or that it was supposed to go to you, Ruth Ann."

"Then how do you know it's for me?" I asked. "The note that was in the pouch must have my name on it, right?"

Doug nodded, "It was the strangest note I ever received. That's why I didn't tell you about it right away. I wanted to do some checking and then I was going to call you into the bank. I only had it a couple days and I never was alone. I didn't want anyone to get an eye on the stone, it's pretty big."

"So," John began, "Doug didn't know if the stone was a fake or not. It could've been some kind a weird joke with costume jewelry."

"Exactly," Doug took over. "I was looking up some gemologists nearby and I had an appointment set up for this coming week. I didn't want to get your hopes up with this beautiful rare piece and it end up being a fake."

"That makes perfect sense, Doug," I said. "But please tell me what the note said. I can't take this much longer!"

John pulled out his notebook and read the details of the note. "I have the actual note in evidence back at the station. But I copied it and I'll let Doug do the honors, unless your head hurts too much?"

"You read it, John," Doug said. "I thought it would stick in my head forever, but that blow has made me foggy."

"Ok, here it goes," John, said. He held out a piece of paper about 4 by 6 inches long, plain white and typed with an old fashioned typewriter.

Dear Mr. Albertson,

The enclosed necklace is a rare, 12.82 carat Aquamarine that was an heirloom for a family my father represented. The Swedish family name, Liljestrom, came from Stockholm, Sweden. A Beda Liljestrom once wore the piece when she immigrated to United States in 1882. We lost touch with the family heirloom after that time, believing it to be sold or stolen.

The estate lawyer, Steven Svenson Jr., representing the Liljestrom family, received the necklace back on September 1st of this year in Stockholm, Sweden. Mr. Svenson has no knowledge of how the piece ended up back at his office. There are no surviving Liljestrom family members in the area, and after a long search we come to find out that there is a Ruth Ann Conroy living in your town of Deer Creek. She is now the rightful owner of the necklace. Ruth Ann Conroy is the granddaughter of Ruth Ann Kraft, nee Lilgestrom (English spelling).

Please forward the necklace with the following information:

12.82-carat weight
Light blue Aquamarine, rectangular shaped
Origin: Stockholm, Sweden
Estimated value: priceless, none of that rarity to compare. (Perhaps in the United States a more precise value can be made).

My father has told me stories of this gem. It has been in the Liljestrom family for generations. Rumors of illegal activities have been linked to this item. Robbery, assaults, and even a murder have been linked with this necklace. These of course are just "stories" that have been passed on through the years. Please take care of the owner when she takes possession, just to be safe, Godspeed.

Sincerely,
Michael Svenson, Esquire
September the fifteenth

The three of us were silent for a long time; none of us were capable of speaking. John was the first to break the silence, "Wow, I've read this letter several times, but each time is as dramatic as the first."

Doug looked at me and asked, "Now do you see why I waited before showing you this?"

"Doug did the right thing, except for contacting the police. We could've investigated and determined whether the piece or the note were legitimate. Now we're in quite the pickle, aren't we?" John asked, looking at Doug.

"I know, I know," Doug replied, shaking his head. "I thought I could figure it all out and then bring this magnificent piece of jewelry to Ruth Ann."

"Doug, I'm not mad, but I really wish you would've called me in and we could've researched the piece together," I said. "This is wonderful, a piece from my family!" I looked at Doug and said,

"And you, John, I could've told you my mother's side of the family is named Lilgestrom, and they're from Stockholm. I also know of Beda, my great grandmother."

"Think about it Ruth Ann, anyone could figure out your family's history. It's the stone we had to verify and the illegal activities surrounding this necklace, too."

"Aren't those just old stories told through the generations to make it sound exciting?" I asked. "I've never heard about any of them or the necklace that I remember."

"You don't remember your mother or your grandmother talking about a family piece of jewelry that has such value?"

"Well, yes, but I never saw any pieces of jewelry and figured they never really existed." I added, "I have many items that were handed down to me but I never had a necklace like that."

"Maybe it was stolen from your great grandmother, Beda, and your grandmother never told anyone. It could be a disgrace to lose a piece like this if it's been around for a long time," Doug said. "There are a number of items in the vault that belong to families here in town. They claim to be family heirlooms but who really knows unless they have been appraised."

"That could've happened," John said. "There's more to discuss and I don't want Doc to come in and kick us out, so let's get at it." Doug and I agreed and let John speak, "First, the necklace is missing or should I state it was stolen. Who found out about this piece even being here, and why did they go to such lengths to steal it?"

"Didn't you see what that lawyer wrote in the letter, it's priceless," I said. "That could bring any criminal to Deer Creek. However, it doesn't answer the question of who knew it was even here." John and I turned our attention to Doug.

"Well, that could be from me," he answered. "I told you I contacted gemologists and one is coming this week. I contacted a number of them and maybe there's some recording of a stone like this disappearing years ago."

"Sounds farfetched to me," John said. "But let's suppose that is true. A gem dealer just happens to have known about a stone of this importance and what, he hires a thug to steal it?"

"I don't know, John, I haven't told anyone else about it. "Even my staff doesn't know."

"What concerns me are all the warnings about the necklace.

We did some research back at the station and your family name, Liljestrom, does have quite the background," John stated.

"You mean regarding the necklace?" I inquired.

"Yes," John said. "That necklace has quite a history. First, I couldn't track how long your family owned the piece. Second, as far as I could go back there were reports of numerous thefts of the necklace, yet your family seemed to always get the piece back."

"And it looks like it just happened again," Doug interrupted. "The piece appeared to have been missing for at least two generations and now it has popped back up. But this time, not in Sweden, but here in Colorado."

"Seems to be accurate," Doug said. "We don't know if the necklace had always been in Sweden. Remember, Beda supposedly immigrated with it back in the late 1800's."

"True, but then there's no mention of it until now and it ended up back in Sweden," John said. "How did it get back there I wonder?"

"Can't your men look into this?" I asked. "And Doug, maybe your gemologist might have answers, too."

"My men are still looking into this." John turned to him and asked, "When is your guy coming?"

"He's scheduled to come to my bank on Tuesday," Doug answered. "But it's Sunday and I'm stuck here in the hospital. Do you think Doc will discharge me before then?"

Doc must've been right outside his door and stuck his head in and said, "Not likely, Doug, you need more time to heal. Just over twenty-four hours ago we didn't know if you'd survive the night. Plus," Doc said looking to John, "Uh, don't most people still think he's unconscious?"

"Yes, Doc, you bring up a valid point," John said. "We're going to have to bring this man to the hospital to meet with you."

"Wait," I blurted, "We don't have the necklace anymore! How can we have a gemologist look at something we don't have?"

"We're going to bring him here to discuss what he knows about the piece. He must have some knowledge of this stone and its importance or he wouldn't have bothered coming here at all. Unless," John asked Doug, "You are paying him a large sum to appraise it?"

"No," Doug said, excited. "I just explained the necklace, the age and description, and within an hour he called me back and jumped at the invitation to come here and appraise it."

"Hold on, Doug," John cut in. "You never told me that. Why would someone do that unless he has a very interested stake in it?" He added, "It appears your gemologist may know more than he said and red flags are popping up."

"It does sound suspicious, Doug," I said. "But that sounds crazy that someone would know about a Swedish necklace, even if the value is high."

"Priceless, Ruth Ann," Doug corrected me. "Remember that note states the value is considered priceless."

"Doug, please tell me you didn't tell the gemologist that?" asked Chief John.

Doug looked about as guilty as the guy who bashed his head in. "I believe I did, John," he said. "How was I to know how valid the letter was or that anyone would have knowledge of the necklace?"

"Well, if your goal was to intrigue him to meet you here, then you succeeded. However, you kind of put yourself in a dangerous position if this gemologist isn't on the up and up."

Doug looked horrible again and Doc kicked us out so Doug could rest. John and I went into the lobby of the hospital and John said, "You know, maybe what Doug did will help us now."

"How?" I asked.

"Well, it's our only solid lead to the person who knew about the necklace besides Doug and the lawyer who sent it. Maybe I'll just be the person to meet with this supposed gemologist."

"Can I be there, too?" I asked. "Considering I'm the owner of it."

"We have two days before I have to decide. Let me get to work on this case and see if the guys at the station came up with more information," John said.

Chapter 5

We drove back to the station and I picked up my car. John felt I was safe until the gemologist came to town. If he was the one who set up the robbery, then I'm sure he wouldn't send any goons back in town until he discovers what we know about the necklace. John did make me promise to go straight home and only go to my store until Tuesday. He would check in with me regularly and if I didn't answer my door or phone, he would break my door in. I told him not to worry, just work on finding out where my family heirloom is and catching the person who put Doug into the hospital.

I left the hospital and drove to the small grocery store in town. Chris Jenkins runs the store and she is married to Roger who owns the hardware store and gas station. They have one son, Ricky, who works in all three places. I didn't tell John I was stopping at the store, but I needed some food and felt it was quite safe to make a quick stop.

I pulled into the lot of the store and walked in. It was dinner-time on Sunday and Chris was about to close the store. She saw me and immediately opened the door for me. "Hi Ruth Ann, you got here just in time. I was about to head out."

"I'm sorry," I said. "I didn't realize it was closing time. Can I grab a few items to get me through a day or two?"

"Of course, c'mon in," she replied.

I took a cart and grabbed some milk, bread, cereal, lunchmeat, and salad items. Then I grabbed some baking supplies. I felt like making chocolate chip cookies and didn't want to bother my daughter. It'll keep me occupied while I put this ordeal in order in my head. I noticed Chris was watching me closely and I could tell she was aching to ask me something.

"Ok, Chris, what do you want to know?" I asked. "It's about Doug, isn't it?"

"Well, yes," she began. "Everyone who comes in here starts

gossiping and now that you're here you can tell me the truth."

"What have you heard, Chris?" I asked, before revealing what I could.

"Geez, Ruth Ann, I've heard so many stories," she said. "I've heard everything from Doug being kept alive by machines to he's up and roaming the halls of the hospital, bored."

"Seriously?" I asked, stunned. "What else?"

"I heard that someone robbed the bank and the contents of the vault are empty and Doug tried to stop the robbers and they hit him on the head with a blunt object." She looked at me and added, "But the consensus is that there was a robbery at the bank and Doug is still in the hospital."

"Correct on the consensus, Chris," I answered.

Chris looked angry and responded, "Are you serious? That's all you're going to tell me?"

"I really don't know much, Chris," I said. "There appeared to be a robbery at the bank but I don't believe the vault was emptied. Doug was injured, but not trying to catch the criminal. He was in his office and the person hit him over the head. He was severely hurt and is still in the hospital."

"But you must know more about his condition because you've been there constantly," Chris stated. "So how is he now?"

"I haven't been there constantly, but I have visited and so has John. Not much information has been given to me about the actual crime. I don't work for the police and John has told me to butt out. However, I do know Doug is stable, not running around the halls. He's still unconscious but I believe he will make a full recovery. It's just taking time for him to come around."

Chris looked pleased. "See, that wasn't so difficult and you didn't tell me anything specific."

"I don't know specifics," I said, starting to feel defensive. I hated all these secrets and lies, but I didn't have a choice right now. I just hope that when the truth comes out and people find out my part in the whole ordeal that they'll still be friendly with me.

"Ruth Ann, you date both the Chief and Doug. You know that people around town are going to look to you for answers. I have a feeling your store will be pretty busy tomorrow." she said smiling. "Hopefully sales in your store will be booming this week. Could be a plug for your business, don't you think?"

"That never entered my mind, Chris. I don't want to benefit from a horrendous crime," I said, helping Chris put my items into the bags. "Maybe I should close the store for a few days. My excuse could be that I'm setting up the store for the holidays."

"I don't know, unless you want to avoid seeing people and repeating what you know over and over. Otherwise, it might be financially beneficial to stay open. You could sell some of your current inventory and then have room for holiday items."

"I have no reason to avoid anyone," I said, a trifle irritated. "I really need to sell off some older items so thanks for the idea. I believe I'll stay open and see what happens." I said goodbye to Chris and headed back to my car. I put the bags into my back seat and was thinking about what Chris said to me when I noticed a car in the street slowly driving by the grocery store. At first I didn't think too much of this, but as I drove home I realized there was a car behind me that looked like the one I just saw at the store.

I decided to drive all the way down Main Street and take the long way back to my house. If the car was still behind me I'd pass by where I live and go straight to the police station. I was mad at myself for letting Chris get me all worked up and not paying attention to what John had warned earlier. He believed I was safe, but he was also worried that the person who injured Doug had spotted me. For all we know this person thinks he murdered the president of the bank. I made a few extra turns down some residential side streets and the car was still close behind me. No one in town would make the turns I did. There weren't that many streets and people here just drove from Main Street to their own street. They didn't go up and down the streets unnecessarily.

I decided to drive straight to the police station and call John from my car so he could meet me at my car. As I drove back onto Main Street I noticed the car had disappeared. Ah ha! That person must have figured out I knew they were following me. The downside is that they're aware that I know someone is after me. I pulled into the police station parking lot and contemplated my next step. Do I risk going home now or do I tell John what I believe had just happened?

I wasn't going to sit here alone for long. I didn't feel safe anymore. It all hit me like a brick. I kept telling John, Doug, and myself that I was fine, that I didn't feel any danger would befall me.

Now it's all changed, unless I just imagined I was being followed.

After a short time debating my situation, I decided to go inside the station and see if John was still there. He would first scold me for going to the store and not straight home. Then he would never let me alone until this crime has been solved and I was safe again.

I walked in and Delores was absent since it was a Sunday evening, but a young policeman, I didn't recognize, sat at the front desk. "I'm here to see the chief," I said.

"Is there something wrong, ma'am?" he asked.

Ma'am? Really? I never liked being called that! "I'm a friend of his and would like to talk with him. Is he still here?"

"One moment and I'll buzz his office," he said, picking up the phone on the desk.

I turned around and walked toward the window facing the parking lot. I wanted to make sure the coast was clear and no stranger was hanging around my car. It should be safe parked in a police station parking lot.

"Ma'am, the chief told me to let you back. Are you ready?" he asked, buzzing the locked door into the main station area.

"Yes," I said. "Are you new here? I don't recognize you."

"Temporary help," he replied. "I'm new out of the academy and your chief asked for some extra help around here. I'm very happy to get the experience, so I jumped on the opportunity."

"That's great, what's your name if I may ask?" I inquired.

"Officer Pinkerton, ma'am," he answered. "Todd Pinkerton."

"Nice to meet you and welcome to Deer Creek," I said as I walked into John's office. John waved the new recruit away and motioned for me to sit down at a chair in front of his desk.

"What do I owe for your visit, Ruth Ann? You should be home by now."

I sat down in the chair and tried to figure out the smoothest explanation so he didn't explode. "Um, I was planning on driving straight home when I realized I needed a few grocery items. So I thought it was harmless to stop by Chris Jenkins' store."

John jumped up out of his desk chair and shouted, "You did what? I explicitly told you to go straight home and you disobeyed my direct orders."

"Whoa. John, I'm not your employee. I can and will do what I want. I didn't think there would be any harm to me if I made a quick stop at a store where everyone knows me," I snapped.

He turned a lighter shade of red and sat back down. "Sorry, I have had a long couple days and if anything happened to you I would never forgive myself."

"I'm fine, John, but," he quickly caught my *but*.

"But? What do you mean but?" he retorted. "Did something happen? That's why you're here and not at home, isn't it?"

"Will you please let me explain?" I demanded. "Nothing happened, really, I just thought I might've been followed from the store and to be safe I came here instead of my house. I may have even imagined it all, I don't know anymore." I added, "You and Doug have me all scared now and I feel I might've been a bit paranoid."

Trying to remain calm, John took a deep breath before he began. "Let me get this straight. You went to Jenkins's grocery store, right," I nodded. "Then when you walked out to your car there was another car you didn't recognize?"

"Not exactly," I said. "I was preoccupied with what Chris and I had been talking about when I noticed a car driving on Main Street by the store going very slowly. I glanced up as I was putting my bags in the car and saw the car."

"Go on," he said calmly.

"I didn't think too much of it and so I started to drive down Main toward the side street to my house. I happened to notice a car in my rear view mirror. I have no idea why I thought they would be following me, but I had a strange feeling. So I drove around a few side streets and the car was still behind me. I panicked a little I have to admit, and decided to drive here to you."

"So the car followed you all around and even to the station?" he asked.

"No, when I made it back to Main Street, the car had vanished," I said, shrugging my shoulders.

"Vanished when?" he asked.

"I'm not sure," I answered. "They were behind me, in and out a few side streets, but when I was about to make a right back onto Main they were gone."

John slammed his fist on his desk and I jumped a little in my chair. "I knew it," he blurted out. "I knew I should never have left you on your own."

"Seriously, John?" I retorted. "We both thought I was fairly safe. That's why you trusted me to listen to you and I blew it. I'm very sorry I didn't go straight home."

"Actually I'm extremely happy you didn't," John said, surprising me.

"What? I thought you were furious with me for not following your directions."

"I was until you told me you were being followed. If whoever it was followed you to your house instead of the store you might've been in bigger trouble than you could imagine."

"Wow, I never thought of it that way," I said. "Then it's a good thing I disobeyed you, huh?"

"Not funny, Ruth Ann," John barked back at me. "Now we know that you're in danger."

"Maybe I was mistaken, John," I said. "Maybe some teenager was just cruising the town."

"Do you really believe that's all it was?" he asked. "Or are you trying to diminish the importance of this incident?"

"No, I just don't want to believe it's true," I said. "What do we do now? There apparently is someone in this town who wants to keep an eye on me."

"You know it probably isn't a resident of this town or you would've recognized the car following you," he said, trying to comfort me. "We have to presume there's a stranger hanging around town. What I'll do starting tomorrow is question people around here. I'll go to each of the businesses along Main Street and see if they noticed any outsiders around. It isn't ski season yet, so most people in town are residents."

"But that means you'll raise suspicion and fear around here," I said. "One of those businesses is my daughter's bakery. I don't want Lynne scared to run her bakery, especially since she has to get there so early in the morning. She'll feel unsafe."

"I don't have any choice, Ruth Ann. The best thing I can do is raise awareness and then people will notice all sorts of things. Many of them will be unimportant, but we'll weed all that out and we may find our person." John was deep in thought for a moment and then blurted out, "Hey, you never told me if you recognized the car that was following you."

"They were behind me with their headlights on, so I had no

idea," I said. "And in the grocery parking lot it happened so fast I can't recall."

"Just try hard and think back to the car going slowly down the street outside of the Jenkins's store. Was there anything about the vehicle, color or size that you can remember?"

I closed my eyes and put myself back at the store and thought about all Chris Jenkins and I talked about. I remember looking up from loading my car and seeing the SUV going down the street very slow. "It wasn't a car, it was a SUV, a white one!"

"That's terrific!" John called out. "I'll put out a watch for any vehicle similar to that. My guys will drive around the area and see if there's a match. You didn't happen recognize a particular hood ornament or brand?"

"No, sorry, just a white, SUV," I replied. "When they were following me I could only see the headlights and a person behind the wheel." I caught myself again, "John, there was only one person in the front seat, a male because I could see a large figure with some facial hair."

John was scribbling so fast on a piece of paper and repeating, "That's great, just great." He dropped his pen and walked over to me and grabbed my arms, and I stood up so he could give me a great big hug. "I'm so proud of how brave you are, Ruth Ann. This'll work out, I promise you." He ran out of his office shouting for Lou or Dave, his closest men working with him on the case. I sat back down and closed my eyes. I was suddenly exhausted and I just wanted to go home and sleep in my own bed. I wondered how long it would be before I'd be allowed to do that.

John was gone quite a long time and when he entered his office he found me dozing off in the chair. It was late Sunday evening and I knew I needed to open the store in the morning. He let me nap for some time and when I woke I wondered where I was.

"Ruth Ann," John said, seeing I was a bit confused. "You're still in my office. I have a plan of how we're going to keep you and Doug safe until we catch these guys. Hopefully not too long, I'm counting on getting some information out of that gemologist guy that's coming on Tuesday."

"And what is your brilliant plan, John? Keep me locked up in one of your cells here at the station," I said sarcastically.

"Don't tempt me, but no, that's not my plan. Can you let me

get it out and then you can question me all you like?" I nodded in agreement. "Ok, Doug is at the hospital until this whole thing is solved. I'll keep a constant guard at his door. The problem is you," he began. "You're the wild card running all over town and talking to people. This guy may get antsy and get to you before you tell too many people and then his cover could be blown."

"Ok, I'm following so far," I said.

"Yes, well as for your safety, I don't see any way around keeping you under surveillance, too. The problem is I don't have the manpower in this small town to keep round the clock guards on Doug and you, and try and solve this case."

"So let me guess," I said. "You want me to move in with you?"

"That did cross my mind, but no," John said. "People gossip too much here so that won't work. However, we need to come up with a reason why you have to temporarily move out of your house."

"No way, John!" I interrupted. "I will not jeopardize my daughters' lives either."

"I know that," he answered quickly. "I wasn't going to suggest that. Can I go on until I'm finished, please?"

"Fine," I snapped. "But get to it or I'll keep interrupting."

His glare told me to stay silent until he was done. "Ok, I think the best solution would be to put you up at the resort for a while under a fake name, and you'll have to stay in your room until I say it's safe." He saw the expression on my face, that I was about to explode, when he quickly added, "It'll be one of their suites so you'll have all the luxuries you deserve."

"Now wait a minute, John," I said. "That'll never work. Everyone knows me here, and I have a business to run. The holidays are right around the corner and I have to be at my store."

"Can't you just take the week off? By then we may have caught the guy and solved the case," he said, knowing I would refuse this ridiculous idea.

"No way, John," I answered. "I will not hide away and close my store. Think of another plan."

"But Ruth Ann, I don't know what else to do. You won't involve your family, and I agree with that. You don't want to stay with me and you won't stay at the resort. Do you have any better ideas?"

I was trying so hard to come up with a plan that would keep me safe, keep my business running, and make John satisfied. It sounded impossible to me, but there had to be a way. We both sat in silence for a while when an idea popped into my head, maybe not the best, but it could work.

"John, I have an idea. Part of what you said works. I'll have to come up with a reason to stay away from my house for a few days. Maybe termites or some sort of infestation that will require my house to be abandoned for a while."

"Ok, so far so good," John agreed. "Where will you stay is the question of the night?"

"I'll stay at my store in my office. I have a couch in there and a bathroom with a shower because I work out almost daily there." I saw the astonished look on his face and quickly added, "Wait, let me finish before you knock down my plan. I'll pretend to be staying at the resort while my house is unoccupied and if anyone really is after me they'll first go to my house and see some sort of sign out front with a pest company logo. They'll probably assume I would take a room at the resort so they would go and check it out next. When they see my name on the guest list and the room number they'll hopefully search it." I took a deep breath and said, "Then, and only then will we know if I really am a target."

John's expression went from outrage to disbelief to possible. I was impressed with myself for coming up with such a devious plan that could actually catch the criminal, too. He sat still and I could tell he was going over in his head all the problems that could occur when he finally spoke. "You know, that's a good plan, Ruth Ann."

"Thank you," I said proudly. "I thought so too, and if I'm truly a person of interest to this criminal he would try and find me no matter where I was."

"Now you raised an alarming point," John said. "What if he realizes it's just a ruse and finds you at your store. Especially since you'll be there during the day anyway."

"I can pretend to drive to the resort, go in, and then sneak back out and go back to the store. Heck, I'll even eat dinner there each night with you and make my presence even more noticeable."

"Not bad, if someone was watching you, they'll see you with the police chief and leave you alone," John replied. "I could pretend to walk you to your fake room and then you can sneak down the employee's staircase and I'll meet you at my car. Then I'll take you back to your store." His facial expression changed. "There are so many holes in this plan it scares me. He could grab you at your store or even in the employee staircase. I'll have to keep a guard at your store, Ruth Ann, I don't have any choice."

"You said you were short handed, John," I said.

"I'll figure it out. If I have to hire an outside guard firm I'll do it. I don't have much time; the gemologist will be here in less than two days." He turned back to some papers on his desk and asked me, "Do you know the number of the resort? I need to have a talk with Richard or Carol Dickson about acquiring a fake room for you. I'll tell them it's police business, but I'm sure they won't buy that. I'll give them basic information and swear them to secrecy for your safety. They'll agree and also be an extra set of eyes at the resort for us."

"What about tonight? Do you have a pest company we can borrow a sign from?" I asked.

"We'll just make one up and print it here, and later tonight I'll drive over there and stick it on your front door. As for your sleeping arrangements tonight, I think it's best that you stay at my place for the night. We can hide you away again without the town gossip exploding," John said.

"You make the call to Richard and Carol and then can you follow me back to my house so I can pack up?"

John made the necessary arrangements at the resort and promised Carol, the owner, that I would talk with her tomorrow. We went to my house, and while I packed, John put the sign up on the outside of the front door and checked the house thoroughly. He didn't think any intruders had been here, but if I had been followed earlier it was just a matter of time before they come here.

By the time we arrived at John's condo it was late and the majority of people were long asleep. John offered his bedroom to me again and he took the couch. We didn't do much talking since it was late and tomorrow we had a lot of work to accomplish.

I fell asleep almost immediately and woke to the sun shining and John in the kitchen making coffee. "Good morning," John said, almost jovially.

"Wow, you're in a good mood," I replied, not as jovially. I wanted my tea and something to eat. "Are we ready for today?" I asked.

"Yep," he answered. "We'll drive over to the resort and put a few items in your bogus room, and go down and eat some breakfast. Then I'll be there when Carol confronts you, and I can control what's said to her."

"You have trust issues with me, don't you?" I teased.

"No, that's not it. It's just that this is an official police investigation and we want their help, but they still can't know everything about the case. So I'll diffuse any questions that shouldn't be answered, is that ok with you?" he asked curtly. "After we eat, I'll follow you to your store and make sure all is safe in there."

"Sounds good, John," I said.

"I put in a request to a company that hires out security guards and they contacted me immediately. There will be a guard inside your store round the clock starting this morning."

"That was fast, but won't it look suspicious having security at my store? I've never had one before."

"If anyone asks, just tell them you're helping out a long-time friend who opened a guard company and they're using your store to help train new guards. Plus, you can add that since the bank was robbed it didn't hurt to have a little extra security."

I thought it was a great answer and told him I'd use it. We headed out to the resort for breakfast and I felt happier than I had in a couple days. Doug was improving, even though most people didn't know that, and I felt safe with all the security around me. I drove my car over to the resort and John followed behind me. I didn't see any strange white SUV around and wondered if all this effort was for no reason. Better safe than sorry, I thought to myself.

We walked toward the front desk as if I was going to check in. Carol was waiting there since she knew our plan. I had a small piece of luggage that I would take up to my phony room and then meet John in the dining room. All went smoothly and we sat down to a wonderful breakfast. I was in need of nourishment so I ordered the pumpkin pancakes. They were my favorite this time of year. I asked for extra syrup and dumped all of it on my pancakes as John and Carol stared at me like I was crazy. "Gee Ruth Ann," Carol started to say. "How can you eat all that and stay so fit?"

I put a big bite in my mouth and smiled. "I doubt I'll eat all this, but if I do I'll just make myself work out a little longer than I usually do."

John chuckled at me because he knew I had a huge sweet tooth. That's why my own daughter opening her bakery was such a disaster for me. I could never work in there for a long period of time. I would eat more than was sold and gain so much weight that I would be one unhappy middle-aged woman!

"So, Carol, since you're standing over us, why don't you just sit down and join in our conversation?" joked John.

"Don't mind if I do," Carol said, sitting next to me in the booth. "So, Richard filled me in on most of your conversation last night, but I have so many questions for you both."

"Now Carol, you know it's an ongoing investigation and I can't discuss it," John said as he stuffed down a piece of buttered toast.

"I get that John, but what I don't get is why Ruth Ann's involved. She's not on staff at the police station is she?"

I answered for John since his mouth was still full, "No, I'm not, but I'm involved in the case because," I hesitated and John nodded for me to say more. "I was the one who found Doug at the bank right after the robber left the building. And there's a slight chance he saw me through the window before he escaped."

John's glare told me to stop at that and say nothing else. Carol on the other hand looked stunned. Her mouth gaped wide open until she was able to speak. "I didn't know that!"

"Nobody does, Carol," John, answered. "Only the police are privy to that information for Doug and Ruth Ann's safety."

"That makes sense. So does Ruth Ann's staying at my resort. You want to flush the guy out so you can catch him," Carol said.

"That's part of it," John replied.

"Richard told me that you put up a fake pest control sign at Ruth Ann's house. You want the guy to go to her house and think she's not there. Oh, oh, then they'll come here and think she's in a room here. If we see any stranger walking around her room we contact you and bam, they're caught!"

"Kind of," John answered, stunned by Carol's excitement over the ordeal. "We also installed a camera just outside her hotel room and one inside. It's under constant surveillance and I'm hoping that if you see any person of suspicion wandering around that you'll call me immediately."

"Sounds exciting," Carol said. "Richard and I'll be your eyes and ears at the resort."

"Great," John said. "One condition, no two," he started to say. "First, do not confront anyone that you feel is acting oddly, you call me a.s.a.p. Second, none of your staff can know what we're doing here. Do you understand what I'm asking of both of you?" John added, "It's a matter of life and death." John wanted Carol's excitement to turn the reality that there's a dangerous criminal out there.

Carol got the point, "I understand. We don't want anything bad to happen to Ruth Ann or Doug. How's Doug really doing?"

John was surprised at her question. He wondered if people doubted what was being told about Doug's condition. That would put Doug in more danger, too. "Why would you ask me that, Carol? Doug's been unconscious for two days now and all I can tell you is that he's stable and Doc Albert is hopeful."

"Why are you so defensive, John?" questioned Carol. "I just thought with what Richard and I know that maybe Doug was better or worse than you were saying. I'm sorry, I don't want to make you mad."

John relaxed his tone and said, "Sorry, I'm just frustrated with the whole situation. This shouldn't happen in our town, it's small and away from big city crime."

I said, "True, but bad things can happen anywhere, and you'll catch this guy soon so we can get back to normal around here."

Chapter 6

We finished our breakfast and Carol assured us that she would keep quiet. John followed me to work and we pulled into the alley behind the store. There was another car parked there that I wasn't familiar with. John told me to wait in my car while he checked the car out. It wasn't Meme's car and she wasn't due in for another hour or two. She had to wait to bring Elijah to daycare so I always let her come in around ten.

John took my keys and entered the back room of the store. About five minutes later he came back out the alley door and saw me standing and talking with another man. He rushed over to find it was just the new security guard next to me.

He looked pale as a ghost until he saw it was the guard. "I thought I told you to stay in your car, Ruth Ann. You don't know if this guy is legit or not." John turned to the guard and asked for identification and he pulled out his badge and ID card. John examined it and handed it back to the guy.

"Ok, this is Paul Welch, your security guard," John said.

"We already introduced ourselves," I said, giving John a nasty look. "Paul ran over to the bakery and grabbed some coffee while he waited for us to get here." I turned to face John and added, "And my daughter asked all about him and he told her he was hired to be a security guard at my shop!"

"Uh oh," John said. "I guess you'll have to do some explaining to her. Just use the story we came up with, it'll work, and act like it's no big deal."

"John, what if she asks what old friend of mine has a security business?"

"Good point, let me see," John said and quickly answered me.

"Don't you have old contacts from your days working at the antique auction place? Maybe tell her someone from back then contacted you and said they opened a local business in Grand Junction. That should work."

I acknowledged it was probably good enough to get by for now. The three of us entered the store and I gave Paul the tour of the place. John and Paul agreed that he should walk the store occasionally, but for the most part, stand near the front door so he was visible. If anyone came up to the front door they would see a guard and hopefully, if they were up to no good, turn and leave.

John left me in the hands of Paul, the guard. He was armed and that made John feel better. You never know, John explained to me when I argued about people seeing an armed guard inside my store. "Really?" I said. "In an antique shop?" He wouldn't respond, but turned and left after he told me to keep my phone with me at all times and always answer his calls. I agreed, and he took off, back to the police station.

It was around nine in the morning and the store didn't open until ten. I thought I could get some paperwork done in my office and told Paul where I could be found. The hour went by quickly and before I knew it, it was time to open the store. Meme arrived promptly at ten and went out into the showroom and left me out back to wait for a delivery from the city. I had ordered a few holiday items and wanted to check them out when they arrived and price them. I was letting Meme handle all the displays now, so I could concentrate on the finances of the business and ways to make it more profitable.

I had to explain the reason for the guard to Meme after she came rushing into the back room. "I'm sorry I forgot to tell you about Paul. It's not a big deal, just a training ground for new security guards. I have an old friend in the city that wanted to use my store to do some of their hands on training. He'll just be here a short time. So if any customers ask, that's what you tell them, okay?" Meme nodded and headed back out into the showroom.

Whenever the front door opens a bell jingles to alert us to a customer. The first customer of the day was none other than my daughter, Lynne. I knew she would be coming by fairly soon since Paul was just in her bakery. I waited until she came into the back so I could talk with her privately.

"Hi, dear," I said. "Isn't your bakery crowded right now? You could've come by later."

"Really? That's all I get?" Lynne snapped. "An armed guard walks into my shop a little while ago, orders a coffee and tells me he's working as a guard in your antique shop." She stood still and waited for my response.

"Um, yes, dear. His name is Paul, and he'll be working here for a few days or so," I said, knowing this wouldn't be a good enough explanation. "I guess you're wondering why I need a guard, huh?"

Lynne corrected me and said, "You mean an armed guard."

"Yes, I believe he does carry a weapon. It's not a big deal, Lynne. He's just here training as a guard for a friend of mine."

"What friend?" she inquired. "I've never heard you talk about knowing anyone in security outside of the police here in town."

"He's from my past working days at the auction house. You were too young to know any of my old contacts." I looked at her reaction and continued, "I still use my research contacts for items that come in the store, you know that much. And when one of my old contacts said they were opening up a security firm in the city they asked if I could use a guard. Of course I said no, but then he asked if I would do him a favor and just use a guard now and then for their training. They know Deer Creek is a small, fairly safe town, and that it would help with some practice." I waited to see if she took my bait.

"Oh," Lynne said, calming down. "That makes sense. Why didn't you tell me about it though? I don't like surprises like this."

"I'm sorry, it was very last minute and with me hanging out at the hospital all weekend I forgot to tell you and Nancy. How is Nancy? I haven't talked to her in days."

"She's been wrapped up reading and grading papers. I haven't seen or talked to her much either."

"Well I'll give her a call later today after she's done at school. How's your business? Any new items for me to taste?" I asked, changing the topic.

Lynne became excited and said, "Yes, I've been working on a whole new line of items. They're different flavors of chocolate balls."

"Excuse me, did you say balls? That sounds a bit inappropriate don't you think?" I questioned.

"No, mom, not at all. They're flavored truffle balls dipped in white, milk, or dark chocolate. I experimented with the Oreo balls in the store and they were sold out before lunch. So then I tried pumpkin, and peanut butter, and vanilla. There are so many combinations I could almost open up another store and call it, 'She's Got Balls!' Isn't that a great idea?"

"Sounds like I should come down and try these balls. You're really thinking of opening another store here?" I asked.

"Well, maybe a specialty store in the resort if Carol thinks it could be profitable. I think it's a great idea."

While Lynne was preoccupied, I suggested I come by her bakery later and try a ball. It was my way of avoiding lying to her any more than necessary. Lynne was floating out of the store on her grand idea when she stopped, looked back at me as I was standing at the front door and asked, "Hey, you never told me how Doug was doing."

So close, I thought. She was almost out of the door but she had to ask me about Doug. I had to think fast and all I said was, "No change, dear."

"Oh, I'm sorry, mom," Lynne replied. "I know how much you care about him and it has to be very difficult for you. I can always go with you and sit with him at the hospital."

"No, that's alright," I said, feeling horrible. "I'm hoping that Doc will give us good news real soon about him. I have a good feeling that he'll be back to normal very soon."

"That's great that you're staying positive. Good for you, mom!" Lynne said, as she left and walked back to her bakery.

Unbelievable, I'm lying to my daughter and she's praising me. If I was Catholic, I would need to be in confession several times a day!

I made a mental note to myself to get over to her bakery at lunchtime to try one of her famous balls! I do love a good piece of chocolate anyway.

After Lynne left, I checked with Meme to make sure all was running smoothly and she said it had been very quiet so far. It was just after ten and I was hoping there would be a few customers. I knew the busiest times for me are ski/holiday seasons and the summer when the tourists flocked to the area. Many of the locals would come in to browse and chat, and I was waiting for the curious residents to arrive. I knew they would come so they could find out more about what happened to Doug.

I had walked back into my office to call Claire over at the hospital and see if I could talk with Doc Albert. I knew Claire didn't know anything about Doug's condition and I definitely didn't want to talk with his nurse, Shirley. She informed me that Doc was with a patient and she would give him the message to call me. I went back to my paperwork when I heard the front door bell. I was curious about who was coming in the store, so I headed out back into the showroom.

The person who had just entered surprised me. It was Lucy Meyer, Doug's secretary over at the bank. I hurried over to her because the look on her frightened face was priceless as she stood next to Paul, the guard.

"Hi Lucy," I said, hoping to distract her. I asked Paul to make a round of the store so I could have a moment alone with Lucy. "Everything alright?" I asked.

She got her voice back and asked, "Why is an armed guard here, Ruth Ann?"

"Oh it's nothing to worry about Lucy," I said. "Just a favor for a friend to help train new guards at their company. There's no problem here."

"Oh," she said, still unsure. "I thought it might have something to do with Doug and how terribly he was beaten."

"No, just a favor for an old acquaintance," I answered abruptly.

"Ruth Ann, I'm so shaken by what happened on Friday night to Doug," she said trembling. "Did you know he was still unconscious and he may not survive?"

"Lucy, Doug will be fine. He just needs time for his head to heal and Doc says he's stable. Doc really believes he'll make a full recovery, so don't worry, just give it time."

Lucy calmed down a little and said, "I'm scared to death to go back to work at the bank with a criminal out there. What if they come back for more?"

"I've talked with Chief John and he doesn't think that'll happen. Not much was taken from what I can guess. The robber probably thinks we live in too small of a town to have lots of valuables."

"Valuables?" she blurted out. "But I thought they stole money?

I have family heirlooms at my house, and I don't want to be robbed!"

"Lucy, get yourself together," I said. I wasn't a fan of anyone losing his or her cool so easily. "Nobody is after your family's jewels. I don't have specifics on the case but John is on it and I'm sure they'll catch whoever it is very soon." I decided to change the topic so I asked her, "What are you doing here? Are you looking for something for yourself or a gift?"

She shook her head violently. "No, no, that's not why I'm here. I know you're close to Doug and Chief John and I was so worried about going to the bank that I thought I'd ask you what you knew. Tom said we should still open the bank and do basic business, nothing that needs Doug's attention obviously, but easy transactions like deposits and withdrawals. What do you think? Is it safe for us to do that?"

"I don't know, Lucy," I said honestly. "Maybe you should be asking that question over at the police station."

"Good idea, Ruth Ann!" she exclaimed. "I'll go there right now! Thanks for the advice."

"Anytime, Lucy," I said.

Lucy turned to leave, acting much calmer. She hesitated and turned to me and said, "Oh, by the way, any new items in here that would be good for my daughter-in-law? Her birthday is mid-November and I thought a gift from your store would be nice."

"You should have a look. I change out items all the time and you know her taste. I could have Meme help you if you'd like."

Lucy waved her hand and said, "Later, right now I'm heading over to the station to speak with Chief John. I'm not taking one step into that bank until I know it's safe."

"Good luck, Lucy," I said as she left the store. One down I thought. How many more times will I have to go through that?

To be exact, there were seven more locals who came into my store just for information and not to purchase merchandise. The armed security guard shocked each one and I felt I reassured them all as to the reason for his presence. I asked Meme if she would be all right with Paul in here so I could pop over to Lynne's bakery. I promised I would bring back treats for both of them.

As I walked into the back room, I was surprised that I haven't heard a word from John or Doc Albert. He must be busy with patients and just hasn't had time to call me back. John promised to check in with me regularly, but maybe his regularly wasn't until lunchtime. I grabbed my phone and went out the back entrance to the alley. As the door shut behind me I had a chill run down my spine. It was a beautiful October day and not chilly at all. I hurried down the alley, only two stores away, to the bakery, Sinful Sweets.

I walked in and found several tables occupied with Lynne's regulars. Many people here chose to eat meals over at the café and come here for coffee and a piece of dessert. Lynne always had new items for the residents to test and she charged next to nothing for her new test items. Today was no different; I noticed that many of the people were holding up one of Lynne's balls. They all seemed to enjoy them from the expressions on their faces. I walked up to her counter and took a seat at a stool.

Lynne's bakery had a dozen or so small four-person tables and seating at the counter for eight. It was a bright, cheery business that made me smile every time I walked in. Lynne's business was doing great and if she thinks she should open up another store, I'll give her my blessing.

Lynne came out of the back kitchen and saw me, "Hi, Mom."

"Business is booming today, huh?" I asked.

"It's the balls, like I told you. People are talking about them and giving me all sorts of suggestions for flavors to try. I think it's great and now I have to make sure it's not just a fad but has staying power." Lynne said, grabbing three balls and putting them on a plate for me.

I picked up the first ball, a dark chocolate covered Oreo filled ball. I took one bite and realized I was in heaven. "Lynne!" I said with my mouth full, "I don't think I've ever tasted something so wonderful as this."

"Thanks, mom," Lynne said, smiling. "Your opinion is the one I've been waiting for."

I finished the first ball and took a sip of hot tea to clear my mouth of the Oreo flavor. "Ok, here goes number two," I said, grabbing the next ball. I took a big bite and said, "Pumpkin cookie filling dipped in white chocolate. This is delicious and I'm not normally a white chocolate person, but this is absolutely delectable." Lynne watched as I finished the second ball and drank some more tea. "You know this isn't good for my diet," I said chuckling.

"Like you diet," Lynne said, laughing. "You could never diet because you would never ever agree to give up chocolate."

"You know me so well," I said, picking up the third ball. "What's this one? It looks like milk chocolate." Lynne closely watched me as I took a bite and found a mint cookie filling inside like the traditional Girl Scout cookies we bought from the junior high girls. "Wow, I love chocolate and mint! These are just as good as the other two. I couldn't tell you which one I like better, Lynne!"

Lynne was thrilled at my reaction to the balls. "You see what I'm talking about now?" asked Lynne. "People are coming in here to see what filling I'm coming up with and what kind of chocolate I'll dip them in. I've already got an idea for a new one for tomorrow. Peanut butter cookie filling dipped in white chocolate."

"Sounds delicious, save me one please," I said. The balls weren't big but they were rich and I just knew that this new business was going to cost me another ten pounds.

"Just come over tomorrow and you can test a fresh one," Lynne said.

"I'll do that," I said. "I've got to get back to the store. Can I bring back a few balls for Meme and Paul, the guard? I'll pay you."

"Nope, these are on the house. This is my test day and I only charge half until I know how well they're received. "

"Let me pay half," I said, pulling out some money from my pocket.

"No mother, let me just have this. You do so much for Nancy and me, I'll never charge you," Lynne demanded. I agreed and thanked her profusely. I said my good-byes and scooted out of the store before people realized I was at the counter and started to bombard me with questions.

I went out the front of the store and noticed my pocket was moving. I reached in there to find my phone vibrating. I had forgotten I put it on vibrate so it wouldn't constantly ring in the store. I looked at the number and saw it was Doc Albert. "Hi Doc," I said, into the cell phone.

"Ruth Ann," he said. "You're difficult to get a hold of."

"What do you mean Doc? This is the first call I noticed."

"I've called you several times, look at your call log when we're done. I just wanted to tell you Doug's been asking to see you."

"Is he alright?" I asked, worried.

"Physically he's doing well. Improving by the day, but mentally he seems stressed. So when you get a chance can you come over to the hospital?"

"Of course, tell Doug I'll be over a little later. I'll close the store around three and head over."

"See you then, Ruth Ann," Doc said and hung up. I looked down at my phone and realized I had missed four calls from Doc and five calls from John! Great, I won't hear the end of this. I'm surprised he hasn't physically come over to yell at me for not following his orders.

I hurried back to my store and entered through the front door. Paul, the guard was standing there at his post but he wasn't alone. John was standing with his arms crossed yelling at poor Paul. I could overhear him before I even walked in the door. "I gave you explicit orders to not leave Ruth Ann alone at any time! Do you not understand that leaving the store and going into the public is dangerous for her? I thought I made my instructions clear, Paul. This is how you fail your training, isn't it?"

"But sir, I'm not in training, I'm a fully licensed armed guard. The training part was just a ruse to tell people," Paul said, trying to get himself out of trouble. "She said she was just going two doors down to her daughter's. I didn't think that would be dangerous, sir."

John was enraged. "The only reason you're here is to guard her, and when she leaves, you leave, got that?"

Paul nodded and was apologizing profusely when they saw me enter. John gave Paul a little shove to move him out of his way and marched to me. "And you," he started to say, waving his finger at me. "You promised me you wouldn't go off on your own. I had your word and you broke it!"

"Please calm down, John. You're going to have a heart attack if you don't get yourself together. I'm perfectly fine. It's daytime and I just went to Lynne's bakery." I held up a bag with the balls I brought back for them to try. "Why don't you try one of these and maybe it'll help you calm down."

"Ruth Ann," he shouted. "I feel perfectly fine, I'm so angry with you I better walk away before I really say something I shouldn't." John turned toward Paul and barked out another order. "Why don't you walk around the store and then make a round outside the store. You know what to look for."

Paul turned and hurried away from us. I wasn't sure if I should speak because if I did I would just infuriate him more. I decided to ignore him for a moment and walked in the back room to see if Meme was back there. John followed right on my heels and as soon as we entered my office he said, "I'm sorry." He added, "Wait, I'm only sorry for how I handled myself, not sorry for your inconsiderate behavior."

That set me off. "Inconsiderate behavior!" I shouted. "I've given up most of my freedom for some wild goose chase that we don't know is even true. Yes, I saw the guy at the bank and I could potentially be in danger. However, I'll not stop living my life. I feel strongly that if they want to get to me, they will. So back off a little, please."

John calmed down and said, "I'm sorry, but if anything happens to you it'll be my fault."

"No it won't John, I have to take some responsibility for my own life and you can order me around all you like, but I don't have to listen." I understood his dilemma but I had to make my point clear. "I agreed to move out of my house for a few days and sleep here on a couch. There's a guard around me for 24 hours a day," John opened his mouth to respond, but I cut him off by raising my hand for him to wait. "Ok, he goofed once. I'm sure Paul learned his lesson. I'll do my best to not take off again, will that suffice?"

"Yes, thank you," he replied, calming down quite a bit. "I understand your frustration, but this guy tried to kill Doug and until we catch him I'll be in protection mode. Can you try and see my side?"

"I see your side, but we need a compromise. I can walk two doors down in broad daylight to my daughter's bakery without an armed guard following me. I won't go anywhere in the dark without you or an official escort, deal?"

"Kind of," John said. "I don't like you roaming around by yourself even during the day, but you're correct, I can't stop you."

"Thank you, John," I said. "I promise I won't take any unnecessary chances if that makes you feel better."

"If it were my choice, I would handcuff you to myself or another police officer until we catch this creep."

"Funny, John, but that won't work will it?" I laughed and finally was able to make John smile. "Oh, I almost forgot, Doc called and wants us to go over to the hospital soon. I told him I could go at three when I close the shop."

"Yeah, Doc called me too and said Doug was stressing out and asked for us. I'll swing by and pick you up and we can go together if that is allowed?"

"You're on a roll!" I joked. "Sounds good, I'll be ready. Hey, what about the guard in here? What are his plans if I'm with you?"

"Paul will trade places with another guard and he'll spend nights at the store. I'll have to check out the new guard to make sure he's legit. After the hospital we can park your car and grab a bite to eat at the resort. You can go up to your room and I can see if there's been any activity in the room. Then we'll get you secretly back to the store for the night. Sound good?"

"Yes, complicated, but I agreed," I acknowledged. "Hey, I thought your guys at the station could see what's going on through the cameras at all times?"

"They can and so far it's been quiet."

John left me at the store for a couple hours and I went to find Meme. Meme and Paul were in the back room trying out the balls Lynne made.

"Ruth Ann, these are so good I can't stop eating them! I doubt they're very good for my diet," she said. "I just can't help myself!"

"Glad you like them. Lynne wants to open another store to sell these balls. What do you think?"

"It'll be a huge hit!" Meme declared. "I'll be a regular customer for sure."

Paul was quiet still, probably over the tongue lashing John gave him. I noticed he ate a bite out of three balls but didn't finish them. I was curious, as an outsider to this town, if he actually liked them. Meme couldn't be impartial because she's a friend of Lynne's. "Hey, Paul, what do you think of my daughter's new recipe?" I questioned him carefully, not using her title of 'balls" because it sounded a bit uncomfortable saying that to a male stranger.

He snapped out of his funk and answered, "I'm not a sweets person, but if I were, they would be top on my list."

"Great, I'll tell my daughter that! She'll love to hear from someone who doesn't have a sweet tooth and doesn't know her. The tourist season is coming up, and I think she wants to add these to her menu."

"She'll succeed for sure," Meme rang in. "Tell her if I had money, I'd invest in another store with her."

"Meme, that's a fantastic idea!" I said enthusiastically.

"Oh, Ruth Ann, I don't have that kind of money."

"No, no, not you, me!" I said. "I could put the money up for her store and she could run it. That's a great idea, I wonder if Lynne would go for that?"

"If my mother offered me money for a store I would jump on it," Meme said. "You should tell her. Maybe you two could look at real estate and see where you could open a store."

"Actually, Lynne came up with a better idea. Open a small store inside the resort."

"That's terrific, anyone who stays there would love a place like that!"

"Next time I see Carol I'll bring it up casually. See what she thinks since she would be the decision maker. Richard only cares about the financial part of the resort and he would love a new business that they could charge rent for a space."

"Maybe you should run it by Lynne first," Meme said. "Since it's her business and all."

"I will," I said, thinking it all out in my head. "But I could still just mention it to Carol. If her and Richard don't like the idea then Lynne and I will come up with something else."

I went back into my office and did some paperwork while Meme handled the customers in the showroom. Every few minutes she would peek her head in my office and count off all the people who had come to browse the store and ask a few questions. Meme would tell them I was unavailable and she didn't know anything about the case. Which was actually true. Paul would wander around the store and check on me and then repeat it all over again.

At exactly 3:00 p.m., John came in the back door from the alley. I let Meme go to pick up Elijah and Paul said he would stay in the store until his replacement came at about 6:00 pm. I told John I thought it was ridiculous that he stayed in the store when I wasn't even there. John shot me down. I was able to convince him to let Paul order food from Wilma's Café so he could eat dinner.

We drove both cars over to the hospital and went straight through to Doug's room. Claire was on the telephone chatting away, so I was able to avoid that conversation for now. With Claire working at the hospital I was never sure what she was told about Doug so I would rather keep contact with her short. Doc was in his office near Doug's room and heard us coming. He waved us in his office before going into Doug's room.

John quickly asked what I was thinking, too; "What's wrong with Doug, Doc?"

Doc Albert closed his door just in case Doug could over hear. John and I sat down on the two chairs that faced Doc's desk. I suddenly felt nervous, I don't know why but I just had a bad feeling.

"I told Ruth Ann earlier that Doug was improving physically, but he seems to be having some emotional problems and I was hoping you two could fill me in on why?" Doc asked, looking from John to me.

John spoke up first, "He's probably concerned with an appointment he was supposed to have tomorrow."

"He can't have any visitors, John," Doc declared. "Plus, I thought he was still unconscious to the outside world."

"He is," John stated. "Doug's not meeting with anyone tomorrow. I'm holding the meeting in his place."

I was shocked by his announcement. "I didn't know that, John! How are you having this meeting with…" John stopped me suddenly and said, "I have it all arranged."

"Oh, ok," Doc, said. "Maybe you need to fill Doug in on this bit of information because if that's what's causing him undue stress, it needs to stop."

"I was planning on discussing that with him now," John said as he stood up. "Is that all?"

"I guess so," Doc said. "Doug's been acting nervous and he's even been imagining people here that aren't."

John flew off the handle on Doc's last comment. "What?" he shouted.

"Doug said he saw some strange person walking down the hall dressed in black, and he even thought he paused outside of his room and looked in."

"Where was his guard?" John asked, frantic.

"Doug said he didn't know, maybe he took a bathroom break,"

Doc replied.

John flew out of Doc's office and into Doug's hospital room. He found Doug sitting up in a chair and looking out the window. As John hurried over to him, Doug turned his head calmly and said; "I could hear you all the way from Doc's office."

"What's this about some stranger in the hall? Why didn't you contact me immediately?"

"I pushed my button and Doc answered it and I told him what I thought I saw and he said it was impossible because there's a guard stationed right outside my door. I don't know what's real or not. That blow to my head still has me all fuzzy."

"Doug, maybe there really was someone lurking around the halls, do you know if there are other patients down this corridor?"

Doug shrugged his shoulders not knowing. "But what about my guard, he would've seen someone walking around the hall dressed in black and stopping in front of my door."

"When exactly did this happen, Doug?" questioned John.

"It was early this morning, like seven a.m.," Doug answered. John stepped back into the hall and talked with the guard on duty. I had walked over to Doug and we both waited silently until John came back. "He says they change guards at seven o'clock, and there could've been five minutes when you would be left alone. It makes sense, first Ruth Ann tells me about a car following her and now you. There's someone in this town that's constantly watching us and knows our schedules. I don't like this at all."

Doug panicked when he heard John say that I had been followed. "Are you kidding me, John? Someone followed Ruth Ann? What are you doing to protect her?"

"We've got that covered Doug, I promise. You need to concentrate on your own condition and I already told those guards that they shouldn't leave you unattended even for one minute. They can change guards at your door, and if they need to leave for any kind of break they need to have Doc or a nurse stand by until they return. Don't we have aides or orderlies around here?"

"John, you can't put a nurse or aide in charge of Doug while the guard's away," I said, realizing how silly that sounded. "What do you want them to do if some guy tries to get to Doug?"

"They can scream and the guard will get back immediately," John declared. "These guards can only go to the restroom or grab food or something to drink out of a vending machine. They know to bring whatever else they need with them. That's why we change shifts every 6-8 hours."

"Good luck getting Doc to agree to that after a criminal walked right in and started cruising the halls looking for Doug," I said.

"I'll take care of it," he snapped in frustration. I felt bad for John because he wasn't getting any breaks in this case. "We need to discuss tomorrow's appointment, Doug."

"I almost forgot about that!" he exclaimed. "Doc won't let me go and I guess I could have him come here. It seems futile since we don't have the necklace anymore."

"He isn't aware of that yet, and it'll give me time to talk with him myself and find out what all he knows about this infamous necklace," John said. "I'm keeping your appointment for you at the bank. I'll use your office and tell him I'm you."

"You can't do that! Isn't that entrapment?" Doug panicked. "Why can't he come here and you can be in the room while we talk about the stone?"

"No way Doug, everyone, and I mean everyone, must keep thinking you're in serious condition and cannot communicate yet."

"But you don't know anything about the necklace or how my bank runs," Doug said flustered.

"I don't have to know about banking or gems. What do you know about the gem, anyway?"

"Good point," he said. "All I know is what was in the note. I just wanted it verified and appraised, then I would've handed it over to Ruth Ann. It's her necklace after all."

"That's right," I cut in. "It's all about my necklace, and so, if John is running the show tomorrow with the gemologist, I plan on attending this meeting too."

John and Doug shouted, "NO," at the same time but it was John who kept going, "There's absolutely no way you're coming anywhere near the bank tomorrow. Do I make myself clear, Ruth Ann?"

"Perfectly, but I'll be there anyway. You cannot order me regarding my own property. If this guy knows anything about the necklace, I want to hear."

"But," John began to say and I stopped him by holding my hand up, "I will be safe because you'll be there and I highly doubt this gemologist was the criminal who stole it and bashed Doug's head."

"You're probably correct, however, he could be the one who ordered someone to do it. In my mind that makes him more dangerous than his hired thug."

"I'm not caving on this one, John," I said. "I'll be there and we can play it off like I have knowledge of the necklace. It may help if I look like I can explain the piece, don't you think?"

"Possibly," John admitted. "You're beginning to be quite a pain!"

"Thank you," I said, smiling. I felt I won this round but I'm sure there will be plenty more to go. "So, maybe we should talk over what we're going to tell this man." I looked at Doug and asked, "Wait, we don't even know this guy's name, do we?"

John answered for him, "I do. I had him and his business checked out to see if he really was a gemologist."

"You going to tell me or do I have to ask the man himself tomorrow?" I snapped.

"Mr. Jeffrey Toggles," Doug answered for John. He saw my boiling point was close and his head couldn't take much more. "He's a private jewelry dealer from the city, and he was also willing to do something that others were not."

"What's that?" I asked.

"Come to Deer Creek."

"Ah, it's a small town and may not be worth the trip," I said.

John added, "Unless he's aware of the stone and its value." Doug and I nodded in agreement.

John got the ball rolling on how we were to handle tomorrow's appointment. First, John would go to the bank in the morning and inspect the camera systems inside and outside the bank. He wanted to capture everyone who entered and exited the bank. The appointment was set for 1:00 p.m. since the man had to travel to get here. John would go over security with Tom, the bank's guard, and his own men would be there undercover as a customer and a teller. Doug agreed so far. I just listened and felt if there were something he was missing I would speak up. Next on John's list was Doug's office itself. He wanted to make sure all personal pictures of Doug that would give John away were put away. Good thinking!

"So, once we have the area outside and inside the bank as secure as possible, then we wait for Mr. Toggles to arrive. Ruth Ann will be sitting in Doug's office and I'll be in the lobby of the bank watching for any unknown person to enter. I'll walk up to anyone I don't recognize and say hello and ask what I could do for them. When Mr. Toggles identifies himself and shows the proper ID I'll escort him into 'my' office."

"I don't know if this will work, John," Doug interrupted. "This makes me very nervous and worried for Ruth Ann's safety."

"I'll be fine, Doug. We're just talking to the man."

"Let's go on," John said, not letting us get sidetracked. "Once seated in your office we'll ask him if he has any knowledge of the piece that we asked him to appraise. I'm an expert at telling when someone is lying or not telling me the whole story." He paused and looked directly at me like he knew I had tried to fool him in the past, which of course I had. I gave him an innocent smile and he continued. "If he passes my expertise test then we'll proceed to find out as much as we can about the stolen necklace before we break it to him that it has indeed been stolen."

"He's going to blow a gasket, John, when he finds out he drove all this way and there's no necklace," Doug said.

John ignored Doug's comment and went on. "I'll see his reaction when I tell him that it was stolen from my bank. We'll not tell him any details on the robbery; do you understand that statement Ruth Ann?" I nodded and smiled. "I don't like that smile, Ruth Ann. I'm dead serious about it, not a word about the actual events of last Friday."

"I get it," I said. "Go on."

He acknowledged my answer with a slight smile. "Ok, let me see where I was. I tell him it was stolen. He'll have one of two responses. One, complete surprise that tells me right off the bat he wasn't involved. Second, anger at coming all this way to find we knew there wasn't a necklace to appraise." He paused, deep in his own thoughts. "The first incidence is complete surprise. Anger will eventually set in, but before that I can question him about who he may know that could steal this type of gem and why. Hopefully we'll get enough information to give us another lead. The second reaction tells me he's guilty in some part of what happened to Doug and the necklace."

"Wow," Doug said. "That sounds like perfectly logical responses to the situation."

"I agree," I said. "I'm impressed at the logic, John."

John smiled and said, "Thanks, maybe that's why they gave me the job as chief, huh?" Here I thought he was being humble, nope.

"So what if he does something different than you expect?" questioned Doug.

"Like what?" John replied. "There really is no other way he could respond." I hope so, I thought to myself. "Ruth Ann and I are going to let you rest. I need to check on the fellow roaming the halls and streets. I'll talk with the guard again to make sure he understands his duty. Lastly, I'll speak with Doc to make sure he knows you're to be watched at all times."

We said our good-byes and stopped by Doc's office. Shirley was in there and told us he was in an examining room with a patient. John told Shirley the instructions for Doc and left him a note on his desk. Before we left John asked Shirley one last question. Who was Doc examining?

"I didn't recognize him, John." Shirley said. "He told me before Doc saw him that he was hiking around the mountain and tripped. He appears to be fine, just a few bruises but he wanted to make sure nothing was broken.

"What did he look like, Shirley?" questioned John, curiously.

"Uh, about 35 years old, dark hair, brown eyes, 240 pounds on the scale I put him on."

"What clothing was he wearing?"

"Jeans and a sweatshirt. It's cool outside, but not cold yet, so he didn't have a coat that I noticed, why?" she inquired.

"Just being careful about strangers around, that's all." John looked at me with a wink and we walked toward the lobby when he stopped near Claire's desk. "I want to have a peek at this patient," John said. "I'm going to stay put and I want you to sit down in a chair and wait for me. We can head over to the resort for dinner after this guy checks out."

"Do you think he's the man that was outside Doug's room and he could be posing as a patient to get access to Doug?"

"That's why I'm going to get a name and see this guy before I leave here. I'm going back in and wait outside the examining room. I don't want to take any chances on this guy skipping out."

I watched as he went back in and I walked over to Claire's

desk. She was working on some paperwork pretending not to listen to our conversation. I planned on keeping our talk light and happy, so I don't spill any information I'm not supposed to.

She looked up as I leaned on her desk. "Hi, Ruth Ann," she said. "You look tired. It's got to be really stressful watching over Doug."

"It sure is," I replied, starting to feel so horrible about lying. "I'm tired, but I have to wait for John because we're going over to the resort for dinner. You know I'm staying there for a few days?" I thought getting that information out would help if anyone were looking for me here. One person tells another and it spreads like wildfire. Claire would be a good leak to get my whereabouts made public.

"Why you staying there?" Claire asked curiously.

"My house is being tested by some pest company. I've heard some strange noises in my attic and they suggested they do spraying and advised me to move out for a few days."

"Oh, that's a shame," she said. "But how nice to get a little pampering over at the resort!"

"Exactly," I replied.

John was taking longer than I expected so I went back toward Doug's room and didn't see John or Doc. I figured they were in his office, so I headed that way. I peeked in Doug's room on the way and found him sound asleep. I was happy he was resting and not worrying about what was going down tomorrow. The guard was at the door and smiled at me. "All quiet, ma'am," he said to me.

"That's how we want it," I replied and walked to Doc's office. I found the two of them with their heads together, talking quietly. Doc was sitting at his desk and John was standing over him and they were examining some papers spread out on the desk.

"Hi," I said, causing the two of them to jump.

"Don't sneak up on us like that, Ruth Ann," John snapped.

"Sorry," I said smartly. "What's taking so long, I'm starving."

"Just a few minutes more please," John said calmly. "Doc and I are just going over a few notes from his new patient."

"Anything with him?" I asked.

John quickly responded, "No, just seeing who he is and what's wrong with him. Doc said he might have a concussion from a fall on the mountain. I'm not convinced that he's telling the truth, and either is Doc. He has classic symptoms but they can be faked somewhat."

"Really, Doc?" I asked. "Someone can fake a concussion?"

"Not really, I think John's worried that he purposely caused a bump on his head to get in here and see me. He's suspicious about anyone who's staying here while Doug is here."

"Staying here?" I asked shocked. "He's here as a patient of yours?"

Doc answered, "Yes, he is. I can't release a person just because John is suspicious. The man has a right to treatment and I think it's best he stays overnight so we can monitor him."

"And John doesn't agree, right?" I asked.

"You bet!" John replied. "He could be the person of interest I'm looking for with the bank robbery."

Doc knew a lot but I wasn't sure how much John had confided in him. Doc has been going along with John regarding Doug's "unconscious" condition, and now Doug saw a stranger in the hall that fits the profile of the bank robber. I wouldn't doubt John has told him more, but I wasn't going to be the person who spills any further details.

John asked Doc if he could question the man and Doc flatly refused. There was no proof the man was a criminal, just a person who took a fall while hiking. Until there was more to go on, Doc insisted we leave him alone. Shirley was there late that night and would keep a close watch on him. She was a mean, surly nurse who won't let him leave his bed. I told John we should just leave Doc to his work and go grab dinner.

"I've called the guy's name into the station. If there's a hit on his name we're coming back here immediately. That's if he gave Doc his real name. It's easy for a criminal to get false identification."

As we were leaving John had a word with the guard and explained the circumstances regarding the new patient. He was to keep a sharp eye out for this guy if he left his room. "Ok, I feel somewhat confident leaving for a while. I'll come back after we get you all settled in for the night."

Chapter 7

"Sounds like a plan," I said, walking out of the hospital. We drove separately to the resort and I parked my car there for the night. We entered the resort and headed to the restaurant. Carol was seating people that night and she was anxious to speak with us. She brought us to a nice cozy table that was away from other tables.

"I'm sure glad you're here," she said, appearing a bit jumpy and looking around the dining room carefully.

John caught on to her nervousness and asked, "Has something happened?"

"No, I don't think so," she said. "But I have to tell you that one of my staff was up on Ruth Ann's floor and caught a man standing in front of her room. He pretended to have dropped something on the floor and mumbled something to my employee and walked off."

"Who saw this man?" John demanded. "Can he give me a description of the guy?"

Carol sat down at one of the empty seats and said, "Keep your voice down, John. We don't want people suspicious, right?"

John lowered his voice; "I'm calling this into the station and see if we have a hit on the guy from our cameras. Did your employee see if he got inside the room?"

"No, he didn't think much of it at the time, and then he realized it was Ruth Ann's room and he came and told me. The guy thought he would be gossiping about a secret rendezvous at Ruth Ann's room!"

My turn to speak up, "What did you just say? Your employee thought a man was meeting me in my room to have an affair?"

Carol nodded and said, "They're new and you know how it works, Ruth Ann. One person sees something that's worth gossiping over and it spreads all over."

"Great, now I'm meeting a mysterious man in a hotel room that nobody knows," I snapped. "This just keeps getting better and better."

"Hold on Ruth Ann," John spoke. "That'll pass if anything actually gets out. I'm concerned about the man that was at your door. Think about it," he said, staring at me.

"Oh, yeah," I replied.

Carol became confused and asked, "Is there more to this story then you're telling me?"

John quickly changed the subject, "Carol, what's your employee's name please? I need to ask him some questions. Is he still working tonight?"

"Nope, he went home for the day, and the person's name is Ben."

"What's his job here at the resort?" he asked.

"He's a busboy and also delivers room service for the kitchen," Carol answered.

"I need you to give me his address. This can't wait, I need to talk with him immediately." Carol nodded and went to the office to get Ben's address and phone number. He wasn't known around town because he just started at the resort about a month ago and was in training. Carol hurried back to us and filled us in on his background.

"He's 46 years old, and has a slight disability. When he came in late August, Richard interviewed him and hired him on the spot. I don't even know if he checked his references."

"Really?" John asked. "Richard is smarter than that. Is your husband here?"

"No, he's over at church in Bible study," Carol, answered. "He'll be back around nine.

John appeared flustered. "Why are there so many twists and turns here?" Carol and I knew that he wasn't looking for us to answer him. It was best to let him get it out and move forward.

"John, Richard has good instincts. Ben has been a perfect employee since he's been here. He's always on time, and doesn't complain about duties he's given. He's quiet and smiles a lot, and there's been no complaints against him."

"Does it say in his file where he came from?" I asked.

"Yes, he came here from Tampa, Florida," Carol answered. "I wonder why anyone would leave sunny, warm Florida and land here in the middle of nowhere?"

"Good question," John said. "I wonder if he answered that

question for your husband during his interview?"

Carol said defensively, "Look here John, Richard and I are trying to help you but if you keep cutting my husband's abilities down, I'll stop this whole charade regarding Ruth Ann's room and the hidden cameras."

I jumped in to try and diffuse the disagreement. "Carol, John's being a bully and he knows he needs to cut it out. Don't you, John?"

He looked terrible and apologized profusely to Carol. She accepted his apology and understood the frustration he was going through trying to solve the bank robbery. "Just watch who you tick off, John," Carol said. "People won't want to help you if you threaten them."

"I agree completely," John said, acknowledging he needed to take his temper down a notch. "I really am sorry, Carol, please forgive me?"

"Of course," she said, perking up immensely. "I wrote down the address for you and maybe it would be best if I called Ben and told him you want to ask a few questions. Maybe that would break the ice a bit since he's slightly disabled."

"Why do you say that, Carol?" John asked. "If I may ask that of you?"

"Yes, of course you may," Carol replied with a happier attitude. "Ben said he never finished high school because he was slower than the other kids and they made fun of him. He dropped out of school and worked odd jobs. He's quite good at carpentry and computers, and he said he loves breaking things and putting them back together. Like an engine, he said he could take one completely apart and put it back together. But since he doesn't have a degree of any sort, nobody gives him a chance. That's why Richard hired him. He figured he could start him out with easy jobs and if he proves himself he can give him more responsibility."

John asked, "He hasn't been diagnosed with a specific handicap has he?"

"Nope, he can't afford medical costs," Carol answered.

"I would prefer if you didn't give him any notice that I want to speak with him."

"Why? That'll just scare him if he sees a policeman at his front door," Carol questioned.

"To be honest, everyone who's new to town is raising red flags with me. Until I know more about this case involving Doug, I don't trust anyone I'm not personally involved with."

"So Ruth Ann and I are safe?" kidded Carol.

"Yes," John replied curtly. "I don't want to give this Ben anytime to think about why I want to speak with him. It's best to get his initial reactions."

"Fine," Carol replied. "He lives over in those lower income apartments on the opposite side of town that you and Ruth Ann live in. They're clean, but the apartments are filled with young married couples or people who are down on their luck. Ben fits the latter, so be kind to him. He's had a rough life and he really appears quite sweet and simple."

"I'll handle him carefully, Carol," John said. "But if he shows any inconsistencies in his responses, I do have to label him as a person of interest."

"Are you talking about what happened with Doug and the bank? He was working on Friday so it couldn't have been him." Carol said.

"Carol, what I care about first is who he saw lingering around Ruth Ann's hotel room. If he answers honestly then I'll leave him alone. But if I spot any sign of him avoiding my questions then I'll have to keep a close watch on him."

"Ok," Carol said. "Just give him a bit of a break because he might scare easily."

We ate a quick dinner, and John and I went up to my room at the resort. Outside the door, John examined every inch and called the station. He wanted reports on any activity that occurred in and outside the room. We entered the room, and as far as I could tell nothing were amiss. John took a thorough but quick look around and left the room. He reminded me that I should go down the stairs and meet him at his car. Try to be quick and keep an eye out if anyone sees me leaving. He'll be waiting at his car.

John waited for me to go into the stairwell. The coast was clear as far as I could tell. He took off for the elevator and out the front door to his car. The stairwell opened up to the lobby but off to the side. The lobby area was quiet, so I hurried out the front door. As far as I could tell nobody saw me leave. I met John at his car, and he took off toward the other side of town where my store and the bakery was located.

"The apartments are down this way, but I figured I can't just drop you off, can I?" I shook my head. "You want to come with me to talk to this Ben character?"

"Yes, maybe he won't be as scared if he sees me with you," I stated.

"You do realize that I've broken so many rules involving you in this case, don't you?"

"I appreciate you letting me in, John," I said. "Everything seems to involve me so I want to help. Plus, if I'm with you then you won't have to worry about me."

"I'm not arguing anymore with you, Ruth Ann. However, if we get to a point where I have to handle whoever injured Doug, then you're out, got it?"

"Crystal clear," I answered. "I wouldn't want to mess up catching this guy."

"Thanks," John said, as he pulled into the Mountain View Apartments. There was no security gate, just a large parking lot and three buildings, two-stories high. They were well maintained, just didn't have amenities like a pool or clubhouse. Carol wrote down Ben's address and we pulled into a spot close to Building 3, Apt. 203.

We headed toward the staircase for Building 3 and walked up to the second floor. Access to the apartments was from the outside. There was no lobby or indoor entrance. They reminded me of motels where you parked next to the room you were staying in.

We noticed there was a light showing from a window at Ben's apartment. John grabbed the knocker on the door and tapped it. There was no answer right away but I could've sworn I saw the curtain move a little. John knocked again a little louder. We heard the locks on the door rattle and the door opened.

A very short, gray haired man opened the door. If Carol didn't tell us he was in his mid-forties I would've guessed he was twenty years older. He was wearing gray sweatpants and a black flannel shirt that hung over his waist. He looked terrified when he noticed the police uniform and gun in John's holster.

In a stumbling voice Ben asked, "Is something wrong-g, sir?"

John replied, "Are you Ben Anderson?"

"Y-e-s," he replied with a shaking voice. "Why are you asking?"

"Do you work at Deer Creek Resort?"

"Yes, I do, is there a problem?"

I wanted to assure Ben there was no problem, but I didn't want to interfere with John's preliminary police questions. John asked if we could come in and talk. He flashed his badge to assure Ben we were here on official business and not to harass or hurt him.

Ben led us into a small, sparsely furnished studio apartment. There was a futon against one wall with blankets spread out and a small television on a TV tray against the opposite wall. Also in there, was an old wooden kitchen table and four chairs near the small kitchenette by the door. There was only one chair besides the futon, and John led me to sit there. He introduced me as his friend and a friend of Carol's to make Ben feel more comfortable.

Ben sat on the futon and looked at me and said, "Mrs. Dickson and her husband have been very kind to me. They gave me a job and now I'm able to pay my rent here." He stopped talking and looked back at John and said, "Please tell me nothing happened to them?"

"No, no, they're fine, Ben," John answered. "I'm here to ask you a simple question. You did nothing wrong, I just need some information from you that would really help me a lot. Can you help me, Ben?" Ben cautiously nodded.

"Ok," John began. "It's actually two questions to begin with, if it's still ok?" He nodded. "Great," John said smiling at Ben. "First, were you working on the second floor of the resort on Friday afternoon?" Ben nodded.

"Carol told me that you noticed a man outside of room 203 and he dropped something on the ground. Do you remember that?"

"Yes, I do. I first thought it was strange that a man was just standing and staring at a room. Then he noticed me watching him and he pretended to drop something and pick it up. I figured it wasn't any of my business, so I moved along."

"Can I keep going, Ben?" Ben nodded. "Ok, what were you doing up on the second floor?"

"I was picking up a room service tray that was left outside a door down the hall."

"That's great, you're doing great so far," John said, still smiling at Ben. Ben relaxed a little and smiled back. "Do you remember what this man looked like and what he was wearing?"

"Yes, I do," Ben spoke up proudly. "That's what caught my attention at first. I was walking down the hall with my head down. I try to keep to myself usually, but when I saw this man I couldn't help but notice he was all in black from his feet to his hoodie pulled over his head. Why would he need a hoodie inside the hotel?" I shook my head to agree with his question.

"I agree, Ben," John replied. "He was inside and shouldn't need to be so covered up. Did you see his face at all?"

"Just for a quick second. Once he saw me walking down the hall he dropped a key chain on the floor and bent over to pick it up."

"Ben, you had said you think he dropped something on purpose. Why do you think that?" inquired John.

"Because it was so obvious," he answered, matter of fact.

"Why, can you be more specific, please?" John asked carefully. I could tell he wanted to be tougher and force the answers out of Ben but knew that could backfire and then he would have nothing.

"Well, when I got to the floor I could see all the way down the hall and he was about halfway down, just standing there looking at the door. If he were going to go in or knock he would've done it. It wasn't until he saw me when he grabbed his keys out of the pocket in the front of his hoodie and dropped it."

"You saw all that?" asked John.

Ben looked nervous. John might've pushed the last question by doubting his word. "Yes," he said. "My eyesight is perfect, my head doesn't always work very fast but I have no problem with what I see."

John, noting his tone and his defensive answer said quickly, "Ben, I believe you. I just need to know everything you saw while you were up on the second floor. I'm sorry if I appeared to doubt your word."

Ben calmed down and smiled. "Most people don't like me because I'm different," he said. "I'm not stupid or crazy, I just don't like complications and it takes me long to make decisions."

"We like you Ben," I said. "John is the Chief of Police here and he just wants to make sure our town stays safe. When Mrs. Dickson told us about what you saw, John just wanted to make sure the resort stays safe, too."

"Oh, yes," he said loudly. "I love the resort. They have all been so kind to me and I don't want any trouble. I don't like trouble."

"We know that, Ben," John said. "We don't like trouble either!"

Ben looked from John to me and asked, "Is that all?"

"One more thing if it's okay with you?" John asked, as politely as possible.

"Yes it's okay."

"You said before that this man saw you? Did you see his face maybe his eye color or skin color? Maybe he had a birthmark or something different than you or me."

"Umm, I saw dark eyes and his skin was our color," Ben said pointing to John and me.

"So, Caucasian?" asked John.

"What?" he inquired, looking confused.

I helped John out and said, "His skin color is white is what you're saying, correct?"

"Yes, a white man, not a black man or a man from China or Mexico."

"Ok, that's great Ben." John looked at me and I could tell in his eyes that he was comparing Ben's description to mine after I saw a person driving slowly outside the grocery store. "Anything else like a birth mark?"

"Oh yeah," Ben blurted out, all of a sudden. "He had a funny drawing on his neck. I could see part of his neck when he looked up and it looked like part of a Viking ship, you know from the olden days?"

"A Viking ship?" I asked confused. "Like from Sweden or Norway?"

"I don't know," Ben said, perplexed. "I've seen pictures of ships like that and they're from long ago.

I looked at John and we both were dumbfounded by this news. A Viking ship is a symbol from Scandinavian countries! Why would anyone get a tattoo like that? Ben referred to it as a drawing, but John and I knew it had to be a tattoo.

John went and patted Ben on the shoulder and thanked him. We told him if he remembered anything else to call the police station and ask for the chief. Ben nodded and promised he would do that. We took our leave and John drove me over to my store. What we found there changed everything.

As we drove behind the store down the alley everything appeared normal. There were lights on in the store; I always left a few on for security purposes. There was a car parked behind my store and I assumed it was the new guard's. John and I entered the back room and walked into the showroom. There was no sign of a guard or anyone. John hurried over to the front door and still no guard. John called out for the guard. Maybe he was up on the second floor walking around. There was still no response and I suddenly felt a chill run through my body. Something was wrong, very wrong.

John told me to stay at the front door and if he told me to run, I run. Where I would run, I had no idea, but hopefully that won't occur. John took off up the stairs to the second floor, no guard there either. I realized that there was a possibility that the guard went to get a cup of coffee over at the Café. The Café was still open, not for long, but maybe the guard needed some caffeine to get him through the night.

I told John this as he hurried past me to go into the back room and my office. He acknowledged what I said, but didn't stop to answer me. I wasn't comfortable by myself in the showroom so I disobeyed his orders and went into the back room right after he did. John wasn't there, but I heard sounds from my office. I peeked inside my office and found John standing next to my desk. "Stay out, Ruth Ann," he demanded. "I found the guard and it's not pretty."

Shocked, I said, "He's on the floor? Did he hurt himself?" I asked questions even though I knew the answer; something bad had happened. John looked to the floor then to me. He walked over to me and I noticed red stains on his arm sleeve. "John, what's that on your arm?"

He looked at his sleeve and said, "I think you know. I need to make a call, you don't move." John stood next to me and called into the station for backup and the coroner.

Once he hung up I blurted out, "Coroner?"

"Yes, Ruth Ann, your guard has been murdered."

"In my office?" I asked. It was the only thing I could think of for the moment. John kept me away from looking, but I needed to know how he was killed.

"He was hit in the head with something, I don't see anything near here that could do the damage it did. It's similar to Doug, but much worse."

"Of course it's worse, John!" I cried out. "He's dead and Doug's still alive."

He stopped what he was doing and came back to me. I believe he thought I was going to cry, but that wasn't happening. I was furious, so furious that someone committed murder in my office. Not only was a man dead, but also my office would now be off limits to me until this investigation is over. How dare they?

John was taken aback at my lack of sympathy for the guy, and how angry I was about the inconvenience of the murder happening at my store. "Of course I feel horrible for this poor man! He was hired to guard me and now he's been murdered."

"I need to open the back door for my men. Are you going to be ok for a minute? Just don't go near the body, please." I agreed and let John go past me while I just stood frozen in the doorway of my office. I felt torn, I wanted to go and see the man on the floor by my desk, but how would I react? I don't recall ever seeing a dead body before, especially such a fresh one. I chose to stay put. I didn't think I would gain anything by seeing such a horrible sight.

It took a couple hours before everyone left my store. I was told to not go into my office until it was cleared, and if I chose to open the store I would have to keep the office closed. I wasn't sure what I would do at the moment. It was late and I had nowhere to stay now and a business that was supposed to open up in the morning. John solved a few of my dilemmas. He dragged me to his car and he took me to the station. We went into his office and I dropped myself down onto the sofa in his office.

"I have some work to do. Can you close your eyes and rest? It might be a few hours and I have no other choice but to keep you with me."

"I agree," I said. "I don't have any choice now."

"Well I'm glad you understand because I'm not in the mood to argue with you. I need to contact the agency the guard works for and break the news. It's a horrible call to make, especially if this guy has a family."

"It wasn't Paul, the first guard. Did you even know the name of this guard?"

"I have a list of names of the guards that were supposed to be alternating shifts at the store," John said, shuffling papers on his desk.

"Here it is. I'm going to make this call in another office if you don't mind."

I asked him to shut his door so I could close my eyes and try to get some sleep. All I hoped for was to put the whole night out of my head because it felt like it was going to burst. I must've been successful, because the next thing I knew John was shaking me gently telling me it was time to go. He said we were going to his place for a few hours of sleep and at this time nobody would see us come or go. I was too groggy to complain, not that I would.

We didn't speak much on the way to his condo or even inside his condo. John had so much on his mind I thought it would be best to leave him alone. Plus, I didn't want to talk anymore. We spent a few hours there and came straight back to the office for John to check with his men.

"This'll take just a minute. I think we should get a bite to eat then head over to see Doug," John said. "Remember, we have an appointment to keep this afternoon."

"I completely forgot about that!" I exclaimed. "It seemed like days ago when we discussed it in Doug's hospital room."

"I believe we need a group meeting before we meet this gemologist. Things just got even uglier."

"Murder and attempted murder," I said. "What am I supposed to do about my store?"

"I think you should keep it closed today. It's not safe and I'm sure you don't want to put Meme in jeopardy."

"Oh my, I forgot about Meme," I cried out. I pulled out my phone and called her immediately. I wasn't sure what I was going to tell her. By now the whole town was aware there had been a murder at my store. That can't be good for business. I know, I sound horrible worrying about my business. I was worried about it all, the store, the guard, Doug, and myself!

Meme took the news quite well since I told her I would pay her for her time while the store was closed. She had heard rumors about police activity at the store late last night. I didn't have much choice, so I told her it was more than police activity, a guard was murdered. She was horrified but a little less when I told her it wasn't Paul, the guard she spent the day with yesterday.

I promised I would keep in touch with her and when she tried to ask more questions I cut her off, saying I was going to the hospital to see Doug. Which was true, but I wasn't allowed to say more to Meme about the case.

I suggested we order take out delivery from the café but John wanted to go the resort. He felt we could eat, check on the room and Ben. Carol was manning the check-in desk and wasn't able to talk. Richard saw us sitting at a table and walked over to us.

"Hi, you two," he said. "I hear there's been another incident, this time at Ruth Ann's store?"

"Yes, Richard," John said gloomily. "There was but I can't go into any detail."

"Just catch whoever it is causing our town to get such a bad reputation. This won't be good for my ski season here at the resort."

"Don't worry," John replied. "This'll be over soon." John felt the need to change the subject and asked, "Hey, is Ben working today?"

"Carol told me you were asking questions about him. Is there a problem with him?"

"Nope, he was very helpful with us yesterday regarding the man outside Ruth Ann's room," John said.

"Carol told me all about it. I hope there's not going to be trouble here, too?"

"It'll be fine, Richard," John said. "So, is Ben here?"

"That's the strange thing," Richard began to say. "He didn't show up this morning. He's never been a minute late and today he totally blew us off."

"What?" bellowed John. "What time was he due in?"

"His shift started at 7:00 am and that was just over two hours ago," Richard replied, worried.

John grabbed my arm and we flew out of the dining room. We hurried over to Ben's apartment. John tried to get me to stay in his car, but I refused. He didn't have time to argue with me. We ran up the stairs and banged on the door, no answer. John kicked the door in easily and held me back. He pulled out his gun and ordered me not to enter until he said it was safe.

I couldn't take it, so I peeked inside Ben's apartment to find John standing over Ben. "Ruth Ann," John snapped. "I told you to stay outside. This is a crime scene now and I don't want any disturbance here."

"I was here last night, so my prints are all over anyway. I won't touch anything. Is Ben ok?" I asked, trying to see Ben, but John was blocking my view. It appeared he was sitting in one of the kitchen chairs, tied up. What I couldn't tell was if he was alive or dead. "John, please?"

"Oh, alright, but don't touch a thing!" he ordered.

"Is Ben alive, John?"

"Yes," John said. "He's got a gag in his mouth and I'm just about to get it untied." I could tell John was struggling to release the gag that was tied around Ben's mouth. "The knot is so tight," John said, finally freeing Ben to speak. He waited for Ben to speak, but only his eyes were showing emotion. "Ben?" asked John. "Can you talk?"

After a moment, when he realized John and I were there to help him, he felt it was safe to talk. "Yes," he began. "I didn't recognize you at first. I was too scared to open my eyes because I thought the bad guys were back."

John looked at me and then back to Ben, "Did you say guys as in plural?"

Ben looked confused, so I clarified. "Ben, was there more than one man here that did this to you?"

"Yes, there were two men and they grabbed me this morning just as I was leaving to go to work," he said rubbing his mouth. "My mouth is so dry, can I have some water before I say anymore, please?" John motioned to me to go to the kitchen and grab a glass of water. "But remember Ruth Ann, don't touch more than you need."

I hurried and found a glass from a cupboard and turned on the kitchen faucet. I brought the cold water back to Ben and he drank every drop in the glass. "Thanks." Ben said, getting his breath back. "That thing they stuffed in my mouth was so tight I couldn't swallow even my own spit."

"It's all better now, Ben," John said, giving him time to recover. "Can you tell me exactly what happened?"

"I think so," he answered. "I was up at my normal time, 6:00, and got myself ready to go to work. I always leave at 6:35 am because I walk to work since I don't own a car or bike. I would love to have a bike that I could ride someday. That would make many things easier for me."

John, trying not to be impatient said, "Maybe we can arrange to get you a bike soon, ok?"

Ben's expression was of pure joy. He said thank you several times. John, trying to get him back on track before he forgets everything said, "Ok Ben, you were leaving at 6:35 right? Then what happened?"

"Yes, I grabbed a light coat because it was pretty cool out and opened my door to leave. I turned around to lock my door and then next thing I knew I was being hit on the head by two men and dragged back inside my apartment. They dumped me into this chair and tied me up. I was too scared to move or say anything." He was very upset and said, "Am I going to lose my job at the resort because I was late?"

"No, Ben," John said. "This isn't your fault. You were attacked and tied up. Richard and Carol will understand and they would never fire you for being late for this."

"That's good. This is the best job I've ever had."

I interrupted their conversation because I felt I needed to ask Ben a question. "Are you hurt anywhere, Ben? Like your head? You said they hit you over the head."

"Yes, yes, my head hurts very much," he answered, rubbing the top of his head. "Can I get some aspirin for my headache?"

"Actually Ben, I think we should take you over to the hospital and let Doc Albert check you out thoroughly."

Ben became agitated and shook his head, "No, no, I don't need a doctor, just some aspirin."

"I'm sorry Ben, we have to have you examined by a doctor now. This is a police investigation." John knew his time was running short with him and asked a very important question. "Did you see the men who did this to you, Ben?"

"No, not much of them. My back was toward them because I was facing my door to lock it. I just saw two men, dressed in black with hats on that covered their faces, too. You know the kind, like they wear in the movies when robbing a bank?"

John jumped on Ben's question, "What do you mean, like the kind they wear when robbing a bank?" I looked at John and shook my head. Ben didn't mean our bank here in town. He was talking about movies and TV shows that have criminals wearing masks to hide their faces. John thought Ben knew more about our bank robbery.

Ben looked to me for help and I explained to John what I thought Ben meant. Ben nodded and John backed down a little. "Oh, ok Ben. You're only saying what you've seen on TV shows, right?"

"Yes," Ben answered.

"So, let's just repeat what you told me. Two men hit you over the head while you were locking your door and they dragged you inside here and tied you up to the chair and gagged you, correct?" Ben nodded vigorously. "Did they take anything from you?"

"No, they asked me a couple questions before I passed out. I'm not sure if I passed out from the head wound or fear." Then he remembered one more thing. "Oh, oh, they walked around my apartment and looked through the cabinets and under the furniture, too."

John said, "You didn't tell me they talked to you. What did they ask?"

"If it was me outside the hotel room the other day, and if I knew the person who was supposed to be staying in that room."

"Oh, my," I blurted out. "John, they're looking for me!"

Ben asked, before John could reply, "But why do they want you? Have you done something wrong?"

"No, Ben," I said quickly. "They may want to hurt me like they hurt you."

"Why, what do these men want?" he asked, looking like a young, scared child.

"Ben, they won't bother you again," John said. "They realize you don't have what they're looking for or know anything more. You're safe now, I promise."

"Are you sure, John?" I asked him quietly. "What if they know we've been here or maybe they know we're here now!"

"Let's get Ben over to see Doc Albert and we can talk about it when he's in the examining room. We don't have much time before the gemologist appointment at the bank and I have to get ready. What worries me is that the guy that's been involved here with all the crimes with the guard, you, and Doug has been joined with reinforcements. Like the gemologist possibly?"

John called in to the station to have them come over to Ben's apartment to thoroughly search for any clues. Maybe there'd be a match in the system for a fingerprint, but it all has been going so badly that I doubted we'd get that lucky.

We took Ben over to the hospital and Doc Albert was waiting for us in the lobby. John had called and alerted Doc about Ben's condition so Doc was fully prepared to handle him with caution. "Hi Ben," Doc Albert said with a huge smile. "I hear you have a bump on your head, do you mind if I get a better look at it?"

Ben agreed and the two of them went into the examining room. John and I stayed back in the lobby. We didn't want to go see Doug until we knew what we were dealing with. John was on his phone most of the time we waited. Time was ticking away and he wanted to be at the bank by noon to get prepared in Doug's office. I said I could wait for Ben, but John told me to come with him to the bank.

"How long is Ben going to stay with Doc?" I asked.

"He's going to keep him there till this appointment is over with at least. I don't know what Doc will do to keep him there, he just wants to get over to the resort to make sure he still has his job."

"I got it John!" I said. "Why don't I call Carol and see if one of them can pop over to the hospital to sit with him and reassure him he still has his job?"

"That's a great idea," John said. "Call them now, could you?"

"Of course," I replied. Within minutes we got all the loose ends worked out. John and I were pulling into the bank, Carol was on her way to the hospital, and Doug was in his hospital room anxiously awaiting our return from the gemologist's appointment. What Doug didn't know was that a guard was killed at my store or anything about Ben. We thought it best to leave Doug in the dark about those occurrences until after our appointment.

"Ok, Ruth Ann," John started to say. "I have a change of clothes I'm bringing in and I need you to stay with Tom, the guard, while I change. My men have been placed in here already and we should be well covered just in case. Who knows, maybe this guy coming is just a gemologist and has no idea what has happened."

"I don't know how else someone would know about the necklace if it wasn't from this gemologist. No one knows about the necklace and remember what Ben said?"

"What part?" he asked.

"The tattoo on the guy's neck that he saw outside the hotel room. The Viking ship, remember?"

"Yes I remember," John said. "I forgot to ask Ben if he saw the ship tattoo on one of the men who attacked him earlier." John pulled out his phone and made a call to Doc Albert. He waited a second and Ben was put on the line. "Hi Ben," John said, upbeat so not to frighten him. "I forgot one last question for you. Did you happen to notice if one of the men who hurt you this morning had that Viking ship tattoo on his neck?" There was silence on John's end for a minute then John said, "Thank you, Ben. You get better and I'll come by and see you very soon." He looked at me and nodded, that was all the confirmation I needed. The man with the tattoo was determined to find me.

I wasn't sure whether I should feel deflated or determined. I wanted to crawl in a hole and wait until this was over, but on the other hand, I was so angry. I was the reason why a murder, two assaults, and a robbery had occurred. It was up to me to fight this and find the evil person who committed these crimes.

John could tell I was unsure about how to move forward. He grabbed his clothes out of the back seat and went around to my door and opened it up. He held out his free hand and said, "C'mon Ruth Ann, let's catch this creep!" That was all I needed to hear, I was all in.

Chapter 8

We entered the bank and found Sue and Christie absent. They were the bank's normal tellers. In their place was a female I didn't recognize and Lou, one of John's men. "Who's that woman?" I asked him.

"It's an undercover detective brought in from the city. I called in for some additional help and thought a female as a teller along with a male made it look realistic. Don't let her appearance fool you, she's one lethal woman."

I took a closer look at her and the smile on John's face. A pang of jealousy ran through me that I had never felt with him. I watched as he walked over to her and they talked for a few minutes.

John walked into the bathroom to change and the woman waved me over to her. "John asked me to keep a close eye on you until he comes out. My name's Judy, Detective Judy Lynch." She held her hand out to shake and I couldn't help checking her out. She was wearing a navy blue pencil skirt with a tight white blouse unbuttoned a little too low for my liking. She had blonde hair pulled up into a tight bun and pretty blue eyes and a perfect nose. She was tall and thin but with a muscular physique, I hated her already!

"Hi," I said with a wide, phony smile. She ignored my smile and said, "Dan and I will keep you safe just in case events turn dangerous. John and I have known each other for years and he has complete confidence in my abilities."

"Oh, that's great," I said. "How long have you and John known each other?"

"Let's see, a good fifteen years at least. He was there when I was just a rookie and really helped me move ahead. You see, my parents were friends with him years ago."

"How old are you?" I asked, regretting the question immediately.

"I'm 35," she said right away. "Never married, been too busy with my career. Maybe someday I'll settle down."

I wanted this conversation to end. I felt stupid asking questions that made me jealous. "I'm sure you will, you're young and beautiful."

"That doesn't exactly matter in my line of work," she stated. "I just hope to find a companion that's as dedicated to his job as I am. Like John here, he loves his job and is great at it." Detective Judy watched admiringly as John strolled up to us in a business suit. Oh really, I thought.

"You ready, Ruth Ann?" he asked leading me away from Judy. I let him take my arm and walk me to Doug's office. I was feeling childish and told myself to knock it off. Judy was too young for John anyway. Plus, she won't be here for long. Once this investigation was finished she would go back to the city.

"Ok," John started to say as he walked around to sit at Doug's desk. "I'm going to sit here and you sit in the chair facing the desk. When the gemologist, what's his name again," John said as he fumbled in his pockets. "Here it is, Jeffrey Toggles. When he enters the office I'll direct him into the chair next to you."

"Sounds good so far," I said.

"If I see any tattoo on this guy's neck I'll casually stand up and pull out my cuffs and arrest him. On the spot," he claimed. "You see me pull out my handcuffs, you head out to Judy and let her cover you, got it?"

I nodded and then we waited. It was fifteen minutes until the appointment time and we were as ready as we could be. Neither of us spoke until John spotted a man enter the bank. From the distance John could only make out a brief description to me, a short, chubby man with a briefcase. He walked up to Judy, thinking she's a teller of course, and Judy pointed in our direction.

The man walked over to us and waited for John to wave him into the office. "C'mon in, sir," John said smiling. "You must be Mr. Toggles?"

The man replied, "Yes." The first thing I looked for was a tattoo on his neck. Negative, I said to myself. He was wearing a navy blue sweater with Khaki pants so I had a clear view of his neck or should I say necks. The man was quite overweight and I know John was thinking the same as me, no way could this be our guy.

John motioned for him to sit down next to me and he introduced me. He kindly took my hand and shook it. I was beginning to think this was a wasted effort. This man looked like a grown-up child. His hair was thin and combed over to one side to cover his balding head. He was no taller than me, at about five foot four, but he weighed at least twice as much as me. I immediately thought about Ben and Doug and knew this man didn't attack them. However, he could've hired men to do his dirty work.

Mr. Toggles was the first to speak. "I understand, Mr. Albertson (he thought John was Doug Albertson, president of the bank, remember), that you have a piece in your possession you would like my expertise in?"

"Yes, well kind of," John, answered. "I would like to know your qualifications, Mr. Toggle, before I go into any further detail."

"Please call me Jeffrey," he stated. "I've been in the jewelry business for most of my life. My parents had a jewelry store and when I was old enough to work I helped them until they retired and then took over the store. I've been in charge of my business for over twenty-five years and deal with all kinds of gems, gold and silver, and estate pieces."

"Sounds good," John said, not really caring. "When we spoke last, I told you about a piece that had come into my possession was explained that it was a very rare gem with a long history. This," John held out his hand to point towards me. "This is the rightful owner of the piece."

Jeffrey Toggles looked at me and said, "Well, it would appear you're very fortunate to have a piece that has caught the attention of the president of a bank, ma'am."

"Please call me Ruth Ann," I said. "Yes, it's a family heirloom."

John said, "We received the piece not long ago and wanted to verify it's a real gem and its appraised value, for insurance purposes, of course."

"Of course," Jeffrey answered. "May I see it please?" He

asked and put his shaking hand out. I also noticed a few beads of sweat forming on his forehead. Uh-oh, I thought, this guy isn't as innocent as he appears. If I noticed it I can only imagine what's running around in John's head.

"In due time, sir," John replied. "I would like to know what research you pulled up on the piece after our phone call. I wouldn't think a man of your caliber would drive all the way to Deer Creek without it being worth your time?"

"What are you implying?" Jeffrey replied anxiously. "Are you saying I came here under false pretenses or that I'm hiding something?"

"Well, yes," John said, matter of factly. "If you pulled up the research I did you'd see that piece produced quite a list of interesting facts. Such as its priceless value and all the criminal activity associated with it over the years."

He jumped up out of his seat and said, "Sir, I don't know what you're talking about, but I assure you I only drove here to see a piece of jewelry you asked me to appraise. I don't care about the criminal history of it and I'll just take my leave." Jeffrey started to storm out of the office when he noticed Lou, John's policeman standing in the doorway to block the way. Jeffrey pulled back a step and turned to John.

"Tell this man to let me exit, please," he said arrogantly.

"I'm afraid not Mr. Toggles," John said coolly. "Please return to your seat."

Jeffrey did not move. John took this as a refusal and said, "So, we can do this the easy way or," he stopped and pulled out his badge and flashed it at Jeffrey. "Or we can take this to the station."

Jeffrey realized he wasn't going to get his way, nodded, and returned to the seat next to me. I wondered if John or Lou were going to frisk him because I sure didn't want to be sitting this close to a man if he could be hiding a gun.

"Ok," John said. "Do you have anything to tell me?"

"Fine," the man said, with sweat pouring down his face. "I did do some research on the piece you're referring to and found out all the information you said." He wiped the moisture from his cheek with a handkerchief he pulled out of his pants pocket and said, "But I haven't done anything wrong!" he protested.

John stood up and took off his suit jacket and casually put it around the back of Doug's chair. His gun was in his holster and Mr. Toggles started waving his hands all over the place. "Look here, I'm just an old jewelry store owner. I don't want any trouble. I didn't ask for this either. All I did was make some calls and then my life turned upside down!"

That wasn't exactly what I expected to hear. What did he mean by his life turned upside down? John sat back down and folded his hands in front of himself on the desk. "Why don't you tell me all about it, Mr. Toggles?"

Jeffrey looked from John to me back to Lou who was still standing at the door showing his gun in his holster, and then back to John. He conceded and began a very long, but amazing story.

"Before I begin, can I ask exactly who you are? I'm assuming you're not the president?"

"I am Chief of Police here in Deer Creek, John Wilkinson."

"That figures," he said quietly to himself. "How did you know I was involved?"

"I'll do the questioning," John stated. "Now, go on with your story."

"Yes, well when the real president, Doug Albertson contacted me about a necklace I didn't think much of it. He said he received a package with strange information regarding the piece. He told me all about the shape, color and size of the gem. I told him it could also be a fake." Jeffrey paused and asked for water. I think he sweated all the fluid out of him. He motioned to Lou and he disappeared from the doorway.

"I asked Mr. Albertson about the note that was inside the package." John interrupted and asked, "How did you know about the note?"

"Oh, he told me he was reading the specifications of the gem from a note that was included with the package. He basically read me the note and I have to admit it piqued my curiosity. I told him someone might be fooling him but until I looked at the piece I couldn't tell him for sure. That was when he asked me to come here at my earliest convenience."

Dan came in and handed Jeffrey a paper cup with some water. He drank it and wiped his forehead. "I told him I would come and we made an appointment for today, as you know."

"Okay, so up to this point you were unaware of the importance of the necklace?" John inquired.

"Yes, kind of. I mean there are always pieces that come from a shady past. I deal mostly with estate appraisals and I've seen a lot in the last twenty-five years."

"Are you admitting that you deal with stolen jewelry, Mr. Toggles?" John asked.

"No, no," he panicked. "I mean, maybe, but not knowingly. I get to see many old pieces and I don't know where they come from and who their owners may legally be. That's typical in my business and you can check that out. I do everything I can to stay on the right side of the law I assure you. That's why I'm so terrified of what's going to happen to me now."

John said, "If you're telling me the truth and leaving nothing out why would you be terrified from me?"

"It's not you I'm worried about," he mumbled, but we all heard.

"Excuse me?" I asked. "Who's threatening you?"

Jeffrey turned to me but was redirected back to John. "Ruth Ann, do you mind?" I kept my mouth shut and let John ask the questions.

"Mr. Toggles, are you telling me that you're being threatened regarding this piece?"

"No, I mean yes, I mean I don't know," he said, shaking his head in frustration. "Can I just explain, but if I tell you everything I could be signing my death warrant."

"Are you telling me your life is in danger?" asked John.

"Yes," he said. "I really do fear for my life. There's already been a murder or two."

"Who has been murdered?" John asked.

"Well, that guard and now maybe the president of this bank. I thought he was spared since I was supposed to have an appointment with him, but now, maybe he's dead, too."

"How did you know about the guard being murdered?" John asked. "That just happened."

"These people are very efficient," he said, lowering his head. "I'm next now."

"Stop stalling," John shouted, slamming his fist down on Doug's desk. "I'm about to haul you down to the station and put you in a cell unless you tell me right now what you know and don't stop or leave anything out. Do you understand me, Mr. Toggle's?"

"Yes," he replied anxiously. "Ok, after making the appointment I made my own calls and did some research on the computer. The background of the necklace fits a description of a very sought after piece. The people I called must've done their own research and somehow the information about this necklace fell into the wrong hands."

"Whose hands?" John demanded.

"Please, let me get this all out. It's becoming very confusing to me." John nodded but didn't speak. "Ok, after I found out some alarming news regarding the necklace via the Internet, I received a visit from an older gentleman." Jeffrey looked nervously to John but he still didn't say anything. "This man came across as very wealthy and at first I thought he was just browsing in my store. I was alone in the store that day, normally I have a sales clerk but he was out ill, so I thought."

"Ok, I have to interrupt now," John said. "What do you mean your clerk was supposedly out ill?"

"I found out later that day that my clerk, who is only forty-five and overall healthy, had a heart-attack."

"Why is that strange?" asked John.

"Because he was a runner, fit and never had a problem with his heart. It scared me because of the earlier visit with this gentleman. He said he was looking for a necklace for his wife of fifty years. He wanted something so special and rare that cost was not an issue. The older gentleman came to my store because I dealt with antiques and he was referred to me." Jeffrey stopped and looked at John and said, "Before you ask, I have no idea who referred him to me."

"Go ahead," John stated.

"I showed him pieces and they weren't good enough. He stressed it had to be something I recently came into possession of and so valuable there could be no price attached to it. I started to become nervous and when I walked to my counter where I installed a secret button that alerts the authorities, two thugs entered the store with guns in their hands. They were pointing those guns at me. I knew I was in big trouble and I also figured out the older gentlemen controlled the two thugs. They walked over to the older man and asked what they should do with me!"

"This doesn't make sense," John said. "This man does or doesn't know you have the necklace in question?"

"I believe he thought I already had your necklace. I knew that was what they were looking for and I told them I didn't have it or would have it. I told them I was called to appraise a piece of jewelry that fits the description but it wasn't at my store. And it never would be."

"I take it the older, hmmm, gentlemen didn't take kindly to that?" asked John.

"No, he didn't believe me. The two hired men grabbed me and threw me into a white SUV that was parked in front of my store. The older gentlemen got into a black limousine and we drove off. I didn't even get to lock my store; do you know how much merchandise I could've lost leaving my store unlocked?"

"Really?" John asked mockingly. "You were just stuffed inside a SUV with two guys who had guns and you're worried about the stuff in the store? I would be a bit more worried about my life."

"Oh, yes, I-I was, but my store is all I have. I guess the seriousness of the moment eluded my brain."

"Where did you go?" John asked.

"I'm not sure, I guess the old man's estate. They blindfolded me and we drove for about thirty minutes or so. I could tell we went up some elevation because of the way the truck felt. When we arrived at our destination I was led into a large room, a library of sorts."

"How do you know it was a library?" John questioned.

"Because there were books lining all the wood shelves. I don't mean a public library; I mean a person's personal library in a house. The room was large with double wooden entrance doors and two walls of books. A massive stone fireplace took up another wall. There was a huge desk in the middle and armchairs in front of it. The two men dropped me into one of the armchairs. They told me not to speak and wait for their boss to arrive. Then, they threatened, that if their boss wasn't happy with my responses, they would handle me personally."

"Did you see the house when you walked through it or were you still blindfolded?" John asked.

"I didn't see where I was until we walked into the library and they closed the doors behind me. That's when they forcefully led me to the armchair and deposited me."

"Was the older gentlemen there?"

"No, remember I said they told me not to speak until the boss arrived."

It was very clever of John seeing if Jeffrey would slip up. But he didn't and John ordered him to keep going.

Jeffrey looked around and squirmed in his chair. "You have to understand what I'm about to tell you. I was forced to cooperate or I would've been killed. Can you understand that much, please?"

"Just tell me what happened," John said with zero emotion.

"The older gentlemen finally arrived after quite a wait. I think he planned on having me sit and sweat so when they asked me to participate in their scheme I would because I'd be so scared. Well, it worked," Jeffrey, said. "The two men were told to leave us alone. They exited the library and I could tell they stayed on the other side of the closed doors because every once in a while I heard their deep voices. The older gentlemen went to a cupboard by the fireplace and pulled out a decanter full of whiskey and filled two glasses. He handed me one and advised me to drink. He said it would calm my nerves. I drank it all in one gulp and he took the glass from me and refilled it. This time I held the glass and asked him what he wanted from me. The older gentlemen told me to call him Axel and asked me to answer him truthfully or I could be in serious trouble."

"Let me guess, he asked you if you had possession of the necklace?" I asked. "Oops, sorry, John."

"Well?" John asked. "It was the logical question, so you may as well answer it."

"Yes, he asked me first if I knew the history of the necklace and where it was. I told him I had just begun researching it because a client was interested in finding its value."

"So that's how Doug was identified, correct?" asked John.

"I'm sorry, I had to tell him. My life was on the line. It may not matter to you if I lived or not, but it just happens to matter to me!"

"Go on." John said, becoming impatient. He stood and started walking around Doug's office.

"I told him I knew the necklace originated in Sweden and had been bumped around for generations. It had come to the U.S. and back to Sweden a couple times. The family that owned it had gone through many misfortunes trying to hold onto the necklace."

"So you do know about the criminal history of the necklace, and the family that owned it?" asked John.

"Owns, John, not owned," I corrected.

John nodded and waited for Jeffrey to answer. "Yes, I knew basic information from my research. But as far as I could tell the necklace disappeared many years ago and until now had been lost. I still haven't seen it and can't for sure tell you it's this missing necklace. But if you show it to me I could probably tell you. Why can't you just show me this piece?"

"We'll get to that later, go on with what happened," John demanded.

"The older man, I'm sorry, Axel, wanted to know who Doug was and why he was inquiring about the necklace. I told him he was the president of this bank and he received the necklace from a Swedish lawyer. They tracked down the true owner of the piece and it's Ruth Ann here." Jeffrey looked at me like I should be feeling lucky, but I felt as if I was cursed.

"So the older gentleman, Axel, knows who I am and that the necklace belongs to me?"

"Yes, I'm sorry. At the time I had no idea what lengths these men would go to retrieve the necklace. Axel untied me and told me I wouldn't be harmed if I cooperated with him. What else was I to do?" Jeffrey asked.

"You could've contacted the police," John mentioned, furious.

"At the moment I wasn't thinking clearly. I asked Axel what help I would be and he told me I was to keep my appointment here at this bank and when the necklace was presented all I had to do was to take ahold of it and they would handle the rest."

John interrupted, "So you came here today with the intention of grabbing the necklace and letting Axel's men run off with it?"

"No, no!" he cried out. "I did agree to keep the appointment, that's why I'm here, but I told them I wouldn't steal it."

"From what you just told me you weren't the one who would steal it. They told you once you got a hand on it they'd take over and handle it. I wonder what they meant by that?" asked John. "From what you just told me we're being watched at this exact moment and they're waiting for the necklace to appear."

"That would be my opinion, too," Jeffrey said. "That means

they may know this was a set up and I'm a dead man!"

"Not necessarily," John said. "We've already got too many people in protection without the manpower," John mumbled. "Jeffrey, if you aren't telling me the whole story I'll see that you spend the rest of your life in jail for accessory, attempted murder, and theft. Do you understand me?"

"I'm telling you the truth!" Jeffrey cried out. "Either way I'm done. I'm either going to jail for going along with these guys or I'm going to be number one on their hit list."

John stood up and walked out of the office. Lou stood guard and I noticed John walk over to Detective Judy. They didn't talk for long and then he walked back in. "I'm going to have you step out of the office for a minute, Mr. Toggles. I want you to wait just outside my door on the chair there." He pointed to a couple of chairs and Lou took him and sat him down. John closed the door and pulled out his phone.

Judy entered the office a few minutes later and reported to John that the men who were stationed around the bank had seen no evidence of anyone out of the ordinary wandering around. They'd checked with the businesses around the bank and all was clear. I wasn't sure if they didn't believe Jeffrey or if Axel and his gang took off when they realized the police were involved.

"This is what we're going to do," John started to say. "We're going to let Mr. Toggles depart on his own. Lou, you'll keep a tail on him and don't let him out of your sight. I'd like to know if he goes back to his business or to Axel's estate. If he's followed, you'll call it in so we can back you up." Lou nodded and went back out to Jeffrey who was still sitting in a chair right outside Doug's office. I thought Jeffrey looked calm considering the circumstances. I made a mental note to mention that to John.

Something wasn't right, I thought. Why would John let Jeffrey go off by himself? Even with Lou following him, it opened the door for Axel or his thugs to shoot him. Maybe John had a different theory, could he be setting Jeffrey up to catch the illicit Axel and gang? Was Jeffrey the expendable one or was Jeffrey one of them? That was the question to answer.

John told Judy to go back to her position as teller for a little while longer. He looked at me and said, "I don't like the direction this is going, Ruth Ann. I started to believe Toggles' story until he landed himself tied up at Axel's house. "

"Why?" I questioned.

"Why would he give his name to Toggles and then take off his blindfold? If he really wanted to get to the necklace and steal it why involve the gemologist at all? He got the necklace so it should be over, why keep the ruse going?"

"I didn't think about it, I guess."

"Look, the facts as far as I can see are that they caught wind of Doug looking into the value of a rare piece of jewelry. Mr. Toggles was the gemologist who responded to Doug and was willing to come out here and have a look at the necklace. Doug gets attacked, the necklace stolen, you've been spotted and now you and anyone around you are in danger. That's why the guard was killed and Ben was gagged and tied up."

I felt a little slighted and said, "I feel like you're blaming me, John."

"No, I'm sorry, Ruth Ann," he said. "You didn't even know about the necklace. You're danger is that you witnessed the actual robbery of the necklace and they know who you are. And, and this is a big AND..." John emphasized, "They think you know who they are."

"But I really don't!" I exclaimed.

"But they don't know that," John reminded me.

"So all these terrible things that have happened since the necklace has been stolen are because they think I can identify them?"

"Yes," John answered.

"But that makes no sense," I said. "They have the dumb necklace so why don't they just go on to their next crime. Even if I could identify them it wouldn't mean they would get caught. They knew they were well disguised."

"Up until Ben saw the tattoo on the guy's neck," John said. "That was a crucial error on their part. Now they can be identified with or without you."

"Oh that makes me feel better, John!" I said. "Now they can kill me, too!"

"No they won't, Ruth Ann," John declared. "I promise no harm will come to you." I know he meant his words, but it didn't mean it wouldn't happen or they wouldn't try.

John motioned for Lou to bring Jeffrey back into the office.

Jeffrey took his seat next to me and John decided it was time to reveal the true whereabouts of the necklace. "So, Mr. Toggles, we haven't brought the necklace out yet, are you still curious?"

"Why yes, of course I am," he said greedily. "But remember what my instructions were."

"Yes, yes," John said. "They would take it from there."

"So why would you put me or your people at risk from these criminals? Just don't take it out!"

"We can't," John stated, waiting for Jeffrey's reaction.

"What do you mean you can't?" he asked, stunned.

"I mean, Mr. Toggles, the necklace was already stolen by your man, Axel."

There it was, I thought to myself. The line I have been waiting for hours to hear from John. I watched as Jeffrey's face went from shock to anger back to shock. He stood up and tried to leave the office but Lou blocked him. Lou grabbed his arm and led him back into the chair.

"Well, Mr. Toggles? Are you aware that your older gentlemen friend, Axel, already took possession of her necklace?"

"NO!" he shouted. "Why would you put me through all this if you don't even have the dang blasted necklace?" He shook his head back and forth and started mumbling incoherent words to himself. I didn't know if he was having a fit or talking in another language. Wait a minute! He was speaking Swedish! I recognized a few words my grandmother used to say and I couldn't help myself I stood up and blurted out, "John, this man knows Swedish, can you hear him?"

John stood up, whipped his handcuffs out of his pocket and grabbed Jeffrey out of his chair and cuffed him. Lou came in and the two of them hauled him out into the lobby of the bank and out the front door. I knew he was too calm. He has to be a part of this, too. But why would he go through all this? Oh, my, maybe it was to flush me out?

I was left alone in the office and suddenly felt vulnerable. I hurried out and made it over to Detective Judy just in time to hear a number of loud booms. It was gunfire! Suddenly, the front window of the bank was shattered. Judy threw me down to the ground and put herself on top of me.

The entire incident happened in less than a minute. Once the gunfire stopped, Judy took off toward the front door. She yelled back at me to stay where I was and then she was gone. I was shaking and didn't want to move, but I was alone in the bank from what I could tell. I carefully stood up and looked around the lobby of the bank. There was glass everywhere and I saw a man down by the front door. I ran over to find Tom, the guard, face down in a pool of blood. He had been shot.

"Tom," I called out, trying to get his attention, but there was no answer. I went to my knees and carefully put a finger on his neck to see if he had a pulse. Thank God, he was still alive. I stood up and tried to find anyone who could help me get Tom some medical help. I looked out of the large opening that used to be the front window. John was on the ground kneeling over another body. Was it Lou's or Judy's? Maybe it was Jeffrey's. I wanted to go outside but knew it wasn't a smart idea, so I went back to Tom to see if he was responsive yet. Once I felt sure that he was still alive I ran to a phone on the nearest desk and called for an ambulance.

Within minutes I heard a siren and wondered if the surrounding area was safe. It had to be or I doubt John would be standing in the middle of the street. He wasn't alone, Judy and Lou were with him and when he spotted me standing in the shattered window opening he hurried over to me. He hopped through the opening and grabbed me in a tight hug.

"Are you alright?" he quickly asked.

"Yes, I'm fine, but Tom's been hit."

John hurried over to Tom and found he was seriously injured, but still alive. "I have to call this in and get Tom to the hospital, Ruth Ann."

"I already called," I said. "They're sending an ambulance and I believe they just pulled up." John turned and ran out to the ambulance and the other police cars that had arrived. I saw the paramedic went first to Jeffrey, who was the person I saw lying on the street. John waved him away and directed them to Tom. As they worked on Tom, John told me Mr. Toggles had been shot and killed. They didn't know where the shots came from, but it happened as they were putting him in the back seat of the police car. There were a number of bullets that hit the car and none of them were hit but Jeffrey Toggles. It was an assigned hit, John said.

"I don't get it," I said. "Why would they kill him?"

"Because they didn't want him to talk. I'm pretty sure they figured out we weren't buying his story about Axel and the two thugs so before he spilled the real story they had to finish him off. This is getting really complicated, Ruth Ann. Too many casualties and I'm no further in solving this case."

"You will," I said, feeling sorry for him. "It'll just take more time."

"At what cost, Ruth Ann?" John walked over to the coroner who was now at the scene. John put me in his police car to be safe just in case someone was still out there with me as the target. I overheard the policemen reporting to their chief that the area was clear with no sign of the shooters. They found where the shooters were located, and it was across the street inside a shed at the gas station. The shed was full of replacement tanks for gas grills. Perfect hideout, since no one would think to lay low inside a gas tank shed.

Chapter 9

An hour later the area was empty except for police tape around the shed and the front of the bank. The coroner took away the body to add it to the guard's body from this morning. That's two just to-day! John came and sat in his car and told me we had to drive over to the hospital. Doug had to be steaming mad by now and Ben and Tom were there, too. "If Tom's stable I'll need to speak with him, and also see what Doc did with Ben. I told him to keep him there until we return, so hopefully Ben's safe and happy."

"Doug will be seriously angry about what went down at his bank. Besides the bank window being shattered and glass all over, there are numerous bullet holes inside, too."

"It'll be cleaned up and a new window replaced before he leaves the hospital," John said. "I've already made the necessary calls and once they inspect and count all the bullet entries, the walls and counters will be fixed. I'm not worried about that, I'm worried about the reaction from Doug when he finds out about his gemologist and Tom."

"We better get over there right away. Doug's at the hospital, he probably already knows about Tom," I said.

"You're right," John said, starting up the car. We rushed over to the hospital and went straight inside. By now he knew about his bank, Tom, and Ben. Also, he had heard the rumors about a guard being killed at Ruth Ann's store this morning. Doc had ordered him to take a sedative so he wouldn't move around too much and reinjure his head. We found out about Doug from Claire who was sitting at her desk in the reception area of the waiting room. She followed us into Doug's room, talking the entire way. "Doc said he had to drug him to calm him down," she babbled. "He was furious when he saw Tom being wheeled in. Let's not forget the fact that Doug is awake! I assume you both were privy to that information already since you weren't shocked by my information?"

"I'm sorry, Claire," I said. "We didn't have a choice. Doug's life was on the line and the police needed to keep him safe. But now, all hell's broken out, so keeping Doug unconscious and safe is over."

"I get that, but what I'm mad about is that I couldn't figure that out, and I work here!"

"It was a closely kept secret," I replied. "Is Doug asleep?" I asked, pointing over at him.

"Yes, Doc gave him a super strong sedative and he told me to tell you and the chief that he wants to speak with you when you get here."

"Where is Doc?" asked John, looking around the hall.

"He's in with Tom," Claire said. "He told me to have you wait for him in his office and I'll buzz him that you both are here."

John looked flustered. He didn't want to waste any time waiting around in Doc's office. Another man was killed and Tom was fighting for his life right around the corner. Doug appeared to be safe with the guard still at his door. According to the guard no one had tried to enter his room outside of the doctor and the nurse.

Claire popped her head in and asked, "Can I get you two anything? Coffee or water?"

We shook our heads and before she left she added, "I think I should warn you that the whole town's a buzz about what happened on Main Street. People are talking about the guard at Ruth Ann's this morning, and about a stranger in town who went to the bank and left dead."

John stood up and started pacing the office. "This is just great!"

"I didn't really notice anybody on Main Street after the bank incident, John. Where were the people around town after Mr. Toggle's was shot?"

"My men stopped all access to the street once shots started firing. We didn't need any passerby's getting shot."

"Good thinking," Claire said as she left the office.

We sat in silence for quite a while before Doc Albert entered his office. John sat down next to me and we watched as a tired doctor sat at his desk. "Wow," Doc said. "That was too close."

"Tom?" John questioned.

"Yes, the bullet came very close to his heart. I was able to get it out, but now we have to wait. See if he regains consciousness and then I'll be able to sleep."

"What's your prognosis for him?" I asked, feeling horrible for what Doc Albert has had to endure with this case.

"If he awakens in the next few hours I'll feel his chances are fairly good for a full recovery. If he stays unconscious I'm worried that between the blood loss and where the bullet was he may never wake up."

"Oh that's terrible," I cried out. "What else can you do?"

"Wait, that's all we can do for the moment." Doc added, "I did my best under the conditions and my limitations here at this hospital. Once he's stable I'll helicopter him over to Grand Junction."

"He will pull through," I stated, watching the looks on both their faces.

Doc explained what happened with Doug and why he had to sedate him. "He'll sleep until tomorrow with what I gave him. Do what you need to do to catch these criminals so I can get my hospital back to normal."

We made one last check in on Doug and Tom, then went to see Ben. Doc had him held up in one of the rooms farthest away from Doug. He was sitting up in bed when we walked in his room. He appeared to be enjoying himself watching TV and laughing.

"Hi Ben," I said. "What's so funny?"

"I'm watching this show about videos people take and send into this show and they televise them. It's very funny," he said smiling. "Carol was just here and she brought me all this food from the resort and told me when I'm all better I get to come back to my job."

"That's great, Ben," I said, looking at the assortment of sandwiches, salads, and brownies that I could surely use at this moment. Chocolate always has a soothing effect for me.

John asked if anyone else had come by to see him and he said only the doctor and his mean nurse were in here besides Carol. I couldn't help but chuckle a little regarding Shirley. Ben sure got that right. She is a mean nurse. He said she handled him too roughly when tucking him into the bed. He thought he would fall off the bed the way she rolled him around. John was relieved that all was good here and Doc planned on keeping him in there for a day or two. He told Ben that his head injury was minor but thought it would do him some good to take a rest. It also gave Doc some time to find out what actually was wrong with him.

We left the hospital and headed for the police station. It was Tuesday night and after seeing all that food in Ben's room I realized I hadn't eaten anything for the whole day. John ordered some food from the resort and had it delivered to us at the station. I made sure he added a plate of those brownies I spotted in Ben's room, too. We sat in his office in silence for some time while we devoured Carol's homemade lasagna that was the special for the evening. Once we were finished, John made some calls while I checked my cell phone.

I knew I'd be in trouble with my daughters, Nancy and Lynne. I was happy that Irene, my sister and her husband were off on a cruise and couldn't be contacted for the next couple weeks. Delores knocked on John's door just as I was checking my messages. "Hi, Ruth Ann," Delores said. "Your daughters have called several times and have almost put out an APB on you."

"I know, it's been a long, rough day," I answered. "I was just checking my messages now. Guess I better get it over with and listen to them chew me out."

Delores laughed and said, "When did it happen where the kids become the parents and the parents become the kids?"

"I know, really," I said. "I've had more action than I've seen in my whole life. However, not the kind of action I asked for!"

Before she left John's office Delores said one last comment, "Oh, I'm to tell you that if you don't call them the minute you get here they'll come here and throw you into a cell until you start behaving yourself!"

Delores turned and left and I could hear her laughing all the way down the hall.

"Great, now I have to deal with them," I said, frustrated. "This is really starting to get on my nerves. I never asked for that dumb necklace!"

"We'll get this over with soon, Ruth Ann," John said, looking up from the work on his desk. "We need to think about how much to tell your daughters. You realize that your daughters could get pulled into this unintentionally."

"What?" I cried out.

"If anything ever happened to you, that necklace goes to them," he replied.

I almost fainted after John told me that. He rushed over to me and put his arms around my shoulders. "It won't come to that, I made you a promise, remember?"

I jumped up and said, "That's it! We catch these creeps immediately. Do you understand me?"

John smiled and said, "That's my girl. You have a feisty, smart, determined personality and that's why you're so important to me."

"You're right about a couple of those traits. I'm smart and I'm determined," I declared. "That's my motivation, to catch these guys."

"WE?" Asked John. "We aren't going to catch anyone. I am."

"We'll see," I said, smiling back at him.

I wasn't sure what I was going to say when I pulled out my phone to call one of my daughters. Which one first? I decided on Lynne since she owned a business two doors from mine and knew a little about what was happening. John spotted me dialing as he sat at his desk working when he said, rather loudly, "Stop!"

"But you know I've got to call them or they'll come here."

"We need to think about this rationally, Ruth Ann," John said, thinking fast. "I think the best thing for your girls is to not see them or talk to them until this matter is solved."

"That's ridiculous," I blurted out. "They're my daughters and I do talk to them quite a lot."

"If you're being followed the last thing we need is for them to see you with Lynne or Nancy. You can call them from my phone here and not your cell. We don't want any trace back to these guys and that includes your phone." He saw my expression of horror on my face and added, "I know this isn't what you want, but I strongly feel it's best. We'll call them both and put them both on the line so the four of us can hash this out."

"Fine," I said, knowing it was best solution, but I wasn't happy. The last thing I want is for my daughters to be in danger. "Call them both and put us on speaker, please."

John called Lynne, then Nancy and explained to them we're going to have a nice chat. I'm sure that'll go over smoothly, I thought. I can only hope they don't rush over to the police station and demand to see me.

Lynne answered right away. It was quite late for her since her hours started early in the morning. "Hi John, I assume Mom's with you there?"

"Yes, she's right here, but can you hang on a minute? I'm going to get Nancy on the line too so we can all talk at one time." John put Lynne on hold and called Nancy. She has been so busy with her class over at the high school I hadn't spoken to her in days. "Hi, Nancy," John said when she answered. He explained that we all are going to be able to talk and that I was with him at the station.

"What's going on Mom?" Nancy asked first. "Lynne and I have been worried sick about you the last couple days. First we hear about Doug, then about a guard being murdered in your store, then the shootout earlier today on Main Street. Please tell me you weren't involved or anywhere near there?"

John answered for me and said, "Girls, your mother's fine, but she's limited to what she can tell you for your own safety. Please don't push the questions or I'll have to end the call. Are we all in agreement?" I was shocked when the girls agreed. John decided to take the lead on my end and told them about the robbery at the bank and how I was a possible witness. That's the real reason why there was a guard at the store.

Lynne interrupted John's explanation about the guard and said, "But the guard was murdered? Why? What's so important that people are being killed?"

"Lynne, I can't tell you that exactly, but I can tell you the people who robbed the bank are serious and they aren't giving up."

"Giving up what?" asked Nancy.

"They believe your mom saw one of the men involved, and anyone else who could have identified them have either been injured, killed, or disabled. Therefore, for your mother's safety, I've put her in protective custody until this case has been solved."

Together they shouted, "WHAT?"

"Yes, girls, listen to John. I'm fine, but after what's happened the last few days I have to agree with John. I don't want either of you to come and see me because if I'm being watched I don't want any connection to the two of you. Is that clear?"

No response from either girl. John took over and said, "Your mother will be in my custody or one of my men's. Her store will be closed temporarily." I interrupted John this time and said, "Why? Can't I have protection there so I can keep my business running?"

"No way," John declared. "One guard was already murdered and your office is a crime scene anyway. You don't want to risk another person's life, do you?"

"No," I replied. "But can I have Meme keep it running and maybe the girls can check on the place?"

"Let me think about that one for a while," John answered. "Let me go on with the immediate problem. Your mother, as you both know, can be very stubborn," he hesitated, waiting for my outburst but I just rolled my eyes and let him continue. "Ok, no response, so as I was saying, your mother's going to be difficult to keep under the radar so I'm trying to figure out the best place to keep her safe. I'm rather busy trying to solve the case so it means I'll keep her at the station with me and the staff, or send her away for a while."

"Absolutely no way am I leaving!" I cried out. "I will not run and hide from these people. I'm aware lives have been lost or at risk, but I will not leave."

"Ok, if that's the case, your mom will be held up here."

"She's going to sleep at the police station?" Nancy asked quietly.

"No, during the day she can be here, at night I'll take her home with me."

"John! I know my daughter's aren't that young, but that sounds inappropriate."

"Really, mom," Lynne said. "It's not that big of a deal for you to stay overnight at a man's place." Nancy giggled and agreed.

"Then it's solved," John said. "You will be staying with me until this is over."

Lynne asked the question John was hoping could've been avoided. "Uh, what is it that Mom saw that is so important?"

"I wish I could tell you," I said. "It really is very interesting, what was stolen from the bank." John's glare at me told me I'd said too much.

"What was stolen?" asked Nancy. "We won't say anything."

"Nice try but I can't divulge that piece of information yet. In due time you both will be the first to know. How's that?" John was hoping they would accept his explanation.

"I guess we don't have a choice, but before I agree to all these conditions you do need to tell me if my mom is somehow attached to the stolen item?" Good question, Lynne, I thought to myself.

"No deal, Lynne," John said. "The less you know, the better."

"Fine," she accepted. "Can we at least call the station and check on you?" Nancy added.

"Of course," I answered. "Call me here or on John's cell phone."

We ended our conversation and John felt it went as well as could be expected. "At least they didn't rush over here. That's something you would've done."

"Funny, John," I replied. "And you're right, I would've been here long ago if it were me and my daughters were involved."

We headed back to John's place later than I wanted. He was busy at the station with his men trying to come up with any answers to today's events. Doc called over to the station and informed us that all his patients were still safe. Tom was still touch and go, but Doc remained hopeful he would wake up soon. We would know in the morning if Tom passed the critical stages of his injuries.

The night went by uneventfully. John took up residency on his couch and I took over his bedroom. The bathroom was a tough room to share. John only had one and I wasn't happy about sharing the space. It was better than sleeping in a cell at the station and using the bathroom there.

The next morning we went straight back to the station. John had Delores and Lou go to my house to pack up more of my personal things so I would have them with me here at the station and at John's. I was grateful I had my laptop delivered to me from the store. I could at least do some of my work here at the station. I asked if Meme could be called and open the store. John hesitated but agreed as long as the first guard we had, Paul Welch, was available.

Meme agreed immediately and Paul was on his way. At least my business could run normally. John didn't feel that there was any more danger there since the guard that was killed there forced the police to have a bigger presence. Meme and I could talk as often as needed, so I felt like I was almost there.

We ate bagels that were brought into the station and I had a box of my favorite tea. John was anxious to see what had occurred overnight with the investigation and at the hospital. "Let's put you in the office next to mine, Ruth Ann," John said. "Nobody has occupied that space in a while so you can spread out and relax."

"That's fine, but can I be in your office when you talk with Doc?"

"Of course," he replied. "That's my first call." John picked up his phone and called over to the hospital. Doc answered right away and said Ben was settled in and Doug was up, but very groggy. He was asking for us and John said we'd be over soon. Tom, the bank guard, was still very critical and Doc wasn't comfortable transferring him yet. He was worried Tom wouldn't survive the helicopter ride. "He's not awake yet, but he's been moving a little. That's a good sign that he could be waking up soon."

"I guess that's good news, Doc," John said cautiously. "Tell Doug we'll be by in an hour or so and try, and keep him calm."

"The sedatives will keep him groggy for a few more hours," Doc said.

John went off to talk with some of his men who had been trying to track down information on the bullets found. I set up shop in the adjoining office and was on the phone with Meme when John came in. "We got some hits on these guys, Ruth Ann," John said, perking up.

"You know who they are?" I asked.

"Well no, but the coroner found a piece of paper that was crumpled in Jeffrey Toggles mouth."

"In his mouth? How would he be able to do that?"

"He must've stuffed it in there after he was shot. He didn't want whatever was written on that paper to be found."

"Were you able to read it or was it too dissolved?" I asked.

"Actually, it's our best clue so far besides the tattoo with the Viking ship," John said. "And we're working with tattoo shops all over Colorado to see if they have records of anyone getting a Viking ship tattoo."

"That's great, finally a break," I said. "Can you tell me what the note said?"

"Only part of it was legible. It was smudged but *1212 Loo...*we could make out."

"*1212 Loo?*" I asked. "What on earth does that mean?"

"I'm guessing an address. My guys are looking into that right now."

"That's hopeful," I said. "If you could get an address we could go out there and catch these guys."

"I don't think so, Ruth Ann," John said. "If this is an address the only ones checking it out will be the police."

"But they may have my necklace!"

"And I'll bring it back to you," John answered in a calm voice. "Why don't we go over to the hospital while my guys are checking on a possible match with an address."

We drove over and ran into Shirley, Doc's surly nurse, in the hallway. "Hi Shirley," I said, in as nice a voice as I could muster.

"Oh, hi, it's you two," she spat out, without stopping.

"What's your problem, Shirley?" I asked. "I tried to be friend-ly to you, why can't you reciprocate?"

"Because I really don't want to, Ruth Ann," Shirley said bitter-ly. "This hospital is in an uproar mainly because of you!"

"Me?" I exclaimed. "How do you figure that?"

John wanted to know, too. Shirley stopped before entering a room, probably Tom's, and said, "We have exactly three patients in this hospital and they're all in here because of something you were involved in. I don't know exactly what that is, but I know enough."

"Shirley," John started. "What have you overheard or is Doc filling you in?"

Shirley looked directly at John and said, "I know that Doug is conscious and was hit over the head when someone robbed his bank and you are lying saying he's unconscious. I also know that Ben was tied and gagged by some criminals after he stood outside Ruth Ann's hotel room over at the resort. Last, poor Tom could die because of the same thugs who shot at him over at the bank."

"How are you blaming Ruth Ann for any of this?" asked John.

"Because I overheard Doug say to Doc that Ruth Ann was spotted by whoever hurt him. I figured out about the hotel room after hearing Carol and Ben talking in his room and just figured that Ruth Ann was probably at the bank when Tom got shot."

"Wow, you think you got it all figured out, don't you Shirley?" I snapped. "For your information..." John halted me tearing into

Shirley and said, "Shirley, Ruth Ann's an innocent victim, that's all. As for your eavesdropping, I think it would be best if you cease doing it. You're listening in on private conversations." The look John gave Shirley would scare anyone, even her. She stormed off and entered the patient's room.

"Whoa," I said, grabbing his arm and squeezing it. "That was a tongue lashing and I sure am glad I wasn't on the end of that one."

"She had it coming," John said. "That's all I need if her life is in danger, too."

"I think she could handle any murderer herself," I mumbled, but John overheard me and grinned back at me.

We went to look for Doc before going into Doug's room. I wasn't sure if Doug would be fully coherent yet, so John suggested talking with Doc first. He was sitting in his office eating a sandwich. "Hi you two," he said with a mouthful. "Hope you don't mind; I haven't had much time to eat."

"Go ahead, Doc," John said. "Before we see Doug can you update us on Tom's condition?"

"He's just not coming around like he should so I've decided to call Grand Junction Memorial. They'll come and get him later this afternoon. I think he's stable enough to make the trip."

"I'm glad he'll get the care he needs, Doc. You've done everything possible to help him," I said. "Plus, maybe he'll be safer away from here."

Doc choked on his sandwich and grabbed his bottle of water. "The way things have been going, I agree."

"Now on to Ben, how's he doing?" asked John.

"That's an interesting case," Doc said. "His head is fine and normally I would let him go home. But since you requested I keep him here a few days, it gave me some time to evaluate his mental condition."

"Find anything out?" John inquired.

"That's just it; he's passed all the tests I've thrown at him. I checked his scans and outside of the bump on his head. He's physically normal."

"Can he be mentally handicapped?" I asked. "I mean he is slow. Can that just be how he is or maybe born that way?"

"Possibly, but I can't see any reason why. Maybe something traumatic happened to him when he was very young that damaged him." Doc finished his sandwich and sat back in his chair exhausted.

"Have you had any sleep, Doc?" I asked.

"On and off in an extra room here. I dared not leave this place until everyone was stable."

"That's very helpful, Doc," John said. "Can we get back to Ben? My question is, can he be faking his slowness?"

"John!" I exclaimed. "That's ridiculous, why would he do that?"

"Maybe to hide something from his past. If he came across disabled an employer may feel no need to check his criminal past."

"That sounds far-fetched, John," I replied.

"Maybe, but I'm still going to run a background check on him. Don't you remember what Carol told us?" I shook my head and said I couldn't recall. "That Richard felt so sorry for him and his story that he hired him on the spot."

"Oh yeah, that's right," I said. "Very interesting."

Doc didn't think Ben was hiding anything, but he was no cop. We moved on to Doug and how we would handle telling him any current information. Doc felt he was healed enough to handle it and just requested we keep it simple and don't get him too riled up. We were painfully aware that Doug would blow a gasket, but we didn't have any choice. We had to fill him in on what happened since we met with Mr. Toggles. Doc said he was aware of most of yesterday's event, but since he sedated him, Doc wasn't sure what he would remember.

We left Doc's office and before we entered Doug's room John asked Doc, "What's up with Shirley?" Doc didn't understand what John was getting at and so he filled him in on her eavesdropping on conversations.

"Really?" he asked, surprised. "I'll speak with her. She knows better than to spy on other people's private conversations. I mean if she was in the room with a patient and people were talking she would have an excuse, but not just standing outside a door and listening."

"Thanks," John said. We entered Doug's room and found him lying in the bed with his eyes closed.

"Maybe we should come back, John," I said. "He's sleeping."

"No, I'm not," a voice called out from the bed. "My eyes are just really heavy, but I'm awake."

John went next to the bed and asked him, "How are you feeling, Doug?"

"Honestly, I'm pretty ticked off at the two of you!" He looked at both of us and Doc quietly left us alone. "Doc may have drugged me to calm me down, and that was a good thing, because I wanted to go find you both and...and," he stopped before he said something he would've regretted. John and I got the point; he was extremely ticked off at us.

"Doug, if you want me to tell you exactly what happened you need to calm down. Doc will come in and stick another needle in you if you don't," John declared.

"Fine."

"Ok, I'm starting with the set appointment Mr. Toggles had with you at the bank. I obviously went in your place and he showed up on time."

"Then he was shot and killed," Doug muttered.

"Please, Doug, let me get through this," John begged. Doug agreed and John continued telling him the events that led up to Jeffrey's death. Doug stayed calm but I could see the anger rising inside of him. I just hoped he wouldn't blow and reinjure his head.

"So," John went on, "When we figured out he was lying, I called him out on it and he spilled his guts about some guy who kidnapped him and forced him to keep the appointment with you. These guys were planning on raiding the bank once Mr. Toggles had possession of the necklace. What I don't understand is why? They already took the necklace, so why go through this elaborate plan?" John waited a moment to see if Doug would answer.

Doug sat up tall in his bed and shouted out, "To kidnap Ruth Ann!"

"That's my thought too, but why?" John asked.

"Because when the guy bashed my head in he thought Ruth Ann saw him and could identify him, so they made Toggles keep the sham appointment. Once they captured Ruth Ann they could dispose of her anyway they choose."

"Exactly," John said. "That's when we took him into custody and as we were putting him in the police car shots rang out. We took cover and tried to fire back, but it was too late. Jeffrey Toggles was hit and killed."

"Don't forget about my bank guard, Tom, he was hit too," Doug said solemnly.

"Yes, Doug, Tom was in the crossfire and once the front window glass shattered Tom was exposed and hit."

"John, I feel horrible about this. How's Delores taking the news? I know they're divorcing, but she still has to be worried sick."

"Delores has been a trooper," John answered. "She's been coming here secretly to see him."

"I didn't know Delores was coming here," I said. "She hasn't said a word to me."

"She's torn," John said. "They aren't exactly getting along, but now that he's been so seriously injured she has had a change of mind."

I asked, "She wants to call off the divorce?"

"That's what she says now. But once he's recovered and back to his normal self I'm sure they'll go ahead with the proceedings," John said.

"I just hope he gets back to normal," Doug replied.

"He's being moved later today," John informed Doug. "Doc thinks he'll get better care in the city."

"Good, I hope it all works out for him," Doug said. "But what about this other guy? Ben?"

"He was in the wrong place at the right time," John answered. "He works at the resort and saw a man with a strange tattoo outside Ruth Ann's hotel room. He reported it to Carol because he thought it looked suspicious. Carol told us randomly while we eating in their restaurant. Unfortunately, they got to Ben, too. They hit him over the head and questioned him about Ruth Ann. He didn't know anything so they left him tied and gagged, that's all."

"What about the guard murdered at your store, Ruth Ann?"

"Horrible isn't it?" I said, not looking for any answer.

John explained about the guard and said they had received some strong clues as to who these guys are. We decided it was enough information for Doug right now since he seemed wiped out, so we asked if it was ok that we leave and return when we knew more.

"Yes, go and find these guys. I don't want anyone else killed," Doug said, as he leaned back in his bed and closed his eyes.

John and I left the room and walked down the hall to take a peek into Tom's room before he was being transported. "Well," John started to say. "That didn't go as badly as I thought."

"Doug handled it well," I agreed.

We stood outside of Tom's room. His door was closed and we were about to open it when Shirley popped out of his room. "Oh, what are you two doing? Not going into this room, are you?"

John wasn't in the mood for Shirley's tirade and replied, "I don't see how it's any of your business."

"He's my patient," she snapped.

"No," John said, "He's Doc Albert's patient."

"Well that's what I meant, of course," she said, walking past us and allowing us to enter. We walked into Tom's room and I was taken aback at all the machines and tubes hooked up to Tom. John noticed my hesitance and grabbed my arm; "It's keeping him alive, Ruth Ann."

"I know, it's just difficult to see," I said. There wasn't much we could do in there so we decided to go and check on Ben. His room was at the far end of the hall from Doug. John did a good job with his guard walking up and down the hall keeping all three of the patients safe.

Ben was sitting up in bed with a tray of food next to him. He was smiling and laughing at the TV again when we walked in. "Hi," he said merrily.

"Hi Ben," I said. "It looks like they're treating you well in here."

"Oh, yes," he said. "I have a nice bed, TV, and Carol brought me some more food from the restaurant."

"I'm very glad, Ben," I responded.

John asked, "Has anyone else been by to see you?"

"No, should there be?" he asked, looking scared. "Are those bad guys going to come here and hurt me again?"

"No, of course not, Ben," I said reassuringly.

"No, Ben," John took over. "You're safe in here, and by the time Doc Albert releases you the bad guys will be all locked up."

"That's great," he said. "I'm in no hurry to leave here. I like it here, everyone is nice and I feel very safe."

John gave Ben a strange look and then asked him, "Ben, do you have any family we should contact for you?"

"No, no I don't have any family," he replied quickly. "I'm all alone and have nobody to help me."

"Why did you come to Deer Creek?" John asked him out of the blue.

"I – I don't know, I just found this nice small town and knew I would like it here. I don't like big cities, they scare me and people aren't very nice."

"I see," John said. "How did you get here, did you drive or get a ride?" I stared at John trying to figure out what he hoped to gain with these questions. Ben was becoming nervous and starting to sweat. Little beads were forming on his forehead. Uh oh, I thought, this is what happened with Jeffrey Toggles when he began to lie.

John noticed Ben's change in demeanor. He became fidgety and refused to answer any more questions. He said his head hurt and asked us to leave. If I didn't physically push John out of the room he would still be forcing Ben to answer his questions.

In the hall John said, "Why'd you do that? I was close to getting some truth out of that man."

"John, you of all people should know that if you push a person too far it will backfire on you. That's what was happening with Ben. He wasn't going to tell you anything and if you kept bullying him you wouldn't be able to talk to him in the future. He would be too scared of you."

"Ruth Ann," John said. "He's hiding something; I just feel it."

"I agree," I said.

"You agree?" John asked, shocked at my response.

"Yes, once you started asking him about his family and why he came here, did you see the sweat forming on his forehead? And he became irritated and all."

"Exactly, you would be a good detective, Ruth Ann," John said. "You know, that was a bizarre trip to the hospital," John said as we got into his car. "Doug took the news better than I thought and we didn't expect much from Tom. I'm glad he's being transported out of here though. But the weirdest conversation was with Ben. I'm far from convinced that he's as innocent or simple as he protests."

"Possibly, I think you should keep an eye on him. I'm getting the feeling that there's more to him than what he's told us." John and I went back to the police station and he headed off in one direction and I went into the office I was borrowing. I decided to call Meme and see how it was going over at the store.

"Hi Meme," I said, as happily as I could muster. "Any business at all today? I know it's only been a day since the guard shooting, but I figured nosy people would wander in."

"Nope, nobody came in all morning, except for Paul."

"I'm glad you have Paul there with you, not because I'm worried about your safety, but because he can lend you a hand." I didn't want Meme worried about her safety. It was mine that was in question.

"This isn't good for business, Ruth Ann," Meme said. "We need to get all this crime stuff solved so we can get ready for the holiday rush. The only good thing to come out of this is that I'm able to decorate the store and move items around. It's going to look marvelous when I'm done and Paul is a big help."

"You have Paul moving furniture?" I asked curiously.

"He's moving furniture, cleaning the brass and silver items, and even steam cleaning some of the carpets," Meme answered.

"That's great, I'm glad he's there. I may have to pay him extra for all his work," I said happily. Paul was doing things that Meme or I had difficulty doing, so I would definitely reward him with some extra money. I wasn't sure how much a security guard made, but I figured he could always use a little extra cash.

I hung up with Meme and made one more call, to my daughter, Lynne. I couldn't contact Nancy until later since she was teaching classes all day. Lynne was at her bakery and picked up right away. "Oh, hi Mom," she said, in bright spirits.

"You sound like things are going well there today," I said.

"It's absolutely packed in here! I can't keep up with the demand."

"Why? Did you make something new for everyone to try?" I asked.

"Not really," Lynne said. "I did make more of my balls for tasting but I do believe it's crowded in here because of you."

"Me?"

"Yes, mother, you," she said. "Everyone's too afraid to go to your store so they go to the next best place for information, me."

"Makes sense I guess. What are you telling people? Because what John told you and your sister really shouldn't be spread around town."

"I haven't said a word, that's the amazing thing," Lynne said. "They won't leave, hoping I'll break and talk and they're eating up a storm while waiting. It's great for business, you know?"

"For your business, mine's going down the toilet so to speak," I said. "Meme told me we haven't had one customer today."

"It may take a little while before people get over the fact that a man was killed in there yesterday. It hasn't been that long, Mom."

"I know I'm just a bit discouraged. It's almost Halloween, and Thanksgiving and Christmas are just around the corner. This is the time of year I make the most money."

"It'll pick up, just give it some time. Anyway, you don't even need the money," Lynne said. "This is just a hobby for you, isn't it?"

"Yes dear," I replied. "Thankfully, I can afford a slow time at the store, I just don't like it."

"Hang in there. I wish you could come by here and sample more of my new creations, but I know you're stuck at the station."

"Me, too," I said, regretting what I was thinking. I wanted to sneak out of here and drive over to the bakery and eat some chocolate. Chocolate always makes me feel better. "I really need some chocolate right about now. Maybe you could drop some off here at the station and pretend you had an order to deliver."

"I could do that," Lynne said. "I'll package up a variety of items, mostly chocolate for you, and bring it over in about an hour. I'm thinking some of these people will leave since they're just spending money and not getting any gossip."

"Oh that would be great!" I said, very excited. "I'll be counting the minutes."

Chapter 10

I went back to my laptop and pulled up inventory lists from the store. It was tedious work, but there was not much more I could do from the station. John peeked in on me and brought me a sub sandwich delivered from the Café. I was starving, so I gobbled it up immediately and went back to my work. I didn't hear a word from John about what was happening, especially about the address. I decided I was done with my work so I started researching addresses in the area with the numbers *1212 Loo.*

I narrowed the range to within 25 miles of Deer Creek. I know it wasn't much of a search, especially with John and his men doing much higher tech searches, but what the heck. Immediately I got a hit! Either John already knew this information or his research guys weren't very proficient at their jobs.

There was a house located on Lookout Mountain Road only nine miles away from here! There was only one house in the area and guess what the number on that house was? Yes, *1212 Lookout Mountain Road.* I zoomed in on the satellite picture of the area and the house or mansion, from what it appeared, was located on the very edge of the mountain so it looked to be hanging in a precarious position. A very large edge, but if there was avalanche, this house would be a goner!

I knew I wasn't the only one who had this information. I found it in five minutes; therefore, John must be hiding this new information from me. I stormed out of the office and found him in his office on the phone. I stood in the doorway, glaring at him until he was finished. "C'mon in, Ruth Ann," John said. "You don't look happy."

"That's all you're going to tell me?" I demanded. "Anything

else you would like to communicate to me?"

John looked stunned. "Such as?"

"Really, are we going to play games? I hope not because I won't take it, and another thing, I'll not stay under your supposed protection if you avoid letting me in on what's going on here."

"What on earth are you talking about?" he stammered. "And by the way, I don't recall you being installed as a deputy recently, do you?"

I didn't want to play this game so I turned around and stormed off. I went back into the office and slammed the door. I had to think. I thought it best to cool off before I confronted John or chose another direction. I would rather handle things on my own. I always have since my husband passed away. If a problem arose, I solved it. So that's what I decided to do.

I sat at the desk contemplating ideas. There was one I kept going back to, but I was stuck on how to accomplish it. Here it is in a nutshell. I need to get out of John's reach and take a little ride up to the house on Lookout Mountain Road, simple right? The rational part of my brain knew it was wrong, but the irrational part didn't care. But how could I get away from John?

I had to come up with a solid plan. I didn't think it advisable to drive out there alone and the only one I could think of that might go along with me was Paul Welch, the guard at my store. He was trained, carried a gun, and didn't technically work for John. His security firm was hired by John, but Paul may do work on the side for extra money. That's it; I'll offer him a large bonus if he cooperates with me and keeps it between the two of us. The biggest problems are getting Paul to go along with my scheme, and getting away from John.

I thought about it most of the afternoon and decided it was too late today to take the ride, but tomorrow would be the day. I kept going over in my head ideas of how I could convince John to let me go off with Paul. I finally came up with a plan that would incorporate a mild disaster in my store that needed my immediate attention. I would let John drive me over there and he would make sure Paul would watch my every move. Which is the truth, he will be with me every second. Just not at the store, ha-ha.

Did I feel I could be in any danger? No. What harm could come of a short drive to just look at a house? I wasn't planning on stopping or attempting to contact anyone who lived there. I just wanted to see the place and find out who was coming and going there. Maybe I would see the guy with the neck tattoo. Then I would confide my whole devious plan to John. He would scream and yell and probably fire Paul, but if it identified the man I'd seen before then it's well worth the risk. I would never let John fire Paul for my foolish scheme though.

I spent the rest of my time at the station coming up with the perfect excuse for John to allow me to go to my store in the morning. It would be a water leak in the upstairs bathroom. I would have to get over there to assess the damage and put in an insurance claim immediately. There was a chance he may say no, but I had to try. I was getting stir-crazy waiting here in the station and staying at John's place. All I wanted to do was get my life back to normal. Boy, was I totally wrong!

I contacted Meme and had her put Paul on the phone. It took a lot of convincing to get Paul to go along with me. He argued and argued that it was wrong and it could cost him his job. After promising large sums of money and persuading him that I would never let John fire him, he finally agreed. He did tell me rather harshly that it was against his better judgment, but he knew it was better that he went along with me than let me go by myself.

We left the station shortly after seven in the evening and John ordered a pizza to be delivered. He refused to talk about the case anymore. I gave him several chances to let me in but he wouldn't budge. I decided my plan was going to happen since John wasn't cooperating. We skipped going over to the hospital and decided we'd go tomorrow morning before going back to the station. The routine was boring me, hospital visit to police station back to John's. Enough was enough.

John didn't notice my anger toward him was building since he was so consumed with the case. He spent most of his time on the phone or the computer. I stormed off to the bedroom in silence shortly after we finished the pizza. What changed his behavior toward me? The only reason I could come up with was he didn't want me involved anymore because they were getting closer to identifying the criminals. Let's see who gets there first!

I woke earlier than normal since I fell asleep so early last night. I got myself ready and went into the kitchen. John wasn't up yet so

I made myself a cup of tea and even made John a pot of coffee. I sat at his kitchen table and waited for John to move around. I was pouring a couple bowls of cereal when he entered his kitchen. "You're up early this morning," he said, looking grumpy. There were bags forming under his eyes and I guessed he didn't get much sleep.

"You look terrible," I said. It wasn't the nicest thing to say, but he deserved it after the way he had been treating me.

John looked at me with a glare and said, "I didn't get much sleep. That couch isn't the most comfortable. It's OK for a night, but not several nights in a row."

"I told you I would sleep there," I snapped.

John realized he put his foot in his mouth again so he took a deep breath and apologized. He said this case was driving him nuts and just wanted it to be solved. I did feel a tad sorry for him, but I was still upset with him for excluding me.

We devoured our cereal and John disappeared into the bathroom. I knew why I ate so fast, but why did he? I was excited about upcoming adventure and getting out of this routine. I hoped Paul wouldn't back out, but if he did I would go alone. John would still believe I was at the store and I would only be gone about an hour.

We arrived at the station by 8 a.m. and the place was buzzing. It seemed like every time I went into the police station there were more policemen working there. John must be loading up his station with men because he's spread himself thin guarding the store, the hospital, and me.

"I'll leave you to your work, Ruth Ann," John said, hurrying to his office.

I didn't even get a chance to reply or ask why he was in such a hurry. I went into my assigned office and called my store. Paul was getting there around now, but Meme didn't get in till around ten in the morning. "Hi Paul," I said when he picked up the store phone.

"Ruth Ann," he said with a low voice. "I hope you've had a change of plans for this morning."

"No way, Paul," I responded. "I'm going with or without you."

"You can't go alone!" he shouted into the phone. "If the chief thinks you're at the store and you go off on some wild goose chase, he'll murder me!"

"Not if I tell him I gave you the slip, Paul," I said. "If you're that much against going with me for an hour, then just say so. It's OK."

"I'll go," he said resignedly. "But let me say this for the record again, I'm against this!"

I was thrilled he was still willing to go along with me. "Thanks, Paul, I owe you one," I said.

"Let's just see who owes who after we pull this one off. I'm only going because I know you would've gone off on your own somehow."

"Got it," I said. "Now I have to put my plan in motion on this end. I'm going to have you call the station and ask for me. You need to sound a little panicked. Make sure you call at the time we discussed, OK?"

"Yes, I'll try," he answered quietly.

"Then I'll rush into John's office and tell them about the horrible water leak that needs my immediate attention. If all goes well and I'm really convincing, he'll drive me over to the store and leave me in your very capable hands."

"And what if he doesn't believe your story?" asked Paul.

"He will. I'll be extra believable." I hung up the phone and told Paul to call in an hour. I sat back in the desk chair counting the minutes. I decided to call the bakery since Lynne never made it over to the station yesterday. "Oh, hi Mom," Lynne said. "I'm so sorry I missed you yesterday. I never had a chance to leave the bakery. We ran out of almost everything so I had to spend the afternoon in the back baking."

"That's OK, I actually forgot anyway," I replied. "I'll try some later if you have time. Do you think you'll be as busy today?"

"I'm not sure, but I'll be ready today. I didn't get home till late last night because I prepared extra for today. I promise I'll get over there after the lunch rush. I made some chocolate chip caramel brownies for you. I know how much you love chocolate and caramel together."

"Oh that would be terrific! I can't wait to eat them," I said. "Have you talked with your sister? I didn't get a chance to speak with her yesterday."

"We've only texted. I was too busy yesterday to talk and she was busy with school stuff. She did ask if I spoke with you and I told her you were fine, just bored."

"Thanks, Lynne, I'll call her tonight for sure," I said, hanging up with her. Only forty-five minutes left until Paul makes his call to the station. Now what should I do?

I decided to go out and see if Delores had made it in today. I know her husband, soon to be ex-husband possibly, was transferred to Grand Junction Memorial yesterday afternoon. She most likely went with him, but I thought I'd go check the front desk. Delores was missing and another woman I met two days ago was sitting there.

"Why hi there Ruth Ann," the voice called out to me.

"Oh, hello Judy," I replied, shocked to see her. "What are you still doing here and why are you at the reception desk?"

"I'll be staying here until John solves this case. They need my help in such a small station." So she calls her boss by his first name? How unprofessional, I thought to myself or was my jealousy seeping back in? "I'm only sharing front desk duties. We all are taking turns while Delores is away with her husband."

"So Delores did go with Tom to the city hospital?" I asked.

"Of course she did, it's her husband. I would go anywhere my husband went, especially if he was hurt."

"Of course you would," I mumbled to myself. Forty minutes to go.

I walked around the station wondering where John was when I felt a tap on my shoulder. It was Richard Dickson, from the resort. "Hi Richard," I said. "What are you doing here?"

"I was just meeting with John; didn't you know?"

"No, I was doing some work in another office and haven't seen John in a while. What's up?"

"Oh, John wanted to know if I knew more about Ben. I told him all I knew, which isn't much."

"How's he doing over at the hospital?" I asked.

"He seems fine. I'm not really sure why he's still there. I could use him back at work, but Doc said his head needed a couple more days to fully heal."

Well, John didn't confide everything to Richard. At least I knew more than he did. "I'm sure he'll be back real soon. Hey, Richard, what do you think of Ben?" He looked confused at my question so I added, "I mean what do you think is wrong with Ben?

He keeps saying he's just a simple man who thinks slowly. What do you believe?"

"To be honest, I haven't given it much thought. That's what I told John. He keeps asking if his behavior has changed since he started working for me. And if I believe he's actually handicapped. Why would he ask that unless he feels he might be involved in something illegal? I don't want someone involved with crime working for me."

"I think he's just paranoid with this case he's trying to solve. He's suspicious of everyone who's new to town."

"That's probably it, just strange." Richard told me he needed to get back to the resort because he left Carol alone there manning the front desk. I told him I'd see him soon for dinner and he hurried off. I was happy he didn't question why I was roaming around here at the station. I didn't think he knew I was in protective custody. Thirty minutes to go before Paul calls the station.

I wandered around the station some more. I couldn't go back to the office and sit and wait. I was too revved up to stay still. I found John in a back storage room looking through some old files. He wasn't alone so I didn't interrupt him. He didn't even notice me. I walked back and passed Detective Judy at a desk just outside my office. Someone else must be manning the front desk now. She gave me a big smile and went back to her computer.

What's with her? She was over twenty years younger than John, but her tone regarding him was bordering on flirtatious. I wasn't thrilled about her being here, and she's another reason why I wanted this case to be over. Detective Judy Lynch will go back to wherever she came from.

I went back into the office and sat at the desk and waited. The next thirty minutes went by slowly until I noticed Dave, the young rookie cop, pop his head in my office and tell me I had a call on line three. I thanked him and noticed Judy watching me through the window of the office. She was still sitting at her desk, but she could see me in the office. John probably arranged that, too. I picked up the phone and turned my back to Judy so she wouldn't see me talking to Paul. I didn't want her to see me casually talking to someone and then run out of my office in a panic.

"Ruth Ann, it's Paul. Ready to pull this one off?" he asked on the other line. I told him I would be making an outburst right now, and to keep the up the act in case anyone was watching.

I shouted in the phone, "What happened! Oh no, I'll get over there as soon as possible." I hung up the phone and ran out of the office. I could feel Judy's eyes follow me as I ran to John's office first. He still wasn't in there. I ran to the back storage room and found him sitting at a table with a pile of folders on it. He saw me rush in and jumped up. "What's wrong?" he asked panicking. "Did something happen?"

"Yes, I mean not regarding what you think, but it's horrible, John," I said, panting. "I need to get over to my store immediately."

John, relieved at my response, sat back down in his chair. "What's this about your store?"

"It's serious, we had a huge water leak on the second floor and Paul said my expensive Persian rugs and dining room furniture have been soaked. I have to get over there and fix this mess."

"Paul can call a plumber, Ruth Ann," John said calmly. "You don't have to go there right now. There's nothing you can do."

"YES THERE IS!" I screamed at him. "It's thousands of dollars of merchandise that have been destroyed. It may not seem like anything important to you, but it is to me. How could you be so callous?" It was time to play the victim and turn this around. If he felt sorry for me, it just might do the trick. "I can't let a temporary guard deal with this situation while Meme isn't in. Please John, can't you let me go over there? You can drive me and Paul will be there with me every single second." I stood at the doorway pleading as hard as I could.

"I don't know, Ruth Ann," he said, thinking very hard about it. "I just don't know if that would be a wise decision. What if I let you go with Dave or Lou for a little while, then you can see what the damage really is?"

"You can't afford to lose more of your men, John," I said, hoping to change his mind. "Plus, you know you need to solve this case, not my store problems. I'll be fine, Paul will be with me."

It took several more minutes of begging, but I won out. John agreed to drive me over to my store and let me have an hour or two only. I said that was perfect and I pushed him to leave immediately. John and I hurried over there, and Paul was waiting in the back storage room off the alley entrance. Just walking in my store made me feel better. I needed to get out of that police station.

"Hi, Paul," I called out, noticing he got himself wet to make the charade believable. That may be an extra twenty dollars in his envelope. Well worth every penny to get John out of here as soon as possible.

"Paul," John said before Paul could speak. "I don't want you to let her out of your sight for one second, do we have an understanding?"

"Yes sir," Paul said, telling John the truth. He didn't plan on leaving my side at all.

"Any sign of trouble, you contact the station immediately, do you understand me clearly?" Paul nodded. "I mean anything; even if a customer enters this store and Ruth Ann doesn't recognize them I expect a call."

"Really, John," I said interrupting. "I do get customers from time to time. What if it's just a tourist staying over at the resort?"

"Then nothing will come of it, but it's not open for negotiation."

"Fine, now will you please go so I can get upstairs and see what the damage is," I snapped.

"I'm going with you, too," John said, throwing a wrench my way.

"But why? I can handle this. You need to get back to the station." If he went upstairs with me the whole thing would blow up and the wrath of John, Chief of Police, would fall upon my shoulders. I couldn't let that happen, but then Paul saved the day. "I've already been up there and stopped the water from pouring out. I used to work plumbing side jobs to pay the bills. All that's up there is wet carpets and furniture."

Thank the stars for Paul! John rethought his plan and said, "Oh, OK, sounds like you have it handled. I have a meeting with my guys soon to go over what's new, so I'll head out." We did it!

John grabbed my arm and said, "You do nothing that would cause me to lock you up in a cell, get that? I want you glued to Paul, and I'll be back in two hours to pick you up." I agreed and off he went. Paul finally let his breath out.

"We can still back out of this, Ruth Ann," he said, terrified of John. "Look at it this way, you're here at your store and you can get some work done here. I know you can't go into your office, but you can see what Meme and I have been working on."

"If all goes well, we'll be back in time for me to see it all and talk with Meme. She's due here soon, so I'll have you leave her a brief note telling her you stepped out for an hour, but will return."

We locked up the doors after Paul scribbled a quick note and taped it to the back door of the storeroom. She was bound to see it and not get worried. I didn't have a car; it was still parked at the resort, so Paul drove me over there in his car and we transferred ourselves to mine. He didn't feel he knew the area well enough to navigate. It was alright with me since I liked to drive and I knew the way.

Chapter 11

We were very careful pulling onto Main Street. We didn't want anyone to spot us. I had ducked down so I wasn't seen pulling into the resort. Paul pulled up next to my car in an empty spot, and I jumped into the driver's seat. Paul locked his car up and hurried over to my car. We drove off and I looked every direction to see if we had been spotted getting out of town.

Once I was assured we hadn't been seen, we headed onto the two-lane road that wound around the mountain. We were ascending the mountain to get to the street that led off the main road. The main road was the only accessible road into Deer Creek that led to Grand Junction. The road was built by cutting around the mountain. There were many times the road was closed due to rockslides or bad weather conditions. Winter is tough in Deer Creek unless you're a tourist. They love the heavy snow for the ski slopes. This time of year we were still clear, but not for long. Toward the end of October, snow can come at any time.

I was happy we were going in the middle of the morning. There were hardly any cars on the road and it was a bright, sunny day. Many of the trees were bare now and I could tell the season was changing into winter. According to my directions, the house was located only nine miles outside of Deer Creek. But driving in the mountains, nine miles took longer than driving on a straight highway. The speed limit was low and I figured it would be a good twenty-minute ride each way.

Paul was quiet and I bet he was going through John's harsh words in his head. If he were caught co-conspiring with me, his head would be on the chopping block. I wanted to lighten his mood, so I asked him some personal questions.

"Do you have a family, Paul?"

"Yes, I have two adult children who live out of state," he answered.

"What about a wife?" I inquired.

"We're divorced. She left me once the kids graduated from college," he replied bitterly.

"I'm so sorry," I said, regretting the question. It sure didn't lighten his mood any. "So, how do you like staying at the resort while you're here in town?"

"Oh, it's very nice," he said, perking up. "The food there is really good and I have a very nice room."

"That's wonderful," I said. "Richard and Carol run that resort meticulously and I eat at the restaurant quite often. Maybe we could have lunch or dinner there sometime before you leave town?"

"That would be nice," he said, staring at me strangely. It dawned on me that I might've just asked him out on a date! That wasn't my intention and I hope he didn't take it that way. He noticed my immediate silence and added, "Of course it would be just as friends since I won't be hanging around here for very long."

"Yes, that's exactly what I meant. You've been such a big help to me. Assisting Meme at the store for starters and this, Paul, I can't tell you how much I appreciate what you're doing for me now."

"It's actually a nice drive and we should only be gone an hour or less. It'll be OK," he said, looking out the window at the windy road. We've only been gone about five minutes, but he was probably thinking and wishing it was fifty-five minutes later!

We were only about a mile from where Lookout Mountain Road should be when I noticed a car in my rear view mirror gaining on me. Whoever was driving was going way too fast for these windy roads. Paul noticed it too and looked nervous. "Do you see the guy in your rearview mirror, Ruth Ann?"

"Yes, I just noticed him. He's going too fast for these roads. Maybe I should pull over as far to the side of the road as I can and let him pass."

"I wouldn't do that, Ruth Ann," Paul said, starting to sweat. "I would slow down and see if they go around you."

I agreed and slowed my speed down to close to 30 mph. The

car was right on my bumper and wasn't going around me. I looked into the car and saw three men in there. Two men were in the front seat and one in the middle of the back seat. They were driving a black sedan that was shiny clean. I decided to roll my window down and wave for them to pass me.

"Ruth Ann, I'm not sure about this. They just flashed you their headlights motioning you to pull over."

"Why?" I said, looking at my dashboard to make sure there were no warning lights lit up. "Everything appears to be fine with my car and it sure doesn't feel like I have a flat. What should I do, Paul?"

Paul panicked a little and suggested we turn around and head back to town. "There's nowhere to do that Paul," I said. "The next turn off is Lookout Mountain Road and it's only a half mile ahead. I'm going to keep going. If they turn when I turn, then I'll start freaking. But there's no reason to do so yet." I think I was trying to calm myself down, too.

About a minute later I signaled and made the turn. The road was a single lane gravel road that led deep into the woods. Oh great, not the best road to travel down. I was hoping for a true paved street where I could drive by the house and not be noticed. The problem was that there was only enough room for one car to drive down and I couldn't see anywhere to turn around. The tree line went right up to the side of the road. Actually, I would call this a driveway and not a road.

"Uh oh," Paul blurted out. "They turned and I have a really bad feeling about this. These guys have either followed you the whole way or they're going to the house at the end of this road. Either way, we're in serious trouble."

"Nonsense, Paul," I said. "If they're just going home then I can tell them I'm lost and ask directions for getting to the city."

"And if they know who you are and what you're up to, then what?"

"I'll deal with that when and if it happens," I said, driving down the road. We only went about a quarter of a mile when I saw the house or should I say mansion? I pulled into a large half circle driveway with a gigantic fountain in the middle. The fountain was closed up for the winter with a brown tarp. The front of the red brick house was framed with massive white columns. The estate was the size of John's condo building!

The car behind us continued to stay behind mine even after I pulled into the circular drive to turn around. I was starting to believe they had another idea in mind.

"Watch out, Ruth Ann," Paul yelled. "The car just whipped around and is blocking you from the front now. I need to contact John quickly before this gets any worse." He pulled out his cell phone and before he could punch in any numbers he spotted one, huge, scary guy looking down on him from the car window with a gun pointed at his head.

I didn't know what to do. My gut reaction was to try and get my car out of the line of fire. They had Paul and me blocked in and I had nowhere to go but out of the car. I had a sinking feeling this was a set up, and that they had followed us all the way from the resort parking lot. How could I be so naïve?

"Ruth Ann, the other guy wants you to open your door. Do as he says. We can hope they're just security here and have no idea who we are. They may think we're trespassers, and if we cooperate they may let us leave."

"I'll try, but the odds aren't looking good for that scenario, Paul."

It was apparent I wasn't moving quickly enough for these guys. The one guy started hitting my driver's side window with his gun telling me to open my car door. He was a large man well over six feet tall, dark hair, dark black eyes staring down at me. He was wearing a black leather coat and black jeans. I wasn't going to mess with him, so I slowly opened my car door.

I got out of my car and tried to look as innocent as a young child. "Is there a problem?" I looked him straight in the eye and kept talking. "My friend and I were on our way to the city and I think we took a wrong turn; can you help us? We didn't mean to trespass on your property."

I waited for a reply but I didn't get one. I looked toward Paul for some assistance when I noticed the guy who was pointing the gun at him had Paul up against the side of my car. "Hey, what are you doing to him?" I exclaimed, trying to get over to him but the man grabbed my arm and held me back.

"It's alright, Ruth Ann," Paul said. "Let them talk."

"So," the guy next to me said. "So you say you're driving to the city, for what?"

"Just a nice day out, that's all," I responded, as cheerily as possible.

"Then why does this guy have a cop uniform on?" the man holding Paul demanded.

"I'm not a cop," Paul said quickly. "I work security for this lady's store in town and we decided to play hooky for a little while and head out to the city for some fun."

"Oh, really," his captor replied, grabbing him and turning him around to face him. "It looks to me like you were doing something else."

"Shut up!" we suddenly heard. Another man exited the car that had followed us. He got out of the back seat and was wearing a charcoal gray business suit. "Take them inside," he ordered.

The two men grabbed both of us by the arm and led us through enormous front doors into the foyer. I would've loved to run as fast as I could, hoping anybody was on the main road, but the chance I could outrun these guys was very slim. The man with the suit said, "Put them in the library," and he added hastily, "now, before they get too good a look around."

The two men led us through a circular shaped foyer toward the right. An wide, elegant staircase was located smack dab in the middle of the room. There was a colossal crystal chandelier hanging over the middle of the foyer, and even during the daytime it shimmered with the light from the windows above the front double doors.

"Hurry up!" snapped the man who obviously was in charge. The guy squeezed my arm even tighter and dragged me into the library. Paul was shoved down into an armchair rather roughly and I was deposited a little less roughly next to him in another chair. "Now get out, but wait right outside the doors," the man ordered. The two men with guns left the room and shut the library doors.

The man in charge walked over to a large, executive desk in front of a wall lined with wooden bookshelves. On one of the sidewalls was a massive stone fireplace with a long, silver sword hung high above the mantel. There was something engraved in the handle of the sword but I couldn't make it out from where I was sitting. The other side, opposite the fireplace, was lined with windows adorned with heavy red velvet curtains. The curtains were open and the sunlight was streaming in.

I watched the man walk behind his desk. He sat down on a leather swivel office chair and looked at Paul and me, seated on the other side of his desk. I wanted to speak, but Paul shook his head when he saw me beginning to talk.

After what seemed like eternity, the man looked down at his desk, grabbed a piece of paper and studied it. He obviously was reading something of importance or why would he be ignoring Paul and me? He set the piece of paper back down slowly and said, without looking up at us, "So you must be Ms. Conroy?"

Paul nudged me and I quickly responded, "Yes, I'm Ruth Ann Conroy."

The man looked at Paul and asked, "And who are you again?"

"I work security at Ms. Conroy's store."

"Ah, so there were more guards than the one who was shot?" he asked, obviously toying with us.

"How did you know that?" I blurted out.

He smiled and said, "It's my business to know everything when it comes to someone messing with my business."

"And what business is that?" I asked curtly.

"It's none of your business just yet," he answered sarcastically. "I'll ask the questions if you don't mind. When I'm ready to entertain a question from you, I'll let you know. So," he said, losing the smirk, "my advice to you is to answer truthfully and completely."

"Fine," I snapped.

"And without the attitude," he added.

Paul's eyes warned me to behave. The man noticed and turned his attention back to Paul. "I really don't have any need for you at the moment, so I'm going to dismiss you." He pushed a button under his desk and the library door flew open. "You need something, sir?" one of the guys guarding the doors asked.

"Take Paul, the guard, and put him into the room downstairs. Have Finn watch over him and keep him quiet." The two guys came to grab Paul, but Paul stood up on his own and started walking toward the doors. He looked back at me and said, "Do what they say, Ruth Ann."

"Good advice, Paul," the man in charge called out. "Come right back after you give him to Finn." The two guys left with Paul and closed the library doors.

"So, it's just you and me, Ruth Ann." He stopped and asked, "Can I call you that or do you prefer Ms. Conroy?"

"Ruth Ann is fine," I said. "But could you please tell me your name so I don't call you something inappropriate?"

"Yes, my name is Axel, that's all you need to know."

I know that name! That was the name Jeffrey Toggles used when he described the man that threatened him. Could Jeffrey have been telling us the truth? I wanted to ask him about Jeffrey, but remembered I wasn't allowed to ask questions, yet.

"Ruth Ann," he began. "I need you to tell me everything about a certain, let's call it an event, that took place at the bank in your town."

"What event?" I asked.

"I'm talking about when your bank president, Mr. Albertson, was seriously injured. You may answer that question."

"I wasn't inside the bank when Doug, I mean Mr. Albertson, was horribly injured and don't forget robbed." Oops, I didn't mean to say that last part.

"Now, now, no lying to me," he said, smirking. "You really don't want me to become upset. That could have dire consequences."

"Then explain what you're asking of me." I corrected.

"I'm asking what you *SAW* that day when Mr. Albertson was attacked and, as you say, robbed?"

I became very irritated and hopped out of my chair. "So that's what this is all about? You and your thugs think I can identify who was in the bank when Doug was bashed in the head and my necklace was stolen!" I really have to learn to watch what I say in the heat of the moment.

"Sit down please," he requested, alarmingly calm. "I'm not going to ask you again to control yourself and just answer my questions. However, you brought up an interesting item, the necklace."

I didn't utter a word because I already caused enough damage. He continued, "Your friend, Mr. Albertson, was at that time in possession of an item I have been searching for. I need to know how he came to possess the item."

"Why do you care? You already got the necklace back from Doug when your men stole it. I'm confused, why you're asking me these questions? You got what you want, and I couldn't identify anyone from that day at the bank. However, you kind of blew it when you sent your men to my town and stalked Doug, Ben, and me. Now at least one of your men can be identified by his Viking Ship tattoo."

"Hmm," Axel muttered. "Ruth Ann, you have a strange way of answering my questions and giving me vital additional information in the process. Your chief would be very upset with you."

"You mean Paul, my security guard?"

"No, John Wilkinson, the Chief of Police," he corrected me.

"He's probably aware by now that Paul and I are missing, and he'll be coming up here to search this place," I added, without his permission to speak.

"You don't worry about that for now," he said. "The more quickly you answer my questions, the easier for you, Paul, and your chief."

"Ask away," I said. "I've already told you all I know."

He laughed loudly, "Not quite." Axel stood up and walked around to the front of the desk and sat down on top of it. "You're under the impression I have the necklace?"

"You stole it!"

"No, you're quite mistaken, Ruth Ann. That's what I'm trying to find out. Who was in the bank that day and took my necklace? I've paid an enormous amount of money to own that piece, and nobody will take it from me again!"

"Wait…what?" I asked, completely confused. "You don't have the necklace?"

"No," he replied. It's strange, but I actually believed him. "It was supposed to come back to me the day Mr. Toggles was to meet with the bank president, Mr. Albertson. But your chief set us up, and Mr. Toggles had to pay the ultimate price. I still have no idea how you found this place though. Please tell me how?"

"May I speak now?" He nodded. "Jeffrey had a crumpled piece of paper stuffed in his mouth after you shot him. He was trying to swallow it, but the coroner found it and was able to read part of it. It had written on there, *1212 Loo*," I answered truthfully. I wanted him to know the coroner found the paper and had given it to the police department as evidence. That way he'd be aware that the police will be here soon.

Axel sat on the edge of his desk without saying a word. He was deep in thought. Does he believe me? I don't see why not. If I had lied, I would put myself in bigger trouble than I already was.

"So Mr. Toggles tried to swallow a piece of paper that had my address written on it?" I nodded. "And the coroner then supplied that information to the police?" I nodded again. "So there is limited time here to figure out what I need to do." I didn't nod that time.

Axel turned and went back to his desk and pushed the button again. The door opened and one of his guys entered. Axel told him to take me to Finn, and keep me there until he requested my presence again. The guy took my arm rather roughly and led me out into the foyer and around the backside of the main staircase. There was a wooden door, and he opened it up and took me down a long narrow flight of stairs.

The lighting was minimal. I had to be careful not to trip on the stairs as he hurried me down. We entered a small, dark, square room lit only with a bulb hanging from the ceiling. The man grabbed my arm a little tighter and went toward one of the cement walls. What was he planning on doing with me against the cement wall?

He felt along the cement wall with his hands and pushed a tiny button. A large chunk of the cement went up into the ceiling, creating an opening into another area. How clever of Axel to build a secret room in the basement. And no one would ever know of its existence without finding that tiny button. Things were not looking very good for me at this moment. My only hope was that they would reunite me with Paul and we could come up with a solution to our current situation.

The secret room we entered was the opposite of the last room. This room was filled with light, fluorescent light that temporarily blinded my vision. It took me a minute to adjust, and when I did I found we were in a room with another man standing over a small pit in the floor. I really hoped Paul wasn't the reason the man was standing over this hole in the ground!

"What's this?" I demanded of my captor.

"Shut up!" the new man spat out. "Put her against the wall here and leave. Tell Axel I'll get the information he needs out of these two or there won't be anything left of them when I'm done."

The other man left abruptly and I tried to see what or who was in the hole. The floor in this room was made of loose dirt, so it wouldn't be difficult to dig a hole. I couldn't make anything out, when the rude man shoved me up against the cement wall and told me not to move. He went over to the hole and put his large arm down and pulled something up. It was Paul. He was conscious but badly beaten. His bruised, but wide opened eyes stared directly into mine and I could, at that moment, read his mind. He was telling me not to argue and tell the man whatever he asked to keep myself safe.

The man dropped Paul on the dirt floor and turned to me. It was at that moment I noticed a very crucial bit of information. The man called himself Finn, and you'll never guess what I saw? A tattoo on his neck of a Viking Ship! It was the man Lou had identified from the hotel, and I believe Doug had spotted him outside his room, too. What a horrible turn of events. This man did not appear to treat his prisoners kindly and I had to hurry to think of something to keep Paul and myself alive.

Finn grabbed my arm and pulled me down to where Paul was lying on the floor. "Look at him," he demanded. "If you want to keep your pretty face clean and unharmed I suggest you start talking."

I had no idea what he actually wanted me to start talking about. I assumed he was told to get information regarding the whereabouts of the necklace. Wasn't he already informed that I told his boss I didn't have the necklace, and that I thought they did? "Look, Finn, if I may call you that?" Finn didn't respond. "OK, Finn, I already told your boss I don't have the necklace. I told him it was stolen and I assumed he was the one who stole it."

"You assumed incorrectly," he replied. "And how do I know you're telling the truth to my boss?"

"Why would I lie when you have us in this precarious position?"

"Huh?" he asked, looking confused.

"Let me try this again," I started to say, wondering if the dye from his tattoo had affected his brain functions. "I don't have the necklace. I wouldn't lie to you or Axel when we're being held and threatened with our lives."

"Hmm," he muttered. I didn't really believe Finn was the smartest guy around, but I wasn't going to chance it. He did a number on Paul's face. Poor Paul was swollen and blood dripped down his face. I couldn't believe how irresponsible I was to get Paul and myself involved in all this. Why couldn't I just let John handle it?

I could tell Finn was confused. He grabbed Paul and shoved him back in the hole and walked over to me. "I'm going to tie you up and check out your story. I don't want any funny stuff from either of you while I'm gone."

"Good, go talk to your boss, he'll tell you everything I said was true." He pushed me back against the wall and put my hands in the shackles attached to the wall. I couldn't move, but I wanted this time alone to come up with an escape plan.

Once Finn departed and the cement door closed behind him, I called out to Paul. At first I did it quietly, but I didn't get a response. I shouted the next time and heard a mumble. "Paul, please talk to me," I begged. "I can't get over to you, but can you make it out of the hole?"

A few moans and groans came out of the hole and he finally was able to speak. "Ruth Ann?" he asked. "Is that you?"

"Yes, didn't you see me a few minutes ago? It doesn't matter Paul; tell me can you get out of there?"

"No, it's too deep." He showed me the tips of his fingers that just barely touched the edge of the hole.

"Can you jump up and grab a hold of the side?"

"I'm standing in wet mud so there's nothing to jump up from. My feet stick to the bottom and I can't move."

"We don't have much time. We have to come up with some sort of plan to get us out of here," I said, panicking. Finn wouldn't be gone too long and I refused to believe there was no way out of here.

"Ruth Ann, maybe John's on his way here. He must've realized you played him and took me up here. That's our only hope right now."

"We can't be sure about that, so we need a plan of our own, too. I just can't think of one yet," I said. I looked around the small room. It was about an eight by ten-foot space with a big hole in the middle. There were more shackles set in the walls, suggesting that this room had been used as a prison before. The only other item in this room was the metal chair that Finn used. But there had to be a key somewhere for these shackles. I searched and searched and couldn't find any sign of keys. Finn probably kept them on his body and there's no way Paul would ever win over Finn to get those keys. That's even if Paul could climb his way out of the hole.

Paul asked if I could see anyway of freeing myself. "I can't see any keys. Did you notice if Finn had them on him or where he might keep keys in this room?"

Paul was silent for a moment and said he wasn't in the room too long before Finn belted him and he fell into the hole. "I'm sorry, Ruth Ann, I'm still a bit fuzzy from being hit and thrown into a hole."

"That's horrible, Paul, I'm so terribly sorry for all this."

Time was ticking and I had to come up with something. I spotted the tiny button along the wall where we could open the door from this end. I had watched Finn push it, so I kept a close eye on it so I could find it in a hurry.

"Look at the chair, Ruth Ann," Paul called up. "Maybe there's keys or something you can use attached to it or under it. Can you see the chair up close or are you too far away?"

"No, but I can almost get my foot out and pull my leg toward it. Hold on a second," I said, as I reached my leg as far as I could and just barely touched the leg of the chair. I kicked it slightly to get it even closer to me. It moved in the dirt with difficulty, but it got within my foot's reach and I pulled it closer to me. The chair tipped over and there it was, a set of keys duct taped to the bottom of the chair. "I did it, Paul!" I cried. "On the bottom of the chair are keys, and I just need to get it closer and figure out how to get the chair from my foot up to my hands. Wait," I realized it was hopeless for me. Paul had to unlock me I had no way of doing it with both my hands shackled. "Paul, I need you to figure out a way to get out of that hole. I need you to unlock me."

"That's not good," Paul answered.

I wasn't going to let Paul be defeated by what seemed to me a couple of inches. If he could just get a couple inches higher maybe he could grab the edge of the hole and pull himself up. Wait, I've got the answer! "Paul, I have an idea. Can you pile up the mud to one side and pat it down and keep doing that until it's solid enough to raise you a few inches? Then you can get a grip on the top of the hole and pull yourself up."

"I don't know, Ruth Ann," Paul said skeptically. "But I'll give it my best. It appears to be our only option unless you see a rope hanging around?"

"You can do it, Paul, but hurry, we don't have much time," I called out, with at least a smidgen of hope.

As Paul worked hard at his task, I was wondering where John was now. He must've figured out I wasn't at the store anymore. It's been several hours now and he had to be quite angry with me right about now.

Chapter 12

JOHN WILKINSON

I drove off and left Ruth Ann at her store with Paul Welch, the security guard. I don't know how I let her convince me so easily. She always had a way of getting her own way. I did threaten Paul strongly, but he had to understand the importance of keeping an eye on Ruth Ann. If he let anything or anyone hurt her, he would pay dearly. I made it back to the station and went straight to the conference room so we could discuss what was new with the case.

Dan, Dave, and Judy Lynch were in the room waiting for me when I walked in. "Hi John," Judy called. "Delores dropped off some of your favorite donuts from that bakery shop down the street. "

"Sinful Sweets Bakery, Judy," Lou answered. "You and Dave are new around here and that's Ruth Ann's daughters place. Lynne makes the best baked goods I've ever had. Our station gets a lot of perks with Lynne around. She sends us her baked items regularly."

Judy turned up her nose and said, "That's not a healthy snack."

"Seriously?" Lou replied. "We're all in good shape here, if we want to treat ourselves once in awhile then who am I to say no?"

"Enough you two," I demanded. "It was nice of Delores to get me some donuts, I'm starved." I picked up my favorite custard filled donut with a chocolate glaze. In two or three bites it was gone. "Those really are good," I said, shaking my head. "Dangerously good or should I say sinfully good? Get it?" They all laughed at my little play on words.

"Let's get down to business," I began. "Dan, I asked you to track down addresses from the coroner's findings, '*1212 Loo*'." Lou picked up a sheet of paper in front of him and held it up.

"Yes, there were three matches that I found within 15 miles of here."

"Really, three?"

"Yes, there were two about 10 miles from here and one about 12 or so miles from here. The addresses are all located on the same property, just spread out over part of the mountain."

Dan pulled out a map of the area and pointed to a spot. "Here, you see?" He pointed to a small road that started about nine miles off the main road to Grand Junction. "But you see it only goes to one house, then you have to go back to the main road and go down another half mile or so and the same name, Lookout Mountain Road, veers off again and leads to another house. The same thing happens further down the main road. It's really bizarre."

"How's that?" asked Judy, leaning over Lou's other shoulder.

"How can three houses have the same house number, 1212?" asked Lou. "Shouldn't it be 1212, 1213, and so on?'

Dave, who was sitting on the other side of the table, responded with a possible explanation. "Maybe whoever owns the land wanted different family members living nearby so they built three houses and just used the same house number."

"Can you do that?" I asked curiously.

Judy stood up and responded, "Why not? If one person owns acres of land with surrounding woods and has extended family living there, perhaps they built a main house and maybe a couple cottages for family to stay or rent."

"That makes sense," I said. "We'll check out all three, do we have a name associated with the houses?"

"That's what's strange," Lou said. "It's listed as a corporation, not a private residence."

"What's the name of the company?" Judy asked before I could.

"Lily's By The Stream," replied Lou. "What a strange name don't you think?"

"What does that mean, 'Lily's By The Stream'?" I asked. "Yes, there's a stream down here in the valley, but aren't these residences up the mountain a bit?"

"Yes," Dave answered for Lou. "The drive up the main road ascends the mountain not back down toward the stream."

"Did you check this business out at all?" I inquired.

"We're checking into that now. It took some time finding the owner of the land," Lou answered. "It all goes back to this company name."

"No name of a person?" asked Judy.

"No," Lou replied.

"OK, let me know when you find out what this company does and we'll plan our course of action before we go up there." I went back, sat down and asked, "What about Ben? He's still in the hospital under Doc Albert's care. Anything you can tell me about him?"

"According to our research there are thousands of Ben Anderson's in the country. I need more information about his age and where he was born," Dave said. Dave was the rookie of the bunch and fairly new to the area. Judy had been a detective for a few years but new to Deer Creek. I was borrowing Judy from the city to help us with this case and she seemed to fit in nicely with our station so far. I don't think Ruth Ann thought too highly of her. In fact, I think she was jealous of her! I kind of liked that, I have to admit. Since I've known Ruth Ann I haven't found anyone else who peaked my interest in dating again. Now Ruth Ann thinks Judy's flirting with me when I know that's impossible. She's twenty years younger than me. Why would she be interested in me? It was a boost to my ego, I have to admit.

Getting my head back in the conversation, I told Dave that I was going to make a quick trip to the hospital and talk with Doc Albert to see if he got any further personal information about Ben. If not, I would go into Ben's room and ask him myself. I still had a couple hours before I went to grab Ruth Ann and bring her back to the station. Hopefully her water leak didn't cause too much damage to her store and the merchandise. Maybe I should've stayed longer and helped Paul, but he assured me he could handle it. Oh well, I'll finish the meeting here and run over to the hospital.

I told the staff to keep digging for any information that could help us find the men who injured Doug, Tom and Ben, and killed the guard at Ruth Ann's store. I left them and headed to the hospital. I was thankful Ruth Ann wasn't with me so I could do my job without her interfering. She was too insistent on being a part of the investigation even though she wasn't a police department employee. That's why I decided to cut her off a bit and started talking less to her regarding the details of the case. I could tell she was getting angry with me, so I was relieved that she was busy elsewhere. As long as she played like a good girl and stayed put. I wasn't so confident with that last part.

Within a few minutes I was waiting in Doc Albert's office. His nurse, Shirley told me he'd be just a few minutes. I was tempted to call over to the store, but then Ruth Ann would call me out and tell me I didn't trust her.

Doc entered his office and sat behind his desk. I was sitting in one of the chairs facing his desk. Doc asked, "Where's your partner in crime?"

"Huh?" I asked.

"Ruth Ann, you know your new recruit over at the station," Doc said, chuckling a little.

"Funny Doc," I replied. "She had an emergency at the store and I let her go and fix it. Don't worry, she's got a guard who won't leave her side."

"That's good, we don't need any more patients in here," Doc said. "What do you need from me?"

"I have some questions regarding one of your patients," I began to say.

"About Tom? He's doing well I'm told. Already seeing signs of improvement."

"That's good news," I said. "No, I wasn't talking about Tom." Doc interrupted before I could go on. "So you want to know about Doug's condition? He's fine, he could normally be released, but you told me to keep him here with the guard." Doc added, "You want him released?"

"No, no," I answered, getting frustrated at Doc's interruptions. "Keep Doug safe here for a little while longer. I'm talking about your other patient, Ben."

"Oh yeah, Ben," Doc said. "He's an interesting case. I can't find anything wrong with the guy, but he still acts like he has a disability."

"Acts?" I inquired. "Why did you use the word act?"

"Typical cop, picking out a word I didn't mean anything by. I meant, his behavior shows signs of possible autism or a past brain injury, but his scans don't show any abnormalities."

"So what does that mean?" I asked. "You think he could be

faking his behavior?"

"No, I don't know, actually," Doc, said frustrated. "He doesn't show any signs of violent behavior, but he keeps claiming he's just a simple guy who was verbally and physically abused when he was younger."

"Did he ever get specific about the abuse with you?"

"No, whenever I broach the subject he gets defensive and shuts down."

I asked, "But he doesn't get physically mad?"

"No, no, not at all," Doc answered quickly. "Just nervous and anxious and then he tells me he doesn't want to talk anymore. I let him be until he calms down. Maybe he needs to be medicated with some anxiety drugs. It could really change his life for the better."

"Maybe, but that's not what I need to talk about now. I want to ask you if you know more about his past, like his birthday or where he was born? Do you know any of those things?"

"No, he claims he's in his late forties, but then he said the strangest thing," Doc stopped for a moment to gather his thoughts to make sure he told me the correct thing. "He doesn't know when or where he was born. He claims his parents abused him, and he was left on his own at a very young age. He dropped out of school because he was bullied and then ran away and started doing odd jobs to make money for living expenses. That's how he ended up here."

"That's what he told me, too," I said, disappointed that Doc didn't get any new information for me. "I think I'd better have another little talk with him."

"Be careful," Doc said. "If you start getting tough he shuts down. That could happen because of his past. If he was severely bullied his mind might automatically turn off. Then you get no-where."

"I'll take my chances," I said, standing up to leave his office. "If he gets out of hand I'll call for you to help him calm down."

I headed toward Doug's room and reminded myself to stop in there before I left. I'm sure Doug was getting restless by now, being cooped up in the hospital not knowing what's happening at his bank or with my case. I passed the guard and got a quick update to make sure all was quiet, and he said nobody had been here except the owners of the resort to bring Ben food.

I tapped on Ben's door to announce I was coming in. He was sitting in a chair looking out the window. "Hi, Chief," Ben said cheerily. "It looks beautiful outside, the leaves have almost all fallen and I feel snow is coming soon."

"You think so?" I responded, walking over to the window and sitting on the ledge looking out with him.

"Oh yes," he said. "I always can feel when the weather is changing. My arthritis acts up and my body aches all over."

"That's not good, maybe Doc can give you some medicine to help with your aches and pains."

"No, I don't like to take anything if I don't have to." He added, "it lets me know I'm alive when I feel either good or bad."

I wanted to keep Ben in a good mood before I started questioning him about his past. We spoke for another five minutes about the weather changes and then I subtly turned the conversation around. "So Ben, when you were young could you tell when the weather was going to change, too?"

He looked strangely at me but answered, "No, I didn't have arthritis as a young kid. That comes with age and all the manual labor I've done over the years."

"So you've had lots of physical jobs?"

"Oh yes, I did whatever I could to make enough money to pay for some place to stay and eat. I never made a lot of money, just enough to get by."

"Ever marry?" I asked.

"Me? No, I never even had a girlfriend. I'm too shy for dating and all. I figured I was put on this earth to be alone and I accepted that a long time ago. I try to make the best of it and working with the Dickson's over at the resort has been the best job I've ever had. They even told me I could stay there if I ever couldn't pay for my apartment. Nice people they are and I really like them."

"Yes, they're nice," I said, trying to figure out a way to get this man to open up about his past. "Since you're new to Deer Creek are you looking forward to snow? Have you ever lived where there was snow?"

"I've lived in snowy areas before," he replied slowly. "Why are you asking me so many questions?"

"Just making conversation and trying to get to know you a little better," I said quickly. "Since you're new I'd like to make sure you have everything you need and see if anyone special in your life might be joining you. But you already told me you like to be alone."

"It's not that I want to be alone, I just am," he said solemnly. "I think I rub people the wrong way so most people don't want anything to do with me. Until I came to this town; people are nice here."

"Yes they are," I said. It was time to cut to the chase, so I risked a question that could upset him. "Ben, you see, I like you, I really do. I just wish I knew more about where you came from so we can help you adjust here and get you involved in town activities. Maybe residents here could hire you as a handyman."

Ben wasn't sure how to respond to me. I somehow managed to ask a personal question about his background all the while telling him I liked him and wanted to help him. I believe I confused him but it worked, for the moment. He hesitated and then said, "I would like to make extra money. I never lived in one place long enough to make it a home. Maybe this town can be my home."

"You know Ben, if people want to hire you they may ask you for some references. Can you give them any?"

"References? You mean past people I've worked for, to tell them if I did good or not?"

"Exactly Ben, can you give any?"

"No, I don't think so, just Mr. Dickson at the resort," he said. "I just hung around different places and got paid cash when I finished a job. They weren't difficult jobs, painting or mowing yards, that kind of stuff. You're scaring me. Did I do something illegal?"

"Did you pay taxes on those jobs after they paid you cash?"

Well that was a huge mistake! He turned pale and began having a panic attack. His head started shaking side to side and he waved his arms up in the air. He started yelling, "I don't want to go to jail, I did nothing wrong. Why does everybody pick on me?" I wasn't able to calm him down, so I stuck my head out into the hall and saw Doc Albert hurrying over.

"What did you do to him? I could hear him all the way in my office."

"I just asked him questions about previous jobs and he flipped out," I said.

"I need to sedate him," Doc said, grabbing a needle and vial from a cabinet in the room. "You'll have to leave now."

"But I wasn't finished," I exclaimed.

"He's no good now, come back tomorrow," Doc snapped, as he tried to grab Ben's arm to give him the shot. "That should calm him down for the day."

Doc waited a few minutes to make sure Ben relaxed and stepped in the hall with me. "It's no good, John," Doc said. "He's either a really good actor or seriously disturbed. Either way, I'm going to call in for a psychiatrist to evaluate him."

"Good plan, let me know when that takes place," I said. "I'm going to pop in on Doug before I go."

"Don't upset him too, I can't take much more of this," Doc said, going back into Ben's room.

I was disappointed that I didn't get much out of Ben. All I got was that he worked all over the place and he was paid in cash. No way to follow him without an actual job and a tax record. Worst-case scenario, I could arrest him for avoiding taxes.

I walked in Doug's room while he was watching TV. "Hi Doug," I said, walking over to his bed.

"John, long time no see," Doug said sarcastically. "Where's Ruth Ann?"

"She's at her store," and before Doug could comment, I quickly added, "The store had a huge water leak and she's panicked about the merchandise that could be ruined. I took her there myself and let her stay with Paul, the guard. He has strict orders not to leave her side."

"Any other news? You know, like catching the guys who put me here and robbed my bank?" I could tell Doug was in no mood for beating around the bush. I think he was feeling a tad confined here in the hospital, but it's still safer here than outside.

"And killed two other men," I added. "No, but we finally have some clues and are closing in on them. I promise, not too much longer."

"I hope so, I have to get back to my bank," Doug stated. "Do you know how the renovations are going after the shootout there?"

"The bank had to be closed for a few days." I knew he would blow up over that, but there was no choice. "It's a police investigation there and Tom is off for who knows how long. We need to find you a new guard before you can reopen the bank. The window's being fixed today and I've had someone there around the clock to guard the bank."

"But where are people doing their banking?"

"We've been telling people that they either have to wait a few days or go into the city if they can't wait. People aren't too happy, but they have to deal with it," I said.

"Hopefully I won't lose too many customers," Doug said, irritated.

"You won't," I replied. "There's only one bank in town so you'll be fine. I bet by next week at this time you'll be back in your office busy at work."

"I'd better be."

"Well, I've got to check in at the station and go pick up Ruth Ann. It's been a while and she should have things under control."

"She can't be too happy with you right about now," Doug said smiling.

"Nope, she's not," I said. "Makes you look pretty good right now, doesn't it?"

"Yep, I'm not only the victim in this, but I'm not ticking her off either," Doug stated.

"No, that would be me," I answered. "She's not very happy with me at this moment. She'll get over it as soon as all this is solved and I recover the necklace. I can't wait to see this infamous piece of jewelry."

"It is amazing," Doug said. "Not worth the lives that have been taken though."

"I agree," I said and stood up to leave. "See you soon, and hopefully I'll have more information for you."

I headed out of the hospital and back to the station. All I wanted to do was check on a few things and then drive over to Ruth Ann's store. It's been a couple of hours so I felt I'd been generous giving her this much time. Judy was sitting at the front desk when I arrived and flashed a huge smile at me. "Hi John," she said all perky. "All's quiet here, too quiet in fact. That always makes me more on edge."

"Why's that?" I asked.

"It's always quiet before all you know what breaks out."

I went into my office and checked for any messages. Judy was right, it was too quiet which made me feel on edge too.. Maybe I'd better get over to Ruth Ann's right away. All of a sudden, I had a very bad feeling. I told Lou to be ready just in case I ran into any trouble. I didn't have any specific reason to anticipate trouble, but I felt uneasy after Judy made that comment.

I made it over to her store in no time. I parked out front this time and went into the store. Meme was in the front of the store changing the window theme," I said. "How's the damage?"

She gave me a funny look and replied, "What are you talking about?"

"The water leak that got Ruth Ann all worked up about so she had to run over here earlier."

"Uh, OK, I don't know what's going on, but everything is fine here and Ruth Ann's not here."

"WHAT?" I yelled, causing Meme to drop and shatter a ceramic vase. "Sorry, did you just say Ruth Ann isn't here?"

"No, she left with Paul and said they'd be back within an hour." Meme had a worried look on her face and added, "But it's been longer than that. I got here about ten and they were gone. I thought they'd be back by then but no go. Now it's early afternoon, that can't be good."

"No, it's not," I snapped. I ran around the back and looked out in the alley. Paul's car was missing. I told Meme to lock up and go home immediately and that I would let her know when I got a hold of Ruth Ann.

I ran back through the showroom and out the front door to my car. I flew over to the resort to check the parking lot for Ruth Ann's car. "I knew it!" I said, feeling stupid. Paul's car was there and Ruth Ann's car was gone. I immediately called Lou and told him to put an APB out on her car. Where on earth did they go?

Chapter 13

RUTH ANN

Paul was on his knees in the mud at the bottom of the hole trying to pile it up as high as he could. He only needed a few more inches until he could reach over the top edge of the hole and pull himself up. Then he could grab the keys and unlock me. All would work out if we weren't rushed for time. We only had a limited amount of time before Finn would return.

"How's it going, Paul?" I called out to him. "Time isn't on our side."

"I'm going as fast as I can, Ruth Ann. This dirt is too wet and won't pile up. Every time I put my foot on a pile it sinks."

"Keep trying," I said, hoping this plan would work. Even if Paul did get out of the hole, and got me out of my shackles, could we get out of this place without being caught?

Minutes passed, and I thought all hope was lost when I spotted Paul's hands coming over the edge of the hole. "Paul, you did it!"

"Not yet, but I think I may be able to reach…" he stopped talking and started grunting and pulling himself over the edge when his hands slipped and he tumbled back into the hole.

"Oh no," I cried out. "Keep trying, Paul."

Before Paul could respond, the door to the room lifted and in walked Finn. That's it, Finn would surely be upset at what we've been doing in here. He looked around the room and spotted the chair turned upside down and the muddy handprints all around the edge of the hole. "You two have been busy little prisoners, haven't you?"

I didn't say a word and neither did Paul. Finn's expression turned ugly and he walked over to the hole and peered in. "Please,

Finn," I begged. "Don't hurt him, I'm the one who turned over the chair."

Finn turned around and glared at me and said, "Are you the one who put these handprints here, too?" he asked, pointing at Paul's muddy prints.

"I did," came Paul's voice from the hole. "Leave her alone, it was all my idea."

Finn slowly walked over to me with an evil glare and raised his arm to strike me. I closed my eyes, hoping that would stop him. As my eyes shut, I heard a jangling noise. He wasn't going to beat me after all! I opened my eyes to find Finn's face inches away from mine and he was unlocking the shackles. He wasn't an attractive man, the tattoo was up close and his warm breath smelled of tobacco. I did whatever I could to remain calm when I asked, "What are you doing with me?" Please don't throw me in the whole with Paul.

Finn didn't respond, but grabbed a hold of my arm and led me out of the room. We were now in the room at the bottom of the stairs. I thought he was separating Paul and me so we couldn't work together to find a way out of this mess. He only hesitated in the room a minute when he motioned for me to go up the stairs. "Where are we going?" I demanded.

"Don't talk," he ordered, and gave me a shove from behind with his hands. I hurried up the stairs and entered a small room behind the staircase that led to the second and third floors. Straight ahead of me was a double swinging door that led to a kitchen. I could tell it was a kitchen because of the aroma that seeped out of the doors. I smelled some kind of fish being cooked, a very strong, pungent smell.

He grabbed my arm and led me into the kitchen. At this point it surprised me, because I assumed we would head back to the library where Axel was the last time I saw him. I had no idea why we were going in the kitchen, but anything was better than the basement.

Chapter 14

JOHN WILKINSON

I was so angry when I didn't see Ruth Ann's car that I couldn't think clearly. I ran into the resort and found Carol behind the front desk of the lobby.

"Carol," I said, getting my breath back. "Did you see Ruth Ann at all today? She might've been with another man, her guard, Paul?"

Carol came around from the desk and pulled me aside. "Not so loud, John," she said. "You're going to scare people."

"Sorry, but I need to know if you saw Ruth Ann."

"Is she in trouble?" asked Carol, looking around the room, searching for her husband, Richard.

"No, not in trouble, but she could be in serious danger," I said, trying to calm down a little. "She was at her store doing some work, when she and Paul took off. Her car was in your parking lot, but now it's missing."

"Oh, no," Carol said. "I haven't seen her at all, but maybe Richard has and he's up on the second floor checking rooms. Let me text him and get him down here right away." Carol pulled out her cell phone, and within two minutes Richard pushed open the stairwell door.

"What's the matter?" he asked.

"John needs to know if we've seen Ruth Ann and her guard today. They took off in her car."

"Yes, I saw Ruth Ann a few hours ago," Richard said nonchalantly. "What's the matter with that?"

I told Richard that Ruth Ann could be in danger and for him to tell me exactly what he saw. "She was in the parking lot. I just happened to be there when a man drove into the parking lot and parked right next to Ruth Ann's car. I only noticed them because there were closer spots, but his car pulled up to Ruth Ann's car. So I watched from the front entrance as Ruth Ann stepped out of the man's car and opened her car door. Seconds later, this guy, Paul you say, walked around to her passenger door and got in. They drove off, that's all I saw."

"What direction did they go?" I asked. "Did they turn back toward her store or did they go toward the schools?"

"I'm sorry, John, I have no idea which way they went. I went inside and back to work," Richard stated. "I didn't really think much of it once I saw Ruth Ann."

"Did she look happy or scared? Maybe the guard forced her to go?" I asked, hoping Richard might remember seeing something that could help me find her.

"Nope, she just got out of one car and into the other. She looked fine, John, if that makes you feel any better."

"Thanks, Richard," I said, walking out of the resort. Now what do I do? I drove back to the station and found Lou at his computer. "Any news on Ruth Ann's car?" Lou said there was no information yet.

"Where do you think she went with that guard?" Lou asked. "You think she got a clue about the whereabouts of the necklace, or maybe they contacted her and they had to meet somewhere."

"She wouldn't do that without telling me," I said, wondering how I could be so easily duped.

"Yes she would, if they told her to come alone," Lou said. "She might've convinced them the guard could come, since he wasn't a cop and it wouldn't be tough to overtake him."

"Thanks for the positive outlook, Lou," I said sarcastically. "But you could be onto something. If she got word about the necklace and these guys contacted her to set up a meeting, she would go."

"The problem is we have zero ideas of where she could go to meet them," Lou stated.

"There has to be something I'm missing. I need a moment to gather my thoughts, then have Judy, Dave, and yourself meet me in the conference room in ten minutes." I took off, back to my office and slammed the door. Where could they have gone and why would she not tell me? I know why, I thought to myself. I started shutting her out of the case recently and she didn't like that very much. So when she got word from these creeps, she took it all on herself. Well, no, she and Paul, worked together. Was she scared or hurt, I had no idea. I had to find her and quick.

I met with the three other staff members, and all we came up with was either waiting for a hit on Ruth's car was or going back to Ruth Ann's store, hoping there was some clue there I missed. Judy and I took on the store while Lou and Dave stayed at the station working on locating her car. Judy was happy to go along. She was used to more action in the city. There wasn't much to do here, except for this case I haven't been able to solve!

Even though Judy had a smile on her face, she told me not to worry; we would find Ruth Ann and Paul. "I'm sure they just went off on some random goose chase. They'll be fine, John."

"You're probably right, but these guys have murdered two people, Judy. And I'm pretty sure they wouldn't care if Doug or Tom didn't make it either."

"Then let's just find them before anything else happens."

We parked in the alley and went into the back storeroom. Meme was gone, but I had a set of keys Ruth Ann gave me months ago. She wanted me to hold onto an extra set because she had a way of misplacing her keys. I never thought I'd have to use them for something as serious as this. Judy went into her office and passed under the yellow tape that blocked the doorway. "I know this is still a room under investigation, but I figure we need to check it out. You didn't go in here earlier did you?"

I shook my head and gave Judy the go ahead as long as she wore gloves. I went into the front showroom of the store and started searching for any clues. I decided to go upstairs and verify there was no water leak. As I suspected, all was dry and well upstairs. Ruth Ann must've planned this out hours ago or maybe even yesterday. Why would she be so deceitful, when she knew how dangerous these guys have been?

I wandered around the store and couldn't find anything. I hoped Judy had better luck. I went back into Ruth Ann's office and found Judy taking some pictures of papers that were on her desk. "What did you find?"

"I think your guys missed some vital clues when they cleaned the place after the guard was killed in here. Look at these papers." Judy said, beckoning me over to the desk.

"It looks like receipts from some antique dealers that's all," I sai,d staring at the papers. "What do you see that I don't?"

"Look at the tiny picture in the corner of the receipt here," she said, pointing to a receipt for an antique cupboard. I leaned over and had to put on my glasses to see what she was pointing at. "What is that?" I asked.

"It looks to me like a family crest. What do you make out of it?"

"Couldn't it be from the company that sold her the cupboard?" I inquired.

"I don't think so. It's different ink than what's on the receipt. There's some blood splattered on it, but it's different. Just look closer. I tried and noticed a crest that looked like some kind of flower with a river or stream.

"Strange, isn't it?" Judy questioned. "Maybe they left a calling card so small that your guys missed it. I don't know what made my eye catch it, but it stuck out to me."

"Good eye, because if I didn't put my glasses on I wouldn't have seen it at all," I said, taking a picture of the symbol too. I wanted to send this over to the station immediately and see if they could research it. Maybe it's a clue to whoever committed these crimes, or just a mark from one of Ruth Ann's dealers. Either way I was going to find out.

Outside of Judy's discovery, we came up empty. We headed back to the station, and I found out from Lou that Ruth Ann's car search still had no hits. "She's disappeared," Lou declared.

"What about the other stuff we're looking into, like the address on Lookout Mountain Road. Did you ever come up with an answer about the name of the company? What was that called again?" I asked.

"Lily's by the Stream," I believe," answered Lou.

"WAIT!" I cried out. "Judy, could that crest you discovered be a picture of Lily's by the Stream?"

Judy said, "It could be. How strange, the crest and the company name associated with the address seem to have a strange similarity don't they?"

"Let's get on this pronto," I snapped. "Judy and I are going to drive up to the address and check it out. Something tells me we've just arrived at our first real clue."

Chapter 15

RUTH ANN

Finn and I entered the kitchen and he kept a tight grip on my arm. I spotted Axel near the kitchen stove with his shirtsleeves rolled up. He was bent over looking at something in the oven, probably the fish. He was cooking?

Axel turned around and spotted us. "Ah, Ruth Ann you're co-operating with Finn I see?"

"Of course I am! I don't want to look like my friend Paul. Did you know Finn seriously beat him?" I glared at Finn, after accusing him.

"Yes, Finn keeps me apprised of what's been going on down-stairs. I heard you and your friend tried to make an escape?"

"Really? You're asking me that question!" I was fuming at the moment and asked, "What did you think I would do, just sit and wait for you and your thugs to kill us?"

"Now, now," Axel replied in a cool, calm tone. "You and your friend aren't in any danger. We just need to come up with a plan of what to do with the both of you. Apparently, your story about not knowing the whereabouts of the necklace might just be the truth."

"I told you, I have no idea where it is, I thought you had it."

Axel took a tray of fish out of the oven and placed it on the long marble island. He turned around and grabbed a pot from the stove and drained the water out of it. He dumped a pile of green beans into a bowl and put it next to the fish. He grabbed some rolls and placed them in a bowl and walked over to the large kitchen table. "Please sit," he said. Finn let me go and I walked over to the table and sat down. "You must be starving," Axel said. "You and I are going to dine, and then I'll tell you what my plans are for you."

"And Paul, too," I added.

"Your friend, Paul, will be taken care of, too," he said, waving

Finn out of the kitchen.

"Please, if that means you're going to keep Paul in that hole, that's unacceptable."

"Ruth Ann," he gestured for me to eat the plate he fixed for me. "It's not exactly up to you on what we'll be doing with your friend. If he cooperates, he'll be fine, but if he chooses to fight with Finn, I can't be held responsible for what he may do."

"Tell Finn not to touch or hurt him!" I demanded.

"Let's get back to you shall we?" Axel suggested, as he slowly took a bite of his fish. "Ah," he said chewing his first bite. "This is what relaxes me."

"Do we really have time to sit and eat a dinner?" I snapped. "Tell me what's going to happen to me."

"Well I'm thinking by now your inept police friends might've figured out where you could've gone."

"So why aren't you rushing to get out of here?" I asked, wondering how he could remain so calm.

"Don't worry about that. I have eyes and ears in your quaint town and I'll have plenty of notice before exiting the premises."

"Who?" I demanded. "You have spies in town helping you?"

"Yes, I do," he answered openly. "And don't bother asking me because I don't intend on telling you." He finished eating and looked at my untouched plate, "Don't you like your meal?"

"I'm not hungry," I snapped. "You probably drugged my food anyway."

"You saw me plate both dinners and I ate mine. Why would I drug myself?"

I was hungry. It had been hours since I'd eaten or drunk anything. I decided I needed my strength so I dug into my food. It was delicious but I wasn't going to let him know that. Once I finished, Axel stood up and grabbed both our plates and walked them over to the sink. That was the last thing I remembered.

I woke up in a soft bed, and for a moment didn't realize I wasn't in my own bed. Wait, I was in my own bed! I sat up and looked around, stunned. I was back in my own bedroom, but how could that be? Was this all a dream?

I got up and ran out into the kitchen and found a plate of pastries sitting on the counter and a carafe of orange juice resting in a bowl of ice. Who on earth did this? I was so confused I didn't know what to do next. I ran back into the bedroom and looked for my cell phone. It was charging on my nightstand and I picked it up. I immediately called John.

He picked up promptly and very slowly asked, "Ruth Ann? Is it really you?"

"John, it's me," I was still groggy and very confused. "What's going on? What's happened to me?"

Panicked, John asked, "Where are you? Are you in danger?"

"No, I don't think so," I said, rubbing my eyes to make sure I really was in my own home. "I'm at home."

"You're where?" he exclaimed.

"I'm at home, in my bedroom. I woke up here just a few minutes ago and I have no idea how I got here."

"Don't move, don't talk to anyone. I'm on my way." John hung up and I hurried to clean myself up and get dressed. I felt a huge headache coming on and realized the last thing I remembered was eating a meal with Axel. Does Axel actually exist?

John arrived a few minutes later and pounded on the front door. I had to take some aspirin for my headache before my head exploded. I hurried and opened the door and John grabbed me in a tight embrace. He released me and looked me over from head to toe. "You look OK, how are you?"

"I'm fine, I think, except for this headache I've got," I answered. I walked into the kitchen and opened a cabinet and took out the aspirin bottle. "This will help me," I said, downing a couple aspirin with the orange juice on the counter. I handed John two aspirin but he waved my hand away.

"Where did that come from?" John asked, pointing at the pastries and juice.

"I have no idea; it was here when I came out of my bedroom."

"You drank it!" he cried out. "It could be drugged."

"I didn't even think about that! I just grabbed the closest thing to me." I rubbed my aching head and said, "Not again, I can't be drugged again."

John took me over to the couch in the family room and plopped me down on the sofa. "I'm not going to be angry with you, yet, but I need you to tell me everything that happened. And do not leave out one single thing no matter how trivial you think it is." Before I began John added, "And what happened to Paul?"

"Oh no!" I howled, holding my head in pain. "I almost forgot about him! He's back at that man's house thrown into a hole in the ground. We've got to go there and rescue him." I jumped up to leave when John pulled me back down. "No, John, we've got to go. I know where he is."

John didn't move. "What are you waiting for?"

"We're not moving an inch until you tell me what happened."

I knew I wasn't going to win, so I explained the whole story in detail; how I planned from the beginning to go investigate the address and how I convinced Paul to go along with me. "He didn't have a choice. He knew that if he didn't accompany me I would go alone. So don't blame him, I made it impossible for him to choose."

"How did you know where to go?" he asked calmly.

"I researched the area with the numbers I got from you. The '1212 Loo'," I replied. "It wasn't that difficult of a search. Once I got the information I was going to talk to you about it, but you were being so evasive. You shut me out, John, so I became upset and decided to do it myself."

"That was a mistake on my part, but the part where you went haring off to a murderer's house is all on you. And you're telling me Paul is still there?"

"I don't know," I said, frustrated. "The last I saw him was when this tattooed man, Finn, dragged me out of the room and back upstairs into the kitchen. That's when Axel convinced me my food wasn't drugged because he also ate it. That wasn't smart of me."

"You didn't know, but usually as a prisoner, one doesn't eat or drink from the captor."

"I'll remember that now," I mumbled.

"I think we should take you to see Doc Albert and have him check you out. You probably were just given a sedative, but best to be sure."

"No, I'm fine now!" I demanded. "I want to go and find Paul."

"You aren't going anywhere," John declared.

"You don't have a choice, John," I stated. "I know where the house is and I know how to get into the secret room where they're holding Paul."

John begged me to tell him how to get in the room without me going, but I refused. If he doesn't want another death on his hands, he'd better let me go. He conceded, under the condition I get a quick check up with Doc Albert. I agreed and we headed over to the hospital.

John called Doc from my house and Doc said to go to the back-lot of the hospital and he would meet us there to let us in. He didn't want either of us to be spotted at the hospital. It was a service entrance and patients didn't use that entrance. We arrived there within minutes and Doc led us quickly into the closest room.

"Now what happened?" Doc asked.

"Ruth Ann here ingested a drug that knocked her out for twelve hours or so. Can you make sure she's all right now? You know how stubborn she can be. She says her only side effect has been a headache and she took some aspirin for that."

"John, I'm perfectly capable of speaking for myself!"

Doc felt the tension building and said, "It doesn't matter who said what. John," Doc said, "I need to examine Ruth Ann in private. Why don't you sneak over to my office and shut the door. No one will bother you there."

John agreed and said he had to set a few things up with the guys at the station anyway. Doc turned his attentions back to me and said, "You don't owe me an explanation, but I'm hoping you'll indulge me in one."

I was confused. I didn't know what Doc knew and didn't know regarding what had been going on. However, he had been so loyal and helpful with his current patients and with all of John's requests that I decided to confide in him completely. I began from the beginning, when I saw the man running out of Doug's office after he beat his head in. The more I said, the bigger Doc's mouth opened. After I was finished I saw the look of horror in his eyes.

"Ruth Ann," he said very slowly. "You're foolish to be involved with any of this!" Really? That was a bit harsh I thought. "John should never have allowed you to be a part of this in any way. You've put yourself in danger, and I think you should pack a suitcase and get out of town until these men are captured."

"Doc!" I said. "How can you say that? This is all about a necklace that is rightfully mine."

"Then let John and his men find it for you. These criminals know who you are. And now they've even taken you prisoner for a day. What I can't figure out is why they let you go."

"That's a good point, Doc," I said. "I don't know why they did that and why they didn't let Paul go?"

"Does John have any theories?" asked Doc.

"I told you it's hard not to get wrapped up in all this. You've been helping us ever since Doug was admitted."

"Yes, but I wasn't aware of everything that has gone down. There have been people murdered and severely injured, and now, taken captive."

"But they didn't harm me," I said, wondering why that was.

"They did drug you, Ruth Ann."

"I was sedated and transferred back to my home. Someone put me in my own bed!"

"But why?" Doc questioned. "I'll bet John is wondering that himself. I think you may not be out of this yet. They may try and contact you regarding your friend, Paul."

"Maybe," I replied.

"If they do contact you this time, you have to confide in John. Maybe Paul's life can be saved if you don't do anything stupid and go somewhere alone again."

"You know if we weren't long-time friends that statement would've really insulted me." I smiled, and said, "But I learned my lesson."

"I surely hope so, Ruth Ann." Doc began his examination and concluded I was just sedated. My body was so sensitive to the sedative that I slept for twelve hours straight. It could also be I hadn't slept much the last week.

John tried to convince Doc to keep me overnight. I told him he couldn't play that game with me. I was fine and wasn't going to stay at the hospital. I planned on going back to my house and contacting my daughters to let them know I was OK. John told me I couldn't do that because we didn't want them to be in any danger. He said he's been in constant communication with them and he had a message from them. "I was in super big trouble with the both of them!" Message received.

John agreed to let me stay at home under one condition. Judy Welch was to bunk at my house for the duration of the case. I immediately refused, but John told me if I didn't agree he would lock me up in a cell at the station. He knew I didn't care for Judy, she was a flirt and I felt she had other intentions with John. I don't care what the age difference; she had a super crush on her current boss. I told him I'd let her stay with me, only because the sooner we solve this case, the quicker she'll leave town. John laughed!

On the way back to my house I asked John if he had any news on Paul. Nothing new and Paul was still missing. He said we'd head over to the mysterious house in early morning after a few hours of sleep. Paul wasn't going anywhere. They needed him as leverage, but John wasn't sure what they were going to swap for him or should I say 'whom'?

Judy met us back at my house and she was perky and ready to 'temporarily' move in with me. John knew this wasn't going to be easy for me. I told John to leave and showed Judy the guest bedroom. I wasn't in the mood to cook or entertain either of them. I went into my bedroom and shut the door. Judy told me she would occasionally check on me, so not to try and elude her. I was tired and just wanted to shower and go to bed. Morning was going to be here quickly and I wanted to get back to Axel's house and get Paul rescued.

I finished showering and plopped down on my bed. I looked at my phone and noticed I had missed a text. I put on my glasses, because without them I wouldn't be able to read a word of it. I bet it was John, checking on me, but I was wrong.

I was shocked at the text. It read, "*Pack your bags, Ruth Ann. We're taking a trip. DO NOT SHOW ANYONE THIS TEXT OR PAUL WILL DIE!*"

I was stunned, I didn't know what to do. Do I rush in and tell Judy or call John? If I did, the sender might know and kill Paul. I couldn't let that happen. Obviously these people are watching all of us, and I needed to wait for more directions. The meaning of the text finally dawned on me, a trip? What trip and where to? Plus, how could they get me to go along with them? I had so many questions and no answers. It had to be from Axel and his men. I already saw what Finn could do with his fists. Paul's face was the proof of Finn's power. I decided to wait for more information. I was never going to be able to fall asleep now. Maybe I should pack a bag, just in case.

I knew I wasn't making any sense. But if I didn't pack something and I was forced to go on this trip then I'd have nothing of my own with me. Plus, packing would give me time to think about what the text implied. But what do I pack, because I have no idea where this trip is? I must have been delirious, because I actually did pack a small suitcase.

I shoved it into my closet so Judy wouldn't come across it and start asking questions. I went and lay down on my bed and grabbed the cup of hot tea I just made. It always soothed my nerves and helped me relax. I needed to stay rationa,l but I was so tired. That was all I remembered, again.

Chapter 16

JOHN WILKINSON

"How did you let her get away?" John screamed at Judy. "She was in her own bedroom with you only a few feet away."

"I don't know," Judy declared, vividly upset. Probably more upset that she let someone get the better of her than because Ruth Ann was missing.

"The cup of tea on her nightstand was almost empty. There are a few drops in the bottom, so I need Doc to test it immediately. She might not have gone off on her own this time. This could be a kidnapping." John ordered Dave, who was at Ruth Ann's house, to bag the teacup.

"John, they must've drugged my water," Judy said. "I remember taking a glass with me to bed, and that's all I remember until you came storming in. I don't think I would've woken up until the morning." John looked at his watch and said, "It's four in the morning, and when you didn't answer my calls or texts I rushed over here."

John and Judy were standing next to the island in the kitchen when Lou walked up to them and said, "There's been no forced entry. Whoever got in here either had a key or knew how to break in without damaging any locks."

"What do we do now, Chief?" Lou requested.

"Dan, you and Dave search every inch of this house and call me immediately if you find anything. Judy and I are driving out to the house up on the mountain. Ruth Ann told me approximately where it is and that there's a secret room in the basement where Paul is being held in a hole in the ground. These guys are barbaric!"

I took off down the main road and noticed the road had a fresh coating of snow. It was the season's first snow and it always takes some practice managing the driving. My car slipped and slid all the way up the mountain, and I made a mental note to myself to contact the agency that salts the roads. It was time they started working for the season.

According to Ruth Ann, the small turnoff to Lookout Mountain Road was about eight or nine miles from town. I managed to get to the turnoff in about twenty minutes. There were no lights on the road showing where to turn and I was thankful Judy spotted it right away. I would've probably passed it a couple times. We drove down the road with the headlights off so nobody could see us coming.

We came upon a large estate with the outside lights on. I pulled the car over to the side of the road before we reached the circular drive. Judy pulled out her gun and I followed suit. "Let's walk around to the back and see if there are any lights on inside. It looks pretty dark inside."

"They're probably sleeping," Judy said.

We carefully walked in the fresh snow around to the back. We passed by large windows on the side of the estate that were covered with curtains so we couldn't see inside. There was a door in the middle of the back of the house. Judy went to one side of the door and I stayed on the other. I carefully tried the doorknob and found the door unlocked. "Be careful John, this could be a trap."

I started to open the door, and after approximately six inches I put my face in to see inside. There was limited light inside and from what I could tell it was a kitchen. I noticed the dim light came from above the stove and the room was empty. Judy and I entered the kitchen and walked around to make sure no one was in there. We left the kitchen through a set of swinging doors and ended up in a small room, maybe a butler's pantry. There was a choice to either head up a narrow staircase or go through another door to the dining room. We went back into the kitchen and found another door just to the right of the butler's pantry.

"It's got to be the basement stairs from what Ruth Ann described," I whispered to Judy.

Judy reached her hand out to open it but John grabbed her arm. "Wait, I just heard a noise coming from the front of the house." They walked through yet another door and entered a very dark grand foyer. "There's a light on in that room over there," I pointed toward a room off to the side. "Should we go in there or go down to the basement first?" asked Judy.

"Let's check out the room up here first. I don't want to get trapped in a basement if anyone knows we we're here." I walked over to the large set of double wooden doors and put my ear up. "I don't hear anything." I grabbed the knob and slowly turned it. "Be ready," I whispered to Judy.

I pushed the door open an inch at a time until I was able to put my head in. It was a library. There was a lamp lit on a large desk on the opposite side of the room. From what I could tell no one was in there. "Looks clear," I said to Judy. We opened the door for both of us to enter and Judy had her gun out and ready just in case. The room was empty, but there was evidence someone had recently been in there.

I walked over to the fireplace and noticed steaming logs that were only half used, and it appeared someone had recently poured water over the them. "Someone threw water on these logs not too long ago." We then went over to the desk. There were some ashes on the desk from a cigar but other than that it was cleared. "This was the room Ruth Ann said they held her and Paul until they took them into the basement. Let's get down to the basement before someone hears us. We can come back to this room later."

We went back to the basement stair door and found it locked. "That's strange," Judy said. "Why would someone want to lock a basement door?"

"To keep whatever's down there from getting up here," I said.

Judy picked the lock in a matter of seconds and I was quite impressed. It would've taken me at least twice as long to pick that lock. Judy noticed my impressed look and she said, "I've had lots of practice doing that."

"Some time you'll have to tell me about the skills you picked up in the city." She smiled and motioned for me to go first.

We took the stairs as quietly as we could. They were old wooden stairs that creaked with the weight of our feet. The darkness was making our descent very challenging, but we made it to the bottom. I had to flip on the flashlight app from my cell phone because complete darkness surrounded us. "Slowly," Judy said as I switched on the light.

"This is the room Ruth Ann described," John said. "She said there's a secret door on this wall." I pointed and walked over to the wall on the opposite side of the room.

Judy asked, "How does it open?"

"That part she wouldn't tell me," I said irritated. "This is going to be impossible to figure out in this light. Maybe we should turn on the light down here so we can see better." I walked over to the string that led up to a single bulb on the ceiling. I pulled the string and the room lit up. We quickly looked around, just in case we were caught off guard from someone.

"It's just an empty room, John," Judy said, looking around. "You sure there's another room down here?"

"Yes, there's a door that pulls up and leads to another room kind of like this one but with a hole in the ground."

"Where these jerks threw Paul, the guard, right?" Judy asked. I nodded, wondering if we would ever figure out how to get in the room and if Paul was still in there.

Judy and I searched the wall for a switch that would lift a piece of the wall up and let us get to the other side. Judy threw her arms up in exasperation and said, "This is hopeless. How are we ever going to find a way in there?"

"Like this," I answered, right after I felt a tiny button about halfway up the wall and gave it a push. The wall rumbled a bit and then a chunk of it lifted into the ceiling, allowing both of us to get inside the next room. Judy jumped in first, aiming her gun and I followed. What we saw shocked both of us.

I ran to the wall opposite the opening and found Paul shackled to the wall and slumped over. I called out to him, but got no response. Judy took his wrist in her hand and searched for a pulse. "He's alive, barely."

"That's good at least," I said. "We need to get him unlocked and get him out of here immediately. Do you see any keys lying around?" We both looked around and the only item in the room was a chair. I noticed the hole Ruth Ann told me about and peered in. "It's disgusting in there. I can't believe Paul was held in that hole for so long."

Judy checked the walls to make sure we didn't miss a hook with keys hanging. Then she walked over to the chair and we heard a clanging noise. "Turn it over," I told her. Judy kicked the chair over, and taped to the bottom was a set of keys. I grabbed them and unlocked the shackles attached to Paul's wrists and ankles. He was dead weight as I freed him, and I could barely hold him up. "How are we going to get him out of here?"

"I'll grab his feet and you grab his shoulders and we'll get him to your car. I don't know if we can hang around here to search upstairs. Paul may not survive that long."

"I agree," I said. "As soon as we put him in my car, you drive back to town and get him to Doc Albert. I'm staying here and look for Ruth Ann and this Axel guy."

"But you can't stay here alone," Judy declared. "It'll take me at least forty-five minutes to get back here!"

"No choice," I stated. "Let me put it this way, I order you to get Paul to Doc Albert. Before you come back, pick up Lou and bring him with you. Call him when you get Paul in the car, and call Doc Albert so he's on alert."

Judy stopped arguing and we started up the stairs. All was still as we retraced our footsteps and went back outside through the kitchen. We carefully loaded Paul into the back seat, and I reminded Judy who to call and I took off back inside. "Be careful," Judy told me as I left her and Paul.

I wanted to go back into the library to search the room. There had to be a clue to their whereabouts. At least we found Paul and we were able to get him out of this place. I made it safely back inside and headed straight to the library. There were still no signs of anybody in the house. They were either gone or sleeping upstairs. I'd search the upper floors when I finished with the library.

I went to the desk and looked in the drawers. There were notepads, pens, paper clips and a stapler in the top drawer. I felt underneath the desk for a secret compartment and success! There was a thin drawer just under the right side of the desk. "What could we have here?" I said to myself as I pulled out the miniature drawer. There was a lock on the drawer but it wouldn't be too difficult to break it open. I put it on the ground, stomped on it, and it cracked open. I picked up the contents of the drawer and placed it on the desk.

Jackpot! I found several pieces of paper, dating back several years, regarding the blue aquamarine necklace. Whoever researched this piece of jewelry didn't have possession of it and they wanted it. They hired private detectives to hunt the thing down and the necklace had been in Sweden then in the U.S., then back to Sweden and apparently now in the U.S. somewhere. It had been stolen so many times over the last hundred plus years that whoever has possession of it becomes a huge target. The lawyer in Sweden who sent the necklace to Deer Creek told Doug that one of Ruth Ann's distant relatives brought the necklace to the U.S. in the late 1800's. Ruth Ann was supposed to take possession of it, but someone stole it from Doug at the bank. I didn't think Axel, if that's his name, had the necklace. Why take Ruth Ann captive? Unless he didn't believe Ruth Ann when she said she didn't know where the necklace is. Or, maybe he knew who had the necklace and needed Ruth Ann to get it back for him. Whatever the reason, I had to find Ruth Ann pronto.

I walked around the library and stood by the large stone fireplace. I looked on the mantel and noticed a plaque resting against the stone. I didn't recall seeing that when Judy and I were in here earlier. I got a closer look and almost dropped to the floor. The plaque was a family crest from Sweden. The name inscribed on the bottom of the piece spelled out Liljestrom. The picture on the front of the plaque showed a river splitting with flowers on the bank of the river. Wait! The flowers have to be lilies and the river could also be called a stream. It was the name of the business this guy ran and the same crest Judy found in Ruth Ann's office.

It was the biggest clue I had found! This crest had to have something to do with Ruth Ann's whereabouts. I grabbed the plaque and hurried out of the library. I wanted to get back to the office, but I had to wait for Judy to come back. I decided I had better check the upstairs levels to see if there was anything else I could use to find Ruth Ann. Who knows, maybe there were people sound asleep up there. I doubt they would let Ruth Ann sleep up there, but I had to check and make sure.

There were two levels above the main floor. I went all the way to the third floor and checked each bedroom. There were four rooms and all were empty. From my search I could tell these rooms had not been used in a long time. There was dust all over the furniture and beds were immaculately made. I went down to the second level and entered the first room. It had to be the master. It was massive with another fireplace that had recently been used. The embers were smoldering and the bed was undone. I found a dresser with drawers pulled open and emptied. This was definitely a man's room, decorated with navy blue bedding, and curtains that were fully closed. I pulled open the curtains part way and light filled the room. It was light outside and the sun was shining. I wanted to stay and search this room more closely, but I had to make sure there was no one in the other rooms on this floor. I headed out the door from Axel's bedroom and went to the next door, locked. The next two doors were also locked.

Why would he lock the doors? Could he have Ruth Ann held up in one of them? I grabbed the pick I always carry and started to gently pick the first locked door. It only took a second and the door lock clicked. I opened the door only about an inch and peeked in. It was a bedroom and I didn't see any movement. I carefully entered the room and walked over to a messed up bed. Someone was in the bed and he appeared to be asleep. I pulled out my badge and gun and positioned myself directly at his head. I gave him a slight nudge and he didn't wake up. His head was facing away from me, so I tried again. Nothing.

I shouted, "Wake up!" No response from the person lying in the bed. I pulled the sheet that was all the way up to his neck, gave it a tug and slowly pulled it down. The man was fully dressed, in black tie and pants. What was going on here? I reached down to his wrist and took his pulse. He was alive. My guess would be this man was drugged. I dropped his arm and looked around the room. It was much smaller than Axel's master bedroom and quite sparsely furnished. I opened his closet and it was neatly arranged, with several black suits, white shirts, and black ties. Ah, it had to be the butler on the bed. Axel must have drugged him and put him to bed. When he woke, the butler would probably assume that he was hungover, because there was a bottle of whiskey and an empty glass on his nightstand. It had to be a set up; the man was too neatly laid out on the bed.

I hurried out of the room and unlocked the next one. There was also a person lying in a bed, but a woman this time. She was clearly a housekeeper from her attire. Once again, a bottle and glass were set on the nightstand next to the bed. This couldn't be a coincidence. There was one more locked door on this floor, and I felt confident I would find another person perfectly set in a bed with alcohol next them. However, I was completely wrong!

The door opened easily once I picked the lock. I didn't hesitate, when I opened the door, I rushed in. I was immediately hit over the head with a large object and I fell to the ground. Thankfully it wasn't so hard that it knocked me out.

"What the…" I cried out. I picked myself up off the floor and put my hand to the back of my head. I was bleeding, but not terribly. I looked around to see if there was still someone in there. I found a woman crouched in a corner holding a brass bookend. "Why did you hit me?" I asked as I stood at the doorway.

She was young, maybe twenty or so. I realized I had made a serious error. I assumed there would be someone else passed out in here and didn't take any precautions. I must've scared this young woman half to death. She didn't respond to me for obvious reasons, but stayed curled up in a corner next to the bed. I saw on the nightstand that there was a bottle of tequila and a glass. "I'm not going to hurt you," I started to say. "I'm a police officer and I came to see if everyone here is OK."

She sat up a bit and eyed the badge I was holding in my hand. I put my gun back in my holster and asked her if she would like a closer look at my badge. She shook her head violently and pressed herself closer to the wall. "It's OK, really," I said. "Did your boss try and hurt you?" I tried asking.

She looked at me and murmured, "He drugged us all."

That's good, I got a response from the girl and I hoped it was just a beginning. "Tell me, why would your boss do that?"

"He's not a nice man. When he wants us out of the way, he pretends to be nice and gives us our favorite drinks, and we all drink and drink together. We wake up in our beds the next morning with massive headaches and think we passed out. This time I only pretended to drink, and now I know the truth of what he does."

"Wait a minute," I said, startled. "Are you telling me that he's done this before?"

"Many times," she replied.

"But why do you go along with it?" I asked, dumbfounded.

"I only suspected he did this, and I couldn't figure out a way to dispose of the alcohol until now. I only pretended to drink, but I actually dumped it out."

"How did you do that?"

"He took us into the dining room and told us to enjoy dinner in there. We never get to eat in there except for times like this. He had a chef make us a real nice meal and put the bottles of booze in the middle of the table. We don't get much time off, so when we do, we enjoy ourselves."

"But didn't you know that he was using the alcohol before?"

"I told you, I only suspected. We're way beneath the level of our boss and he gives us a home and a job. I'm grateful to him for letting me live in such a nice house. Before this, most of us were homeless. My employer came to our shelter and took me and my two friends and gave us jobs."

"Are your two friends in the other rooms up here?"

"Yes,"

"And your boss hired all three of you and lets you sleep on the upper levels, right next to his room?" I asked suspiciously.

"Yes, is that wrong?" She asked innocently. "We do good work for him and we're loyal, until now. I saw him slip powder into our glasses down in the dining room. He waited until we had a few and then figured we were too drunk to notice. But I dumped my glasses into a large cup I hid on the chair next to mine. I made sure I sat by the end so I'd be able to use an empty chair."

"Very smart of you," I said. "So you saw him put a substance in your drinks and your two friends drank it?"

"I did," she answered. "And I watched them drink. I felt bad you know." She lowered her head, visibly upset.

"But why didn't you tell them your suspicions before they drank the drugged drinks?"

"I planned on telling them what he did after they woke up. I stayed in my room longer than usual and was waiting to hear them move around in the hall. I heard my employer leave really early this morning, so I could've left my room, but I was too scared. He has some mean men that work for him and I didn't know if they were keeping an eye on us."

"Mean men?" I asked. "Are you talking about a man named Finn?"

She looked at me apprehensively and replied, "How do you know about Finn? And by the way, why did you come here? Did someone call the police?"

"No, it's a long story and I'll get into that with you, but I need to know if there's anyone else in the house besides you three?"

"No, I don't think so." She added, "The gardener doesn't live here and he usually doesn't come in the house."

"May I ask your name and what your position is in the house?"

She stood up and sat on the edge of her bed. For a moment I thought she was going to pass out. "Are you OK?" I asked.

She shook her head and said, "Yes, I'm just confused."

"Please understand that I'm here only to help you and your friends."

"Okay, I believe you," she said sweetly. "My name is Helena and I'm the maid. I do the house cleaning, laundry, and some cooking with Ms. Angstrom."

"Angstrom, is she Swedish?" I asked curiously.

Helena looked at me strangely and replied, "I have no idea. Why would you ask me that?"

"Because your employer, Axel, appears to be from Swedish descent."

"Axel? I call him Mr. Eklund."

"Mr. Eklund, He's of Swedish descent, correct?"

"I don't know that either," Helena snapped. "I only started working here this past summer and I keep to room where my employer's not in. He doesn't like me cleaning around him."

"Ah, so what about the other man in the room up here. Is he the butler?"

"Yes, that's Bert, He's Mr. Eklund's butler."

"We should go and try and wake the other two so we can all have a talk about your boss and what you've seen going on around here." I motioned for Helena to walk out the door first. She obliged and we went to the room next to hers. It was Ms. Angstrom's room. Helena pulled a key out of her pocket and unlocked the door. However, it wasn't locked anymore and she eyed me apprehensively. "You already unlocked the door? But you don't have a key."

"I'm a police officer and know how to do that. I needed to make sure that whoever was in these rooms were still alive."

"Oh, okay," she said as she walked over to the bed. She grabbed the sheet and pulled it back a little. "I feel horrible that I let this happen to her."

"But it won't ever happen again," I said. "Can you call her name and see if you can arouse her?"

Helena shook her shoulders lightly and called her name out. It took several tries but finally Ms. Angstrom opened her eyes. "Helena," she said sitting up. "What are you doing here?"

"You need to get up, there's a problem," Helena replied.

She looked away from Helena and spotted me. "Oh, my!" she yelled, grabbing the sheet and throwing it over herself again. "Who are you?"

"It's okay," Helena said. "He's a police officer and we need to talk to him. Hurry up and meet us in the kitchen. I'll put on some coffee after we get Bert up."

We left Ms. Angstrom wide eyed and mouth opened. We went into Bert's room and Helena was able to wake him quickly and told him the same story about meeting us in the kitchen right away. Bert didn't seem as frightened by my appearance but that could be because of the mix of alcohol and sedatives.

It took them a few minutes to meet us in the kitchen. Helena had a pot of hot coffee ready and put out some pastries on the kitchen table. I dug in since I've been up for hours already and was quite hungry. Bert and Ms. Angstrom studied me as I ate without saying a word. The housekeeper, Ms. Angstrom, just sipped her coffee and watched me. Finally, Bert, the butler, joined me in eating the pastries.

I stood up from the kitchen table and announced who I was. "I am Chief John Wilkinson of the Deer Creek Police Department." I pulled my badge out and handed it first to Ms. Angstrom, and she passed it to Bert.

He glanced at it for only a moment and asked, "What are you doing here? Did something happen while we were asleep?"

Helena sat down at the table and put her hands up to her face to hide the tears that were streaming down. Ms. Angstrom noticed and asked, "Why are you so upset, Helena?"

She just shook her head and said, "I didn't mean for it to happen! I'm so sorry."

"Sorry for what?" Bert questioned. "Just get on with it," he snapped. "I've got to see to Mr. Eklund, he must still be in his room."

"No, he's gone," I answered for them. "He took off a few hours ago with a friend of mine. That's why I'm here."

"What friend? Where did he go?" Bert asked, choking on a mouthful of pastry.

"It's a very long story and I'll tell you part of it after you answer a few questions for me." They all nodded and we sat down around the table. "First, Helena tell me how you all came to working here for Mr. Eklund."

Ms. Angstrom looked at Helena and asked, "What did you tell him?"

"That we met at the shelter, and Mr. Eklund visited there and took the three of us home to work for him."

Shocked, Bert and Ms. Angstrom exchanged glances. I immediately asked what their looks were about. Bert was the one who answered me. "Yes, we were at the shelter. But not because we were homeless and had no money."

"Why else would you go there?" I asked, pulling out a notebook and writing this all down.

"Helena's young and doesn't know why Bert and I were there," Ms. Angstrom said. "Bert and I came over from London to try making a living in America. We only arrived here this summer and had a difficult time finding positions for a housekeeper and a butler. In Europe it's quite common, but not so much here in America."

"So you just came here a few months ago?" I asked.

"Yes, we both did. We don't have any other skills and thought we'd be happier here. We only went to the shelter to get some food and a place to stay temporarily. We knew it was just a matter of time before we'd land a position. And we did." Ms. Angstrom clearly had an attitude of entitlement. She held her head high and sat so rigidly I felt she would snap in half.

"Helena," I directed this next question just to her. "Were you aware of all this?"

"No, sir, I was not."

"Why would we have to tell a maid our personal history?" Bert barked. "She didn't come with us from Europe."

"My impression, sir, is that Helena felt you were a family of sort, rescued from a shelter and brought here to this fine home to work together." I looked at Helena who still had tears running down her young face. "Is that how you felt?"

She nodded and put her head down on the table on folded arms. "Stop that!" Ms. Angstrom snapped. "We're all close, but you're just a young girl, and Bert and I have been through alot together. You know us well enough since we've worked together here. We just didn't tell you where we came from."

"Where exactly did you come from?" I inquired, starting to feel uneasy about the two of them. Maybe they weren't as innocent as Helena thought.

"I thought you were here to ask us about Mr. Eklund and your friend?" Ms. Angstrom asked. "Bert's and my history aren't any of your business unless you suspect us of some wrongdoing."

"This is my investigation, ma'am," I stated. "If I need a question answered you'll do it, or I can just take you into the station until I find the information out myself."

"Fine," she snapped. "Bert and I came from an elderly gentleman's home back in England. He passed away and we were out of a job. That's all there is, nothing sinister, just his heart gave out due to old age."

"So if I need the name and address of this employer, you can cooperate?" I asked.

"Yes, of course," Bert answered for Ms. Angstrom. "But he was all alone without any family and now that's he's dead I don't see how it'll help you."

"I'll determine that later," I replied. "Let's get back to the time you've been living here." They both relaxed a little and Helena lifted her head up and wiped her face.

"Does your boss live here alone?"

"He has two men that live here off and on," Helena answered first.

"Helena, is one of them Finn?" She nodded and Bert and Ms. Angstrom glared at her.

"What's your problem with her answering these questions?" I asked, frustrated.

"She should not divulge private information. You can question Mr. Eklund directly," Ms. Angstrom said.

"He's not here and once again I'll make myself perfectly clear. If you do not answer my questions to my satisfaction, then we'll take this meeting down to the station."

"Chief," Bert interrupted. "I didn't notice a police car parked out front."

I ignored his question and continued. "So, Finn and someone else who works for Mr. Eklund stay here off and on." They all agreed and so I asked, "Who's the other man?"

"I don't know his name," Helena said. "He always follows

Finn's orders and just grunts. He looks really scary and I avoid him all the time. I don't like the way he looks at me, so I run the other direction when he's around."

I looked at the other two and they claimed they didn't know his name either. I figured I wasn't going to get too much out of them so I concentrated on Helena. "So these two men were here when you first came here in the summer?" They all nodded. "Have any of you ever been in the basement?" That did it! The looks on their faces answered my questions for me. "What have you seen down there?"

"I only went down there one time and it was because Mr. Eklund ordered me to clean up a mess on the floor."

"What kind of mess?" I inquired.

"Finn took me down and I was so worried about being alone with him I didn't pay much attention. I had a bucket and mop and there was a puddle of some kind of liquid. It was dark down there and just an empty room so I figured Finn spilled some oil or something."

"Why would you say oil?" I asked.

"Because it shimmered and was a dark, sticky sort of liquid."

"When was that?"

"Actually it was just a couple days ago," Helena answered. "I didn't think much of it. As I said, I wanted to get away from Finn."

"What about either of you? Been in the basement lately?"

"Not really," Bert replied. "My duties involve the upstairs rooms and the front door."

"Do you get a lot of visitors?" I asked.

"Why would you ask that?" Bert snapped back at me.

"Because you just said your duties include the front door. I would assume you would be assigned to the front door if you get visitors."

"The front door is one of my duties, I said," Bert answered. "I do a number of things, most of them are for Mr. Eklund."

"So you have a lot of contact with your boss?" I asked.

"Yes, of course. I'm his butler."

"Have you been around him lately when a woman was here in the house?"

"Let me think," he said, thinking. I was wondering what excuse he would come up this time for avoiding my question. I was surprised when Bert said, "There was a woman here over the last couple days. She was in the library with Mr. Eklund and I prepared tea for them."

I pulled out a picture of Ruth Ann and showed Bert and the rest of them. "I've seen her!" Helena cried. "She was taken into the library when I was in the foyer dusting. I saw Finn take her toward the basement door shortly after that."

"That's great, Helena," I said, praising her. "Did you see her after that?"

Ms. Angstrom cut in and said, "I saw her leave the house. She walked out on her own accord."

"Excuse me?" I asked. "Are you saying you personally saw this woman walk out the front door and leave?"

"Yes," Ms. Angstrom replied curtly.

I stood up and went behind Ms. Angstrom and pulled out the empty chair next to her and sat down. "Now why don't you start telling me the truth? This is your last chance. Do you understand me clearly?" I looked her straight in the face, not more than twelve inches apart.

"I don't know what you're implying, Chief."

"I happen to know for a fact that this woman was drugged and carried out of here. I'm assuming by Finn and the other man."

Bert cleared his throat and looked at Ms. Angstrom and said, "Stop Bertha. We need to come clean."

Bert and Bertha? Are these people real? The only one I trusted so far was Helena, and I believed she was realizing that she was alone in this questioning. "I'm confused," Helena said. "Did this woman walk out or did Finn carry her out?"

Bert answered for Bertha, "I was told to pull the car around and wait inside the car. I waited for about ten minutes when Mr. Eklund walked out and Finn was behind him. He wasn't alone. He was carrying this woman you showed us in the picture. She appeared to be unconscious."

"Are you sure?" I asked.

"Yes," Bert replied. "I became uncomfortable and Mr. Eklund noticed my uneasiness, and told me it was all OK. He told me that she drank too much and they were going to take her home. They placed her in the very back of the limousine and told me get in, too."

"When was this?" I asked.

"Yesterday," Bert said. "But there's more."

"Bert!" Bertha snapped. "That's enough. I think we should wait until Mr. Eklund comes back and tells his version."

'There isn't another version, Bertha," Bert retorted. "Just the truth, and I'm going to keep going."

"That's good, Bert," I said, smiling at him. Finally the barriers were crumbling down. "Go on."

"We drove into your town, Deer Creek. I remember her house, and how Finn and Mr. Eklund entered the front door. They were only gone a minute or two when they came back in the limousine and told me to drive off immediately."

"So they brought her into the house and came out without her, right?"

"Yes," Bert responded. "But that wasn't the only time we were there."

"What did you do?" Helena cried out.

"I didn't do anything but drive as I was ordered to."

"You're doing great, Bert," I said. "Tell me about when you went back."

"Yes, it was strange because Mr. Eklund woke us all up and told us to be ready for a little party in about an hour or so. It was after midnight and we couldn't say no, but we all were concerned. Why would he want to party in the middle of the night?"

"I know why now," Helena said. "That's when he drugged our drinks and put us into our own beds."

"How do you know that?" Ms. Angstrom barked. "He wouldn't drug me."

"Why not?" I asked quickly. "Helena saw him do it, too."

She shot Helena a nasty look and shut her mouth for the moment. "Bert, please go on," I said.

"He told me we had to go back to the house to make sure the lady we dropped off earlier was doing all right. I kind of thought it was nice of him at the time. We took off with Finn, of course, and when we pulled onto her street, he asked me to turn the headlights off. We pulled into the driveway and Finn and Mr. Eklund disappeared inside. They came out not much later."

"They had the woman again, didn't they?" I asked.

"Yes, but she walked out."

"She walked out on her own?" I asked, surprised.

"Yes, but she was very unsteady. Like she was still drunk."

I thought to myself that must have been when they slipped Ruth Ann and Judy some kind of drug. Ruth Ann must have been partially sedated when they took her from her house. "Did you ask them about her condition?"

"Absolutely not," Bert responded. "I need this job and I do what he asks."

"Even when it's illegal?" Helena asked him.

"I don't think about what he asks me to do. I just do it and turn the other way. Helena, you're young and naïve. When you get to my age it's all about survival."

"Bert," I interrupted. "Your way of going about business is not only illegal, it's immoral. You see a woman seriously impaired not once, but twice, and you just go along with it?"

Bert didn't answer. Ms. Angstrom did for Bert, "What are you getting at Chief? Bert told you more than you asked and now you're trying to make him the criminal?"

"He took part in an illegal kidnapping. I say that's more than I can let go."

"Are you going to arrest me?" Bert asked.

"I'm going to take you down to the station, and you'll be fully interrogated. Are you an American citizen?"

"Well, no," Bert said. "I'm here on a work visa for the year."

"We'll check that out, too," I said. I looked at Bertha and asked her the same questions and she also wasn't a citizen.

"Helena, should I ask you the same question?"

"I'm not from London, I was born here, in Houston."

"Well then you're a citizen," I said. "I need to find out more information about last night. Bert, was Mr. Eklund alone or were the other two guys here with him, and what were they doing up until you were woken up to drink and drive?"

Bert was about to answer me when suddenly a thought entered my head. "Wait a minute, Bert. You said you all drank and then your boss drugged your drinks. Helena said you both were passed out and were put into your beds. However, you just told me about the party, and that you had to drive to the house to check on the woman again. How does that work?"

Bert moved anxiously in his chair and admitted, "I wasn't

drugged at our party. In fact, I knew he wanted to slip Helena and Ms. Angstrom something to help them sleep."

"Bert!" Bertha shouted. "You knew he drugged me? How could you do that to me after all we've been through?"

"Listen, Bertha," he pleaded. "I didn't have a choice. He told me if I didn't go along with his plan he would have us both shipped back to England. I figured it was just one night, and you would wake up refreshed and OK this morning."

"Well I didn't, did I?" Bertha snapped at Bert. "I have a major migraine and you betrayed me."

Helena sat silent and watched the two of them go at each other. Helena felt fine this morning since she wasn't drugged or hungover. "Enough you two!" I yelled, loud enough to shut them up. "I don't care who drugged who and who knew. We need to get back to the woman who was held captive in this house. Do any of you know when your boss took off earlier this morning and where he went?"

Blank stares all around after I asked them. It was at that moment a door opened at the back of the kitchen. Judy stormed in with her gun in her hand, ready to fire. "Hold off, Judy," I hollered.

"John, are you okay?" She called, out of breath.

"Yes, I'm fine, so you can put that gun away."

She looked around the kitchen table at the three strangers and asked what on earth was going on. I explained and said, "We're just about to get to Axel taking off with Ruth Ann and find out where they went."

"Ruth Ann?" asked Helena. "That's your friend who's missing?"

"Yes," I replied. "Now, do any of you know where they disappeared to?"

Helena shook her head violently and said, "No." Bert and Bertha Angstrom looked at each other and didn't say a word. I called them out and said, "I saw the looks exchanged. Now why don't you tell me what they were for?"

Bert looked at Bertha and she looked back at him. "One of you, do it now!" shouted Judy as she went and stood behind Ms. Angstrom.

"Fine," she snapped. "I was under the influence of drugs and alcohol, but Bert here gave me a brief rundown of what happened to the lady as we came down here this morning." Bert popped up out of his chair as Judy shoved him back in it. "Speak, now," she demanded.

"After we brought Ruth Ann, that's her name correct?" I nodded. "OK, after Finn brought her inside, Mr. Eklund ordered me to pack a suitcase for him. We went up to the master bedroom and Finn lay Ruth Ann down on his bed. I went into the closet and pulled out the large suitcase and packed his clothing and toiletries."

"How many clothes did you pack?" Judy questioned. "I mean was it for a long trip or a short one?"

"I can tell you exactly what I packed if you need to know, but I would guess it was at least a couple weeks' worth of clothing."

"Was Ruth Ann conscious at all at this point?"

"No, she was asleep on his bed. Mr. Eklund and Finn talked to themselves for a short time then Finn left the room. I only heard a few words of the conversation since I spent most of my time in his closet."

"What did you hear?" I demanded.

"Fuel the jet for the long flight over, and telephone to the house for the staff to get it ready for him and a couple guests."

"So let me get this straight," Judy said. "This Mr. Eklund, aka Axel, wanted Finn to make sure their jet was fueled up for a long trip and that when they arrived at their destination they were to go on to another one of Axel's homes where he has a different staff. He was to phone them and prepare the staff for him and a couple other guests to stay at his home? Is that correct?"

"Yes," Bert answered. "But don't ask me where, because I have no idea."

"Are you aware of other homes your boss owns?" I asked.

"Well, yes, he has several," Ms. Angstrom replied for Bert. "He has this estate here and one in New York, but I think that's just a condo. He also has homes in the south of France, Rome, and Sweden."

"Did you say *Sweden*?" I asked.

"Yes, he's from there originally, I believe."

Bert sarcastically said, "You could've figured that out by name "Axel Eklund"!"

Judy gave him a knock on his back with her gun, and as he

turned to rise she shoved him back down saying, "Don't be stupid! Any more sly remarks and this gun will be knocking you unconscious, got it?"

Bert rubbed the top of his back with his hand and didn't say a word. "Let's get back to the home in Sweden," I said, trying to get back on track. "What do any of you know about it and where is it?"

Bert said, "I know he has homes, but I haven't been privileged to learn where they are yet. I was hoping in time to visit them with him, since I'm his butler."

"OK, Bert, after you finished packing, what happened next?" I inquired.

"He excused me and I went downstairs to get the limousine ready. He said they were going to leave shortly and I was to drive them to a private airstrip just outside of Grand Junction where he keeps his plane."

"He has his own plane?" Judy inquired.

"Yes, he travels all over the world, so he prefers to travel privately. I waited in the foyer for Mr. Eklund and Finn, who was now carrying Ruth Ann, to arrive. We went to the limousine, but Mr. Eklund told me I was to stay here and go have a drink. Finn was going to take them to the plane."

"So they just left and you went where?" I asked.

"I went upstairs to my room and found the bottle next to my bed and poured myself a drink, then another one or two. I woke up this morning pretty out of it. Finn probably put something in mine, too."

"Poor you," Bertha said with a sarcastic tone in her voice.

Another thought popped in my head about Bertha, Bertha Angstrom. I had to see her reaction to my next question. "Bertha?" I wanted her to look directly at me when I asked, "You're Swedish too, aren't you?"

"What does that matter?"

"Just answer his question," Judy ordered.

"Yes, I was born in Stockholm, Sweden. Two loving parents, who both were killed in a car accident when I was just 18 years old, raised me. I ended up having to take a job to support my two younger brothers. I left Sweden in my late twenties and found a job in London with the elderly gentleman we already told you about.

Does that answer your question?"

"Part of it," I replied. "Do you have any connection with the Eklund family from Stockholm?"

"I never said they were from Stockholm, Bert did," she said, realizing I was trying to get her to slip up. "But their estate is just outside of Stockholm and everyone knew the family because they were very wealthy. I didn't know him personally."

"What about other family members?" I inquired.

"That was years ago, I'm pretty sure we didn't run around in the same circles. My family was poor, and after my parents died we were even poorer, if that's possible. However, we were never homeless. I was able to make enough money to get my brothers through school. Luckily, I just had to pay for our lodging and necessities since in Sweden school is paid for by the government."

"What happened to your brothers?" Judy asked.

"They're still in Stockholm," Bertha answered. "They're in their forties with careers of their own."

"Did they ever marry?" Judy asked. "Any kids?"

"No, they didn't marry," Bertha, replied coolly. "They were too busy with their own lives and were always a bit selfish, if you ask me."

"Do you still keep in contact with them?" I asked curiously. Since they were in Sweden, maybe Ms. Angstrom's more involved than I originally assumed.

"Why the third degree about my family?" Bertha asked, becoming frustrated. I didn't answer but awaited her response. She rolled her eyes and admitted, "Yes, once in a while. Mr. Eklund has been very kind to let me call them from here without charging me." Of course he has, I thought. How strange that these different pieces of a puzzle were starting to come together. It couldn't be a coincidence that Bertha's from Sweden and she has brothers who live and work in Sweden, too.

"So you have two brothers that aren't married and live in Stockholm?" I asked to verify. "You didn't mention what your brothers did for a living."

"They own a couple of pawn shops," Bertha answered. "It's not a respectable career in my opinion. That's why I don't talk about them."

"Pawn shops?" I asked curiously, as Judy realized what this

could mean. "So they take in other people's merchandise and hold on to it for a time or sell it, correct?"

"I guess so," Bertha replied. "I don't get involved in their business.

Judy was about to go at Bertha when I cleared my throat and stopped her. "Let's get back to your boss, shall we?"

"I'd like to get on with my work this morning. How much more time do you need from us? Helena has several bedrooms to make up and this kitchen to clean." Helena gave Bertha a nasty look and stood up to start on the kitchen. I let her go to the sink since I wasn't too concerned with her. The suspicious ones were still sitting at the table barking out orders to Helena and requesting more coffee. Bertha wanted aspirin for her headache, so she asked me to hurry up and finish.

"As of this moment, Ms. Angstrom, you're not in charge. Do you understand me?" Judy demanded. Bertha snarled and nodded, while Bert was disinterested in all of us. He sat at the table eating another pastry and sipping his coffee. He admitted that without his employer in the house, he wasn't too busy.

"So," I began again. "All you know is that your employer and Finn took Ruth Ann to an undisclosed airstrip and were flying out of the country."

"We told you, Bert heard him say to fuel it up for a long trip, he never said out of the country. Maybe he went to New York?" Bertha stated.

"Let's assume he did leave the country," I said. "Judy, I need you to call this in and see if there was a flight plan on Eklund's plane." Judy stepped out of the kitchen to make her call. I told the other two they could go about their business, but not to leave the house. Bert didn't move an inch and Bertha took off toward the stairs leading up.

"She didn't hesitate to leave, did she?" Helena asked as she cleared the cups off the kitchen table. "I'd watch her, maybe she went to warn someone."

"Why would you say that?" Bert asked her, while I watched.

"She seems very bitter this morning and she might be calling her brothers as we speak to warn them."

I asked her, "Why do you think she needs to warn her brothers?"

"It's just my opinion, but after watching what went down here you and that detective lady seem awfully interested in her brothers' business. Ms. Angstrom admitted she didn't care for their business, so maybe they've done something wrong and she's warning them."

"Very intuitive," I said to Helena. "Why don't you just go and find her and let me know? I'll wait here for you."

Helena took off her rubber gloves and hurried out of the kitchen. Bert laughed and said, "Trying to get that girl to play detective, now? She's as dumb as a rock! All this stuff happens right under her nose and she doesn't have a clue. She sees a woman being carried out of here unconscious and she turns the other way!"

"Look who's talking?" I snapped. "You helped your boss take an unconscious woman out of here and actually drove them to her house. Not once, but twice you went along with your boss."

"But I knew he wasn't a good man. Helena chose to keep her head down and ignore what was going on here. My plan is to always know what's going on, and if I have to go along with his inappropriate actions then I will, but I keep mental notes of everything."

"Let me get this straight," I said. "You know he's a criminal, but if he asks you to go along with him you will, but you tell yourself you're not liable since you're just following orders?"

"Exactly," he cried out, rather loudly. "I never said I was a perfect gentleman. I worked for a crotchety old man back in England and he groomed me into being a true, nosy butler."

"What did your previous employer die of again?" I asked suspiciously. Maybe Bert and Bertha did the old guy in and came here knowing exactly who they wanted to work for. Bertha came from Sweden and her brothers own a pawnshop. I wouldn't put it past them if they, at one point, held Ruth Ann's necklace in their greedy paws.

"Old age," he said. "I already told you that."

"How old was he?"

"Over 90," he said. "Is that good enough for you or do you suspect Bertha and I killed him?"

"One more sarcastic comment and I'm throwing you in jail," I threatened. "In fact, that's exactly where you and Bertha are going until I check out your alibis, and past involvement with your 'old man' employer that died of 'old' age."

"You have nothing to arrest me for," Bert stated.

"Are you sure about that?" I argued. "Let's begin with accessory to kidnapping and I could even throw an attempted murder charge on you."

"What? I didn't try and kill anyone. All I did was drive the limousine under my employer's orders."

"And what about the two murders so far?" I pressured him on.

"What two murders? I don't know anything about any murders."

"Your boss murdered a guard and Mr. Jeffrey Toggles who was following orders just like you did. But Mr. Toggles failed to complete his task. Is that what you want to happen to you?"

"No I don't," Bert cried, changing his tone from sarcastic to cooperative. "I don't want to go to jail either. What can I do to stay out of jail?"

"Finally, I got your attention."

"Please, Chief," Bert pleaded. "I can't go to a jail cell. I won't survive in one of them."

"We're going to take a drive into town and take your statements. I'll decide what to do with the three of you after everything checks out. My main goal right now is to find out where your boss has taken Ruth Ann."

Judy walked into the kitchen and said that Lou and Dave were looking into the flight plan. "We need to bring these three back to the station with us now. I want to get on this right away. The plane could be over the Atlantic Ocean by now."

Judy said quietly to me, "You think they're headed to Stockholm, don't you?"

"I'd bet my badge on it! But why do they need to go all the way over there? It's not like Ruth Ann can lead them somewhere, she's never been there as far as I'm aware."

"Maybe Ruth Ann hasn't told you all about her past before you met her," Judy stated.

"No way, she's been here for over twenty years. Before that she was married with two small children living in California."

"I'm not saying she's lying about her past, John."

"I know things are spiraling out of control, Judy. There have been too many curveballs with this case. It started with Doug receiving a family heirloom, and all he was supposed to do was to give it to Ruth Ann. But that Swedish lawyer included the note disclosing the necklace's violent history, and all the people trying to get their greedy hands on it. This is insane."

Judy went to look for Helena and Bertha Angstrom, and I led Bert out the front door. The police car was there and soon Judy came out with her two people. "Judy, you sit in back between the two women and Bert will sit up front with me. Don't try any funny stuff while we're on the move. We'll be at the station in about twenty minutes."

"Don't we get a phone call or something?" Bertha questioned.

"You're not under arrest, as of yet," Judy said. "We just want to ask a few more questions and check out your stories. If everything comes out clean, I'm sure you'll be back here before long. That's if you all cooperate.

"And if we don't?" snapped Bertha.

"Stop it, Bertha!" Bert snarled. "Enough, if you don't answer all their questions to their satisfaction we'll be thrown in a jail cell. You know I can't be put in one of those."

"Why?" Helena meekly asked.

"He's afraid to be in a closed space," Bertha answered. Obviously divulging a secret Bert didn't want disclosed. He looked like he was going to burst and attack his friend Bertha for saying that.

"Why?" Helena asked again. "Did something happen to you?"

"Yes," Bert replied before Bertha could tell his story. "When I was a young lad in England my father would throw me in a narrow cupboard in the kitchen when I misbehaved. It was dark and small and I couldn't breathe very well. Ever since then I've been terrified of enclosed spaces."

"Well let's make sure you don't have to be put into one," Judy said, smirking.

"What I don't understand, Bert, is why would you knowingly break the law then?"

"Because I didn't think I was breaking any laws by just doing the driving."

"Accessory, ever hear of that?" Judy responded loudly.

Chapter 17

RUTH ANN

I awoke in a large, luxurious bed. I could barely sit up to see where I was, but I forced myself to sit upright and have a look around. I couldn't tell if it was night or day because the curtains were drawn and there was no light seeping in from the windows. There was a dim light coming from an open door off to my right. I swung my legs over the side of the bed and tried to stand up. I was very unsteady, that I knew, but I had to try. I held on to the bed for a step or two and headed toward the light.

I entered a small bathroom. I went over to the sink and splashed cold water on my face, and that's when I saw my reflection in the mirror. I almost scared myself! My hair was a mess and someone must have changed my clothes and put me into a flannel nightgown. I noticed that an assortment of toiletries had been laid out for me on the counter. There was a toothbrush and toothpaste that I dove in and used. I had a terrible taste in my mouth. There was shampoo and even a nice supply of makeup. It wasn't my makeup, but it was an expensive brand in unopened containers.

I wanted to take a shower and get myself dressed and cleaned up. Then I would get out of this room and find out where I was. I felt perkier after splashing water over my face, so I walked into the bedroom and flipped on a switch on the wall. The room lit up and I looked around for some of my own belongings. I found the small suitcase I had packed in a corner. I grabbed it and took out some clothes.

After I was showered, I walked to the door and tried to open it. It was locked. I was trapped in this bedroom. I bent over and looked at the knob to see if there was a key in the door, but no luck. I banged on the door and called for someone to let me out. After a few tries I turned and decided to search my room. It was large, darkly decorated bedroom. It looked very masculine, and I wondered if I was back in the house Axel owned. It wasn't familiar to me, but the house had several rooms.

There was a cherry wood six-drawer dresser with a mirror attached to it and I checked out each drawer. There were linens and towels in most of the drawers. I entered a huge walk-in closet and it was empty. I couldn't find anything that would help me get out of this room. All I could do was make a lot of noise in hope that someone would hear me.

I must have banged on the door for a solid ten minutes before I heard a key inserted into the lock from the other side of the door. I stepped back and waited to see who was going to open the door. I didn't have access to anything that could be used as a weapon, so I told myself to stay strong and wait and see what would happen.

A large woman dressed as a housekeeper opened the door and told me to follow her. I tried asking where she was taking me, but I had the hardest time understanding her. She had a thick accent, Scandinavian I believe, but she stopped answering my questions about where we were going after I had to ask her to repeat herself several times. We walked down a long hallway and I counted eight other doors besides the one I was in. She led me to the end of the hall, and we went down a flight of stairs that ended on a landing. From the landing we could go in two directions. One set of stairs led down on a narrow set of wooden stairs. The other stairs, going up, were wide and carpeted, with ornately carved, wooden spindles on the railing. We descended on the wooden, narrow staircase, not the ornate one.

At the bottom of the stairs the housekeeper grabbed my arm and told me to wait here a moment. If I had known where I was, and where a door was I probably would've made a run for it. But after being drugged for I don't know how long, I didn't think I would do very well running anywhere.

I was standing in a small room; a butler's pantry I would call it. There was a swinging door on the other end of the room that I could only guess led to a kitchen. The housekeeper was only gone a short time when she beckoned for me to follow her. We entered the kitchen, and there sat Axel on a stool, at a very massive, white marble island.

The brightness of the kitchen temporarily blinded me. It was daytime, and the sun shone through the many windows of the kitchen.

"Come and sit down next to me, Ruth Ann," he said, motioning me over.

"Where are we?" I asked, knowing this wasn't the same kitchen we had been in previously.

"Ah, you noticed the change," he said smiling at me.

"This isn't the same house I was in earlier. Are we in one of the other houses on your estate?"

"Not exactly," he said. "This is my home, yes, but not anywhere near the place you visited before."

"I don't exactly call kidnapping me the same as me visiting your house."

"The first time you came to my home, you and your friend, Paul, did come voluntarily," he reminded me.

"Yes, but we didn't make it out of my car before your goons grabbed us and took us as your prisoners. Then you drugged me and brought me back to my house, only to drug me again and bring me...wherever we are now?" I forgot about Paul, where was Paul right now? "Axel, is Paul here, too?"

"Nope," he replied, picking up a white porcelain teacup and sipping the hot beverage inside. "He's back at my other place, and I would guess that right about now your police chief is discovering him."

"I never told him how to get in your secret room in the basement. Paul could die if nobody finds him."

"Trust me, he won't die, and I happen to know they'll find him and he'll be taken care of."

"But how do I know you're telling me the truth? You've killed before."

"I admitted to the unfortunate demise of Mr. Toggles, so why would I lie about your friend, Paul? He'll be fine."

I had no choice but to believe him and go along with him for now. "Thank you."

"Please eat something," Axel requested as I eyed a plate of eggs, bacon, and toast. "It's delicious after such a long trip. You must be ravenous."

"Long trip?" I asked.

"You were asleep most of the time, so you would have no idea how long we've been gone."

"You mean I was drugged," I reminded him again. "Are you going to give in to my curiosity and tell me where we are?"

"Of course, I want your stay to be as comfortable as possible," Axel said, smiling at me in such an innocent manner. "We are just outside of Stockholm."

"*Sweden*?" I asked, shocked.

"Yes," he answered. "Now, before I say anymore, I need you to eat and then you can meet me in this house's library." Axel hopped off his stool and left the kitchen. "Inga, look after our guest. When she's finished eating, bring her to me." She nodded and shoved my plate of food a little closer to me.

Axel was right about one thing, I was starving. I picked up my fork and dove into the eggs. I didn't think he would continue drugging me, so I ate it all. Inga took my plate and put it into the sink and told me to follow her. She was a large, homely woman of about sixty or so. I followed behind her as we exited the kitchen and went into the foyer of the house. It felt oddly similar to his other home. A large, grand foyer and staircase with a living and dining room off the foyer and a set of wooden doors that led into his library.

Axel was sitting behind his desk in the library and a roaring fire was warming the otherwise cold room. The opened drapes allowed the sun to shine in, and I could tell from the view that we were out in the middle of nowhere. Escaping could be difficult. There was snow covering the ground and that's when it really hit me that we're not in Deer Creek anymore, unless we got several inches of snow in the last day.

Axel noticed me staring out the windows and said, "So now you believe me? We're in Sweden and not your little town anymore."

"Yes, this is definitely not Deer Creek," I said, walking over to his desk. "But I don't understand why I'm here."

"In due time," he said. "I'm waiting for another person to arrive and then we'll get to the bottom of your missing necklace."

"Who?" I asked. "Who's coming here?"

"Don't you worry about who. There's been a slight delay, but I'll get it worked out right away." Axel said, as he grabbed his cell phone and walked toward the library doors.

"Wait, where are you going?" I called out to him. Just as he left, Inga walked back in and stood at the doorway with her arms crossed, barring me from leaving.

Chapter 18

JOHN WILKINSON

Once back at the police station, I had Judy take them to the inter-rogation room. I wanted to speak with Lou and see if he had in-formation regarding Eklund's flight plan. "Yes, I got the infor-mation you asked for."

"So tell me, where did they fly?" I asked.

"It's kind of crazy," Lou answered. "First, they flew to a pri-vate airstrip outside of New York City. They were there only an hour or so, then took off across the pond and ended up in London. But they didn't stay there either. I found fuel receipts that verified the plane refueled and took off for Paris, then on to Stockholm."

"My guess is that they were buying time, thinking we would spend a while in each of those locations. But it wasn't difficult for you to figure out, so why did he play that game?"

"The flight plan ended in New York, sir," Dave answered for Lou. "If Lou didn't dig a little deeper, we wouldn't know they were over in Sweden."

"But how can they not file a plan with the FAA?" I asked.

"I'm sure he knew someone or figured another way around the rules," Lou replied.

"Judy's in the interrogation room with our three guests from Eklund's house. I'd like to question them apart, then together. I want to see if any of them slip up. I thought at first Bert, the butler was suspicious, but now I'm leaning toward the housekeeper, Ber-tha Angstrom."

"What about the maid, Helena?" Lou inquired.

"I think she's just a maid," I answered. "She figured out some shady stuff was going on once she started working at the house, but besides that, I believe she's innocent."

Dan and I walked into the interrogation room and what I saw stunned me. Judy was on the floor, unconscious, and Bert and Helena were gagged and tied to their chairs. Bertha was nowhere to be found. I ran over to Judy and found a lump on her head, but no other injuries from what I could see. "Judy, Judy, wake up?" I called, grabbing her shoulders and trying to sit her up.

It took a few tries, but she finally opened her eyes and tried to stand. "Stay put, Judy," I said, holding her down. "You had a blow to your head and you need to stand slowly."

She touched the back of her head and felt a huge lump. "What on earth happened to me?"

"It appears you were duped by Bertha," Lou replied, almost grinning.

I noticed Bert and Helena were shaking their heads forcefully. I walked over to both of them and pulled the gags out of their mouths. At once they cried out, "Bertha didn't do that to her!"

"Excuse me?" Judy questioned. "If it wasn't Bertha, then who hit me?"

"Judy," I asked her, astonished. "Don't you remember what happened right before?"

"No, I'm a bit fuzzy," she replied, rubbing her head.

"I can tell you," Bert interrupted. "She was looking down at those papers on the table when another man entered and took out his gun and hit her over the back of her head."

"What man?" I demanded.

"He had a police uniform on," Helena said. "It was a man, dark, tall, in his thirties I would guess."

"Bert, is that what you saw?" I asked.

"Yes, a man about six feet tall, maybe 225 lbs., dark hair and eyes, wearing a police uniform came in and we didn't think much of it. Judy didn't seem surprised by him, but she was looking down. The next thing I saw, he took his gun out and whacked her on the head."

"Sir," Dave said, clearing his throat to get my attention "Do you think someone's working here wearing a bogus uniform?"

"That's exactly what we need to figure out," I demanded. I took Lou out of the room and left Dave there, but with the door open. I didn't want any more accidents in this room.

"Dan," I said quietly. "We need to investigate everyone I hired from other stations to help us out. Do you notice anyone missing?" I looked around the station room and Lou walked around the whole place. I didn't want to leave the interrogation room doorway. I saw Judy sitting on a chair now and looking more herself. I suggested Doc Albert check her out, but she declared she would be fine. "Just a big lump," she answered, embarrassed that someone could fool her so easily.

Dan came back over to me and said, "Sorry to tell you this Chief, but there's one man missing."

"Who?" I demanded immediately.

"The sergeant from Tinker's Cove."

"Sergeant Royce?" I inquired. "Did you notice him here earlier?"

"Yes, he was just on front desk duty and now he's nowhere to be found. I checked everywhere, even the bathroom and storage rooms."

"Great, just great," I yelled in aggravation. "I'm going to call over to Tinker's Cove and see if they can fill me in on him."

I told Lou to stand guard outside the room and make sure Judy was still doing OK. I hurried into my office and called over to the chief at Tinker's Cove. When this case started I was short of men and called some local stations for help. I was happy that about a half dozen men came into the station and helped with the work here and at the hospital. Sergeant Royce had been here from the beginning and seemed like a professional. Why would he grab Bertha and run? The only conclusion could be that Eklund used him as an inside guy, and it worked to his favor once the three staff members started yapping about Eklund's activities. But why take only Bertha? It had to do with her and her brothers from Stockholm. I felt it in my gut; they all are involved with the missing necklace and Ruth Ann's disappearance.

I walked back into the interrogation room and told Judy, Lou and Dave that the chief never heard of a sergeant Royce. We concluded that when the other men came into our station, this fake cop just added himself to the roster and we didn't check him out. What a horrible, fatal mistake that was.

"What's going to happen to us?" Helena asked, terrified that some harm was going to come to her.

I took my staff to the side and we had a mini conference. "This is what's going to happen. I'm going to Stockholm and one of you is coming with me. The other two have to hold the fort down here.

I feel quite safe that all the dangerous participants have fled the area now, so there shouldn't be any more problems here in town."

"I'll go," Judy offered right away. "Dan and Dave know this town and can keep things running smoothly. I'm a detective and can handle these guys. They got the best of me two times now, but never again."

"Judy, I'll take you," I said, but Lou protested.

"Sir, with all due respect, Judy's been drugged and hit on the head. Is she the best candidate to have your back?"

Judy glared over at Lou, but before he could speak I diffused the situation. "Judy had no idea Sergeant Royce was a dual agent and neither did you two. Also, she has a point, you two are familiar with this town and the people here know you. I don't know how long I'll be gone, and I need to keep things as normal as possible. All I want to hear about is traffic tickets and nothing else while I'm gone!"

Dave didn't say a word. He was still considered a rookie, but Lou's nose was clearly out of joint. I tried to explain that he would be in charge and that seemed to help his ego. "Fine," Lou agreed.

"We need to get moving," I said.

"What about us?" Bert called out.

"Yes," I said, forgetting about the two of them. "I'm going to let you both go back to your boss's house and wait there. Nobody's around and it should be quiet. Use the time to look for another position on the computer. I have a feeling you won't be working for Eklund anymore."

"I'll end up back at the shelter!" Helena cried out. "I don't want to live there, not after living in such a wonderful house."

Judy told her, "Don't worry, Helena, We'll find you something around town here. I'm sure the chief will help you find work here, too."

"Definitely," I said. "I know everyone here in town, and we'll get you a job as soon as I return. Go back to the house and enjoy the peace and quiet."

Bert didn't ask for our assistance. From his advanced age, I assumed he was close to retirement and was ready to move on somewhere far away from here. Judy called and got us flights to Stockholm. It was late afternoon and we were lucky that we were able to catch a red-eye flight out of Grand Junction through Denver then on to New York. From there it was a non-stop flight to Sweden. We should be there in about twenty-four hours.

"Go pack a bag Judy. I'm going home to do the same." I turned to Lou and told him I would be back in an hour or so, and to go over everything he may need while I was gone.

I decided to make one more stop before I headed home to pack. I drove over to the hospital to talk with Doc Albert, then Doug, Ben, and Paul, the guard. "Hi Doc," I said, walking into his office.

"Haven't seen you around here much," Doc said. "Your guard Paul is healing nicely. May have to keep him here a couple days for observation."

"That's good," I replied. "How are the other two patients?"

"Ben is content. In fact, I think he believes he's at a resort or spa here. He's happy all the time. Doug, on the other hand, is ready to break out of here and tell you a thing or two."

"That's what I'm here for. If Doug's healed, he can resume work at the bank. Ben too, he can be released and go back to work for Richard and Carol over at the resort."

"Really?"

"Yes, that's why I'm here. The people who were causing all the trouble have fled the country and I'm going after them. I'll be gone for a few days or so."

"What about Ruth Ann?" Doc asked, concerned. "Is she going with you?"

"Not exactly," I responded. "I can't tell you too much, but know this, she'll be home safe soon."

"She's already gone?" Doc exclaimed, giving me an alarming glare. "Are you telling me that these killers have Ruth Ann?"

"Doc, I can't tell you. I have no reason to believe she's been harmed. She's only being held because they think she can help retrieve that necklace."

Doc stood up from behind his desk and looked furious. "Go get her and bring her back."

"That's the plan. So, can you release Doug and Ben?"

"They'll be home before dinner."

I left Doc's office and went to Doug's room. Before he could unleash his anger on me, I told him he was going home today. I didn't want to tell him anything, but that didn't work. He was furious with me for letting Ruth Ann get kidnapped. I assured him these guys would pay for it dearly and Ruth Ann would be home soon.

I poked my head in Ben's room and Doc was right. Ben was in there, happy as can be, watching TV laughing away. However, unlike Doug, Ben wasn't too happy about going home. "I'm scared they'll come after me again," he said.

"They won't," I assured him. "They have left town and you'll be safe."

I told him I would have my men come and check on him regularly until he felt secure. He was thrilled he could go back and work at the resort. Ben felt safe there and wanted to make some money so he could better himself. I told him that was terrific and maybe he could settle down here and start a career. Maybe become the town handyman. He was happy about that, so I took my leave and went home to pack.

Within a few hours, Judy and I were on a plane to Denver.

Chapter 19

RUTH ANN

I waited in the kitchen for some time with Inga, the housekeeper, keeping watch over me. Finally, Axel walked into the kitchen. "I'm glad to see that you ate your breakfast."

"I need my strength," I replied. "Where did you go? Did the other person you were waiting for arrive?"

"She'll be here soon," he answered. "Until then, you may go wherever you want, as long as you stay inside this house."

"You trust me to stay here?" I asked, surprised.

"I'm not a fool, Ruth Ann. I have cameras all over this house and a full staff to make sure you don't leave."

"Oh," I said, not knowing what to make of my freedom here. But I was thrilled that I would be able to investigate the house where I'm being held prisoner. Maybe I'd find a way out, even if it took a while.

Axel left the kitchen, but told me that when his other guest arrives, we'll all meet again. Until then, I was on my own. I hopped off the stool and went toward the kitchen door as Inga watched my every move. I entered into the foyer and walked toward the front door. Inga was standing at the door to the kitchen and said, "Do not go outside."

"I'm just looking out the window."

She turned around and disappeared back into the kitchen. I looked outside the window on the side of the front door. Snow covered most of the driveway, and from where I stood I could see no other homes around. We were in the woods, like in Deer Creek.

I decided to go into each room on all the floors. Axel didn't give me any restrictions, except to not go outside. I had time to kill and didn't want to be cooped up in a bedroom. The nearest room from the front entrance was the living room. It was a large, rectangular shaped room with massive windows on the front wall. There was a grand piano in the corner near the window. The room was warm, almost welcoming, which surprised me. It was a room that I would've said a woman decorated, with the bright colors and floral couches. There were several armchairs around the room and it had an inviting atmosphere. Next was the dining room. It was another large room, but the windows were now on the side wall. In the center, was an enormous dark wood table with twenty chairs around it. The crystal chandelier over the table was just my style, and I would love to have that in my shop back home. I walked to the other end of the room and through the door. I was back in the butler's pantry, where I could go into the kitchen or up the back staircase. I chose to go up and not back to Inga.

The second floor is where I stayed earlier. There were nine rooms up there, and I was put into one of them. As I walked along the hall, I noticed the other doors were locked. I didn't know why they would be locked, but they were. I was at the very end of the hall, near my room, and noticed another door that I missed before. I reached to turn the knob and found the door unlocked. I opened it very slowly and was surprised to find another set of stairs that led up.

Axel never told me not to go in certain areas of the house, so I decided to explore where the stairs led. It was a dimly lit wooden staircase that was quite narrow. I went up about fifteen stairs and came to another closed door. I figured it would be locked, but I was wrong. I opened the door and found myself in the attic. A massive bedroom had been constructed up there.

It also appeared someone was currently occupying this room, too. "Hello?" I asked, wondering if there was someone in there I couldn't see. No answer, so I tried calling out again. Whoever was staying in this room wasn't in there now. I probably should close the door and go back downstairs, but my curiosity got the better of me. I entered the room and knew immediately that it was a woman's bedroom. I walked smack dab into the middle of the room, and found it curious that a woman would be hidden up here.

A king size bed was next to me in the middle of the room, and the linens were all messed up. The floral comforter was folded and put at the end of the bed. The lighting up here was minimal because there were only a few tiny windows covered in pink, sheer curtains. I leaned on the bed post and looked around the rest of the room. There were several old wooden chests, a large antique dresser that I would also love to have in my shop, and a set of wooden rockers underneath one of the windows. Just as I was heading over to the dresser to take a peek inside the drawers, I heard the door creak open and there stood Inga, glaring at me.

"What are you doing in here?" she demanded. "You aren't allowed up here."

"Axel never told me to stay away from any particular part of the house. Only that I couldn't go outside."

"He wouldn't want you up here. Go now!" She ordered, and walked over to me and tried to grab my arm.

I pulled back and told her, "NO!"

"Don't make me hurt you," Inga demanded. "Mr. Eklund told me to keep you under control, and if you didn't obey me, I must forcibly make you."

"Fine," I stammered. "I'll leave here under one condition. Tell me who lives up in this room." Inga remained silent. "I can tell it's a woman. Maybe it's his mother or sister or even his wife?"

"It is none of your concern. We go now," she said, and got ahold of my arm this time and pulled me back down the stairs. She left me on the second floor and turned and locked the door to the attic, and put the key in her apron pocket. I knew there was more to this than she was allowed to tell me. I decided to go find Axel and ask him.

I headed back down the main staircase and into the foyer again. I marched over to the library, but the doors were shut. I was about to reach up and knock when a voice stopped me. "You can't go in there."

I turned and found a middle-aged man dressed in a black suit and tie with a stark white shirt. "I need to speak with Mr. Eklund."

"You can't go in there right now, He's busy."

"Is he alone or is someone else in there with him?"

"That, Madame, is none of your business," he declared with an air of arrogance.

"I'll tell him you're looking for him. May I suggest you wait in the living room and I can bring you a cup of tea?"

"Yes," I said. "That would be nice." He led me into the living room, and I chose to sit in an emerald green wingback chair near the front window. It was adjacent to the grand piano and it allowed me to look outside to watch for the 'guest' Axel was waiting for, unless the guest was already in the library.

The butler returned with my tea and I thanked him. I wanted to stay on as many people's good side as I could, just in case I might need a favor in the future. I sat and drank my tea and watched the front drive. I didn't want to miss anyone who may come or go.

Shortly after I finished my cup of tea, I heard the doors to the library open. I hopped out of the chair and peeked around the open entrance from the living room into the foyer. The library was across the foyer and I saw Axel and another man talking as they walked toward the front door. "Just keep her as comfortable as possible. I'm not sure how much longer we can keep her going," the man said to Axel.

"I will, doctor, thank you for coming here again, and for giving her the best care under these circumstances."

"I wish there was more I could do, but we'll make sure she's as comfortable as possible. Good day," the doctor said, as he left through the front door.

Axel started to walk toward the library but changed direction and headed to where I was standing. I hurried back to the chair and grabbed my empty teacup. "Ah," Axel said. "You're in here. I thought I heard a noise or two coming from this direction."

"Yes," I said. "Your butler brought me a cup of tea while I waited for you."

"You want to see me?" he asked curiously. "My other guest hasn't arrived yet, but it should be soon."

"That's not what I wanted to speak with you about." I waited for him to respond, but he quietly walked over to the matching chair next to mine and sat down. He looked to me as if he was strained, almost weak. I don't know the man very well, but he always came across as very polished and confident. I looked at him closely and noticed he wasn't as young as I originally thought, maybe closer to his mid to late sixties. His gray hair was well maintained and quite thick. He had dark circles under his eyes, like a person who hadn't slept in a while. I had the feeling it didn't even have to do with me, but that another situation was challenging him.

Axel took a deep breath and sat up straight and asked, "What can I help you with?"

"I was looking around your house and discovered a secret set of stairs off the second floor. They appear to lead to an attic, but," I was promptly stopped.

"That door is off limits to you." Then he added, "And the door's supposed to be locked."

"But it wasn't and you told me I could go wherever I wanted to as long as I didn't go outside."

"Wait, I know why it wasn't locked," he said to himself, but loudly enough for me to hear. He looked directly into my eyes and told me it was none of my business.

"But who lives up there?" I asked. "You have a woman stashed in your attic!"

"Leave it alone," he demanded, and stood up and left. I wanted to follow him, but the tone in his voice told me I wasn't going to get another bit of information out of him. Actually, I hadn't gotten any information from him. Obviously, there was another secret in this house besides me.

I watched him go back into his library and slam the door. I leaned back in my chair, and was about to close my eyes when I heard a noise coming from outside. I stood up and walked up to the window and saw a large black limousine pull up and an older woman got out of the back. She walked up to the front door, and the mysterious butler appeared out of nowhere and opened the door for her. "Is he in the library?" she demanded. The butler nodded and led her to the closed doors. He didn't knock, just opened the door and let the woman in.

I rushed out into the foyer before the butler could disappear and caught up with him, just as he was going back into the kitchen. "Wait," I called out. "Please, can you tell me who that woman was that just went to see your employer?"

He gave me a nasty glare and said, "No, I cannot," and disappeared into the kitchen. I wasn't going to let him off that easily, so I hurried in after him. The butler wasn't alone. Inga was sitting at the kitchen table drinking a cup of coffee and asked Sherman to sit down. So that's what this butler's name is, Sherman.

They must not have noticed me at the doorway, because they started a conversation. I slowly took a step back, so I was actually in the butler's pantry. I closed the door behind me and let it stay open only an inch or so. Maybe I would overhear something of importance for me.

"Sherman, what can I get you?" Inga asked.

"Just a cup of coffee will do," Sherman said, as he sat down across from Inga at the large table. Inga stood up and grabbed a cup and saucer from the middle of the table, and poured him coffee from the carafe. "Here you go," she said, sliding the coffee across the table.

"She's here," Sherman said with a coarse tone.

"I heard the front door and figured she was back. I assume she's in with him?"

"Yes, they're in the library."

"Do you think she'll tell him anything new?" Inga questioned.

"All I've heard is that she was able to get out of that local jail and fly here fast. She needs to get ahold of her brothers so they can take the next step."

"But do they have the item or are her brothers' scamming him?" Inga asked.

"It's a risk he's willing to take. I think Bertha would scam her own siblings to help Mr. Eklund. She's quite taken by him."

"Well I hope they do something quick, I'm not sure how long Mrs. Eklund can hold out."

"I overheard the doctor tell him that all they can do for her is keep her comfortable. He's still buying it, but I don't know how much longer we can keep this up."

"Poor dear," Inga said. Really? Inga has empathy for someone? She comes off like a large, tough female, not a person who feels sorry for anyone else.

Who's Bertha I wondered? It must be the woman in the library right now. I wonder what jail freed her? They said it was in a small town. Wait! Could it be this woman came from Deer Creek, and she escaped from John at his police station?

So much was running through my head that I missed when they changed the topic to the mysterious woman who lives in the bedroom upstairs. They called her Mrs. Eklund, so was that his wife or mother? It's obvious she has some kind of condition, because they've all said that the doctor is keeping her comfortable. But where was she when I was up in the attic? If she's as sick as they think, why wasn't she in her bed? I had to get back into that attic and check it out. I knew they locked the door, but I should be able to pick it. I'd seen John do it many times.

I hurried back up the stairs to the second floor and down to the end of the hall, where the door was shut. It was still locked, so I went into my bedroom to look for a bobby pin. I always had them with me in my toiletry bag, and I found one right away. I carefully looked down the hall to make sure the coast was still clear, and put my pin in the little hole in the middle of the doorknob.

I heard a click immediately and the door was unlocked. That wasn't so difficult, I thought to myself. I'm not so sure I'd let John know that I picked up his trick. I carefully opened the door, and closed it behind me so I wouldn't be spotted. I could see a light through the door at the top of the stairs and wondered if the mysterious Mrs. Eklund was back in her bed. At the top, I wasn't so quick to open the door. I felt for the doorknob. It was loose, so I opened the door a little bit, just enough for me to look in. I saw the bed in the middle of the room, but it was still empty.

Was I mistaken about who was staying in this room? Maybe it was Bertha, and not Mrs. Eklund who occupied this room. If it was Bertha's room, I was on limited time up here. I threw open the door and rushed in, so I had a chance to search the room. What I found when I entered the room almost dropped me to my knees.

"Who are you?" A young woman spoke, terrified. I was momentarily stunned and couldn't speak. "I said, who are you and what are you doing up here? I have never seen you here before."

I needed to come up with a quick explanation and I just couldn't think of one. I was so surprised that there was someone in this room that my mind went blank. The woman standing by one of the small windows was young, maybe in her thirties at most. She was wearing a white linen nightgown and had long blonde hair that was tied in a low ponytail with a satin ribbon. "I'm sorry," I said. "I must have gone the wrong direction and gotten lost." That was all I could come up with.

"Seriously? That's all you got?" The woman said sarcastically. "There's no way you could end up here lost. There is a locked door at the bottom of the stairs you have to get through. You must have stolen a key."

"No I didn't," I stated, slipping the bobby pin in my pocket. "I was up here earlier and that housekeeper, Inga, made me leave. But you weren't here."

"No, I had a doctor's appointment and he brought me into another room to examine me."

"Oh," I said. "I overheard a little about a Mrs. Eklund, and that she's sick. Is that you?"

She looked me over and realized I must not be a part of Axel's staff and said, "Before I tell you anything, you must tell me who you are and why you're here."

I let it all spill out! "I've been kidnapped by a man named, Axel Eklund, and I live in the United States. He brought me here against my will. I've been ordered not leave the house, but I do have the freedom to roam inside."

"Wow," she said, plunking herself down on the rocking chair she was standing by.

"Are you alright?" I asked, knowing I had just dropped a bombshell on her.

"I'm fine," the woman said bitterly. "He's gone too far this time."

"Excuse me? What do you mean by that?"

"I have a feeling I know why you're here, but you can confirm that in a minute. We might not have too much time before Inga comes looking for you. I need to tell you a few things."

"Go on," I said, knowing time was precious and I wanted to gather as much information as possible.

"I am Mrs. Eklund, the second."

"What do you mean by the second?" I asked, confused.

"I'm Axel's second wife. His true love passed away a year ago and he married me on the rebound. I'm quite a bit younger than him and I used to work for him. He would always flirt with me, so I knew once his wife was gone he would want me. I didn't really want to be with him, but I didn't have much money left and he offered me quite the lifestyle, until..." she hesitated a moment and looked at me intently. "He's not a nice man you must know. He comes across confident and gentlemanly, but once you get too close, he's evil."

I was surprised this woman opened up to me so quickly. It did sound a bit rehearsed and robotic but I went along with her. "Why did you have to marry him?"

"The money, plain and simple. I came from a humble household with a mother, father, and six other siblings. My father worked several jobs just to keep food on the table and a roof over our heads. Once I was old enough to make my own money I took off. I landed this job as Axel's personal maid and he told me if I did well I could enter his business and become his assistant."

"He told you this at what age?"

"I was twenty-one when I started working here. My parents made me wait I finished my schooling. I got a degree in business, and the thought of working in Eklund's Corporation, as an assistant to the owner was a big deal around here. The Eklund name is well known in Stockholm. They're very rich. "

"Why would you start out as his maid then?"

"He told me he would have to trust me personally before professionally."

Seriously? She believed that? "Was his first wife still alive?"

"Yes, she was alive for years before she passed. It's been almost one year since she died."

"What did she die of?" I asked curiously.

"She wasn't that old, only about sixty-five, but she died of natural causes I was told."

"Didn't you think that was kind of strange?"

"Yes, but at that point I didn't question it. He was so generous and kind to me that I didn't care. His first wife was horrid. She would boss all the staff around and claim she was the one with the money and her husband married into it. She would look at me with hatred, because she knew her husband had more than just professional feelings for me."

"What was your relationship with him at that time?"

"I was still his personal maid, but he let me into many business deals, too. You could say I was half personal assistant, half personal maid."

"Did you have a relationship going while his wife was alive?"

"I don't really want to answer that," she snapped, stood up and walked over to her bed. "I need to get myself to bed before they come up and check on me."

"Wait, you don't appear too sick. Why do you have to be stuck in bed?"

"That's a really long story and we just don't have the time to talk anymore."

"But I need to know more, I've been imprisoned here and I want to go home. Can't you help me?"

"Listen, I'll give you an extra key, so when the coast is clear you can come up and we can talk more." She opened a drawer in the nightstand next to her bed and pulled out a key. "Here, take this, but don't tell anyone about me or this key. It'll just put your life in more danger. More than it already is. I'll explain later so go, please."

I took the key and started walking toward the door when I just had to ask one more question. "Are you actually sick?"

She smiled and said one word, "No." I had a feeling that was going to be her answer.

"But no one else knows that except you, me, and that doctor of yours right?" She nodded and told me to leave before I was caught. I wasn't sure what I believed, but at the moment it made for an interesting situation here.

I hurried down to the bottom of the stairs and cracked open the door. No one was visible, so I headed into the hall after re-locking the door. I went into my bedroom and shut the door. I couldn't believe what had just happened. There was another person being held hostage by Axel Eklund, but this one happens to be his 'ill' wife.

Chapter 20

JOHN WILKINSON

Twenty-four hours later Judy and I landed in Stockholm. We knew Bertha must've arrived here not too much before us. I needed to find Eklund's home and see if Ruth Ann was being held hostage there. This was getting too complicated, and I knew I should be contacting the local police, but I didn't want more complications.

I wasn't sure if Bertha was going to Eklund's home or to her brothers. She admitted they owned a pawn shop here in Stockholm. She also claimed she wasn't close to them because of their business. I had to throw all that out because it was now obvious Bertha was in on it. I knew there was more to her. She was unwilling to cooperate from the beginning.

"So now where?" asked Judy.

"We find his house and see if Ruth Ann's there. Or we could look for the brother's pawn shop that Bertha mentioned. I don't have a name for the shop, so I say we find Eklund's home. "

"Are we going to the local police here for help?" Judy inquired.

"No," I stated.

"You know we could get into trouble for not doing that," Judy commented. "But I get why you're not."

"Thanks, let's get out of the airport and find out where Eklund lives. I'll hail a cab and ask the driver if he knows where he lives. He seems to have quite the reputation around here so I'm confident people know where he resides."

We hurried out of the terminal and caught a cab. I asked if they knew where a Mr. Axel Eklund lived and the driver glared at me like I asked where the President of the United States lived.

"No, no," he said with a thick accent. "You can't go there. It's outside of the town and heavily guarded. Nobody's allowed there."

"Why?" Judy asked.

"Mr. Eklund is very private man. His family is very rich and they don't like visitors."

"How would you know that?" I asked curiously. "Do you know him?"

"Me, no," he said nervously. "Everyone around here knows not to get involved with them. They're a scary family and many bad things happen to people who deal with them."

"Seriously? Like what?" Judy asked, trying to remain patient.

"OK, let me put it this way. The family has a bad reputation for people who don't do what they want. They get rid of people. One day they just disappear and the police never do anything about it."

"Are you saying the Eklund's are a mob family?" I asked.

"No, I don't know exactly. I just know they don't mess around when it comes to business and their private lives."

"You sound like you know this personally?" I questioned. He was driving before we told him where to go. I could tell he was agitated and wished he never picked us up.

"I don't want to talk about this anymore!" he cried. "Where do you want me to take you?"

"Eklund's estate," Judy demanded. "If you can't go all the way take us as far as you can go.

"Fine," the driver said.

We didn't ask the driver any more questions but watched where we were heading. The driver flew in and out of lanes, and I could tell we were heading into downtown Stockholm. He pulled over at a large intersection and told us to get out. He told us we could easily get another cab in this area. He didn't want to have us as customers any longer. I even flashed my badge, but the guy wouldn't budge. Judy and I hopped out of the cab and wondered what happened to this guy that frightened him so much.

"Now what?" Judy asked, looking around at our predicament. "We're in the middle of a city where we don't speak the language, and we might not have much luck asking for directions to Eklund's place. He seems to have frightened most of the people around here."

"Let's go into this café and grab a bite to eat and figure this out." I said, pointing to a corner cafe.

Chapter 21

RUTH ANN

I sat on the bed and went over what had happened in the last hour. First, a doctor held a meeting in the library with Axel Eklund. Second, Axel came and spoke with me while I was sitting in the living room. He appeared tired and withdrawn, but snapped out of it when I started asking questions. Third, a woman named Bertha arrived from the United States. She was held in a small town jail and somehow escaped and came here. Fourth, and most importantly, there's another woman in a bed upstairs pretending to be sick so she can escape her life with her husband, Axel Eklund. He had a first wife who seemed to have power over him, and Axel must've been lost after she died, unless he was the one who finished her off. The mysterious woman upstairs told me that his first wife died in her sixties of natural causes. That alone seemed fishy.

I was holding onto the key the woman gave me, and caught up in my own thoughts when I heard a loud bang at my door. It startled me and I hurried to put the key into pants pocket. I wanted it with me at all times just in case I had the chance to sneak up to see her.

"Yes" I called out.

Inga opened the door and told me her boss wanted to see me in the library, and that I was to go right down. "Is he alone?" I asked Inga.

"That's none of my business," she declared. "Hurry up and go."

"Fine," I snapped back, and hopped off the bed and walked right past Inga. She followed me all the way down until I knocked on the library door. Inga ushered me inside and then disappeared toward the kitchen.

I entered the library and found Axel behind his desk, and a

woman sitting comfortably in one of the chairs in front of his desk. Axel stood up as I entered and told me to take a seat next to the woman. I did as I was told and sat down next to her. She appeared to be in her sixties with sharp facial features and gray hair, fixed into a tight bun. She had a horrible scowl on her face as she watched me sit next to her. "Hello," I said directly to her, wondering if she would answer me.

"Ruth Ann," Axel said, instead of her. "This is Bertha; she'll be helping us with the missing necklace. I want you to tell her all you know and she'll fill you in on what she knows."

I had a strong feeling I had seen Bertha before, but I couldn't put my finger on exactly where. Before I dove into the whole story, I asked her if we had met before. "That's irrelevant," she snapped.

"Bertha, please don't be rude," Axel said. "Ruth Ann has been very cooperative so far and we need her if we want to get my necklace back."

"Excuse me?" I asked. "I do believe I am owner of the necklace. Why would you think it's yours?"

"Because I paid an enormous amount of money for it and I'm now the rightful owner."

"And from whom did you buy it? I was told a lawyer here in Stockholm sent the necklace and the papers to my bank president and they clearly stated I'm the heir to the necklace. If you paid money for it, then the money should've been in my hands by now." I quickly added, "And I can assure you I have not received a large sum of money from anyone."

"That necklace has been handed back and forth from my family to your family for centuries. The last true owner was me when I paid for it."

"Who could you have paid for it? There are no other relatives except for my daughters and me." The second I said that, I regretted it.

"Did you say your daughters?" Axel asked curiously. "What do they know about this?"

"Nothing!" I cried out. "They don't even know I'm missing. Leave them alone otherwise you'll get nothing else out of me. You can kill me before I allow anyone to hurt my girls."

"I don't plan on hurting your daughters, Ruth Ann. Do you think I'm so stupid that I didn't already know you had two daughters? Let me see...they are twins, Lynne and Nancy, correct? Yes, one is a teacher and the other owns a bakery in your little town. Need I say more?"

I shook my head and decided it best to let him speak instead of me. I had a tendency to put my foot in my mouth and I didn't want to make it any worse.

"OK, let's get back to business. I have a right to the necklace, and you, Ruth Ann, are going to help me."

"But I told you I have no idea where it is. I have never even seen it. The last person to see it was Doug, the president at the bank."

Bertha didn't seem surprised at any of our conversation. "Excuse me, Bertha," I began to say. "Why do I get the feeling you know all of this?"

"Tell her," Axel snapped.

Bertha turned her attention to me and said, "I just arrived from Mr. Eklund's other home, the one where you were detained."

"That's where I saw you!" I called out. "You were there, at the other house, where Paul and I were being held. You're the housekeeper!"

"I guess that's what my position could be called."

"But why are you all the way over here and why were you in jail? Oh my, you were being held by the police in Deer Creek weren't you?"

Bertha nodded and added, "Yes, by your friend the chief and that female detective."

"Judy?" I questioned.

"Yes, Judy, she had an attitude that made me want to slap her. She has a very smart, sarcastic mouth!"

I couldn't argue with Bertha on that. "I still don't understand why you're here, and what did John arrest you for?"

"I wasn't arrested. Your friend Paul was discovered inside the house. He's fine, by the way. Your chief and Judy questioned me, Bert, who is Mr. Eklund's butler, and a naïve maid named Helena." She rolled her eyes and looked at Axel. "I never understood why you would hire someone like her. She's not smart enough to count to ten."

Axel ignored Bertha and told her to continue telling me about why they were taken to the police station. "Paul, your friend, was found in the basement and taken to the hospital. He really is fine, before you interrupt me about that. They found the three of us drugged in our beds. Mr. Eklund here felt it necessary to put a sleeping aid in our late night drinks."

"Bertha, I told you I had to do that to keep up our plan," Axel stated. "Anyway, you told me Helena discovered what I was doing and didn't take the drink. She couldn't be that stupid then, right?"

"Whatever," Bertha said. "Your chief started asking lots of questions and decided it was best to take us to the station for further questioning. That's when Mr. Eklund helped arrange to get me out."

"How did you get out?" I asked curiously.

Axel answered my question and said, "I had a little inside help at the police station."

"Are you telling me one of John's men let her go?"

"Not exactly, I had one of my men do it. He was pretending to be one of the cops helping out at the station. Enough of that, let's get back to the necklace. There have been too many distractions."

"I agree," Bertha stated. "When do we get started with our plan?"

"What plan?" I asked.

Bertha glared at me and told me I would only be allowed bits of the plan. If it were up to her I wouldn't be here at all. I still didn't understand why I was here in the first place. Axel pulled out a file folder and opened it. "The last time the necklace was seen was in Deer Creek. The bank president, Doug Albertson, was attacked and the thief took off with the necklace. Ruth Ann happened to be a witness of that crime." They both turned their attention to me.

"I didn't see much, except for a man dressed in black holding a shiny object. Our eyes met for a second and then he was gone."

"So my guess is that this man has been after you, since he thinks you're a person who can identify him," Axel said.

"Wait," I cried out. "Are you telling me that you aren't' responsible for the attacks back in Deer Creek?"

"Some yes, and some no," Bertha answered.

"I do believe Ruth Ann asked me that question," Axel barked. "I did take care of Mr. Toggles. He knew too much, so I admit to his demise. However, I had nothing to do with the attacks on the bank president and the night guard at your store."

"But your guys mishandled Ben and Paul?"

"And the little crimes of kidnapping you a couple times," he chuckled. "We only questioned Ben to see if he knew where you were and what he knew. He was pretty much worthless. You brought Paul into our business by bringing him up to my house in Colorado. I didn't have the guard at your store murdered. There was another serious injury at the bank, Tom, correct?" I nodded. "He was only hit by accident."

"Not that any of this excuses you, but now I feel a little better about helping you retrieve my necklace," I said.

"Correction, *my necklace*," retorted Axel.

"I still don't understand that. Am I allowed to hear the history of my great-great grandmother's piece of jewelry?"

"That's a terrific idea, Ruth Ann," Axel said. "Bertha, I'd like to talk privately with Ruth Ann. Why don't you go and rest for a while?"

"But…" Bertha said. "Why are you dismissing me?"

"You know it all, so go have a rest and we'll meet together soon," Axel said, and stood up. He walked around to her chair and escorted her out of the room. He asked me to join him on the couch facing the huge stone fireplace. I stood up and sat next to him on the couch.

"It's more comfortable here and the story is quite long. Would you care for a drink first or tea?"

"No I'm fine," I said, turning my body so I faced him on the couch. I didn't like that I was beginning to care a little for this man. How could I? He kidnaps, murders, and steals from people! But something about him told me he wasn't the evil man his second wife believes he is.

"I believe you've been told the part about your distant grandmother wearing the necklace over to America in the late 1800's, right?"

"Yes, Beda was a young bride or bride to be, and she wore this legendary necklace on a boat to come and live in America."

"Yes, but before that you have no understanding of where the gemstone came from. This is where my family enters the picture. We come from a long history of Eklund's in Sweden. My very distant relatives acquired the gem probably a hundred years earlier than your family. The Eklund's have always been a prominent family in Sweden. So was your family, the Liljestrom's. The two families never got along. Your family and my family were competitors in shipping. My distant relatives and your distant relatives were ship builders. Back then it was extremely competitive. People would kill to get a contract and that's exactly what our two families did to each other. If you go back far enough, you would see a history of violence that would make me look like a saint."

"How do you know all this? And how do I know you're telling me the truth?"

"Why would I lie? We both have the same goal, to retrieve the necklace. Whether it's your family or mine, it needs to come back to us."

I was shocked to hear him say it could go to either of our families. He must be desperate to get this necklace back, but why?

"Your great-great grandmother Beda was given the gemstone as a wedding present and wore it over to America. She was the last known person in your family to possess it. My grandfather told me that Beda sold him the gemstone when she lived in Chicago where Beda with her husband."

"What? You're telling me your family bought the stone from her, but why?"

"They were a young couple and needed money, so my grandfather purchased it for a large sum of money."

"How much are we talking about?" I asked, wondering if his grandfather ripped off a young, poor bride.

"Not relevant anymore," Alex snapped. "Let me finish the story please." I nodded, just because I wanted to hear the whole story. "My grandfather gave the gem to my grandmother, and she treasured it for years until it was stolen. My father told me it was Beda's son who stole it from them, but the facts get fuzzy around this time."

"When did all this occur?" I asked.

"In the 1920's I believe. Beda's son, Ronald, was around twenty-five when he broke into my grandparent's home and robbed them." He saw the shocked look on my face and quickly added, "Now don't get mad at me. This is what I've been told, and I had to believe my father just like you would've believed your grandmother."

"Wouldn't Ronald have an arrest record he was the one who stole the necklace?"

"Never reported, I was told."

"That makes no sense. If this piece was so valuable, why wouldn't they try to arrest Ronald?" I inquired, not knowing what to think or believe.

"Because my grandparents knew it was Ronald, and like I said before there's a lot of history between our two families. Let me go on," he said, becoming flustered. "Where was I, oh, Ronald purportedly stole the necklace and brought it home to his mother, Beda. So, now it was back in your family's possession in the late 1920's. My father explained that my grandfather wasn't going to take this anymore, and vowed to get the necklace back for his wife. The facts get fuzzy, but according to my father, he said there was a back and forth battle between your great-great grandfather and my grandfather. They both played dirty and it was my grandfather that ended up dead."

"What?" I exclaimed. "My great-great grandfather killed your grandfather?"

"They played horrible games with each other, and my grandfather ended up falling off one of his ships as it was racing against your family's ship. It wasn't one of the large ships from the business, but a smaller, private boat and they were racing against each other at high speeds, and my grandfather fell overboard. That's all I know. My grandmother died the next year and she would never discuss the matter. My father was a young man of twenty, and he took over the business after that."

"So that's the business you're in, building vessels?" I asked.

"Yes, that's part of it," Axel said.

"Then why would you resort to violence and even murder?"

"There's so much more to the story than you know. I just gave you some of the history. Don't you want to know who ended up with the necklace after the boating accident?"

"Yes, of course," I said. "I figured it would be my family since your grandfather died."

"Nope, wrong again. The necklace was taken overboard when my grandfather went over."

"What? It was lost at sea?" I cried out. "The necklace might never be found!" Wait, I thought to myself. That didn't happen.

"Sorry, I got caught up in your story. We know somebody did find it and sent it to me in Deer Creek."

"Exactly," Axel replied. "Now this is where my story gets really interesting. Seriously, how could it get more interesting? It was already so farfetched I had a hard time believing any of what he told me.

"Please go on. I can't take much more," I exclaimed.

"My father told me both our families believed the necklace was lost forever. Then something amazing happened when I was in my early twenties. I had finished school, and just started working at my father's company. He was grooming me to take over eventually. I was a salesman to start, and I was out at a pier in Stockholm meeting someone to negotiate some parts for our latest ship. I was looking out over the water when a woman walked by, and she was stunning. She was a tall, slim, blonde woman who carried herself with such confidence that I couldn't help but stare as she walked by me. She must've spotted me staring and she stopped, turned around and smiled at me."

"On the pier you said this happened?" I asked, wondering why he was telling me this part of the story.

"Yes, I couldn't tell you at the time why she was walking on the pier. It wasn't a tourist spot, it was in an industrial area and the pier was very long. We put our new ships in the water in the area, so I knew it well. She waited for me to say something, and I was young and a bit daring, so I walked up to her and said hello. That was when my eyes went to her neck."

"No," I said. He's not going to tell me what I'm thinking. "Please don't tell me she had on the necklace?"

"Yes!" he declared. "Before you ask me, you probably are wondering if I knew what the necklace looked like? I had seen pictures of it, and I knew the minute I saw it that it was the necklace. If you haven't seen it, I can assure you it would take your breath away. The size alone is enormous, about 13 carats, a brilliant sky blue color and the cut made it shimmer no matter how it's laying. I knew I had to find out how this mysterious woman came into possession of my family's necklace."

I corrected him, even though I shouldn't have at the moment. "Our family's necklace." He let me do it without snapping at me. He was so caught up in his own story that he let that one slip.

"I asked her name and we started talking. I didn't want to lead on that I was after her necklace. My mind raced and all I could do was try and flirt with her and make sure I see her again." He stopped long enough for me to interrupt.

"Please, don't keep me in suspense."

"Sorry, got caught up in the moment. Brings back a lot of memories for me."

"Wait, don't tell me that this woman was your wife?"

"How did you figure that out so fast?" Axel asked, surprised. "Yes, this woman eventually became my wife. It took two years to convince her to marry me. She came from an even wealthier family than my own. I knew from the minute I talked to her that I wanted to spend my life with her, regardless of the necklace. What I didn't know was what she was capable of."

"Are you telling me that she tricked you too?"

"Yes, but I didn't know that until after we were married. You see, I actually fell deeply in love with her and I didn't care about her money at the time. I truly believed she loved me too, but then years later she crushed me and she made my life a living hell ever since."

"I'm confused," I said. "What happened once you were married? You both seemed happy and the money wasn't an issue, especially if you both came into the marriage with money."

"Yes, I never made her sign a prenuptial agreement, but her father made me sign papers."

"That makes no sense! If you signed, then she should've signed, too."

"I told you I fell hard for her and my brain wasn't thinking clearly. My parents were furious with me."

"So in time you and your wife developed problems?" I asked.

"That's saying it mildly. We took a long honeymoon and came back happy and ready to start our new lives. I had my father's business to take over and she was an heiress. I couldn't see any problem we couldn't solve until we moved into my family home. My parents retired and moved to a penthouse apartment in the city and left us alone here, in this huge house."

"So the house we're in now is where you and your wife lived?"

"Yes, and the moment we did she made my life a living hell."

"How and why?"

"Let me just say that she planned to run into me that day on the pier. She wore the necklace on purpose, because she knew it was something my family desperately wanted back."

"That's quite a coincidence," I said. "How did she know that the necklace was from one of our families?"

"Exactly, and to this day I have no answer to how she knew. But I didn't even know it was her deliberate plan to find and marry me, until a little over a year ago."

"But it's been years, how did you find out?"

"From the time we moved here she pointed out that her family's wealth could squash my family. She felt she had all the power in the marriage, since I signed away my rights to any of her money, but she could rob me blind of my own money. That's why my parents were so mad at me when I didn't make her sign papers too."

"Are your parents still alive?" I asked, knowing the probability was low since Axel had to be in his late sixties himself.

"No," he said angrily, but calm. "She threw my parents out of the penthouse and put them in a horrible nursing home. She claimed they couldn't take care of themselves and needed full-time care."

"You didn't agree?"

"No, they were older, but still lucid and active."

"Then why on earth would you allow her to put them in a home? They're your parents not hers."

"She didn't give me a choice. If I didn't agree, I could leave the house and give her my family's business because she held all the cards in the relationship."

"What I don't understand is, why did she do it? Why marry you when she had plenty of money and didn't need you at all."

"That's the billion-dollar question. I was stuck, but she wasn't."

"Before she died did you make peace with her?" I asked.

"No," he quietly said. "Her heart stopped one night while she was sleeping and all I kept thinking when they told me was, what heart? She didn't have one. The doctor said she had heart disease and it ran in her family. She was such a high stress person that it caught up with her. You could kind of say karma."

"Hmm," was all I could say, because I was wondering not only about her sudden death, but also about his second wife. I couldn't ask any questions about her, since I wasn't supposed to know about her. But she did tell me they had a relationship for years. I couldn't help but wonder if her heart giving out wasn't a planned death. I took it another direction, to see if he would open up even further. "So, did you ever marry again?"

He glanced at me strangely, and reminded me his wife only died a year ago. "But your marriage was over years ago, really. Maybe someone else came into your life and made you happy."

He stood up from the couch and went over to a cabinet behind his desk. He pulled out a decanter full of a dark liquid. "I could use a brandy, would you like one?"

"No thanks," I said.

"Ruth Ann, I'm done for the day. I would like to continue this tomorrow with Bertha. We need to remember the task at hand, retrieving the necklace."

"So you must have an idea of where it is?" I asked, hoping for some information.

"I have an idea, but you'll have to wait to hear about it. Why don't you go freshen up? I'll have Inga come and fetch you from your room when dinner's served."

I felt finality in his words, so I left the library and headed back to my room. It was nearing five o'clock in the evening and I was getting hungry. I was conflicted and wanted to go to my room and think. As I walked down the hall to my room, I looked at the closed door at the end of the hall. I wanted to get back up to his second wife and talk more. It would have to wait until later.

I went into the bathroom and washed my face and changed my clothes. I was happy that I had my own clothes to put on. I sat down on the sofa under the window. It was dark outside and I wondered where John was? Could he be nearer than I thought? I wish I had him here, just to talk over everything I learned today. Was Axel such an evil man or was he just heartbroken from his first wife? How did his second wife play in with the whole scenario, too? I had more questions than answers, and told myself to stay focused and I would find all the answers out in time.

I knew I couldn't risk going upstairs to see his new wife, but I couldn't get her off my mind. Why didn't Axel tell me about her? And more importantly, why was she hiding and pretending to be sick? Axel thinks she's dying, but I learned she's only faking her illness, but why?

I was so caught up in the mess here, that I almost forgot the reason I was here in the first place. I pulled out a piece of paper from the nightstand and wrote down all the connections. Maybe there was a pattern that I couldn't see yet. Possibly it'll lead to the missing necklace. I felt I could figure it out if I had all the missing pieces. The main piece I didn't understand was lying upstairs in a bed pretending to be terminally ill.

Promptly at six o'clock Inga pounded on my door. I had just finished writing down everything I could recall and shoved the papers under the couch cushion. I didn't want to put them in the nightstand or under my pillows because Inga was probably searching them regularly. I told Inga I would be right down, and then I heard her thumping footsteps fade as she went down the hall.

I started down myself and wondered who would be joining us at dinner this evening, and why I'm even included. I was still a prisoner in his house, but Axel was treating me as a guest. It was very confusing to me. I believed I could escape, but something or someone was telling me not to. I needed to stay and see this through.

Inga was waiting for me at the bottom of the stairs, and led me into the dining room instead of the kitchen. I was the first one to arrive and noticed the table was elegantly set for six. Six? Who would be joining us? I immediately felt underdressed. I was wearing a pair of black slacks and a green sweater. This room was screaming out for me to be in a long party dress and diamond earrings. Oh well, this is all I've got.

Inga pulled out one of the chairs on the side of the long table. I sat down and thought the table could seat at least twenty, but we were cozied up together with the six place settings. Axel, Bertha and me makes three. Who were the other three? I was soon to find out.

Bertha was the first to arrive after me. She sat directly across from me and didn't say a word. I was thrilled when Axel came in, dressed in a black suit and tie and broke the silence. "Good evening ladies," he said, smiling. "I'm sure you're both hungry and Inga runs a tight kitchen, so I'm sure it'll be delicious."

I asked, "I see there are other people joining us. Do I know any of them?" I doubted his second wife would be one, but that would make for an interesting dinner.

"Ah, you noticed, Ruth Ann," he said, sitting himself down at the head of the table. "In due time you'll know. Actually, Bertha, your guests are tardy."

"They'll be here," she snapped, with an ugly scowl on her face.

Axel looked toward the door facing the foyer, and I turned my head and saw a familiar face. "Finn," Axel spoke. "Please take a chair next to Ruth Ann."

Finn walked to the chair furthest from Axel, but next to me. He didn't speak, but I had to admit I began to sweat. This was the man who beat up Paul and threatened me numerous times. I wanted to stand up and leave, but I thought it might not be the smartest thing to do. I was able to get a close look at the Viking ship tattoo on his neck, and something dawned on me. Could there be a connection between Axel and Finn that has to do with his family's business? Why else would Finn be sporting such a specific tattoo?

Finn caught me staring at his tattoo and he said in a slow, deliberate voice, "You like my tat?"

I couldn't think of anything to say, so I said the first stupid thing that popped in my head, "That's a huge tattoo, why did you get a ship printed on your neck?"

Finn let out a vulgar laugh and looked at Axel. "Ruth Ann," Axel said, over Finn's laughter. "Not much bothers Finn. He's as tough as nails."

"Oh," was all I could mutter, embarrassed. I turned my attention away from Finn and his tattoo. In my opinion, I would've thought Axel had better taste in dinner companions. Maybe Finn has a bigger role here, and in time I hoped I'd find out.

Sherman walked into the dining room and announced the missing two guests. They walked into the room and Bertha stood up to greet them.

"Finally," she snapped. "You both are late."

They shrugged their shoulders and one of them said, "We had to wait to close up the shop. You know we don't close till six o'clock." The one that answered Bertha was an enormous man, well over six feet tall and three hundred pounds, if I had to guess. The other man was much smaller, not much heavier than me and his head was shaved. He walked over to Axel and shook his hand

and took a seat at the table next to Bertha. "David, nice to see you," Axel said, as he shook the man's hand. "Have your brother sit on the other side of your sister."

Did I hear correctly? Brother, sister? Bertha's two brothers just came to dinner here? Once again I had so many questions and I hoped by the end of this dinner some would be answered.

Bertha sat between David, the smaller brother, and Andy, the larger brother. Andy barely fit in the chair and was across the table from me. Bertha didn't say much during the first course which was a tasteless broth. I remembered my younger days, when relatives would say Swedish cooking was bland, and now I knew that they were telling the truth! I was hungry and hoped the rest of the meal would be tastier. The next course that was an ordinary salad. It was okay, but you can't really mess up a dinner salad. No one spoke until after we had finished the main course of Swedish meatballs over a pile of egg noodles.

Axel initiated the conversation by asking me what I thought of Inga's cooking. "It's very good," I lied. It was far from good, just barely edible if you really want the truth.

"She's a talented cook," Andy said, with a mouthful of noodles. "I enjoy when you ask us to dine with you."

"You're welcome, Andy," Axel said. "Did Bertha explain why you both are dining with us this evening?"

"Nope," David replied. "Just figured you had another object for us to appraise and sell."

Axel glanced at me to see if I was listening, and of course I was. He added, "Not exactly boys." Did he just call them boys? I do believe from my observation they were about fortyish.

David looked over at Bertha, who was staring straight down at her empty plate. "Bertha, did you forget to tell us something?"

She lifted her head and looked straight at Axel and said, "No, Mr. Eklund wanted to speak to you both. I'll let him fill you in."

"Yes, that's correct David," Axel said, ignoring Andy. I was getting the impression that David was the brains in the family and Andy the brawn. David was half the size of Andy. They sure didn't look like they came from the same mother.

"We'll talk in my library," Axel said very coolly, as he stood up and wiped his mouth one last time with his cloth napkin.

I rose, and was about to follow them when Axel stopped me.

"Ruth Ann, we'll talk in the morning. This meeting is not for you."

"But," I said shocked. "I don't understand?"

"Tomorrow, you may go upstairs to your room." Axel left me standing alone in the dining room, questioning why I wasn't included in the meeting.

I wasn't alone for long; Inga entered the dining room from the kitchen. "You need to go," she said, beginning to clear the dishes. "I need to clean this up." I went out into the foyer wondering if I could listen at the door, when Sherman, the butler, appeared out of thin air. "May I help you?"

"No," I snapped. "I'm going upstairs."

"Good evening," he said, with a disturbing smile. He knew I was planning on listening, because he caught me red-handed. I returned the smile and went upstairs to my room. "Perfect," I said out loud as I walked in my room. It was at that very moment when I remembered that I had put the key to the secret upstairs room in my pocket. This seemed the perfect time to go and talk with Axel's second wife. Inga was busy in the kitchen and Axel and Bertha were in a meeting. I'd never seen Sherman up on this floor, so I had some time. I hurried out of my room and over to the door that led up to his wife.

The key she gave me worked and I headed up the stairs. The woman was sitting up in bed with a computer upon her lap. I startled her for a moment until she saw who it was. "I'm sorry," I said. "Should I knock before I come in here?"

"No, it's okay," she said, closing the lid of the laptop. "I didn't want anyone else seeing me with a computer."

"Why not?"

"Axel and the his staff think I'm sick and not capable of doing much of anything except resting. The doctor snuck this in for me so I could use it."

"That must be some doctor you have."

"He's been good to me and he knows Axel's reputation."

"Did he also take care of his first wife?" I asked.

"Yes, that's another reason why the doctor is on my side. He isn't quite convinced that her death was of natural causes."

"Really?" I asked. "Does he believe Axel drugged her?"

"Yes, but all the blood work and reports were destroyed soon after she died."

"How could they be destroyed? Doesn't it go to a coroner and police?"

"There was a fire at the coroner's building, and not only were the paperwork and tests destroyed, but she was burned and so was the coroner."

"You can't be serious?" I asked, totally shocked by this occurrence. "How could the police ignore something that strange?"

"I agree with you, but as I told you before, Axel and the family name have a strong influence around here."

"Earlier I forgot to ask you your name, may I find out now?"

"Oh, I'm sorry, I didn't realize you didn't know my name. It's Prunella. Prunella Eklund."

"Thank you," I said.

"Are you sure it's safe for you to be here?"

"Yes, they're busy right now, so I hurried up here to continue our conversation. Where did we leave off?"

"Why I'm stuck up here pretending to be sick instead of being the lady of the house." Prunella said, stuffing the laptop under her bed.

"Exactly," I responded. "Please, I want to hear it all."

"As long as you're sure you won't get caught up here."

"Even if I was, I can tell them I was curious about the room up here and didn't know who was staying here."

"That won't work, but let's hope it doesn't come to that." She threw her legs over the side of the bed and stood up. "I need to keep walking or I'm afraid I won't have any strength when I can finally leave here."

"I know you have a lot to tell me, but why can't you leave?"

"You see how you're a prisoner here, but have freedom of most of the house? I also am a prisoner, but I have no freedom."

"But you're his wife!"

"It all changed after his first wife died." She looked at me as she walked over to the tiny window and then shivered. "It's getting cold out with winter arriving."

"Yes, but please get back to the story. I don't have that much time."

"I was very happy until about a year ago. I was a young, vibrant person who looked forward to a full life with travel, kids and a man I truly thought was my one and only. I know what you're thinking," she said, sneering at me. "He's twice my age, but I need you to believe it didn't matter to me. I really loved him and not his money."

"Money does make it easier though," I couldn't help but say.

"Yes, you're correct, but he was a man trapped in a horrible marriage, and despite his age he was very active."

"How could your life go from being on top of the world to this?"

"I think you know why," she said, lowering her head and putting her hand to her neck. "I'm not who I said I was," she admitted.

"You're confusing me Prunella. Please just tell me what you're getting at."

"I lied to you earlier," she said. "I didn't come from the family that I described to you."

"Why did you lie? You barely know me and I've done nothing to have you doubt my trust."

"I wasn't sure if you were sent here. Maybe Bertha or Axel put you up to this to catch me. But if you didn't tell on me earlier, then I feel I can trust you. But I need to know, are you telling me the truth about being a prisoner here, too?"

"Of course I am!" I exclaimed. "I don't live in Sweden, I'm from a small town in Colorado."

"I'm sorry, but you have to put yourself in my shoes. I've been up here for months, playing this sick game with Axel, Bertha, and the others. I don't know who I can trust."

"Were you telling me the truth about the doctor? Is he really helping you keep your secret?"

"Yes, I wouldn't have made it this far on my own." She sat down on the rocking chair and motioned for me to sit on the matching one next to her. "Please, let me hurry and tell you more." I sat down and let her continue. "Can I call you…?"

"Ruth Ann," I replied.

"OK, my name really is Prunella and I'm really his legal wife. I have a family that is also known to you." She observed my reaction and held up her hand to stop me from speaking. "Please, I need to get this all out before it's too late."

"Fine," I agreed, out of sheer curiosity.

"I'm just going to tell you who I really am, then I'll tell you how I got to this point. As I said, my name is Prunella, Prunella

Liljestrom Eklund." She stopped, looked directly into my eyes and waited for my response.

"What, wait, what?" I cried out. "Did I just hear you say Liljestrom?"

"Yes, I'm related to you Ruth Ann. Distantly, but we're from the same family here in Stockholm."

"How did you know I was from this family you're talking about?"

"I know more than you think. I've got a few spies myself here in the house and they told me of your presence."

"Who?"

"In due time. Let me explain. I did come here to work for Axel Eklund, but it wasn't just by chance. My parents raised me to believe the Eklund family was evil and not trustworthy. You have to understand I didn't understand why until I was just about twenty-one."

"That's when you came here to work as his personal maid, correct?"

"Yes, good memory, Ruth Ann," she said with a kind smile. "I knew when I worked here my purpose was to get on the inside of all his business and personal transactions. It was known around this area that his wife was a powerful, wealthy woman who held all the cards when it came to Eklund's life. At the time I didn't care about her at all. My goal was to penetrate Axel's life, not hers. Boy, was I wrong about that." Prunella hopped up out of the chair and started walking around the room. "You see, our family and the Eklund's were bitter rivals when it came to the family business. They played dirty and got all the contracts, so my family would lose money and the hope of expanding our business."

"Are you talking about the shipping business?" I asked, wondering if what Axel told me about our families being competitors was true.

"Yes," she said surprised. "You do know more than I thought."

"I know very little, please go on," I asked.

"My grandfather, and even further back than that, fought battles, deadly battles over the contracts. Usually my family lost because the Eklund's bribed or cheated to get them. So as you can see, the Eklund fortune climbed and we lost more and more money. Once my father took over the business, we had barely enough money to keep the company afloat." She stopped and said smiling, "Sorry for the pun!"

"Didn't Axel's grandfather die in a boat race against my great-great grandfather?"

"How on earth did you know that?" Prunella questioned.

"I'll tell you that after you're done."

She eyed me suspiciously, but kept going. "So, when I was of age my father had me come up with a fake background and sent me here to live and work. I knew I could get into his business dealings if I could get him to trust me."

"So that's why you accepted the job as his personal assistant?" I inquired.

"Yes," she answered. "The more contact I had with him, the more I would learn. That's exactly what happened."

"Did he fall in love with you or did you mistakenly fall in love with him?"

"That, Ruth Ann, is where it all came crumbling down." She plopped down on the side of her bed and put her hands on her face.

"Please don't cry," I said, walking over to her and sitting next to her. "I understand how things change and if you did love him it's OK to feel sad."

Her head popped up and she declared, "I'm not sad about that man! He betrayed my family and I was stupid. I didn't stick to the plan and I got burned. But it's all going to turn around now. Especially with you here."

"*Me?* What help can I be?" I asked, confused.

"More than you can ever imagine." Prunella put her hand on my hand resting on the bed and said, "Ruth Ann, we're family. Can I trust you'll be on my side no matter what?"

"Of course, Prunella. Family always sticks together."

"Thank you," she said. "But I must hurry, there's still so much more."

I looked at the time on my watch and it was getting late. I wondered how much time I had before someone would come looking for me. Prunella noticed my anxiety and said, "If you'd like to go we can talk tomorrow."

"No, let's give it a little more time. Please go on, from when you started working here and realized his first wife was more involved than you thought."

"Yes, after I started working as his personal assistant, his wife started getting suspicious of the two of us. She was a mean person. She would yell at the staff constantly about ridiculous things such as her tea wasn't at a certain temperature or there were fingerprints on the furniture, and she would have them clean everything over and over. She humiliated the staff and she wasn't any better with Axel. I felt sorry for him, even though I was told my whole life that he was a monster."

"Did Axel just let his wife get away with it?"

"He had to, or she would rob him blind. He confided in me that she had control over his money and he didn't have any choice but to let her act that way. He tried over and over to talk to her about her attitude, but she dismissed him as if he was part of her staff."

"I hate to say this, but you're forming a case against him regarding her death."

"I know. It's petrified me since the day she died. I believe there's more to her death than he said. He just destroyed the paper trail, and even the coroner, so nobody can prosecute him for her death."

"Too convenient," I said. "Didn't anyone tell the police about their suspicions about the fire at the coroner's office?"

"No one would dare do that or they would be a dead man."

"There are ways to not be found out," I said. "Like witness protection, or the person could have remained anonymous, and Axel wouldn't know who ratted him out."

"He'd find out, trust me."

"I have had conversations with Axel, and he just doesn't seem like the villain you have painted him out to be. I'm very confused. He seemed like the victim when he told me about his wife."

"So he talked to you about her?" Prunella asked curiously.

"Yes, not much, but he told me about our family's history and how he met his wife."

"Wait! He told you about how they met?" Prunella cried out.

"Yes," I said, regretting my words. I now had to tell her about the necklace, because that's why Axel supposedly talked to her in the first place back on the pier. I looked at her seriously and said, "We need to be honest with each other, Prunella. There's one major fact we both haven't mentioned."

"The necklace," Prunella said, before I did. "You know all

about the necklace, don't you?"

"Yes, I do," I admitted. "My story only goes back a couple weeks though, not decades."

"How so?" she asked.

"I never knew the necklace existed until a friend of mine, who happens to be our town's bank president, received the necklace from a lawyer here in Stockholm."

"I bet I know which lawyer," Prunella mentioned. "Was the lawyer's name, Svenson?"

"Maybe, I don't remember exactly, but how would you know? Don't tell me yet, we keep getting side-tracked." I went back to my story and told Prunella how Doug was robbed and assaulted, and the necklace was stolen. "The lawyer's letter mentioned that I was the only relative left, but how come you didn't get it if you're a Liljestrom?"

"That would be complicated and I'll explain when you're done," Prunella said.

I told Prunella the whole story about Mr. Toggles getting shot by Axel's men and that a guard was killed protecting me because I became a target. I told her about my conversations with Axel, and that he admitted to having Toggles murdered, but that there were others involved and they were the ones who robbed Doug, the bank president. The story took a while, but when I was through Prunella was stunned.

"Wow, that all happened in such a short amount of time. And you never even saw the necklace?"

"Nope," I said. "All this over something I've never seen or knew about. The whole thing is ridiculous if you ask me. How much could this necklace be worth to cause such trouble?"

"That's the million-dollar question, Ruth Ann," Prunella said. "Axel thinks it's priceless. He has told me there have been attempts to appraise it, but no one has been able to put an actual dollar amount on it. I do believe Axel has found someone who claims they can do exactly that though."

"So that's why he needs the necklace so badly?"

"Yes."

"But how do you know this if you're trapped up here and also a prisoner of his?"

"Remember I told you I have eyes and ears in this house who

report to me whenever Axel has people visit him."

"Sherman, the butler?"

"I'm not going to tell you, Ruth Ann, just in case things fall apart. I don't want to get anyone in trouble."

"Fine, but what I haven't told you is that Axel, Bertha, me, Finn, and two additional men were at dinner tonight."

"Who? Do you know?"

"Yes, they claimed they're Bertha's brothers, David and Andy. I also overheard David ask Axel what he wanted them to look at or sell."

"Really? I'll have to find out about that." Prunella anxiously noticed the time and said, "You have to go now. They'll be checking on you and me, too."

"But we have so much more to discuss, like how you got to this point, here in bed sick? Also, why didn't the lawyer did give the necklace to you instead of sending it all the way to Deer Creek, Colorado!"

"Not now, go, we'll talk tomorrow. Why don't you come up here before dawn and we can talk? I'm not sure how much time we have until we're discovered or Axel uses you for whatever he has planned."

I agreed to meet her in the early morning. I didn't think much would happen in the next eight to ten hours. I left her in her bed and hurried down the stairs. I carefully looked before I opened the door at the bottom of the stairs. All clear, so I went straight to my room. I thought I made it without being caught, but I was mistaken.

As I stepped inside my room, Inga was sitting in a chair in the corner tapping her hands together impatiently. "Where have you been?" she snapped. "I've been waiting for you for over a half hour. Must I get Mr. Eklund and notify him of your disappearance?"

I panicked and said, "No, I was just walking around the house. I was full from dinner and needed to burn some energy. That's all I was doing."

"Don't lie to me," she sniped. "You barely ate your dinner. I cleared all of your plates and you were the only one not to finish."

"Maybe I don't eat as much as the others," I tried to say.

"NO!" Inga stood up and walked toward me at the door. "I

know where you've been. You went back up the stairs, didn't you? But how did you unlock the door and what did you find up there?"

Inga infuriated me and I blurted out, "You mean whom did I find upstairs?" That did it! I just blew it.

Inga grabbed my arm and dragged me out into the hall. "Please," I begged. "Don't tell Mr. Eklund. I'll do anything you ask." She didn't say a word, just pulled me down the hall but not in the direction of the main staircase, but to where I just came from. "Wait, where are you taking me?" I asked.

Inga pulled a set of keys out of her apron and put a key into the lock and opened the door. "Up," she ordered me. I gazed up at the stairs and then back to Inga behind me. "Please don't do this," I pleaded.

She gave me a push from behind and I had no choice but to go back up to Prunella's room. At the top of the stairs was the last door between Prunella and us. Inga reached around me and swung open the door. "Enter," she told me.

I saw Prunella ahead lying in her bed without her computer and her eyes shut. She was doing a good job pretending to be sick and when she opened her eyes she sat bolt upright. "What's going on here?" Prunella exclaimed.

Inga shoved me over to the side of the bed and said, "What should I do with her?" Wait…what did she just say? Why would Inga ask Prunella what to do with *me*?

"Well, Ruth Ann, you discovered my secret weapon!"

I looked from Inga to Prunella and said, "Are you telling me your spy in the house is *her*?"

Inga took offense to my comment and said, "And why not?"

"No, I'm sorry. I didn't mean it like that. It's just I'm surprised that you would betray your employer, that's all."

Prunella chimed in before Inga could and said, "Ruth Ann, Inga's wonderful to me. Don't you remember what I said about his first wife mistreating the staff? That's when Inga and I grew close. She's like a mother to me!"

"Inga?" I questioned.

"Once again," Inga said. "Why not? Miss Prunella's a smart, beautiful young woman and I would die for her."

"I'm sorry, I just don't get it," I said confused.

"Ruth Ann, Inga and I formed a bond a while ago and she

knows about my bogus illness. We're completely united and I wouldn't be here if it wasn't for her."

"So now you're telling me Inga, the doctor, you, and I are the only ones that know you're not really sick?"

"You told her that?" Inga said, pointing at me.

"Yes, Inga, Ruth Ann's family and we have to treat her as such."

"I'm the one that told you who she was family," Inga stated. "But I wasn't sure if she was trustworthy."

"Of course I am, Inga," I intercepted. "I'm here as a prisoner, not a guest. Just like Prunella is, being treated like a prisoner."

"Yes," Prunella said. "The only reason I'm alive is because Axel thinks I'm extremely ill."

"And we have to keep it that way," Inga demanded, looking directly at me.

"I won't tell anyone," I declared. "But there's so much going on I'm getting a migraine."

Inga looked anxiously at Prunella and said, "Are you sure about this woman, Prunella?" Prunella nodded. "OK, I need to tell you that Mr. Eklund had those two men back at the house again and they're Bertha's brothers. I don't know if I believe that or not, but you know what business they're in don't you?"

"I know who they are because Axel has done business before with them. I only recently found out they're Bertha's brothers. This could be a problem. They may know more about the necklace and that's why Axel had a private meeting with them."

"Wait," I interrupted. "Axel claims he doesn't know who has the necklace. He said to me that he had an idea who may."

"He must be suspecting Bertha's brothers and that's why they're here. I wonder what happened in their meeting?" Prunella asked. "Do you think Shermie can tell you?"

"Excuse me, Shermie?" I asked.

"The butler, Sherman, he's actually on our side too, Ruth Ann," Prunella said, watching Inga's not so happy expression. "Inga, please, let's speak freely between all of us here."

"OK, but if you betray Prunella and the rest of us, I won't be responsible for my actions," Inga said, waving her finger at me. "There can be no other people in on our secret, Prunella."

"There won't be, I promise."

"I'll go and find Sherman and see if he has any information about the meeting in the library. You both stay put here and I'll be back in a few minutes," Inga said, hurrying out of the room and down the stairs.

Prunella got out of bed and started pacing around the room again. "I have a bad feeling about this Ruth Ann."

"All of it's bad," I said, joining in on her pacing. "I've been kidnapped, people have been killed, and you're trapped up here in a huge lie. If he finds out about you he'll kill you, won't he?"

"I'm sure of it."

"You haven't finished telling me how you got to this point. All I know is up to when his wife died. Were you still in love with him then?"

"Yes," she said. "I believed him when he said he had no part in her death. I had already disappointed my family by not destroying him when I had the chance, but when they found out I was in love with him they disowned me."

"Now I have to ask again, why was I sent the letter from the lawyer stating I was the only Liljestrom alive outside of my daughters and wait, my sister, Irene? I forgot about her. Why didn't she get the letter instead of me?"

"Svenson knows I'm still alive. He thinks I'm on my deathbed and that's why he sent the letter to you. In regard to my parents, I haven't told you all of it yet. Within the last year both my parents were killed in a horrible car crash. I'm all that's left, and Svenson did contact me about the necklace."

"But I thought Axel's first wife had the necklace?"

"She did until she died. Axel claimed ownership of it after that, and then last year he was robbed, and it went missing. I have no idea how Svenson got ahold of the necklace, but somebody must've given it to him with the agreement it goes to you in the United States."

"And now it's lost again!" I cried out.

"Not exactly," Prunella said, sitting back down on her bed. "Those two men downstairs may be the key to this. We should wait until Inga comes back. In the meantime, let me tell you how I got here." I nodded and sat down next to her on the bed.

"Up till the death of his wife Axel was wonderful to me. He was miserable in his marriage and I was his hope. His wife had her suspicions, but he wouldn't talk to me about that. He didn't really care if she knew he had feelings for me as long as she didn't take everything from him. I told him she could destroy him if she became jealous enough, but he didn't think that would happen. He never told me why she stayed with him when she could've left him penniless."

"Didn't that raise a red flag to you?" I asked, suspicious of Axel's motives.

"I guess I wanted to think only the best of him and not worry about it. I was pretty stupid, I know."

"We all do naive things when it comes to love," I said, patting her hand gently. "It's what you're going to do now that matters."

"Crush him," she said quietly, but with a forcefulness not to be reckoned with.

"Go on with your story, please," I said.

"After she died, Axel asked me to marry him and I said yes, of course. We were married immediately."

"How soon after her death did you marry?"

"One week after she was buried we were married, here in the house. It was lovely. Inga, Shermie, and the rest of the staff were very happy for us."

"How could it all end so abruptly?"

"We were happy for a couple months. Then I noticed his personality changed. He became distant, didn't sleep in the same room with me anymore, and he started mistreating the staff. Not as badly as his first wife did, but the staff was worried it would get that way again. I tried over and over to reach out to him, but he pushed me away. Then, about six months ago, he started having private meetings in his library at all hours and he grew angrier and angrier. I started to be afraid of him and pulled away. He didn't like that and threatened to lock me up in my bedroom until I started behaving myself. Really, behave myself? He treated me like I was a five-year-old. I started planning to leave him, even contacted a divorce lawyer. Axel found out and completely lost it. He had Finn watch over me and that's when I discovered what made him so angry. The necklace was gone and he blamed me."

"You? But why would he blame you?"

"Because I did take it, Ruth Ann," Prunella admitted. "I took it because it was mine, not his. This necklace was a part of my family history and his family kept taking it away from us."

"So he caught you with the necklace and that's when you concocted the story about being deathly ill and needing the money to
pay for your medical expenses, right?"

Prunella stared at me in amazement. "Wow, that's exactly what
I did! How did you come up with that yourself?"

"Besides the obvious, you and I being family, it wasn't that
hard to figure out really," I said, smiling to see if she understood
my statement about us being family members. She was too far-
gone in her story to get my little joke.

"I knew I could rely on Inga and Sherman, but I had to get the
doctor to go along with it. Once Axel caught me, he demanded I
give back the necklace. I refused, of course, and he went berserk.
He came after me and wrapped his hands around my throat and the
only reason I survived was because I fainted."

"You really fainted or you pretended to?" I asked.

"No, I really did faint. He cut off the oxygen from me and I
dropped. Axel must've had feelings for me, because he panicked
and carried me back to the bedroom we used to share. He readily
agreed to call my doctor to make sure there was no damage done."

"Let me get this straight," I said. "He tried to kill you, but when
you fainted, for real, he regretted it and tried to make it up to you?"

"YES!" Prunella bellowed. "I knew I had to do something drastic or he would try again to get me to give him my necklace back."

"How did you get the doctor to go along with you?"

"That's just it, when Axel agreed to use my doctor I knew I had
a plan that could work. My doctor happens to be a friend of my
family, too. Remember what I told you earlier? Many people
feared or despised the Eklund family; my doctor was one of them.
I got lucky, that's all."

"So your doctor came up with a horrible disease that'll kill you
eventually?"

"Yes, a debilitating, life threatening disease that affects my
nervous system. I'd lose my ability to walk, talk, and function like
a normal human being."

"And he believed that?" I said, wondering if Axel really did believe them, or did he have a plan of his own in the works?

"He really did," she said. "The doctor showed him test results
and x-rays of a very sick individual, but not me. He believed it all

and actually expressed to me he would wait until I died to take the necklace from me."

"And you thought you were safe under these conditions?"

"No way," Prunella declared. "I had to have a solid plan to keep the necklace safe, without Axel knowing where it was. If he did, then all he had to do was kill me and take the necklace. As long as I lived he knew I wasn't going to tell him where it was. I claimed I had a lawyer that would turn it over to him once I died naturally. He also had to treat me with respect and provide a comfortable place to live out my last days."

"And you picked the attic?" I asked, surprised she would pick a dark, old attic to live in.

"I love it up here, Ruth Ann. It's been renovated for me and my needs and I don't have to see Axel or his thugs like Finn ever, except for his regular visits to check on me."

"He comes and visits you often?"

"Yes, it's pathetic. I don't know who's faking it more, him or me. He pretends to be concerned about my health and I lie in bed acting weak and needy. I should win one of your Oscars for my acting!"

"You mentioned, Finn," I said. "What do you know about him?"

"He's related to Axel; did you know that?" Prunella asked, watching an expression of shock rise in my face.

"He's what?" I asked, stunned. "I knew that Viking Ship tattoo had some kind of significance.

"Yes, it's all about the family business. Finn is Axel's nephew. Axel had a sister that died tragically in childbirth, and Axel took in Finn as his younger brother, but actually he's his nephew."

"Wow, Axel neglected to mention any of that to me," I said, wondering if that was intentional. I was hearing two sides to the story and my gut told me to go with Prunella's side, especially since she was family.

"Ruth Ann, you've only been here a couple of days and I've spent my whole life here. I know you want to understand what's going on here, but it's too much to tell. All I would like from you is loyalty to our family and we'll be fine. Trust me, not Axel, and we'll survive this and come out with our family's necklace. Can you do that for me?"

I wanted to tell her yes, but something in my brain hesitated. Prunella jumped on my moment of silence and snapped, "Ruth Ann! Are you doubting me?"

Immediately I said, "No, that's not it at all. I just was thinking about what you told me and comparing it to what Axel told me, and I know in my heart I'll be on your side. How would I choose otherwise? Axel has kidnapped me more than once now, and Finn has hurt people I care about."

Prunella calmed down and said, "Thank you, Ruth Ann, that's all I need to hear. I'll assure Inga and Shermie that you can be completely trusted, and they'll protect you from now on just as they do for me."

"That would be nice. I could use some help around here and information, too. I have one major concern…" I said. "If you don't have the necklace anymore, where is it now and how did somebody take it?"

"I was wondering when you'd ask me that. Once Axel agreed to my terms about living up here and accepting that he had to behave or he would never see his precious necklace again, I had to come up with a plan to get me and the necklace safely away from here forever."

Prunella saw the light bulb go off in my head. "Yes, Ruth Ann, I think you might have figured some of this out in your head by now. I hired the lawyer, Svenson, and I gave him the necklace. He sent it to you after a long research of our family tree. I told him originally I didn't want to know where he was going to send it, but he had to send serious warnings with the necklace about the history of the dangers associated with possessing the piece."

"Did Axel know about it?"

"Yes, eventually," she said. "That's how Axel ended up in Deer Creek. He purchased the house in the mountains and set up the entire scheme of retrieving the necklace from you once you got it."

"But somebody else beat him to the punch, right?" I asked.

"Yes, and he thinks it was someone hired by me."

"Was it?" I asked, curious myself.

"No, it really wasn't. But I couldn't convince Axel of that and he started threatening me again. That's why I'm in fear of my life again. If I don't have the necklace, why keep me alive up here?"

"What are you going to do?"

"Keep Inga, Shermie, and you as informants. Once we know his next move, I'll take action. The doctor was just here earlier, and convinced Axel that I don't have much time left. We're hoping that will buy us some time and he won't try to kill me himself, or have Finn do it like he usually does. Finn's his hit man."

"That isn't reassuring, Prunella. What if Inga or Sherman don't see or hear his plans? He could poison your food or send Finn up here in the middle of the night."

"Inga tests every morsel of food that comes up here. Besides, she cooks all the food here, and he thinks he can trust her, so if he did want some unknown substance put in my food, he would probably tell Inga and she would innocently go along with him."

"He would know she was a part of this if that happens."

"Why would you say that?" asked Prunella.

"If you didn't die from the food, then he would know Inga didn't put the poison in it."

"Or I didn't eat it," she answered. "I'm not worried about Inga and the food. I think the doctor convinced him to leave me be since I'm at the end."

"Let's hope so. I mean, let's hope that this thing with Axel ends, not your life. Now that I'm here maybe I can get him to trust me and maybe he'll confide in me?"

"Ruth Ann, please don't overstep with him. He really is a very dangerous man. I know he can act kind and even generous, but it's always a ruse. He'll stop at nothing to retrieve the bloody necklace, even killing you or me. Don't forget that."

"I won't," I said, thinking about my next move with Axel. He did tell me quite a bit earlier today about how he met his wife. But he stopped short at how he planned on getting the necklace back. I think it has to do with those two 'brothers' of Bertha. I'll just have to spend more time with Axel, starting tomorrow morning.

I told Prunella I was going to leave and get some sleep and I would pop up early in the morning. Just as I headed toward the stairs, Inga hurried in the room. "Where are you going?" she asked as I stood on the first stair going down.

Prunella called out, "Inga, bring Ruth Ann back for a minute and tell me what you discovered." Inga took a hold of my arm and dragged me over to Prunella's bed. I couldn't figure out why Inga kept dragging me all over the place. It was becoming quite annoying.

"I talked with Sherman, and he found out that Mr. Eklund and the two men had quite the heated conversation. Once they went to the library I was told Mr. Eklund slammed the door and had the men begging to leave."

"How did Sherman know that?" I asked curiously.

"He was in the library for most of their meeting. Sherman was ordered in there with Mr. Eklund before they all entered. He was to get a fire going and pour brandy for his guests. Sherman was in the background when they all entered and he slammed the door. Instead of retreating, Sherman stayed and waited for him to ask for his brandy. Mr. Eklund sat behind his desk and kept slamming his fists down so hard, the desk shook."

"Did Shermie tell you why?" Prunella asked.

"All he heard before he was summoned out of the room was that Bertha and her two brothers were to hand it over and that he knew they were involved somehow. Eklund asked them if their motive was purely financial and if they had already sold it."

"Oh that's good, Inga!" Prunella exclaimed. "Axel thinks Bertha's two brothers got a hold of the necklace and pawned it off on to some rich person. Axel must be livid if they did sell it. So you don't know what the brothers said to Axel after Shermie left the library?"

"He tried to listen at the door, but you know those doors are so thick, it's hard to hear everything. He did say the smart little guy spoke and told Mr. Eklund that he didn't know what he was talking about and that's when Eklund screamed at them and ordered them to leave, and if they didn't give him the truth by tomorrow they would be taken care of."

"Taken care of?" I asked, wondering if I heard her correctly.

"Yes, kill them," Inga said, all excited. "Bertha's brothers left in a hurry and Sherman opened the front door for them, and waited for them to drive off. He heard the big, dumb one say that he could handle Eklund and don't worry about it. They would do what they had to do."

"I wonder what that means," Prunella said, hopping out of bed and walking over to the window. She plopped down in one of the rocking chairs and said, "They have my necklace or maybe they used to have it. Those idiots probably sold it at a value nowhere near what it's worth."

"It's not good, but if we could get to these brothers before Axel does something drastic, maybe we could find out if they sold it and to whom. Or if we're really lucky, maybe they still have it and are just waiting for the highest bidder." I thought the news was good and the best information we had received in a long time.

"Possibly," Prunella said, rocking away steadily. "We need to find out about Bertha and where her loyalty lies. If it's to Axel, we're in trouble, but if it's to her brothers', maybe we can make an appeal to her. But how can we find that out?"

"Bertha's a nasty one," Inga spat out. "She comes in here and bosses us around, and she's only a housekeeper."

"I think Bertha's more than just a housekeeper, Inga," I said. "My guess that's just her cover."

"Really?" inquired Prunella. "That's a good observation, Ruth Ann. Maybe we need to pay closer attention to whom she talks with here."

"I think she's close to Finn," I said. "They seem to be in the same place all the time. Bertha and Finn were together in Deer Creek and now they're both here. I think Bertha's definitely on Axel's side, I'm sorry to say."

"It does look that way," Prunella said, disappointed. "We've got to come up with something and quickly."

"The only way to get to these brothers is outside of this house. What about that doctor of yours? Can he call on the guys at their shop and pretend to be a millionaire looking for a unique piece of jewelry?"

"Ruth Ann, that's pretty far-fetched, I think our best bet is to wait for them to come back here. Maybe we can get their attention before Axel sees them. They have to either come back tomorrow or run."

"What if they run? Then we're done for!" Inga cried out. "Let me bring these brothers here. I can get them alone and force them to talk."

"Inga," Prunella said, horrified. "I don't want you hurting any-one"

"But they've played dirty, maybe it's time we do, too."

"There's got to be another way," Prunella said, getting back into bed. "I'm exhausted, let's get some sleep and maybe something will come to us in the morning."

Chapter 22

Inga and I left Prunella and headed down the stairs. Inga followed me into my room and I waited for her to leave. She stood inside my door and shut it. "You won't betray her?" Inga asked in a low, calm voice.

"No, Inga, I promise," I replied, surprised at Inga and her loyalty to Prunella. "I just can't think of a way out of this without getting to the brothers and finding out if they have or had my family's necklace. This is so ludicrous, everyone fighting over a silly necklace."

"Not so silly to them," Inga said. She was about to leave but turned back and added, "I can bring those brothers here. Maybe you and I could question them without anyone else knowing."

"How could you do that?" I asked curiously, knowing it wasn't possible anyway.

"I have ways," she said. "I have some family in the area who can grab these men overnight and bring them to me."

"That sounds serious, Inga, what if your family members get caught?"

"They won't," she said, shutting the door behind her.

"That's absurd," I said out loud.

It was very late and I was exhausted. I went to the adjoining bathroom, took a quick shower, and put on my nightgown. I lay down in bed and thought of John. Where was he and was he even close to finding out where I was?

I dozed off for a few hours when I heard a slight knock at my door. I've always been a light sleeper, so the knock woke me immediately. I hurried over to the door and found Inga standing outside my door. "Follow me," she whispered.

"Wait, I'm not dressed," I said, looking down at my nightgown. Inga looked anxious, but told me to hurry up and throw on a robe. I rushed over to the closet and grabbed a woman's robe that was hanging in there. It wasn't mine, but I wasn't picky at the moment. Inga pulled me out into the hall and put her finger to her mouth, signaling me to be quiet. Axel's room was on the other end of the hall and we had to be careful not to be caught.

"Where are we going?" I asked Inga. She shook her head and led me down the stairs heading toward the kitchen. We didn't stop there. Inga opened another door off the kitchen and we hurried down another steep flight of stairs. There was barely any light, so I had to be careful not to trip on the robe as we made our way down to what I assumed was a basement.

Inga stopped at the bottom of the stairs and grabbed a string that was attached to a bulb on the ceiling. We were standing in an enormous unfinished basement. At first, it appeared to be just a large room with four cement walls. But after my eyes adjusted to the light, I noticed in the far back corner of the room was a group of people. It was too dim to see who they were, but Inga didn't waste any time and motioned for me to follow her.

"Don't speak, Ruth Ann," Inga whispered. "You have a tendency to talk too much. Let my cousins handle the situation right now."

"What situation?" I murmured.

"You'll see," was all Inga said.

As we slowly walked to the other side of the basement, I saw a circle of five people around two chairs in the middle. Those chairs weren't empty. There were two people sitting in those chairs. She didn't do what I thought she did? She had her cousins kidnap Bertha's brothers!

"Bertha?" I called out softly. "Please tell me you didn't do what it looks like?"

"We didn't have a choice. I didn't actually do it, my cousins did," she said, smiling large, yellowed teeth at me. It was the first time she smiled so widely that it showed her stained teeth, and I would rather she didn't do that again. "They're something, aren't' they?"

"Your cousins?" I asked, wondering what she meant.

"Yes, of course," she snapped. "They are intimidating and will get all the information we need out of them."

"They haven't hurt them, have they?"

"Not yet," she said, peering over one of the cousin's shoulder. "They look unharmed but terrified."

One of the men stepped back and stood next to Inga. "We'll get them to speak, just give us a little time and they'll be singing so loud they'll be heard all the way back to their stupid little pawn shop." He waited for Inga to respond, but she didn't. She kept her eyes on the two men and waited for one of them to talk.

"Inga," he said. "They have no idea where they are and why they're here."

"Have you asked about Miss Prunella's necklace?"

"I waited for you to come so you can ask them."

"But won't they know me? I served them dinner earlier tonight," Inga said. "And she can't be seen by them either if we want to keep them ignorant of where they are," Inga added, pointing to me.

"Fine," he said. "I'll put their blindfolds back on and then you can speak with them freely."

I watched closely as they put the blindfolds back on as the brothers yelled and kicked at the cousins' legs. One of the cousins smacked the big brother, Andy, across the face and a trickle of blood ran down the side of his face. Andy shut up and let them tie the blindfold without fighting back.

"OK," the cousin who talked with Inga said to the two brothers. "You'll answer the following questions or suffer the consequences. Do you understand me?" Neither brother moved an inch. *Slam!* The cousin hit the smaller brother in the stomach. He immediately coughed and threw up a small amount of liquid onto his shirt.

"Yes," Andy quickly replied for his injured brother. "We'll do what you want. I don't understand what you want from us though. Did we rip you off with something from our store? This seems a bit extreme if that's the case."

"Shut up!" the cousin responded. He must be the leader of Inga's cousins. I heard Inga call him Luke. Andy pulled back a little in his chair, expecting another hit. Luke laughed loudly and motioned Inga and me to come forward. "These women have questions for you, answer them or I won't be so nice anymore."

"Yes, whatever you want," Andy said, sensing his brother's pain from the last hit.

Inga grabbed my arm and we pushed our way into the middle

of the circle, standing right in front of the two men. I wasn't sure about being in this predicament, but since I was here I figured I might as well hit them with a stunning question right out of the gate.

"Where's the necklace Eklund wants?" *Boom!* Inga and the rest of the group, including the two blindfolded men looked my way in horror. "Yes, I asked you that," I said. "Tell me where the necklace is!"

Inga pulled me aside far enough to ask me if I was stupid. "Why would you do that?" I told Inga I was going for the shock factor to see if their bodily responses would give them away.

"Look at them," I whispered. "They're fidgeting and shaking their heads violently. They know something, just look." She turned her head and watched the two brothers try to fight their way off the chairs. They couldn't move because they were tied around the middle of their bodies to the chair. They were still blindfolded, but arms and legs were free and flailing around.

"Yes," Inga said staring at them. "Maybe you're correct. They look like they're on fire and need to escape."

I smiled and watched the two brothers squirm for a moment or two longer. Finally I repeated, "Speak or you may not be happy with the outcome."

"Wait," Andy blurted out. "Don't hit him again. I can take it, but he can't. I'll tell you what you want."

David turned his head wildly toward Andy and told him to shut up. "No," Andy replied. "I'm tired of all the threats. It's just a stupid piece of jewelry!"

"Great, Andy, you just secured our fates."

"I have no idea what you mean, Dave, just tell them."

"I'm not saying another word. If they want to beat me to death, they can."

Luke took this as his opportunity to enforce a consequence. *Slam,* again…Luke took a metal pipe and hit David, the smaller one, across the back and he fell over, chair and all, onto the floor, writhing in pain.

Andy couldn't take it and shouted, "STOP! I beg you, please leave him alone!"

Inga pushed me aside and barked, "Then tell us what you know, now! No more games, start talking!"

"Alright, I'll tell you everything," Andy exclaimed. "If I tell you'll you let us go alive."

"As long as you cooperate," Luke said. "Talk, now." Luke walked up to them and pulled off their blindfolds.

"Fine," Andy said, leaning back in his chair, watching as Luke placed David upright in his own chair. "It started months ago. Dave was contacted by some lawyer. He told him he needed us to recover a very valuable piece of jewelry. We were told we had to go to the United States and get it from a bank in some hick town in Colorado."

I was about to say, "Deer Creek," when Inga put her hand over my mouth to keep quiet. I shoved her hand away and nodded. I knew I had a tendency to talk too much, but this time I had to force myself to wait.

"Dave told the lawyer he was crazy and why would we go all the way to Colorado to get a necklace. Well, we soon found out what necklace he was referring to."

"You knew something about this necklace? From whom?" Inga asked.

"Yes, of course we did. Axel Eklund showed it to us in the past. Our sister works for him." Dave kicked Andy in the legs to get him to shut up, but Andy kept going. "It's some pricey piece that everyone was fighting about. I told Dave to forget about it, but he couldn't. He said we didn't have a choice, but to go get the necklace and bring it back to this lawyer."

"Why didn't you have a choice?" Inga questioned.

"Let's just say that lawyer had a large amount of evidence regarding our business that could put us away for years, possibly our entire lives. So Dave agreed and we flew over the pond and ended up in a town called Deer Creek."

I couldn't take it any longer. Inga noticed my urgency and nodded. She hadn't allowed me to speak too much up to now. I tried to make my voice lower and forceful. "Were you the one who bashed the bank president in the head to get your hands on the necklace?"

"Yes, that was me," Andy said, proudly. So these were the eyes that met mine as he was escaping from the bank. Finally, we meet face to face, but he couldn't identify me this time.

"Did you kill the security guard and hurt a man named, Ben?" I asked.

"Yes," Andy answered. He added, "Who are you? How did you know what we did in that hick town?"

Luke didn't like his tone and raised his hand to hit his face. Andy must have sensed this and pulled his head away. "Sorry," Andy said remorsefully. "I would like to know who you are and how you knew what happened in Deer Creek?"

"It doesn't matter anymore," Inga snapped. "You admitted to taking the necklace and killing people. I didn't know owning a pawn shop allowed you to become hit men, too."

Dave spat some blood onto the floor and got our attention. "We didn't have a choice. My big, dumb brother here already told you that. If we didn't do what this lawyer asked, we would be sent to prison for the rest of our lives. We didn't have anything to lose."

"What happened to the necklace when you got back to Stockholm?'' Inga asked.

"We brought it to a designated drop off spot and left," David replied. "We didn't even see the lawyer and don't even know his real name. He used a false name I assume, but he had all the paperwork sent to us to incriminate us. We didn't have a choice."

"What name did he use?" I asked. "The lawyer, I mean."

"Svenson, how generic a name here in Sweden," David stated.

"Did you say, Svenson?" Inga asked, stunned at his confession.

"Yes, what about it? I told you there's a million Svenson's out there," he acknowledged.

Inga and I looked at each other in amazement and became speechless. Was this the same Svenson Prunella was using to send me the necklace in the first place? Why would this lawyer send me a necklace he wanted to keep for himself? It couldn't be the same man.

"What did you do after you dropped off the necklace? Did you wait to see if anyone picked it up?" Luke asked, since Inga and I had stopped our questioning to gather our thoughts.

"Yes, of course we did," David barked. "It couldn't have been the lawyer. He must have sent some kid to do it, because whoever grabbed the package couldn't have been more than fifteen."

"And that's it? What if it was just some random kid and he ended up with an expensive piece of jewelry?" Luke demanded. "How stupid are you two?"

"Look, we did what we were told to do. Now, we answered all

your questions, so let us go," Andy insisted.

"We'll tell you when we're done with the two of you," Luke bellowed.

Luke walked over to Inga and me and asked what we wanted to do now. I wasn't sure, Inga looked puzzled, too. "Can we keep them here for a little while?" Inga asked. "I need to talk to Miss Prunella."

"We don't have time, Inga," I interrupted. "What if someone comes down here?"

"No one ever comes down here, Ruth Ann," Inga stated. "It's only been used for storage, and Mr. Eklund would have Sherman come down here and get whatever he needed. He would never come down here, it's too dirty."

"As long as you're sure," I said, looking at the two men tied up in the chairs. "We really do need to talk with Prunella. Does she know what you've done here?"

Inga looked at Luke and back to me. "No, I made the decision after I left you. I contacted my cousin, Luke, and he told me he would do whatever we wanted."

"If we leave can we keep your cousins down here a little longer?" I asked.

"It's not quite six in the morning and Mr. Eklund doesn't start moving till around eight. I think we're good for a little while longer. They can leave through the back door off the kitchen, so they won't be spotted."

I agreed, and Inga and I took off up the stairs to Prunella's room. She must've heard the door unlock from the bottom of the staircase, because she was waiting on the other side of the door at the top. Inga was the first to enter and almost took a hit from one of Prunella's canes. "Wait," Inga cried out. "It's just Ruth Ann and me!"

She stopped just in time and put down her cane. "What on earth are you both doing here at this time? Did something happen?"

Inga asked Prunella to go back and sit down on her bed while she explained what she had done. She assured Prunella that I wasn't any part of the plan. We waited for Inga to finish her story, and only hoped Prunella wasn't going to be too upset at Inga.

I was wrong. "Inga," Prunella said. "I cannot believe you went to all that trouble to help me." Prunella hopped off the bed and hugged Inga so hard I thought she was going to knock her over.

"Wait," I said, stunned. "You're okay with Inga and her cousins kidnapping those two? Even if they're not guilty?"

"Why not?" asked Prunella. "They've played dirty with me, so it's time I matched Axel's games and beat him to the punch, so to speak."

"There's one thing Inga didn't tell you, and I'm afraid it's very important," I stated. "Svenson was the lawyer that hired the brothers to retrieve the necklace from the bank in Deer Creek. They're the ones who killed the guard, injured the president of the bank, and another man. I'm not even sure if there weren't others who were hurt or killed along the way."

"What?" Prunella asked, stunned. "It couldn't be the same Svenson as my lawyer!"

"Quite the coincidence, if you ask me," Inga answered.

"But it makes no sense," Prunella said. "Why would he take the necklace from me and send it all the way to you in Colorado? He could've kept it from the beginning and concocted some story that it was stolen from him."

"Maybe it's not the same Svenson. That's why we came up here so early. We need you to contact your lawyer and find out if there is another lawyer named Svenson out there."

"Well, it's a common name here," Inga admitted. "There could be more than one Svenson in Sweden who's a lawyer."

"I don't know," Prunella, said looking disappointed and worried. "I'm going to call him now and leave him an urgent message to contact me."

I didn't think much of that comment until I wondered how could she call him. Wouldn't Axel know she made a call from the phone here? "How do you plan on calling him?"

"I have a cell phone of course," she replied, surprised at my question.

"How did you get one of those?" I asked curiously.

"Inga bought me one that can't be traced and has tons of minutes. I'm fine with that since I've only used the phone to call the doctor or Svenson."

"What should we do with Bertha's brothers while we wait?" asked Inga.

"Oh, I almost forgot about them," I exclaimed. "We need to

take them somewhere else."

"Why?" Prunella asked. "They're safe down there. Just tell Luke to secure them so they can't get away or be heard. I don't want to let them out of our sight until I've heard from Svenson."

"I'll go tell Luke," Inga said. "Ruth Ann, you should go back to your room and act like you're just waking and getting ready for breakfast."

"Yes, good idea," Prunella agreed with Inga. "Ruth Ann, act normally. Don't give anything away and please don't do the talking if you have to meet with Axel. Let him tell you his version. The last time you two talked, Axel was telling you he had an idea of what may have happened to the necklace. Let him think that's all you know. Can you do that?"

"Of course I can," I said, smiling. "You never know what else I may learn from him, too."

"Definitely, keep him talking and you listening. For all he knows, you're ignorant to everything," Inga suggested.

"Sounds like a plan," Prunella said. "Let's meet up here after breakfast unless Axel has other plans for Ruth Ann. That could present a problem if he takes some kind of action with you, Ruth Ann."

"From what Sherman told us Mr. Eklund's giving them until later today to tell him where the necklace is. If the brothers don't show, I doubt he'll do anything with Ruth Ann right away," Inga said.

"True, we may have an extra day to figure this out. Axel will be furious when he can't find those brothers. He may take it out on Bertha! Ha, that would be something I wouldn't want to miss," Prunella said, chuckling.

"Inga, come back as soon as you can even if Ruth Ann can't get away."

"I'll go speak with Luke and then serve breakfast. After that I can sneak away," Inga, said walking toward the stairs. "You coming, Ruth Ann?"

"Yes," I replied. "I hope to see you after breakfast also." I wondered if Axel was going to speak with me again this morning before he figured out the brothers were missing. He'd be livid, assuming they took off on their own accord. Instead his second wife, housekeeper, and little ole me abducted them!

Inga left me at my door and told me to hurry and go directly to the dining room. She was going to quickly speak with Luke, and once the brothers were secure she was going to tell Luke that he and the other cousins may leave. Inga would tell them to be on hold for further instructions regarding what they were going to do with them after that.

Even though I only had a few hours of sleep, I was full of energy. I didn't know what the future held for me, but for the first time in years I felt alive. Losing my husband so young left me alone and focused on raising my girls, without much of an existence of my own. I would never trade being with my girls, though; I just knew there was more out there for me than being a mother. This has been thrilling and even though my life may be in danger, I wasn't afraid at all.

I got myself ready and headed into the dining room. It was just about eight in the morning now and we were right on schedule. I walked into the dining room and Axel and Bertha were already sitting at the table. Axel had a newspaper up to his face and Bertha was staring at her empty plate. She didn't look very well this morning. I wonder if she knew her brothers were missing and she was too afraid to say anything.

"Good morning," I said cheerily, startling the other two at the table. I didn't have to be a grump even if I was a prisoner in his house.

Axel dropped the paper and smiled. "Well, it is a good morning isn't it?"

"I noticed the sun was shining and a fresh layer of snow blanketed the grounds."

"Yes, it does make one feel invigorated," Axel, said. "Please, Ruth Ann, sit down on the other side of me. Bertha, you could say good morning to Ruth Ann, too."

She lifted her head and forced a smile. "Oh, yes, good morning."

"Bertha, why so glum?" I asked sarcastically. "Did you not sleep well?"

She glared at me and snapped, "I slept just fine."

"Enough of that Bertha," Axel said with a nasty look in her direction. "I don't want anything to dampen my day." He looked around for Inga and rang a dainty glass bell that was set on the edge of the table. Inga popped in just as he rang the bell.

"Yes, breakfast is served," Inga declared, carrying all three of our plates. "Is Mr. Finn joining you this morning?"

Axel squirmed in his chair uncomfortably with her question and replied, "No, he's out this morning."

I pretended to ignore his reaction to Inga's question and dove into my breakfast. I was hungry and Inga did a much better job preparing my food this morning. I must be on her good side now and she showed it in her food. Inga made my favorite, pancakes with tons of syrup. There were four, large, buttermilk pancakes without butter, but with loads of syrup in a gravy boat.

"It's my favorite," I told Inga, pouring the syrup over the top pancake. "Thank you for all the syrup!"

Inga's glare made me tone down my happiness over receiving pancakes. We couldn't give away any relationship in front of Axel.

He didn't pay attention to my comment about the pancakes and went back to reading his paper. He had a plate of eggs, toast, and sausage. I watched as his fork would appear from the bottom of the paper and disappear when he brought it up to his mouth.

"So," I said. "What are my plans for today, if I may ask?"

Inga practically dropped the carafe of coffee she was carrying. I shouldn't have asked any questions, but my mouth has a tendency to speak before my brain tells me whether I should or not. I hoped he didn't hear my question, but I was wrong. Axel folded his paper and placed it neatly on the table. "Well," he said looking directly at me. "You and I are going to have a short conversation after we finish eating, and then I'll be occupied for most of the day. I'll talk with you in the library as soon as you're done. If you ladies will excuse me now..." Axel said, as he stood up and left the dining room.

Bertha couldn't exit the dining room fast enough. Once Axel was out of sight, Bertha jumped out of her chair and headed toward the kitchen. She definitely acted out of sorts. She must be aware that her brothers had either taken off out of fear or that Axel's men had abducted them.

Inga waited until the coast was clear and walked over to my seat and grabbed my empty plate. "What was all that about?" Inga snapped. "Bertha was nastier than normal."

"I think she knows her brothers are missing."

"Already?" Inga asked. "It's only after eight in the morning. Do you think she tried to contact them before coming here for breakfast?"

"That seems highly likely, don't you think?" I said, returning her question.

"You have another problem, Ruth Ann," Inga said, looking down at my empty plate. "Wow, you can really eat pancakes!" she said, getting off topic.

"I was hungry! What's my problem?" I asked Inga.

"You have to go to the library and speak with Mr. Eklund, and I need to go up and talk to Prunella."

"That's fine, maybe I'll learn more and as soon as I'm done I'll come up there."

"I hope it's that simple, Ruth Ann," Inga said, walking out of the dining room.

Me, too. I sat at the table a minute or two longer, before getting up and walking through the foyer to the library. The doors were wide open, and I stuck my head in and Axel waved me in. As I walked in I noticed he was on the phone, so I tried to listen in.

"Just wait outside the doors, I'm sure they'll be in soon, Finn," Axel said softly as I walked up to his desk. "I'll check back with you in thirty minutes. Stay patient and keep a close watch on the place." He hung up the phone and motioned for me to sit in one of the chairs in front of his desk. I noticed he was still in a fairly decent mood, but not as cheery as he was in the dining room. The phone call might just be the beginning of a day he didn't anticipate.

"Ruth Ann," he began. "We haven't spoken too much in the last twelve plus hours. What have you been doing with yourself?"

Uh oh, I thought to myself. He couldn't know what I've actually been doing. Inga would've warned me if I had been spotted going up to see Prunella. "Nothing much," I answered coolly, trying to come across like I'm tired of being here.

"You must've done something to occupy your time."

"I've just walked around the house and browsed through some of your books. Otherwise just slept and ate," I responded, hoping he would accept that.

He seemed to accept my answer and said, "Well, I expect to be done with all this in the next day or two, and then you can go home. I know you're here against your will, but I hope we're making it as comfortable as possible."

"Yes, it's fine and I actually forget at times that I'm your prisoner."

"Prisoner is such a harsh word," he said. "Let's just say I borrowed you for a few days."

"Why do you need me anyway? Yesterday you told me you had a theory of who had our necklace, and I hope by now it's a fact and not just a theory."

"I'm very close to knowing the exact whereabouts of the necklace, Ruth Ann. I do need you just in case you're the only one the necklace will be handed over to."

"If it was a legal transaction I could see my presence being useful. However, this all seems a bit illegal, and then I don't see how I can be indispensable."

"Just give me a few hours, Ruth Ann," he said. "Then I'll have all the answers you need."

If I was an intelligent person I would've stood up and left, but no, my mouth didn't want to leave just yet. "Axel," I said, getting his attention back from his papers on the desk. "Can I ask you a question or two?"

"It depends on what the questions are, but go ahead."

"Yesterday, you seemed quite upset that your wife deceived you and married you for all the wrong reasons. What happened after she died? Didn't you just get the necklace?"

"I was happy she was out of my life, but sad, because I did love her deep down."

"Did you get the necklace after she died?"

"Yes, but not for long," he said, appearing agitated with my question. "Why the questions? I already told you the necklace was stolen and now I'm pretty sure I know who has it at this very moment."

"That's great!" I exclaimed. "I can't wait to see this famous piece of jewelry."

Axel smiled and relaxed a little. "I'm sure you can't."

"I thought you were going to talk to me with Bertha this morning? She seemed agitated at breakfast. Is everything okay with her?" That wasn't the smartest topic to bring up.

"She was acting strangely at breakfast, wasn't she?" Axel said, as if a light bulb went off in his brain. He jumped up and ordered me to leave.

"But we aren't finished yet," I said, trying to get him off Bertha's radar.

"Later, Ruth Ann," he ordered. He came to my side and grabbed my arm and hurried me out of the library. He slammed the doors shut, and I knew had I tipped him off about something potentially going on with Bertha and her brothers. Sherman was standing right outside the library and pulled me quickly aside.

"What did you do?" he barked at me.

"I didn't do anything," I replied innocently. "We were just talking and then he jumped out of his chair and told me to leave."

"I'm not buying that, Ruth Ann," Sherman said. "What exactly were the two of you discussing when he suddenly threw you out of his library?"

"Bertha," I said quietly.

"Excuse me? Did you say Bertha?" I nodded. "What did you say that got him so upset regarding Bertha?"

"I didn't mean to say anything! I just asked him why Bertha was so out of sorts at breakfast earlier and he flipped out."

"Why on earth would you do that?" Even though he said it quietly, it felt as if he was yelling at me. "You basically told him that Bertha knew her brothers were up to something. Now he's panicking and he can become very dangerous when he thinks he's been duped."

"He has no idea what's really going on with the two men," I snapped back. "Inga's up talking to Prunella right now. I better get up there."

"I'll stay right here and see what I can overhear. And if we're really lucky I'll overhear what his next move is going to be. Tell Inga and Prunella I'll report back to them as soon as I have something to convey."

I hurried up the stairs, ran down the hall to the end and found the door unlocked. Inga must've kept the door open so I could get in without wasting any time. I found the two of them near her bed and I could tell Prunella was distressed.

Inga was the first one to spot me and asked me what happened with Axel. I told both of them what transpired and waited for them to scold me, too. Inga wasn't happy, but Prunella took it okay.

"We'll come up with our own plans once we know what his next move is going to be. I know Shermie will find out. He always does," Prunella stated. "I have other news, Ruth Ann, come and sit down."

That didn't sound positive. I walked over the edge of the bed and sat down next to Prunella. Inga paced back and forth in front of us until I told her to stop. It was very unnerving watching her go back and forth.

"What's the bad news, Prunella?" I asked.

"I heard from my lawyer," she began to say. "I don't know how else to say this except to just spit it out. Svenson is on my side, but he's not the only Svenson in his practice."

"What?" I asked, confused.

"Michael Svenson is my lawyer. Steven Svenson is his cousin who also is a lawyer."

"There are too many family relationships going on here. I'm getting quite confused!"

"I know, but the truth is Michael Svenson, my lawyer, was shocked when I told him the whole story. He isn't in practice with his cousin because he can't stand him. Steven Svenson has clients that aren't of the legal nature, if you understand me."

"You mean like the mob?" I questioned.

"Yes, exactly."

"So what does this all mean?" Inga asked, towering over the two of us.

"It means that Michael is the one who took the necklace and sent it to you, Ruth Ann. Then Steven hired Bertha's brothers to get it back."

"So Steven and Bertha's brothers have the necklace!" I cried. "We can get it back before Axel does. We have those guys sitting in the basement right now!"

Inga spoke before Prunella had a chance, "Yes, I can go down and get them to tell me where it is. They claim they gave it to the lawyer at some drop-off, but I don't believe them. They either have it or sold it."

"Michael's confronting his cousin, probably right around now. He told me he'd contact me as soon as he's done."

"He better be careful," I said. "This Steven has had people murdered to get the necklace."

"He knows all about it," Prunella said. "He doesn't think he's in any danger because it's his first cousin."

"Greed doesn't always care when family is involved," Inga declared. "I'll go now and force it out of them. I'll look in their eyes, and I can tell if they're lying or telling me the truth."

Inga started toward the door, but Prunella told her to wait a minute. "Ruth Ann," Prunella said. "Go with her. Between the two of you I think we might get some truth from them."

"I agree," I said.

Chapter 23

Inga and I left Prunella and headed down the stairs toward the kitchen. We had to separate so no one would become suspicious of us. When I arrived in the kitchen I had a plan to ask for a hot cup of tea in case others were in there that couldn't be trusted. When I stepped into the kitchen, I found Inga at the sink and Bertha seated at the wooden table. Sherman was also in the kitchen, filling a silver pot with coffee.

"Oh, I'm sorry to bother you, Inga, but could I ask for a cup of hot tea?" I asked.

Bertha stood up from the table and said, "Inga's busy right now. She's got something she needs to do for Mr. Eklund. Can't you get it yourself?"

"Of course I can," I replied. "Inga, go ahead and do whatever you need to. I'll manage just fine." Inga gave me a nasty glare and took off out of the kitchen, but not to the basement.

I walked over to the many cabinets, and opened and shut several of them loudly before I came across the cups. Bertha became frustrated with me and stormed out of the kitchen. I noticed Sherman was taking a long time getting his coffee from in the pot. "Sherman," I whispered. "Are we safe to talk?"

"No, thanks to you," he snapped at me.

"What did I do?"

"You forced Mr. Eklund to make a move with Bertha's brothers earlier than he expected to. He has Finn outside their pawn shop right now, and from what I overheard after you left, he has probably already broken in and searched the place. You know what that means don't you?"

"No, should I?"

"He'll know they're missing. They live above the shop in a two-bedroom apartment, and once he doesn't find them at the store he'll most assuredly search their apartment. It was going to happen eventually once the brothers didn't show up here later, but now it's just too soon."

"I didn't mean to set Axel off, Sherman, it was a slip and I realized it the moment it left my mouth."

"It's done, now we need to figure out our next move before we all get caught."

"It's fine. We now know that the brothers were hired by Steven Svenson and they either have the necklace or know where it is. All we have to do is get back down to the basement before they're discovered."

"Steven Svenson? I thought his name was Michael Svenson?"

"Steven is Michael's cousin according to Prunella, and he's pretty nasty. Prunella talked to Michael earlier and he knows all about what's going on. He was going to confront Steven."

"Is that wise?" Sherman asked.

"I agree that it's dangerous for Prunella's lawyer to question his cousin. He's a murderer."

"Exactly! I don't like where this is going, Ruth Ann. The brothers know what's going on and I bet Inga's going to pop in here soon and head down there. I would go too, but if we are all missing it will look suspicious."

"I'm going down there, too," I said. "Here's Inga," I added, watching Inga hurry back into the kitchen.

"Is she gone?" Inga asked, looking around for Bertha.

"Yes, let's go," I said, walking toward the basement door.

Inga and I hurried down the stairs and found the brothers tied to their chairs and gagged. Luke was standing over them. "Luke," Inga said, walking over to him. "I thought you'd be gone."

"Didn't think that was safe. These guys are sneaky. I didn't trust leaving them alone down here. What's the plan?"

"We're going to get some answers. They know more than we thought, and it's time for the truth," I said to Luke.

Luke picked up the metal pole that was down in the basement next to the furnace and waved it around the two men. "So," he said, taking the pole and poking the bigger one in the stomach. "Are you ready to talk or should I skip the pleasantries and just start hitting?"

Andy, the larger brother with the pole aimed at his stomach, thrashed his head up and down. "OK, I'm going to pull the gags out of your mouth, but if you do one thing to tick me off I'm not going to be held responsible for my actions." Luke's efforts to scare them upfront appeared to work. He pulled off the gags and Andy took a deep breath and coughed.

"What do you want from us? We told you we don't have the bloody necklace anymore."

Inga stepped up to Andy and said in a low, terrifying voice, "You're lying."

"About what?" David asked, getting Luke and Inga's attention away from his brother.

"We have information that isn't consistent with your story. Let me give you one name that might change everything, Steven Svenson."

We watched their initial responses to the lawyer's name. Andy's eyes opened wide, and he opened his mouth to speak then snapped it shut it. David, the obvious brains of the two, took a sneakier approach. "Who's that?" he asked, playing ignorant.

Luke was true to his word, and without any warning raised the pipe and whacked Andy in the back. He cried out in pain and fell over in the chair. He lay on the basement floor, cringing in pain and yelled at his brother to stop the lying. "Please, Dave, just tell them what we know!"

David watched as Luke picked Andy up in his chair and put him upright. "Next time it'll be much harder," Luke said, grasping the pipe in one hand and tapping it on his other hand.

"Fine," David said, realizing they weren't going to get out of this without telling us the entire truth. At least what we had to accept as their truth.

"Let's start at the beginning," I said. "From the time you were hired to retrieve the necklace from the bank president in Deer Creek, Colorado."

David went over the whole story while they were in Deer Creek. It didn't get fuzzy until they returned to Stockholm with the necklace. "I don't believe you dropped off the necklace and waited until some kid picked up the package." I said.

"That's the only time we made up lies," Andy said, watching

Luke closely. "We didn't drop off the necklace anywhere. Once we retrieved the necklace, we contacted Svenson and he told us to keep it in our safe at the shop."

Luke looked at Inga and me to see if we believed him. "Go on," I said calmly. "Is that where the necklace is right now?"

"No," David answered angrily. "We did as we were told," he continued. "But someone stole it from us!"

"What?" I exclaimed in horror. "Who?"

"We have no idea," David replied. "We assumed it was Svenson, but when he asked about the necklace we knew it wasn't him. He wanted to come by the shop and look at it, but we kept making excuses."

"When was this?" I asked.

"A few days ago," he answered. "If it wasn't Svenson, then it had to be Eklund. That's why we came here for dinner last night. We thought he was going to confront us about how we obtained the necklace and why it was in our safe."

"I can guarantee it wasn't Mr. Eklund," I replied. "He's panicking about that necklace and thinks you two have it."

"Us?" Andy shouted out. "He figured it all out and knew it was us that went to Colorado, didn't he?"

"He told me that he had a theory and it involves the two of you. I never said anything to confirm or deny it."

"But we're in his house!" David exclaimed. "If he finds us here, he'll kill us. He thinks we still have the necklace, and when he discovers it's not at our shop or apartment he will kill us because we won't be of any use to him."

"Bertha must have figured all that out and that's why she had such a worried demeanor about her this morning," Inga said.

"Bertha!" Andy cried out. "Keep her away from him!"

"I'm not quite sure which side Bertha's on, yours or Eklund's?" I asked.

"Of course she's on our side," Andy said. "She's our older sister."

"I don't know," I said, watching how they reacted. "I think she's in love with him."

That did it! David screamed, "That's the craziest thing I've ever heard! She hates him."

Inga smiled at me for my questioning. "Why does she hate

him?" I asked, seizing the bait.

"Because he didn't choose her, he chose that rich woman and married her for her money and that stupid necklace! That necklace has to be cursed, because anyone who touches it suffers," David said, knowing I had sucked out more information than he intended on giving us.

"I knew there had to be more to your story," I said. "Bertha did love him years ago, but Axel chose his first wife because she possessed the necklace."

"Yes, she was young and fell in love with the man for who knows what reason. I told her it was impossible to marry into that family, they only marry rich people and we're not rich," David explained.

"So instead of marrying him she became his housekeeper?" I asked.

"Yes, she did. She believed in time he would see his first wife for who she was and leave her. Bertha was ready to be there for him when that happened."

"That didn't happen, even after all those years did it? Axel never loved Bertha and after time her love turned to hate, didn't it?" I asked, even though it was obvious what the answers were.

"Yes," David said sympathetically. "His wife died last year and Bertha waited for him to declare his love for her, but he never did. The jerk went and married another woman!" Aha! Finally, someone acknowledge Prunella!

"Excuse me?" I questioned, pretending I didn't know what he said.

"That's a secret not many people are privileged to," David responded. "Eklund went and married some woman he was having an affair with for years. His first wife knew about her, but she didn't care because, from what Bertha told me, she was cruel to him and all of the staff."

"Really?" I said.

"Bertha spent years trying to figure out why this woman -- his first wife -- was married to Eklund. He had money, but she had way more money than him. She wore that stupid necklace all the time because she was afraid he would steal it from her if she didn't have it on her body."

Did Bertha ever find out why she was married to him?" I

asked.

"Yes, she did and it was ridiculous," Andy interrupted. "He married her because she knew about the Eklund family and their business dealings. The Eklund's had a reputation of being corrupt and swindling people out of lots of money. His first wife's family was no exception."

"I thought you said she was wealthier than Axel?" Inga asked.

"She and her parents were, but they had to rebuild their fortune after Axel's grandfather destroyed her grandfather's business and everything they owned."

"Wow, this is amazing," I said. "Why did Axel's grandfather destroy them?"

"Because he could. They're just that kind of family, evil," David replied. "His first wife somehow came into possession of the necklace and that was her in with Eklund. She knew he wanted that piece more than anything. It was a part of his family history and he had to have it back. She used the necklace to lure him in, and it worked. That's when she set her plan in motion to make his life a complete hell."

I glanced at Inga and I could tell she was in shock, too. There were so many twists and turns with this case I didn't know what direction to go. I decided to ask them what they knew about Prunella.

"Who's the woman Eklund married recently instead of Bertha?" I inquired.

"She was his personal attendant for years. Bertha and everyone else knew she and Eklund had an affair going on. Nobody would've thought Eklund would marry her though. It's a sad story though, the second wife became ill and Eklund has her locked up in a secret location. Bertha told us that the doctor was here yesterday and told him she would pass away any day now. So sad, she's quite young from what I know." David stopped talking, and I watched as he became choked up. I almost forgot they were killers for a moment and felt sorry for him.

"Wait," I said suddenly. "How do you know all about his second wife?"

"Bertha keeps me informed," David answered, squirming in his chair a little.

"Why?" Andy asked his brother, who appeared in the dark

about his brother's knowledge of Prunella. "I didn't know about his second wife and her being sick."

"Not you, too," Inga broke in, frustrated. "You knew his second wife and had feelings for her, didn't you?"

"Maybe a tiny attraction, but the only person who knew that was Bertha," David stated. "It was nothing, I just thought she was nice and very beautiful. Once she married Eklund I didn't think much about her until Bertha confided in me that she was very ill."

Luke anxiously said, "Can we get back to the topic at hand, the necklace and who has it now?"

"We don't have it, I swear!" David cried.

"OK," I began to say. "If you two don't have it, and Mr. Eklund doesn't have it, then who took it out of your safe and where is it now?"

We looked at each other dumbfounded. I believed that the only explanation possible was that Steven Svenson went to the brother's shop and took it out of their safe without telling them.

"Impossible," David responded. "We would know if anyone touched the safe. It records every time it opens and I would've seen that. Somebody else must've broken in, but I don't know how, unless…" David hesitated and looked at his brother. "Andy, you didn't open the safe and show the necklace to anyone did you?"

Andy, still recovering from Luke's blow shook his head violently. "No, no, I didn't show anyone. But, the safe could've been broken into, Dave. The program that shows the safe's activities broke down a couple days also and that's why you haven't seen any activity. The last time we opened the safe was the last time the recorder worked."

"What?" David screamed at his brother. "You stupid oaf! Why didn't you tell me the safe was broken? Do you know how many valuables we keep in there? It could destroy us. Actually, now it has."

"I'm confused," I said. "Are you telling me that the last time you looked at the necklace was when you got back from Deer Creek and put it in the safe?"

"Yes, until we opened it up and found it missing. Svenson wanted to come and have a look, so I went to retrieve it and it was gone. That's when I made up excuses to Svenson, and we were lucky that he was held up with another case for a few days. Andy and I thought we were in the clear for a short time, and we could find out what happened to the necklace. I checked the activity on the safe immediately, and it didn't show anything, so I couldn't figure out who took the necklace. I didn't know the safe program was broken, and now anyone could've stolen the necklace during that time."

"But you immediately suspected Mr. Eklund?" Inga asked.

"Yes, of course," David replied. "He's smart enough to be able to break any code on the lock and that's why we willingly came here to dinner last night. To see how he acted with us, and we thought we might be able to tell if he was the one who broke in and stole the necklace out of our safe."

"But he threw you a curveball when he demanded the necklace back and only gave you until today to do it, right?" I asked.

"Yes, but he could still be fooling everyone," David said. "Maybe he's just playing a sick game and does have the necklace."

"Does Steven Svenson know that the necklace has been stolen from your safe?" I asked.

"Not yet," David replied. "I'm sure he will very soon and I don't want to be the one to tell him. He'll kill us for sure."

"Unless we can find out where the necklace actually is," I said. "I just don't understand who else could be involved. If it's not you two or Eklund or Svenson, who else is there?"

"Maybe his second wife," Andy quietly spoke.

"Who?" Luke asked.

"I said, maybe his second wife took it."

"How?" Inga demanded. "She's deathly ill and why would she do that anyway?" Inga had to keep up the charade that Prunella was still sick.

"Because she married him for his money. She didn't count on Eklund being a terrible husband or her getting sick," David said. "Wait a minute, what if she's not really sick?"

"Impossible," Inga said immediately. "There's been a doctor here continuously and even Eklund feels sorry for her."

"How do you know he feels sorry for her?" David asked suspiciously.

"All the staff knows that," she snapped back at him. "She wouldn't have the strength or the means to go to your shop and break into your safe. That's ridiculous!"

"Maybe not," David replied. "Who else do we have to suspect now? It could be possible."

"Well, I'm not going to waste my time on that theory. We need to figure out who took it and where it is."

Luke pulled us aside and asked us what we wanted to do with the brothers. We couldn't leave them here for too long, but if we let them go we could be in trouble ourselves. They would rat on Inga and me in an instant, or even more dangerously bring Prunella into the list of suspects. That had to be avoided at all cost.

We decided to leave them down here for the afternoon, and then come up with another solution. Luke said he would stay for a little while longer, but then he had to leave. Inga told him whatever time he could give here would be great, and when we were ready to get the brothers out of the basement she would call him.

Inga and I walked up the basement stairs, and Inga opened the door first to make sure the kitchen was empty. I followed her after she waved me through the door. We were alone in the kitchen and I really wanted to ask her some questions that were bothering me.

"I think we need to keep them until it's dark out so nobody sees them being taken out of here."

"Yes, Luke will wait until after dinner. Mr. Eklund will be furious by then, once he thinks the brothers made a run for it. I wonder what he'll do to Bertha."

"Bertha!" I exclaimed in a low voice. "Maybe she's our necklace stealer?"

"No, you think?" Inga asked.

"Why not? She's their sister and they would never suspect anything of her. She has probably visited their store in last few days, too. I think we need to find her and ask her some subtle questions."

"Oh, I don't know about that, Ruth Ann. Won't she wonder why we want to know?"

"Leave it to me. I'll come up with some sort of explanation."

"You know, it does make sense," Inga said, rethinking her original position. "She could be our thief and not even her own brothers would suspect her."

"Exactly," I said. "I bet she did it to give it back to Axel, because she still loves him. She would look like the hero if she did that!"

"We must warn Prunella."

"Yes, you go to Prunella and I'll meet you up there after I find Bertha."

"I can't go up there yet," Inga said. "I still have to act normal around here, and that means preparing luncheon. Maybe you'll have a moment alone with Bertha during lunch if Mr. Eklund leaves early. He's going to be more and more impatient as the day goes on if he can't reach Bertha's brothers."

"I agree, Inga," I said. "He may not even show up for lunch."

"Yes, he will," Inga, replied. "I have his request for lunch on the counter, so he's planning on it."

"I guess we don't have any choice. I hope Prunella is doing okay upstairs. She must be dying to know what's going on."

Inga was about to respond when the kitchen door swung open and I rushed over to the table and grabbed a cup for tea. We couldn't let on that Inga and I were on friendly terms. I sat down and poured a cup from the pot, and when I looked up I saw Sherman stomping over to Inga.

"Where have you been for so long?" he asked as he noticed me at the table. "You, too?"

"We were down in the basement, you knew that," I answered.

"This whole time?"

"Yes, a lot has transpired and to be honest, Sherman, we don't know what to do next," I replied.

He looked at his watch and told us he had a few minutes before Axel needed him. "Get to it," he said. "Don't leave anything out."

Inga and I told him all that transpired in the basement. As we went along with our explanation, Sherman's face grew redder and redder. "This is horrible!"

"We know, Sherman," Inga said. "But what do we do now?"

"We keep those goons in the basement until we know they won't be a problem for us. We need to get through luncheon and ascertain how Mr. Eklund is doing. If his demeanor has changed and he's anxious and irritated, then we can assume he suspects Bertha's brothers will skip their appointment with him."

"Then what?" I asked. "If he's acting like everything's okay, we can find out if Bertha is the one who stole the necklace from her own brothers?"

"Exactly what I'll do," Sherman answered. "Leave Bertha to

me."

"We need to warn Prunella," Inga said nervously. "I'm worried she won't be safe if Mr. Eklund suspects something's up."

"He won't think the brothers have anything to do with Prunella. He thinks she's helpless and ill."

"As long as you're sure," Inga said to Sherman.

"Yes, I was in there when the doctor was here, and he was genuinely upset about the news she had only a few days to live."

"That's good," I said. "After lunch I'll go up and see her and fill her in on what's been going on."

"Okay, we have a plan. Let's try and stick to it until we have more information about Bertha's connection with the necklace, if there is one. But I think she's the one we need to talk to," Sherman stated. "She's been acting funny and I know that she's been torn between Mr. Eklund and her brothers before."

"Before?" I inquired.

"Eklund has had previous dealings with her brothers at the pawn shop. They tried to pull a fast one on him once, and Mr. Eklund didn't take too kindly to being duped, so they have been on the up and up with him ever since. I believe Bertha warned them how dangerous Eklund can be when he's backed up against a wall."

"I can't imagine what he'll be like once he finds out the brothers are missing and so is the necklace!"

"I have a good idea," Sherman replied. "He'll hunt down the brothers and whoever else is involved and kill them all!"

"Let's make sure we're not in that group," I said. "I'm going to head into the dining room and see if Bertha's already in there. Maybe I can speak with her privately before Axel shows up."

"I want to deal with her myself, but it wouldn't hurt if you talked to her, too. As long as you're careful about any specifics."

"I can handle her."

I took off into the dining room and it was still empty. I took the same seat I had for breakfast and waited. I waited for at least a half hour when Axel walked into the room. He smiled at me and sat at the head of the table. I was on his right, and earlier Bertha had been on his left, but her seat was still unoccupied. Axel asked, "Where's Bertha!"

I shook my head and Inga walked in and answered for me.

"She's probably around here somewhere. I'll get you both started and look for her." Inga placed our lunches in front of us and I dug in. She made a quick chicken salad and plopped it onto a large lettuce leaf.

Axel dug into his lunch and appeared a trifle agitated. "What have you been up to this morning?"

"Not much," I replied, chewing a mouthful of chicken salad. "I've spent most of my time in my room or in the kitchen getting tea. Have you decided what you need me for yet?"

He glared curiously at me and responded, "Soon, very soon."

That was all he was willing to say. I wasn't going to push him because the last thing I wanted to do was make him suspicious of what I'd been up to around the house. I could tell things were heating up just by the lack of communication from him. After he finished his meal he stood up, gave me a little smile and said, "We'll talk later."

"OK, I'll be here," I replied as he walked out of the dining room.

Inga immediately came in and was panicked. "I couldn't find Bertha!"

"What?"

"I think she's gone, but where?"

"We need to go and check on Prunella, hurry," I said, getting up from my chair and heading toward the main stairs.

Inga followed and we went up to the second floor hall and hurried down to the end. Inga went to unlock the door to the stairs to Prunella's room but found the door opened a couple of inches. "Oh, no," she cried.

"Hurry," I said, running up the stairs behind Inga.

We opened the door at the top of the stairs and immediately looked to the bed where Prunella should be lying. The bed was empty. "Where is she?" Inga shouted, scanning the room.

"There," I pointed at the rocking chair under the window. Prunella was sitting upright in the chair with her mouth gagged and her arms tied around the back of the chair.

We ran over to there and I gently pulled the gag out of her mouth, and she took a huge breath and exclaimed, "Bertha, it was Bertha!"

Inga furiously worked on the knots on the back of the chair to release her arms. Once she was freed, Prunella stood up and grabbed my arm tightly. "Bertha came up here about an hour ago and the look in her eyes was horrifying."

"What did she say?" Inga asked.

"She accused me of faking my illness and she said she knew I did something with her brothers, and once she found out what I did, she would come and finish me off. After that she'd tell Axel everything."

"How did she figure it all out?" Inga inquired.

"She said she's been watching you and Ruth Ann for the last day and knew you both were coming up here. She hasn't been able to get ahold of her brothers and is frantic for their lives. Not just because of us, but because fears Axel's wrath if he gets ahold of them."

"Where did she go after she tied you up?" I asked.

"I don't know," she answered. "I think she went to search for her brothers."

I looked at Inga and asked, "You don't think she knows they're in the basement, do you?"

"We need to go now and check. If she does, we're in such trouble!"

Inga and I told Prunella to stay put and we'd come right back. We didn't think Bertha would come back that fast, and once we knew her brothers were still in the basement, we could plan our next move. Prunella agreed and told us to hurry.

We ran down as fast as we could, and grabbed Sherman from the kitchen. He was getting upset because he couldn't find any of us and informed us Axel had locked himself in the library. "Bertha!" he bellowed. "She did that to Ms. Prunella?"

"Yes, she's fine, but we have to get back to her before Bertha does," Inga declared.

We flew down the basement stairs and my fears came true, Bertha's brothers were gone. All that was down there were the gags and the loose ropes that had bound them to their chairs.

"We're too late," I cried.

Inga ran to the far corner of the basement, and in the darkened corner discovered her cousin, Luke. He was curled in a ball, unconscious.

"Luke," Inga called, taking his shoulders and turning him

around. "Please Luke, wake up!"

I went over to them and asked, "Is he alive, Inga?"

"I don't know," she said, panicking.

I knelt down and grabbed his wrist and felt for a pulse. "He's alive," I said. "His pulse is weak, but he's still alive."

Inga grabbed an item that was underneath him and held it up. "It's the same pole Luke used to hit them."

"I had a feeling they did that," I said. "When I picked up his arm, I felt a puddle of blood and knew he'd been hit."

"It looks like they got him in the back of his head, and I've always heard that heads bleed a lot."

"We need to help him," Sherman said, coming closer to us. "But how are we going to get him out of here without being spotted?"

"I don't know," I answered. "The three of us need to carry him up the stairs and get him to Prunella's room. She can contact that doctor of hers and he can help him."

"That's our only option right now," Inga said shakily. "We can't let anyone see us."

"We'll be careful," Sherman said. "Let's do this."

I looked around the basement and found some old towels thrown by the furnaces and grabbed them. We wrapped Luke's head and body as well as we could, so the blood wouldn't drip on the floors as we moved him. Inga's was the strongest, so she took his upper body and Sherman and I each took a leg. We made it up into the kitchen and Sherman ordered me to let go and make sure the coast was clear. I headed out of the kitchen first. All was clear as we made our way up to the second floor without being spotted by Axel.

"OK," Sherman said out of breath. "Almost there."

Once we were on the stairs leading up to Prunella's room I thought we were safe. We entered her room and Prunella rushed over to us to see who was wrapped in the towels.

"I thought you had one of the brothers," she exclaimed. "Oh, Inga, it's your cousin, Luke."

"Yes, ma'am," Inga said, as they set him down on the floor. "He's not waking up and we need your doctor to come and help him." Inga looked at Prunella with pleading eyes. "Will you help him?"

Prunella leaned over Inga and placed her hand upon her shoulder and smiled. "Of course." She went over to her nightstand and pulled out her hidden phone. A minute later she responded, "He's on his way."

"Can he get to you without Axel catching him?" I inquired.

"Yes, he's done this before." Prunella said.

"I'll go down and wait for him," Sherman stated. "The normal spot, right?"

Prunella nodded and explained to me that when her doctor has been here before, he parks down the road and enters through the kitchen. Sherman would be looking for him and bring him straight up.

"Now that we have Luke under control, tell me, what happened?"

We told Prunella how we found Luke and that Bertha and her brothers hit him before they escaped from the basement. "This is terrible," Prunella professed. "They're gone, and now what do we do?"

"We go after them," Luke replied, as he tried to sit up from the floor.

"Whoa," Inga said, pulling him back down. "I'm so happy you're awake, Luke. We have help on the way, but can you tell me what happened down there?"

He slowly sat up with Inga's help, and took ahold of his head with one of his hands. "Wow, they gave me a good one. I guess I had it coming after bashing them a couple times."

"I know you're in a lot of pain, Luke," I said. "But do you remember what happened down there?"

"Yes, everything," he said clearly. "I was walking around the basement trying to find cell service when the door to the basement opened quietly. I only knew someone was coming down the stairs because of the light that crept in. I assumed it was one of you," he said pointing at Inga and me. "But then, out of nowhere, this woman came running at me waving a gun at me. She told me to drop my phone and the pipe I was holding or she would shoot me. Well, I did like she asked and she ordered me to untie the two men."

"Did you know they were her brothers?" I asked Luke.

"Once I realized who was pointing the gun at me I knew. I also knew I was in serious trouble."

"One of the brothers hit you with that pipe, didn't they?" I asked.

"The big one, Andy. He couldn't wait to give it to me."

"Did they tell you anything before you were hit?" Prunella questioned.

"Yes, the big one has a giant mouth!"

"Don't leave us hanging, what did you find out?" Inga asked impatiently.

"Once I untied them, Bertha told them to tie and gag me up. David refused and told Andy to bash my head instead."

"Oh my, they thought you were dead didn't they?" Prunella asked.

"I believe their intention was to kill me, but I'm a tough breed. Before they hit me, I had to free them, then they circled me and questioned me thoroughly."

"About what?" I asked. "Last we spoke with them they claimed they didn't know who had the necklace."

"I can answer that now, too," he replied. "Bertha has the necklace!"

"I knew it!" I cried out. "Did her brothers know she had it?"

"I'll kill them if they did," Inga said, fuming.

"No!" Luke answered. "They were furious with her. I almost thought I could get away without them even noticing. They were screaming at each other, but just as I slowly stepped away Bertha grabbed my shirt and pulled me back."

"Bertha's stronger than I thought," Inga said grudgingly.

"She was so full of adrenaline I think she could've taken us all down."

"What happened after she told them she has the necklace?"

"First, they wanted to know how, since it was supposedly locked up safe and sound back at their shop. She told them it was when she visited them a couple days ago. They thought they could trust her, and left her alone to man the shop while they went up to their apartment to grab a bite to eat. When they came back down they didn't suspect anything, and Bertha walked out of the shop as if she did nothing wrong."

"That simple, huh?" I asked. "Amazing."

"Yes, she took the necklace and it's been in this house the entire time," Luke said. "Her brothers were fuming mad at her, but once they calmed down a bit they were happy to know that at least they knew where the necklace was."

"Then what?" Inga questioned.

"The two brothers wanted to make a run for it and contact that lawyer of theirs."

"Steven Svenson?" Prunella inquired.

"I guess so, the name Svenson sounds familiar. I have no idea about the first name, though."

"It has to be Steven," Prunella added. "He's the one who has been killing people to get his hands on the piece."

"I agree," I said. "Do we know how to find this man?"

"I'll call his cousin right now," Prunella said, grabbing her phone and walking away from us.

"Wait," Luke said too loudly, then grabbed his head. "Bertha told her brothers not to contact Svenson."

"Why not?" I asked.

"She wants to give it to Eklund if he'll accept her proposal of marriage."

"What?" Prunella cried out. "He can't marry her if he's still married to me!"

"Bertha figured you would be dead one way or another," Luke replied. "She knows you're faking your illness, but she still said you would be dead within the next day or so."

"That's ridiculous," I snapped. "She would have to come up here and find her first!"

Prunella sat on the edge of the bed holding the phone in her hand. "Why didn't she kill me before? She had me up here alone and she just left me."

"Maybe she wanted to make sure her brothers were safe and far away from here before she came back here to finish you off," Luke said.

"That's got to be her plan," I agreed with Luke. "We need to get you out of here right away."

"Where are we going to go? Axel has this place under heavy surveillance. We won't be able to take two steps outside without being caught."

Suddenly, Sherman entered the room with the doctor behind him. "Did I hear you correctly? You don't think you can get out of this house without Mr. Eklund catching you?"

"Yes," I answered. "We've got to get Prunella out of here before Bertha comes back and tries to kill her."

"How do you think I got the doctor up here? I have ways of getting in and out of this place without being detected by cameras."

The doctor hurried over to Luke. He looked at Luke and said, "You got a nasty blow to the back of your head." He put on a pair of latex gloves and inspected his head. "Looks OK, probably more external damage than internal."

"Will he be alright?" Inga questioned the doctor.

"I believe he may have a sore head for a few days and a slight concussion, but he'll survive."

"Thanks, Doc," Luke said, trying to stand up.

"Go easy," the doctor said, grabbing his arms to help him up. "You may be a trifle dizzy and nauseous as you stand."

"I'm okay, we need to get out of here," Luke said, stabilizing himself.

"I agree," I said. "Where did Bertha take her brothers?"

Sherman and the doctor were filled in on the activities up till now. "Maybe Bertha and her brothers went back to the shop and their apartment," said Sherman.

"Finn's there looking for them," I replied. "We overheard him on the phone earlier."

"Finn," Prunella said. "I forgot about him. He's a loose cannon. If anyone gets in his way, he'll kill them."

"I know," I agreed. "He's hurt people I care about back in Colorado."

"Bertha probably knows Finn's there waiting. They may sneak up on him and overtake him. Andy's a bully and can whip a mean pipe!" Luke stated. "I have the bump to prove it," he mentioned while rubbing his head.

"Should we all go to the pawn shop and see if there's any activity?" I asked. "We need to get out of here, quickly."

"I think I should stay behind and be the lookout. Mr. Eklund doesn't suspect me at all, so I can help by staying here," Sherman insisted. "Inga has my cell number so we can stay in close contact. Once he finds out Ruth Ann and Prunella are missing he's going to go ballistic!"

"I should go," Inga declared. "I'm as strong as a man and we need some muscle since Luke's out of commission."

"I'm not out of commission, Inga," Luke demanded. "I can go."

The doctor put his hand on his shoulder and told him, "Absolutely not. You'll do more harm than good. I'll go with you too, Prunella."

Prunella's eyes lit up and she gave him a huge smile. It was at that moment I realized why this doctor was so helpful around here. I bet Prunella and he were in love.

"George, are you sure? This could be very dangerous."

"That's exactly why I'm going, Prunella. I can't let you three go without me," George, the doctor, declared. "No exceptions, I'm going. Plus, I have a vehicle parked just down the path here."

"Perfect," I stated. "Let's get out of here."

Inga and Sherman huddled together and agreed to let Sherman stay behind. I agreed too, because he was getting up in age and may not handle physical challenges very well. I wasn't sure I was up to those challenges myself, but I didn't have a choice. This all has to end and sooner than later. I really wish I knew where John was.

Chapter 24

JOHN WILKINSON

Judy and I spent the day researching Axel Eklund and his family. We went to the local library and finally ended up at the police station, pleading our case. After getting laughed at the police station, we realized we weren't going to receive any assistance from the police.

"Eklund probably has them all paid off," Judy declared.

"It sure appears to be that way."

"We're on our own, John," Judy said. "We need to be really careful who we talk to, because from what I've seen and heard around here people either fear him or are paid to be on his side."

"Let's find a place to stay and we can plan our next move," I said.

We found a small hotel in downtown Stockholm and grabbed the last room available. "We'll have to share, Judy. You take the bed. I'll crash on the couch."

"Whatever," Judy replied. "I'm more than willing to share the bed, but if you're more comfortable on the couch, that's your choice."

We took the information from the library and the notes we'd taken on people we'd talked to, and spread them out on the table in the hotel room. "Not much to go on, but there has to be something here we can start with," I told Judy.

"We know his place is about twenty miles from town. He must be there with Ruth Ann. I'm sure he's well-guarded, so just showing up may not be wise."

"We'll rent a car in the morning. I'll go down and reserve one and pretend we're American tourists. Hopefully we can find a person willing to give us places to see, and maybe one of those has to do with Eklund's estate or business. His shipping business is around here, too."

"Sounds like a plan," Judy said. "I'm bushed."

I left Judy and went into the tiny lobby and asked if I could rent a car from someone near here. "We can do that," the woman said from behind the desk.

"That's great," I replied. "Have any suggestions of places to visit near hear? We just got here from New York and want to see how the locals live."

"Oh, you're thinking about moving to our city?"

"Possibly," I answered. "We like to visit places and see how people live, not just the typical touristy sites."

"OK. Let me think," the young woman said. "I can recommend some really good places to eat and then the shipping industry is huge around here."

"Really?" I asked casually.

"Oh yes," she began. "I thought since you're from New York that might interest you. There are some small boating companies, lots of shopping around the piers and of course the largest shipping company."

"Who has the largest one?" I inquired.

"Oh, that's Eklund Shipping Company," she stated. "They practically own the whole area."

"Wow, they sound pretty important. Never heard of them, anything worth visiting?"

"Yes, they have huge ships on display there, including an old Viking ship. There's a museum that shows how ships have evolved over the years, too."

"Sounds like an interesting place. How do I get there?"

That was all it took. I was able to have a car ready in the morning and directions to Eklund's business. I thanked the woman and went back to my room. Judy was sound asleep, but I was too full of adrenaline to sleep.

I lay down on the couch and started thinking about Ruth Ann. Was she safe and unharmed? I was getting closer and closer to rescuing her if she could just hang in there a little while longer.

Chapter 25

RUTH ANN

Prunella went into a small closet and came out a few minutes later dressed and ready to go. I took a moment to run down to my room and grab any essentials I may need, just in case I wasn't able to get back here to retrieve my possessions. Inga and Sherman went down to the kitchen so they wouldn't be too obvious about being involved with us.

George waited for Prunella and they came down and knocked gently on my door. We took off down the back stairs toward the kitchen. There was no sign of Axel. Sherman told us he was still locked in his library.

"We need to go," George said anxiously. "I don't think it would be wise for Eklund to walk in and see all of us, especially his dying second wife!"

"Agreed," I replied.

Sherman took us out the back door and showed us how to avoid the cameras positioned around the grounds. He went back in the house after wishing us luck, and telling Inga to stay in close contact.

"I will," she promised.

"If they come back, I'll call you immediately," Sherman said as he went back into the house.

We followed George down a grass path that led to a small road. His car was parked alongside the road. Prunella hopped in the front and Inga and I climbed into the back. "Where are we going?" I asked.

"We're going to drive over to the brothers' pawn shop to see if we can identify Finn or any of the others there. If the coast is clear, we'll go inside," Inga said.

"What if Finn's roaming around outside?" Prunella asked.

"We will go around to the alley and see if we can get in that way," George decided. "There's always an entrance from the alley, and if we know Bertha and her brothers aren't there, then it'll safe for us to go in. Especially if Finn's just hanging out front."

We drove about twenty minutes when I noticed that we had left the countryside and had entered the fringes of a town. "Their shop is on the outskirts of downtown Stockholm," George said. "They're located in a shadier part of town."

"That's just great," I said sarcastically. "But it doesn't surprise me."

"There's not much traffic, and few people hang around here. We'd be noticed if we pulled up near the shop. I think I'll do a drive by, and all of you need to look out for Finn."

George turned from the main road to downtown Stockholm, and went down a small side road. He told us to start looking, but don't make it too obvious. I was beginning to regret our decision to drive over here!

"There's their shop," Prunella called, pointing to a rundown two-story brick building. "It's a dumpy little place, isn't it?"

"I would think that they would have a much nicer building with all the merchandise they keep in there," I said, hunching down in my seat. "I don't see anyone out front, do any of you?"

"No," George replied.

"Either do I," Prunella said. "I think we should still drive around to the alley and park there. If we can get in I say we do it. We don't have too many choices left."

George turned down the next street and went around to the alley leading to the back of the pawnshop. "Here we are," he said, driving past the back of the shop and parking behind a tattoo shop. "We can park here. People will think we're going into the tattoo place. There are quite a few spaces here for customers."

It was a cold, cloudy day outside. It was a week before Halloween, and my goal was to get back home and open my shop before Halloween. I buttoned my coat and got out of the car. George suggested only a couple of us go in at a time, just in case Finn or the others surprised us when we went inside the shop.

"I'll go in with you, George," I said.

Inga argued with my decision, but in the end I won out because she didn't want to leave Prunella behind. George and I walked over to the pawn shop's back door and turned the knob. I expected it to be locked, but it wasn't. "Suspicious?" George inquired. "Maybe Finn's inside waiting for Bertha and her brothers."

"I sure hope not," I replied. "You still want to go in, don't you?"

"Definitely," he said. "Let's go." George turned the knob and opened the door a little. It was a heavy metal door and I was afraid it would make noise when it opened. George poked his head in and reported that it looked like a storeroom of some sort, and it was dark.

"Let's go in," I suggested. George opened the door wide enough for the two of us to enter. I frantically looked around for signs of human activity, and found nothing but a mess of a storage room. "These guys are pigs!"

"It's awfully cluttered back here. I wonder how they can find anything."

"Most people who live in chaos believe they have it all under control. I bet if they were asked to find something they would believe they could."

"Chaos is chaos," George mumbled. "Typically I've found that when people's work or homes are in chaos, their lives are chaotic, too."

"I couldn't agree more, George."

We looked around the room, but it was a futile effort. It was such a mess we wouldn't be able to distinguish new information from old. "I think it's time to wave in Prunella and Inga. What do you think, George?"

"Let them wait until we check out the main part of the shop. If it's still safe, you can run out and grab them."

George went through a swinging double door that led to the main part of the shop. "It's dark in here, too."

"Maybe that's a good thing," I said nervously. "I really don't want to run into Finn."

George walked all around the shop. It was a small room with glass cases surrounding the outer walls. The front door was a large, metal door with a deadbolt locked in place. "Nobody came in that way," I said, pointing at the door.

"That explains why the back is unlocked. Somebody's been here before us."

"The question is who? Finn or Bertha and her brothers?"

I wanted to find the safe where Bertha stole the necklace. I looked around the walls for a safe or a picture where a safe could be hidden. I spotted a number of pictures, but the one that stuck out was of a large Viking ship. "What's with Viking ships around here?" I called, motioning to the picture on the back wall next to the double doors that led into the storage room.

George snickered and we walked over to the picture. He took it off the wall.

"I knew it!" I exclaimed. "The safe's behind it."

"That was almost too obvious," George replied. "Let's see if we can get into it."

"I doubt it," I said. "It looks like a number is required to open the safe and it could be an endless task trying to guess at that."

"Or," George said, smiling broadly. "It could just happen to be open!"

"What?" I exclaimed.

"Yep, the safe was already broken into. The whole thing appears to be busted."

We looked inside excited to see what we would find. "Empty," I snapped. "Completely empty."

"That's strange," George said. "You would think there would be something in there, even if it wasn't valuable pieces of jewelry or coins."

"Ya, like papers or money," I retorted.

"Somebody's definitely one step ahead of us."

"It has to be Bertha and her brothers. They must've come back here and quickly emptied it. But where did they go?"

"That is the million-dollar question," George stated.

"What about their apartment? How do we get to it?"

"I think it's out back. There was another door in between this shop and the tattoo parlor."

We hurried back outside and reported what we found to Inga and Prunella. They chose to join us in searching the brothers' apartment. We went to the door in the middle of the two shops and opened it. It was also unlocked.

"I need to go first," George said, pushing Inga aside. She was ready to fly up the stairs and fight.

"I'm stronger than any of you," Inga retorted.

"I'm sure you're right," George responded. "But I feel it's my duty as a gentleman to go first."

"Fine," she snapped, and moved out of the way.

I was the last to go up the narrow staircase that led to a single door at the top of the stairs. George carefully opened the door, and once he felt it was safe he waved us all in.

"Whoa," Inga said. "Somebody trashed the place. Not that it was a nice place to begin with. Look at all the furniture turned up-side down and the drawers and cabinets emptied and tossed all over the floor."

I looked around the tiny studio apartment and tried to take it all in. Two sofas had their cushions torn off and exposed pullout beds. The TV entertainment center, filled with top of the line equipment, was smashed so badly it was of no value anymore. Whoever ransacked this place knocked over the entertainment center and destroyed all the electronic equipment.

In the kitchenette area, the few cabinets in there were hanging off their worn hinges and emptied. Plates and cups were shattered and littered all over the countertop and floor.

"Wow," George said stunned. "Somebody got out a lot of rage here."

"Well, that clears Bertha and her brothers," I stated.

"Why's that?" Inga inquired.

"Why would her brothers trash their own place?"

"I didn't think about that," Inga answered, picking up a fallen kitchen chair and turning it right-side up.

I noticed a bathroom off to the side, near the living room. I walked in and it was in the same condition as the rest of the place. The mirrored medicine cabinet was torn off the wall, and whatever contents used to be in there were now spread over the counter. I picked up a pill bottle and read the label. It was Xanax, a mild sedative. I opened the bottle and noticed there were only a couple pills left out of the sixty that were prescribed. Hmmm, I thought. What else were they taking? The name on all the prescriptions bottles was for Andy, Bertha's younger, but much larger brother. He must have serious anxiety issues because there were two other pill bottles with his name on them, filled with drugs for depression and nervousness. I filed that information in my head for future use.

There was nothing else of use in here, so I went back into the living area and started sifting through the rubble. "We should look for any clue to where they might be going," I said.

"Good idea, Ruth Ann," Prunella responded. "I'll look in the kitchen area."

I went to the mess on the floor where the entertainment center used to be. Inga and George were righting the furniture and searching each piece as they did.

I picked up a drawer that used to be in the entertainment cabinet and pulled out a pile of papers. They were instructions for their TV, cable, and speakers. I was about to set the drawer back down on the ground when my hand felt a piece of tape. I sat down on the ground and turned the drawer over. The tape held a white, long envelope. I ripped it off and held it in my hand. Instead of calling everyone over, I chose to read what was inside first. It could be another set of instructions or some other useless information.

I was mistaken.

I held in my hand a lease for another property. It was a rental space near the water in Stockholm. Why is this so secretive? Could it have anything to do with Eklund's shipping business? Or maybe it was something as simple as place to open another shop? I called everyone over and revealed what I found.

"Ruth Ann," George said as he grabbed the paper from my hands all excited. "Do you know what you just found?"

"A rental property lease from what I could read."

"Yes, but you don't understand the significance of this lease," he replied. "It's located near the shipping docks, where Eklund puts his into the water,"

"Really?" Prunella asked, looking over George's shoulder trying to take a peek at the paper.

"I know exactly where this is," he said. "Where did you find this, Ruth Ann?"

I told them how it was taped secretly to one of the drawers and that I figured it was useless, but George and the others disagreed with me. "What does it matter? It could just be where they want to open another shop."

"I doubt it, Ruth Ann," Inga said.

"Too much of a coincidence," George stated. "If it was as simple as that why would they go to so much trouble to conceal it?"

"Good point," I acknowledged. "But why do they need to hide it?"

"Couple reasons," George began. "David was possibly hiding it, even from his brother, Andy. Or both knew about the lease, and they were worried this place would be searched. I would go with the latter. Maybe they didn't want Bertha or that lawyer, Steven Svenson, finding it."

"It can't be Bertha, because she's with them right now, and if that's where you think they went, then she's aware of it too," I said.

"We need to get over there right away," Inga said. "I don't want to lose them again."

"Yes, let's go," Prunella said, heading toward the door. "I want that necklace in my hands by tonight!"

"Or my hands," I said quietly, so no one would hear. It's my property, too.

We rushed down the stairs and loaded into George's car. "How far is this place?" I asked.

"The docks are on the other side of town. I'll go around the city, so we should be there in about thirty minutes."

"That long?" I inquired.

"City traffic, Ruth Ann," Prunella said. "We may not be an American city, but Stockholm's quite large."

I sat back and closed my eyes for a minute. I'm getting too old for these adventures. At first I felt alive and invigorated, but now I just wanted to go back home and see my daughters and open my store. I heard that if you envision something deep into your brain, it'll all come true. I sure hoped it would, soon.

We were about there, when George pointed out Eklund Industries. It was a massive building about a block away from the water. "He builds his ships here and then transports them to the water, and off they go to whoever purchased them. Quite a business he's got," George remarked.

"Why would he risk all of this for a necklace that can't be that expensive," I questioned.

"Ruth Ann," Prunella chimed in. "The necklace has so much more value than money."

"I know it's been swapped between our families for over a

century. I get that, but is it really worth all of this?" I questioned, glancing at his empire.

"Yes, it's gone back and forth between our family and his, but it's a matter of pride and priceless value," Prunella explained. "Axel's father and grandfather fought to the death to keep the necklace in their family and our side wasn't any better."

"But who's the actual owner of the necklace?" I asked.

"Our family of course," she answered. "It was your great-grandmother, Beda, who received the gem as a wedding present from her family. As far as I know, the necklace originated in our family first, not Eklund's. But Axel will tell you different."

"I wish your lawyer, Michael Svenson, would've just given the necklace to you, Prunella."

"Why is that?" She asked inquisitively.

"Because I wouldn't even know it existed and nobody would've been killed or injured over it in my hometown. Plus, I'd still be in Deer Creek working at my little antique shop."

"But you wouldn't have met me, Ruth Ann," Prunella declared, a little hurt.

"I'm sorry, Prunella," I said, feeling badly that I hurt her feelings. "That's not what I meant. I just wish we could've met without all this drama."

"You've saved my life, Ruth Ann," Prunella said. "I'll always be grateful that you ended up here to help us. We couldn't have done it without your help."

"Thank you," I replied. "I'm not sure how much help I've been, but I'm happy you and I have been acquainted now. We'll always be family."

"Yes, we will," she said.

"Okay," George interrupted. "I'm going to drive by the address on the lease and you'll see how close it is to Eklund's business."

We drove a block from the end of Eklund's property, and there was the rental property address. "They rented a place right in between his building and the water where he puts the boats in," Inga stated. "That can't be good."

"No, Inga," George replied. "They did it on purpose, but why?"

We sat in silence as we drove by the short block of old brick buildings. They were run down, two-story flats that were probably sought after housing years ago. But years of being near the water, and not being taken care of made these buildings very undesirable. I was surprised they hadn't been torn down for other opportunities. They would make a nice location for a waterfront restaurant or new Brownstone housing.

"We can't park here," Prunella said from the front seat. "Your car will be spotted immediately."

"I know, this isn't the best street to rent a property unless they had other plans for it," Inga said.

"Like taking down one of Eklund's ships," George mentioned. "Why else would they rent here? It's no place for a pawn shop." George drove by and turned down the last little street before the docks. There was an alley behind the building, and he parked the car there. "Ruth Ann, why don't you and I take a walk around the place and see if we spot any activity." There was no other car parked back in the alley, but we couldn't be sure if the building was empty or not. They could've parked their car somewhere else.

"How can we get in there to see if they've been here, or are still hiding out." We walked all the way around the building without seeing anyone. There was a moment, however, when I felt a chill run up my spine and I looked around and still nobody was around. We ended up back in George's car, trying to come up with a plan.

"This looks quite dangerous," George declared. "Maybe we should be contacting the police now."

"No way!" Prunella cried out. "Axel has the whole police squad under his pay. They won't help us at all."

"If my friend, John, who's the Chief of Police back home was here, he would help."

"I'm afraid that won't do us any good, Ruth Ann," Prunella said. "He's back in the United States."

But was he really?

Chapter 26

JOHN WILKINSON

I woke Judy early the next morning. The car wasn't going to be out front until ten in the morning. That would give me enough time to fill Judy in on my conversation with the desk clerk and grab some breakfast.

"That's great, John," Judy declared, putting a bite of fried egg in her mouth. "I think we may finally have a lead in finding Eklund and Ruth Ann."

"It's all we've got. We'll start with the museum and see if we can work our way into his office. Maybe he'll even be there, wouldn't that be interesting?"

"I don't think it'll be that easy," Judy answered. "But maybe we can find some useful information about what he's been up to, and where he may be keeping Ruth Ann."

"Let's get going," John said, paying the bill. "I want this to be over with by the end of the day."

"Sounds like a solid plan."

We exited our quaint hotel and a four door, white sedan awaited us in the street. The morning desk clerk handed us the keys and gave us another map to use for sightseeing. I thanked him, and Judy and I left the hotel.

"This map shows his building is just on the other side of town," Judy stated. "We can be there in a few minutes unless traffic is bad."

"We're in the middle of Stockholm in the morning. I'm not sure what kind of rush hour they have here, but the roads look pretty good right now."

We drove down the street, and Judy directed me toward the

business district located on the water. "Eklund's business is only a block or two from the water," she said. "He must need it close so he can put his boats into the water."

"I guess so," John said, maneuvering through the traffic.

"The traffic's picked up as we get closer to the water," Judy said, looking up from the map.

The trip over to Eklund Industries took a little longer than I thought, but we were finally there. It was a massive structure, and Judy led me to the entrance where the museum was located. We parked the car in a large lot and went to the front door of the museum.

"No," Judy cried out. "It doesn't open until one in the afternoon."

"That's just great," John exclaimed. "Let's walk around the area and see if we can spot anything of interest."

Judy and I walked around the entire business, and saw where the ships were taken from the enormous opening at the back of the building. "They must put them on huge trailers and carefully transport them to the water. Let's walk over to the docks," I said. "It's just a short two block walk from here."

We made our way down a small street. In between Eklund's building and the water was a rundown street with old brick buildings. "I'll bet back in the day these were high rent apartments," Judy declared. "I doubt anyone would live in them now. I wouldn't want to walk around here late at night."

"Probably not the safest area to be in."

Once we passed the brick buildings, the docks were visible. Judy and I walked to the edge of the water bank and looked at several ships tied up to the long pier. "Are these all Eklund's ships?" Judy inquired.

"I bet they are," I said, counting six ships of all sizes."

"Wow, John," Judy said. "What if he has Ruth Ann on one of those?"

"I hope not," I replied.

"Actually, if those are ships he's built for other businesses I'm sure he wouldn't stash Ruth Ann there. They probably move them out pretty quickly."

"Possibly," I said.

We walked around the area until just before one o'clock. "It's time," I said, looking at my watch. "Let's get back over to the museum. I'm getting an anxious feeling that something's about to break."

"I hope you're right, John."

The museum was on the opposite side of the building from the water. It took us a few minutes to get over there. We entered a three story gigantic room. "Wow," Judy exclaimed. "Look at this place."

"It's quite a business he's got for himself," I said. "There's even a gift shop here. Probably makes quite a lot of money off that, too."

Immediately upon entering the museum, we saw a life-size Viking ship smack dab in the middle of the room. Surrounding the ship was a pool of water and a bridge that led up to the deck of the ship. "He spared no expense in here," Judy declared, walking up to the ship. "Are we going up the bridge to have a look?"

"Might as well," I answered. "We need to check the whole place to see if we can come up with any clues of what to do next."

There weren't many people here and we stuck out, so we pretended to be a typical married tourist couple. Judy oo-ed and ahh-ed at the ship. I had to admit it was impressive. We spent a couple of hours inside the museum, even going into the gift shop. That's where we were able to speak with an actual employee of Eklund's.

I picked up a tiny replica of a Viking ship and brought it over to the counter to pay. I asked, "How much is this?"

The girl behind the counter appeared to be in her early twenties. She immediately answered us in English. "It would be thirty American dollars."

"That's a lot of money for such a tiny ship," Judy said, holding it up in front of her examining it closely.

"Oh, no," the girl replied. "It's very good quality, ya?"

I took the ship from Judy and gave her a quick glare. "It's a very good looking ship. Is it one that this company made years ago?"

"Everything in here is either from an old ship or part of a new ship," she said tersely. She looked at me strangely and asked, "Where are you from?"

"Oh, we're from New York City," I answered quickly. "Have you ever been to our country?"

The girl relaxed a bit and answered, "No, but I want to some-day. I've always lived here, in Stockholm. After a while it gets boring."

"I bet it does for someone as young as you," I replied. "I'm sure you'll get many chances to travel in your future."

She pepped up and said, "I sure hope so!"

"So, can you tell me more about Mr. Eklund and all his boats?"

"He's a very rich and powerful man around here. I only got this job because my father works in the shop as an engineer. He helps design the ships."

"That's wonderful for you and your dad," Judy interrupted. "I bet it's quite a luxury to work at this company."

"Yes, we get many perks working here," she replied. "I get paid a good salary just to sit here and sell souvenirs. My father's well paid, but he can't talk about his job very much. I only know that he works on the ships' designs and how to build them."

"Why can't he discuss his job with you and your family?" Judy inquired curiously.

"It's the rules around here. Mr. Eklund makes every employee sign a paper that demands you remain loyal and quiet about what goes on here. "She rolled her eyes and giggled, "I really don't know why, it's just a bunch of ships being built. Seems silly to me, but oh well."

Judy laughed too and said, "I agree, but rules are rules, right?"

"I guess so," she snarled. "I don't know who he thinks he is, telling us what we can and can't say though. I don't like that rule."

"So you have to follow that rule, too?" I asked inquiringly.

"Nope, he thinks I'm just some stupid, young girl who doesn't know anything," she said, smirking. "I know lots, let's just say that!"

"Really?" Judy asked, getting a little closer to the counter and leaning against it. "Tell me something juicy," she started to say. "This trip has been kind of boring for me. I could use something stimulating."

"Well, I don't know," she said, looking around the shop.

"Please," Judy begged. "We don't know anybody around here, so who could we tell? I just want something to keep me awake for the next tour we go on."

"I get that," she said, perking up. "OK, since you're strangers and all, what can it hurt?"

Perfect, I thought. Judy did an excellent job convincing this girl we're nothing but harmless American tourists. I took a step back so the girl didn't think I was as interested in what she was going to say to Judy. I pretended to be looking at a case of old miniature ships.

"So, please tell," Judy said, smiling as innocently as she knew how.

"OK," the girl started. "My boss, Mr. Eklund, thinks I don't pay attention to what he says when he comes around here. I've always been told to listen and learn, that's what my mother always taught me."

"Good advice from your mom," Judy added.

"Yes, it was. Mr. Eklund comes down here often to see how many people have visited his museum. Whenever he does, he pops in the store to check out the sales in here, too. Usually he ignores me completely, because he's always on his phone. I think it's quite rude of him to not even say hello to me or tell me I'm doing a good job."

"I agree," Judy replied adamantly.

"Thanks," she said, smiling. "Sometimes he comes in here with his bodyguard, a guy named Finn."

Bingo, I heard one name I was familiar with. We're definitely getting somewhere. Judy knew it and remained quiet so the girl would keep talking.

"This Finn is one scary looking guy."

"Why's that? And why does your boss need a bodyguard?" Judy asked curiously. "It's just a shipping company, right?"

"Yes, but I think there's more going on here than just building ships."

"Really?"

"My father told me to mind my own business around here and I'll do just fine. But that's not me. I keep my eyes wide open and watch what's going on here and over at the docks." She took a breath in and continued, "Why else would Mr. Eklund need a bodyguard? This Finn, I think he's related to him somehow, has a huge neck tattoo of a Viking ship, and it's the nastiest thing I've ever seen. It doesn't help that he isn't attractive either."

Judy eyed me and I smiled my approval to her. Keep going, Judy, that's all we need to do.

"Well, he has been here at odd hours and when I've been over on the docks for one reason or another I've noticed loads of boxes being put onto one of the ships."

"It could be parts or something related to the ship," I replied.

"I don't think so," she said, matter-of-factly. "It's always the same ship. It's one that Mr. Eklund uses for his own personal reasons. Don't ask me why, just not one of the boats that have been built for somebody else. Most of the boats that are moved over to the docks leave within a few days. We constantly move them in and out. This boat has been here the whole year I've been here. It only leaves for a day or so and then comes back."

Judy asked curiously, "What do you think is in the boxes?"

The girl looked around and leaned over the counter and whispered; "My friends and I have gone to the docks at night to watch a few times. There are several men carrying these boxes on to the boat and they carry guns. Why carry guns if they're just loading boat equipment?"

"That's very observant of you," Judy answered. "Why bother watching them? Or have you heard rumors around town about illegal things Mr. Eklund is transporting?"

"I never said it was illegal," she snapped and stood straight up.

Uh oh, Judy better bring her back and calm her down. "I'm sorry," Judy said very sweetly. "I thought that's what you were implying, that's all."

The girl relaxed and said, "I guess you're right. "You're not a cop or anything like that, are you?"

"Who me?" Judy said, grabbing my arm and squeezing it. "We're just newly married and traveling around Europe. "Did you hear that John? Cops?"

"Sorry, we're just plain old boring American tourists looking for some excitement."

"OK," she said relaxing. "I could get myself in tons of trouble if Mr. Eklund found out I was betraying him."

"How could he find out?" Judy asked.

The girl pointed to a camera in the corner and said, "That's how."

I couldn't believe I missed the camera in the store. Judy tried to play it off and laugh but the girl stopped her and said, "Don't worry, it's been broken for like a week or more."

"It doesn't matter to us," Judy quickly said, shrugging her shoulders. "We don't know anybody from here."

"That's good. Mr. Eklund has a reputation around here that isn't so squeaky clean."

"Why's that?" I asked, joining the conversation.

"He gets mad at people regularly around here. If you're not performing perfectly or to his standards, he'll either fire you or have Finn bully you. It's really not fair, but he pays really well."

"That's why you and your father stay working for him?" Judy inquired.

"Yes, but my dad's very careful about how he does his job. He doesn't want any trouble. I think he's worried about me because he knows I have a big mouth."

"You have a right to speak your mind," Judy said, smiling. "It's a good trait to have and that'll get you far in your future."

"Thanks!"

"Have you ever seen what's in those boxes over at the docks? Or where they came from?" I asked curiously.

She looked at me and hesitated a moment. "I've seen large Eklund Industry trucks and that's where the boxes are unloaded from. My friends and I think its drugs!" She waited for our reaction but we didn't give her much. "Doesn't that surprise you both?"

I elbowed Judy and we both said at once, "Of course!" I added, "We don't want to alarm you, but you and your friends should be careful to not get caught watching them in case it's drugs in those boxes."

"We won't," she declared. "It's kind of exciting actually. Not much to do around here, so this has been something we do when I notice the trucks all lined up at the back of the building. That means something's up when several trucks are just waiting there."

"How often does that happen?" I asked.

"Once a month exactly."

"That sure sounds suspicious," Judy stated.

"That's what I've been telling you both. I really don't know why I started talking to you about this."

"It's our fault," I said. "We were just a little bored ourselves.

Why else would we have come to a museum about ships?"

"So when's the next truck shipment?" I asked the girl.

"That's the funny thing," she began to say. "I haven't seen Mr. Eklund here in weeks, and tonight is supposed to be the next truck shipment over to the docks."

"Are the trucks lined up out back?" Judy asked.

"Yes."

Judy and I looked at each other, and I was sure we both had the same thought. We need to be here for that shipment. Eklund may return and bring Ruth Ann with her.

"One last thing," I inquired of the girl. "What time do they usually unload the boxes?"

"Why? Are you thinking of coming back here?"

"Maybe, if we're still awake at the time," Judy answered quickly before I could mess it up. "Will you be here, too?"

"Maybe, I'm not sure this time," she said. "But it's always at midnight."

"Thanks," I told the girl, smiling. "Maybe we'll run into you and your friends later."

"Possibly, but be careful not to be seen by any of them. I don't think they're the forgiving type of people if you get caught."

"We will," Judy said.

We said our good-byes after purchasing several items from her. I didn't want any of the items, but felt it was our duty to buy from her since she was so helpful.

Once in the car Judy suggested we take another walk down to the water. I agreed since we knew Eklund wasn't in his building and hasn't been in weeks. "Pretty obvious where's he's been," I said to Judy.

"In Deer Creek, at his other house."

"Yep, but now he's back here and my gut tells me he'll be in this area later tonight."

We walked out of the parking lot and onto the short block before the water. It was midafternoon and there was no one around. "I wonder if they'll ever tear these properties down and make it more attractive."

"I think they should build up the businesses in the area. Put in a restaurant and a few shops. It'll help beef up the business around here and make it a safer area," Judy said.

We were just leaving the block, and the water lay about a hundred yards ahead. A car was coming down the street. It was the first one I've seen around in a while. It was coming from behind so I couldn't tell who was in the car, but I had a sudden chill run up my spine.

"What is it?" Judy asked me.

"I just had a weird feeling." I added, "Did you happen to see who was in that car that just passed us?"

"All I saw was a car full of people. They turned down that little street right here," Judy said, pointing to the street on the left. "I think it goes to an alley behind the buildings."

"Oh well, at least it wasn't Eklund and his companion, Finn," I said. "Let's get back to the car. I think we should keep ourselves under cover. I'm going to drive around the area and see what we can find."

"Sounds good," Judy replied.

We made our way back to the car and I drove down the street and turned down the same small street that the car we just saw went. "There," I said. "That's the car that just went by us. They must rent one of these deserted buildings."

"John," Judy said, eyeing the car carefully. "There are two women in the car. I don't recognize either of them, but they seem deep in conversation. I don't think they even saw us drive by."

We drove back to the main street that leads to downtown Stockholm. "Let's stop and grab a bite to eat and go over what we know," I said, pulling into a café.

We ordered an early dinner and went over and over what the girl in the museum shop told us. "I think we're stuck until later tonight. What do you think?"

"I'm not sure, Judy," I said, thinking about that strange feeling I had when the car passed us by. "I have a feeling that car we saw on the deserted block had something to do with what's going on."

"John, it was just a car full of women," Judy answered. "We know Ruth Ann's with Eklund and Finn. Maybe those women are employed down here. If you know what I mean?"

"Oh, you think they are..." I stopped before using the word prostitute.

"Really, John, you're so archaic. You can say the word hooker."

"You could be right. There are a lot of men near the docks from what the museum shop girl said."

"We'll find out soon," Judy said, biting into a juicy cheese-burger.

Chapter 27

RUTH ANN

"So what are we going to do?" Inga asked, leaning over the back of the front seat behind Prunella.

"I think we need to go and check the place out," I stated, even though I knew George was opposed.

"Ruth Ann, what if Finn or Bertha and her brothers are up there?" Prunella asked.

"We can go in the front or the back and just peek in. If there's no one around, we can see if this is even where they went. We don't know that for sure either."

"We've come this far," George said, changing his mind. "Let me go by myself. If I find the coast is clear, I'll come back down for you all. But if I don't come back in ten minutes, get out of here immediately."

We protested, but agreed with George. He was going to try and get inside the back door. We weren't sure what the building was used for. Was it an apartment or a business that had been deserted? George moved the car short distance from the doorway, just in case someone was watching and spotted us sitting in the car. He handed me the car keys and told me to sit behind the wheel. George took off back toward the door and disappeared inside.

"This is crazy," Prunella declared. "One of us should have gone in with him. What if they kill him?"

"Prunella, we don't know if they're in there," I replied. "Let's give him the ten minutes then we'll decide what to do."

"He told us to leave," Prunella stated. "You don't intend on doing that, do you?"

"No way. He's only here because of us and I would never

think of abandoning him."

"I agree," Prunella bellowed.

Here we sat, three minutes, four minutes…" I'm not liking this," I said. "He should've been out immediately if there was no one in there."

Five minutes, six, seven…ten. "It's been ten minutes, Ruth Ann," Inga said, turning off the timer on her watch. "Let's go in and rescue him!"

I agreed with Inga, but I really wanted to run. I opened the car door and Inga and Prunella followed suit. We made our way over to the back door. It was a metal door without a lock. "I'm going in," I said.

As I gripped the door handle the force of someone coming out pushed me back. "Watch out, Ruth Ann," Inga cried.

"It's only me," exclaimed George. "I thought I told you to leave if I took longer than ten minutes."

"You really think we would do that, George?" Prunella questioned him with a smile.

"No, I guess knowing you three like I do now, you would be reckless and fight your way in."

George closed the door behind him and huddled us close together. "Someone's in there."

"What? Who?" Prunella demanded.

"When you get inside this first door, there's a small stairwell. You can take a steep flight up to the second floor or go through another door that leads into a lower level apartment."

"Which way did you go?" I asked.

"Both," he replied. "I went inside and went straight ahead to the door there that opened into a studio apartment. There was nobody in there and I doubt anyone has lived there in a very long time. I only did a quick look around, but the only living thing in there was a rat. I went back into the stairwell and quietly ascended the stairs. At the top of the staircase was another door. This door I didn't open."

"Why not?" Inga asked eagerly.

"Because, when I got to the top of the stairs I heard voices."

"No?" I exclaimed. "Whose, could you tell?"

"Bertha and her brothers from what I overheard."

"What about Finn?" Inga asked. "Did you hear his voice?"

"No. I'm assuming he hasn't been here. You wouldn't believe what they were talking about!"

"Wait," Prunella cried out. "Are we safe standing here?"

George looked around and decided Prunella was right. We hurried back to his car and got in. George drove a little further down the alley. We were now at the furthest point in the alley before leaving the block. "I think we're safe here until we decide what we're going to do."

"Okay, c'mon George, tell us what you overheard?" Inga demanded.

"I stood outside the door and I could hear loud voices. They were fighting with each other. I knew I was safe because they couldn't hear me over their own yelling."

"Yelling about what?" I asked.

"Bertha wants to go back to Eklund and present him with the necklace and the brothers refuse to let her. They told her it was theirs to sell and not her decision."

"What about the lawyer that hired them to retrieve it in the first place?" I asked.

"They mentioned him, too," George said. "They said they'd take care of him after tonight."

"Take care of him? And what's tonight?" I questioned, knowing the answer to my first question.

"Why would they have to kill the lawyer?" Prunella asked. "Just tell him the necklace was stolen. Why does there have to be all this violence?"

"I agree, Prunella," I replied. "This has been the most ridiculous kidnapping. I've loved meeting you all, but the killing has to stop!"

"Let me get back to what I heard," George stated. "Bertha's adamant about going to Eklund. She still thinks he could grow to love her, but her brothers just laughed at her. They told her she'd be a fool to go to him. He would agree at first, but once his greedy hands got the necklace he would kick her to the curb."

"Not that I'm agreeing with those men, but that's probably true," Inga declared. "You can't trust Mr. Eklund. He'll never have your back, only his own."

"David is clearly the brother in charge. He insisted they stick to the plan and finish their business tonight, then take off and never come back here again."

"Wait, what business?" I requested again.

"I'm not quite sure about that," he answered. "Something about a shipment tonight they're planning on intercepting."

"That makes no sense," I said.

"I think this is a much bigger operation than just your necklace, Ruth Ann," George said. He saw Prunella's expression and he amended, "I'm sorry, Prunella, it's your necklace, too."

Prunella smiled and reached for my hand from the front seat. "We're in the same family. Either one of us can possess the necklace. I don't care anymore."

"Me, too," I said. "If we keep it, we can share it. Or if you need the money we can sell it, too."

"That's if we ever get it back," Inga stated.

"We will!" I said with certainty.

We turned our conversation back to George. "What else?" I asked.

"Bertha's still fighting for her cause, but she agreed they had to get through tonight's shipment and then they'd decide. She told them they'll make a ton of money tonight and they don't need the necklace."

"A ton of money?" I inquired, again. "They must be robbing someone, but who?"

"I know!" Prunella shouted out. "I bet they're involved with stolen merchandise, such as jewelry, and they're intercepting a shipment of jewelry tonight. They'll rob the people tonight and take off with it. Then they'll sell it once they get away from here."

"That has to be what they're doing," I said. "What else can it be? Drugs maybe?"

"I doubt it," Inga replied. "Bertha wouldn't let her brothers get mixed up in drugs, it has to be stolen goods like jewelry. They own a pawn shop so it makes perfect sense."

"I agree," Prunella declared. "We'll wait and see what happens tonight."

"I bet Axel and Finn will be there, too," I stated. "We'll all be there. I bet Axel's fuming right now, with us missing, too."

"He had to have figured out that you were working together by now," George said. "I doubt he knows I'm involved. We should keep it that way just in case I need to get back to the house for any reason."

"Yes, George," Prunella answered. "What do we do for the next several hours?"

"I'm hungry," I called out. "We haven't eaten in hours and we have about six hours to waste."

"Let's go get something to eat, maybe not so close to here, just in case," George said, starting the car and pulling out of the alley. "I'll drive into downtown and we'll stop at a burger joint. I know of a good one."

We agreed to eat and unwind a bit before tonight's activities. It was just before dinnertime and it shouldn't be too crowded yet. George drove about fifteen minutes away from Axel's business and the docks. He pulled into a spot on a very crowded street right in the heart of Stockholm.

"It's always crowded downtown, Ruth Ann," he said, watching my apprehension. "It's better that we melt into the crowd a bit anyway."

The four of us went into "The Burger Shack" and sat in a booth. I was looking forward to a Swiss cheeseburger on rye bread. That's always been my favorite way to eat a burger. Along with a pile of French fries of course!

"What's our plan for later?" I asked, finishing half my burger already.

"I think we should get over to the docks around eight and hang out until we see Bertha, her brothers, and Eklund. We know he'll be there, it's his shipment I believe they're planning on hijacking," George declared.

"What do you think Bertha will do when she sees Mr. Eklund?" Inga asked. "If her brothers are planning on stealing his shipment she can't be a part of that if she wants to marry the guy."

"I have no idea what she's planning on doing," Prunella responded. "Maybe she'll stay back and not even head over to the docks. That building is less than a block from the dock."

"True," I added. "If she thinks Axel will be there, she won't be seen with her brothers. He's going to be fuming mad anyway about all of us, and the precious necklace that's still missing."

"That's why he'll be here tonight," George stated. "He may think something's up, and he'll be armed and ready to go with his buddy, Finn."

"What are we going to do there?" I asked curiously. "We're not armed or capable of defending ourselves against all of them."

"I think we should find a safe hiding place near there and wait and see what goes down," George responded.

"That sounds good to me," Prunella said. "Then we can talk about what we should do as it happens."

Inga looked furious and stated matter-of-factly, "I want to rip those little brothers' heads off!"

"Whoa, Inga," George exclaimed. "We can't do anything foolish or we risk getting hurt or killed."

I looked at Inga and begged her to stay calm. "I know you want Prunella safe, so I can honestly say to you that if you do anything rash it'll make our situation worse than it is now."

"She said quietly, "I wouldn't risk any danger to Miss Prunella, I promise."

"Good," George said, looking at each one of us. "We agree to wait it out and not rush into danger." We nodded and continued our meal.

Prunella, who happens to be skinny as a rail, finished an entire half-pound burger and most of her fries. "I didn't peg you as a burger and fry eating girl," I said laughing. "Where do you put it all?"

"It's been a long time since I've been out of Axel's house and free to eat like this." Prunella looked across the table at Inga and said, "Not that your cooking is bad, Inga. I just wanted a big juicy burger, that's all."

"It's okay," Inga said, actually smiling. It's rare to see such a large, masculine looking woman smile so sweetly. She had such deep feelings for Prunella and wanted her to be safe and happy. I hope when this is over the two of them can remain together.

We hung out at the burger joint for a long time. Finally, we stood to leave. George paid and we walked out into the dark, cool night. "Do we need to get any supplies since we still have about an hour to burn?"

"Blankets, water, and maybe a gun would be nice," Inga said.

"No gun," Prunella demanded. "We're not going to get involved in a gun battle. We'll all be killed!"

"I agree," George replied. "Anyway, I have blankets in the trunk and I also have a gun back there, too."

Prunella stared at George in astonishment. "You own a gun?"

"Of course I do, Prunella. I bought one the minute I started doing business at Eklund's home. I felt safer knowing I had one, just in case."

"I'm so sorry to put you in that position, George," Prunella said sweetly. "I never wanted to get you involved."

"You didn't have a choice, Prunella. It's okay, I made the final choice to be involved."

We drove around town for a while and then headed back toward the water. It was just after eight in the evening when we passed Eklund's Industries.

"Where should we park the car?" George inquired.

"What about in Eklund's parking lot? It's huge and plenty of cars are still parked there."

"That's because they work twenty-four hours shifts. There's always a shift working, even on holidays," Prunella mentioned. "Remember, I was Axel's assistant for a while."

"That's right," I said. "Did you know anything about mysterious shipments at night?"

"No, Ruth Ann, Axel never filled me in on that end of his business."

George pulled in a spot between two cars. We grabbed a couple blankets from the trunk (I'm pretty sure I noticed George grab his gun, too) and started to walk toward the water. We didn't want to be spotted, so we went down the alley behind the buildings on the way down to the water.

"Where are we going to hide?" Inga inquired.

"There's got to be several places. Let's get close and see what we can find," George said

We were close to the long pier when we noticed several trucks making their way down to the water. "Look," I said, seeing them first. "We need to take cover before their headlights spot us."

We rushed behind a large dumpster about fifty yards away from where the trucks were lining up. "It's still early, but now we wait and see what happens," I said.

Chapter 28

JOHN WILKINSON

We finished our food and decided to head back to the water to find a hiding place near the pier. "We really don't know the timing or if anything will go down tonight," Judy said, wiping her mouth.

"I know in my gut that this will be over with tonight, Judy. Take my word for it as a cop, it'll be over."

"I hope so."

"The longer this goes on, the worse the outcome for Ruth Ann," I said, getting into the driver's seat of the rental. "You know the statistics, Judy. It's been too long already."

"She's a tough lady, John. I'm sure Ruth Ann's giving them hell!"

I laughed a little to myself, picturing Ruth Ann as a prisoner to anyone. She wouldn't take that for one minute and yet it's been days. We drove back to Eklund's business and parked in the lot. It was still full of cars since the factory had shifts around the clock. "Safety in numbers," I said to Judy, parking next to another car.

"We could be waiting a long time if that girl told us the correct time," Judy declared, looking at her watch. "It's only ten minutes after eight."

"We don't have anything else to do at the moment, and I would hate myself if we missed Eklund."

We walked down the deserted street and headed for the long pier. I noticed a line-up of Eklund Industries trucks down at the pier. "They're already here."

"Let's get closer, John. Guns out?"

"Definitely," I replied, grabbing my gun. "These guys are killers."

Judy and I made are way to within fifty yards of where the trucks were lining up. "There's lots of places we can take cover. Why don't we head over to those sheds?" Judy pointed to a row of storage sheds that were on the right side of the pier.

"It's a good spot. We'll still be able to see what's coming off those trucks."

We snuck around the backside of the trucks and stood between the first two storage sheds. There was a three feet wide space between each of the sheds, giving us plenty of space to hide.

"Now we wait," I said. It was eight thirty according to my watch.

Chapter 29

RUTH ANN

I wanted to get a little closer to where the trucks were parked so we could see what was being hauled off of them. I spotted a large blue tarp covering a very large object much closer to the pier. It was pretty dark out and I couldn't make out what was underneath. "Maybe we could go on the other side of the tarp," I suggested.

"I don't know if the four of us will be concealed there," George stated. "What about those storage sheds on the other side of the dock? I bet we could easily see from there."

"The problem is getting to the other side of the dock. We'd have to walk by the trucks to get over there," Inga commented.

"That could be a problem," he said. "I do agree with Ruth Ann that we need to get a little closer. From here we can't see what they'll be unloading."

We chose to take cover by sneaking over to the blue tarp. George and I went first, and we planned to wave the others over if it were a safe location. The tarp was halfway between where we currently were and the pier. I ducked down low, and we took off toward the tarp.

"We need to see what's under this tarp," George said, peeking under it. "If it's something they'll need for the boat, then we may not be safe here."

"What's under there, can you tell yet?" I asked impatiently.

"It's just wooden pallets," George replied. "I doubt it's anything they would use tonight. It's only covered so the water doesn't rot the wood."

George waved the two women over, and shortly we were settled on the side of the tarp, waiting. It was now eight-thirty at night according to George's watch.

"We need to keep a lookout, not only for what they'll be unloading, but for Bertha's brothers, too," George said. "They could be almost anywhere."

"We could each watch a different location," I said. "When there's activity at one of them, whether it's unloading the trucks, Axel or the brothers, then we'll shift our attention there."

"Unless more than one thing happens at a time," Inga muttered.

"What?" I asked her.

"Bertha and her brothers might come up the same time as Mr. Eklund does from another area. We need to watch every direction."

"Fine," I said. "How about when anything happens we start recording with our cell phones?"

"Oh yeah, that's a great idea, Ruth Ann," Prunella declared. "That way we can go to the police and show them what's happening. They can't disregard us then."

"Sounds like the best plan I've heard in a while, Ruth Ann," George said.

We leaned against the pile and watched not only the trucks, but also the street of deserted buildings and the ships on the pier. Inga kept a lookout from behind. We didn't want anyone sneaking up on us. The time passed slowly, but finally we noticed the drivers of the trucks get out and lift the back gate of their trucks. They were starting to unload.

"Look," I said, pointing at the trucks. "It's time. We need to see if Andy and David show up, too."

"Axel, too," Prunella added. "He should be here."

"There he is!" I cried.

"Shhh," George said, grabbing my arm down.

"Sorry, I got excited." We watched as Axel and Finn got out of one of the trucks located directly opposite us. They walked around and inspected each truck's contents. There were loads and loads of boxes piling up next to the trucks. Several men were working quickly and Finn was yelling at some of them. "Get it moving!" "We don't have all night!" Finn would holler.

"Any sign of Bertha and her brother's?" I asked, watching Axel closely.

"Not yet, but they have quite a bit of work still to do," George replied. "They'll probably wait till some of these workers take off."

"Makes sense," I said. "I wonder if Finn and Axel stay with the boxes until the ship leaves?"

"If all those boxes are drugs or stolen merchandise, I bet they do!" Prunella exclaimed. "The lights on the farthest boat on the pier were on now. That must be the ship the boxes will be loaded onto."

"Has to be," George answered. "So they must unload the trucks and then haul the boxes to the ship and load them on there. This could take a while."

"There must to be a dozen men. I'm sure they move pretty quick with Finn threatening them," Prunella declared. "He keeps yelling at them to move faster. Tell him to help if he wants it done faster."

"Look at all those boxes," I commented. "There must be a hundred or more already unloaded."

"What kind of business are they running?" George questioned, not expecting a response.

Inga halted her focus on her lookout and added, "An illegal one! That's why he's so rich and buys everybody off. This is why we couldn't go to the police. He would find out and we'd all be dead."

"He'd have to catch us first," I told Inga. "We did pretty good getting away from him earlier."

"He wasn't expecting it. Now he's got to be absolutely furious, and if he caught up with us we'd be in serious trouble," Inga remarked.

"We'll be fine, Inga," Prunella said. "Let's just wait and see when Bertha and the boys show up. They won't be looking for us after Axel gets his shipment robbed."

"Wait," I said, interrupting her. "How are Andy and David going to take over this shipment? There's Axel, Finn, and all the men working, and I bet they're armed."

"Once they get the boxes on the ship, the truckers will take off. All that'll remain will be Eklund, Finn, and the crew on the ship. If the brothers surprise them, it wouldn't be impossible to carry off," George explained. "Or, they have more men joining them."

"That's a possibility," I said. "We're in way over our heads here. I suggest we stay here only as witnesses and not get involved."

"I agree," George said. "I have a gun, but that won't do us any good if we're up against several armed men."

"But we can't let them get away with it," Inga demanded. "Either Eklund gets off with his stolen goods or Bertha and her brothers do. They have to be stopped."

"We'll stop them. It might not be here tonight, but if we have a video of what happens, then we can turn them in without risking our lives," George explained. "I know you want them to pay, but we need more help for that to happen and we're not exactly in the best position right now to get that."

"If I ever see an opportunity to catch one of them, I plan on taking them down," Inga declared. "One at a time suits me just fine." Inga had a wild look in her eyes that assured me she could succeed in hurting any one of the men.

"How long has it been since they started unloading?" I asked.

"It's almost ten and it looks like the unloading is complete. They're piling the boxes on dollies and starting to pull them down the pier toward the boat," George noticed. "They're putting three boxes on each dolly, and with a dozen men they should be done in an hour or so."

"Any sign of Bertha or her brothers yet?" Prunella asked this time. "They have to be around here somewhere."

"Maybe we should take a look around?" I inquired. "Two of us could sneak around the trucks to the other side and take a peek by those storage sheds."

"That's risky, Ruth Ann," George said. "I think we're safe here."

"But we're getting nowhere," I said frustrated. "Maybe we can see better from over on the other side, and spot where Bertha and her brothers are."

"What good would it do?" Prunella asked. "We can't do anything to them if we see them."

"I can!" Inga declared. "If I had a chance, I could easily take down those two spineless men. Especially if they didn't see me coming."

"Inga, please," Prunella said. "We can't alert attention to us. If you get into it with her brothers you may raise attention to us, and Axel and his men will come running. Then what happens?"

"Okay, I get it," Inga said, resigned. "I'll behave and not go after them for now."

We sat down next to the pile, low to the ground while we watched the men wheel down box after box and put them on the ship. Axel and Finn had moved to the ship and we couldn't see them anymore. I felt they were getting close to being finished when I suggested we have a look around one more time.

"There isn't anyone hanging around the trucks," I explained. "We can walk to the other side of the pier from here and have a look around. I just can't sit here and wait any longer!"

"Fine," George finally agreed with my suggestion. "It looks like nothing's going to happen anyway. I can't see Bertha or her brothers running down the pier toward the boat waving a gun and holding up a ship."

"That would be a sight to see," I said. "Finn would gun them down long before they were near their precious ship."

"OK, Ruth Ann, why don't you and I go and check things out?"

"Why can't I go, too?" Inga asked, frustrated. "You two always get to go and check things out."

"Here's a plan," I interrupted. "Why don't we all go? There are more hiding places over there anyway between those storage sheds. If we see any sign of Bertha and her brothers we can duck in between the sheds."

"I agree," Prunella said. "It's probably safer over there."

The four of us carefully walked toward the side of the trucks opposite of the pier. There were no men hanging around since Finn had them hauling the boxes to the ship. We went around a few trees and were about to reach the sheds when a headlight from a car almost hit us. "Get down!" George shouted, pulling Prunella to the ground.

Inga and I dropped as fast as we could as we watched a dark colored sedan pull up near the line of trucks. The car stopped at the pile of pallets under the blue tarp. "Wow," Inga said. "We would've been in big trouble if we stayed over there."

"You're welcome," I said to the group. "Do you think it's Bertha and her brothers?"

George tried to see who was in the car, but nobody exited the vehicle. We crawled toward the storage sheds, when out of the blue a light shone in our direction and spotted us. We were caught!

George pulled his gun out of his jacket pocket and hid it behind his back. He didn't want whoever was about to approach to know he had a gun. We stayed on the ground on hands and knees. All we could make out was two pairs of legs walking toward us, shining a bright light at us. It had to be the light from their cell phones or a flashlight. As the strangers got near, George whispered not to make any quick moves. "We don't want them to react to us. Just stay frozen until we see who's coming toward us."

It felt like the two people were walking toward us in slow motion. All I could feel was the pounding of my heart and I needed to breathe. I started to make out the shapes as they approached. It was a man and a woman from what I could tell, and then the most unbelievable thing happened. One of them wore a leather jacket with the Deer Creek Police Department emblem and name, Chief J. Wilkinson on the front!

Chapter 30

I jumped up before George could stop me and ran toward him. Unfortunately, I saw John before he saw me, and he raised his gun to fire. "Stop right there," he shouted.

"John, no, it's me, Ruth Ann!" I cried, holding my arms high above my head just in case.

He lowered his gun ever so slowly and stood, frozen, in shock. Judy, yes, Judy the detective I didn't care for, was with him and spoke first. "Ruth Ann?"

"Yes, it's me," I said, lowering my arms and walking closer to them.

"Ruth Ann?" John said quietly, putting his gun away. "I must be imagining things...Judy, is it really her?"

Judy smiled, patted him on the back and gave him a little shove toward me, "You just got a miracle."

"I'll say," John said, grabbing me and squeezing me so tightly I thought I'd burst.

"Whoa, John," I said, trying to regain my breath. "I'm fine."

"I can't believe you're standing smack dab in front of me! I've been searching so long, and out of nowhere, here you are!"

"Yes, but what are you two doing here? How did you end up here?" I asked, totally confused.

"It's a very long story, Ruth Ann," Judy answered.

George, still kneeling on the ground cleared his throat. "Hmmm, can we all get up?"

"Oh, I almost forgot about you guys," I said, turning around.

John motioned for Inga, Prunella, and George to stand. "We need to get to a safer location first."

John grabbed my arm and we walked over to the storage sheds and took cover between the first and second shed. "I still can't believe you're here with me."

"I know," I said, smiling at him. "It's been a very long few days, and I have so much to tell you, but first we need to get through what's happening right now."

"Yes," John said. "Eklund's dealing drugs illegally and they're loading them onto that ship now," John stated, pointing over at the large, lit up ship on the pier. "Judy and I discovered this from various people and we ended up here tonight on a hunch Eklund would show up. We planned on grabbing him and demanding he take us to you. But somehow you escaped with these people?" John eyed the others and asked, "Who are these people, Ruth Ann?"

"Yes, John, this is Inga, Axel's housekeeper. Prunella, that's a very long story." John was about to speak, but I held up my hand to stop him. "And this is George, he's a doctor. Don't ask, sounds very strange, but when I tell you how this all happened, it'll make sense.

"This is the strangest group of people I've ever heard of," Judy mumbled.

"We need to see who's in that car on the other side of the pier," George said watching the vehicle in the distance. "I'll bet my medical license that it's Bertha and/or her brothers in there."

"Excuse me, who?" Judy asked before John could.

I asked George, Inga, and Prunella to keep an eye on the ship and the car while I did a quick rundown of what's happened over the last few days. I couldn't tell them everything, just the basics, but they grasped what had happened and agreed we should wait and see who does what first.

"If Bertha's brothers are here we can stop them before they get to the ship," Judy said. "Then we can demand they turn over the necklace and arrest them. I'm sure the local police can't deny us that right of power."

"If they have it with them, which I highly doubt," Prunella mentioned. We turned to her and she quickly added, "Why would they risk bringing it here? If any problems emerged they could lose the necklace again."

"True," John answered her. "But they'll know where it is and we can easily handle the two of them."

"And Bertha, if she's with them," Inga said. "She won't give up that necklace easily since she wants to use it to get to Mr. Eklund."

"I doubt the man would marry her and feign love just for the necklace. The man's a millionaire, what's a necklace?" Judy questioned.

"Ha," Prunella laughed. "That necklace is more important to them than any amount of money."

"That, Ruth Ann, you'll have to explain at another time," John stated.

"Wait!" George called, pointing at the car. "The driver's door just opened up."

"I can't see who's getting out," Inga said, pushing her way to the front of us to look around the shed.

A few seconds more and a figure we knew stood up and waited next to the sedan. "It's David," I said. I quickly explained to John and Judy that it was one of the brothers, the smart one, not the bigger, bully, Andy.

"Andy's there, too," Prunella pointed out. "He just got out of the back seat behind the driver's side. They're talking between the two of them, but why would Andy be in the back seat?"

"That's why," I said. "Bertha's walking around toward her brothers. She must've been sitting in the passenger's front seat."

"Let's go get them," Inga cried out. "It's all of us against them!"

"No," John declared, grabbing Inga's arm. "We wait and see what their next move is."

"But then they'll be on the ship and we won't get any of them," she complained.

"Not necessarily," Judy said, smiling. "We get them with the merchandise as they come off the pier. We need to catch them after they stole Eklund's goods. If that makes any sense whatsoever!"

"Yes, it does," I replied. "Axel's shipping out stolen jewelry or other merchandise, and now Bertha and her brothers are stealing from him."

"Exactly," Judy said and explained, "We can catch both parties for stolen goods then they all go down for a very long time."

"That's if we catch them," George mentioned.

"We will," Judy declared, loading her gun with ammunition from her pocket. "They will not get one foot off that pier."

We must have looked a pretty sight. Leaning over the edge of the storage shed, we were lined up from the ground up as Bertha,

David, and Andy opened the trunk and grabbed a rifle and a couple guns. We watched as they loaded them, and David and Andy walked toward the pier. Bertha stayed back at the car. "She didn't go with them," I said. "Why?"

"Isn't that obvious, Ruth Ann?" Prunella answered. "She doesn't want Axel to think badly of her. She's still holding out hope that she'll end up with him."

"Did you forget one very important thing?" George mentioned. "Eklund's still very married, to Prunella."

"I tend to forget about that myself," Prunella stated, and turned to look at George. "That'll be taken care of as soon as this is all over."

George grabbed Prunella's hand and gave it a squeeze. I didn't know who noticed him do that, but I sure did. I knew there was more between those two than a doctor-patient relationship. Prunella spotted me staring at the two of them and gave me a slight smile. I wanted her to be happy. She had a rough childhood. Her parents taught her so much hatred toward another family. It was time for her to enjoy her life. Maybe when this is all over I could convince her to move back to Deer Creek with me. She has family there now, and we could help her live a normal, happy life.

But first, we need to get out of our current dilemma. I didn't want any of us to be a casualty. In a strange sort of way, I felt close to all these people and would be happy if they could come back home with me. "The brothers are walking up the pier," John said, getting my head back in the game. "I'm going to get a closer look now."

The brothers were smart, waiting in their car until all the trucks departed. They thought they had to only deal with Axel and Finn. But what they didn't know, was that we were here, too.

Judy followed John after explicitly telling us to stay where we were. Within a second they disappeared into the shallow water, and were creeping up to the side of the pier. The waves were high, and water splashed vigorously against the wooden pier. Once I saw Judy slip and fall after a wave hit her at the knees. John grabbed her arm, which I didn't care for, but I knew he was a gentleman, and he helped her up. They patiently waited for David and Andy to get all the way down to the ship before they pulled themselves up onto the pier from the water.

"I hope Bertha doesn't spot them," George said, keeping a sharp eye on Bertha.

"She won't," Inga said. "She's getting inside the driver's side of the car."

"Probably wants to be ready for when they come running down the pier with their stolen goods," Prunella said.

"Little does she know they won't get that far," I replied.

We stayed at the front of the sheds to get a better view of the ship. John and Judy practically crawled up to the aft of the ship. The brothers were nowhere in sight. We didn't have any choice but to wait and see what happens.

Time passed slowly. What could be taking so long? Prunella and George were talking quietly amongst themselves, and Inga was with me, watching for any movement either at the ship or the car. I settled back against the shed when, out of nowhere, I heard a loud bang come from the direction of the ship. "What's happening? Can any of you see anything?"

The four of us ran toward the pier and jumped down on the sand at the edge of the water. We made our way into the icy water until the edge of the pier was about shoulder height for me. I didn't think I'd be able to pull myself up onto the pier from this height, but none of us knew what our next move would be. "I can't see anything from here!"

George pulled himself up so that he was hanging on the edge of the pier. "I can see," he stated. "It looks like someone is running off the boat onto the pier. Stay down," George demanded.

We waited as we heard footsteps get louder and louder as whoever it was ran down the pier toward land. George had ducked down to stay undercover, but as the runner came closer he peeked over the edge. "It's Axel!"

"What?" I cried, as quietly as I could. "Why would he run off?"

"He's going towards Bertha's car," George told us. "What's happening? Why would he go there?"

We moved ourselves to a lower part of the pier where we could see over the edge. We watched as Axel got into the passenger side of the car.

"Did she start the engine?" I asked.

"Not yet," George answered. "I'm going to get a better view of the ship. Stay here," he demanded. "I'm going in."

Prunella tried to stop him, but he pulled himself up on the pier too fast and ran towards the ship. "Maybe we should all go?" Prunella asked, frantic.

"Yes, let's go," Inga agreed. She'd been ready to get in the action for quite some time now, and nobody was going to stop her.

Just as the three of us stood on the pier, dripping wet, we heard more loud bangs. "That's gunshots," I cried. "I don't know if us running up there is going to help anyone."

"I need to make sure George is OK," Prunella demanded. "You can stay back, but I'm going in."

Prunella ran ahead of us and Inga and I followed. By the time we arrived at the plank that would take us to the ship I was breathing heavily. It was longer down the pier than it appeared, and I was desperately trying to catch my breath. All those workouts on the elliptical should've prepared me better than this.

We jumped onto the lower deck of the ship. I tried to count the rows of windows to see how many stories were on the ship and I counted ten. "This ship is huge," I stated. "How are we going to find them?"

There was no time for a response, because suddenly a door flew open and we dropped ourselves down on the ground near a large metal box. "Look," I whispered. "It's the brothers."

"If Axel and the brothers are out, where are John, Judy, and George?" Prunella asked anxiously.

"Don't forget about Finn," Inga said.

"Something's not right," I said, looking at the men hop off the ship and hurry down the pier.

We waited for a minute when the door flew open again and John, Judy, and George exited. I stood up and was about to run over to them when Inga pulled me down. "Look," she pointed. "Finn's behind them with a gun!"

"Oh, no," Prunella cried out. "He's caught them."

"But I didn't see anyone come off the ship with any merchandise. What were they doing?" I asked curiously. "This is all too strange."

We watched as Finn rushed them off the ship, and as I stood up I accidentally knocked over a metal bucket full of water. The three of us froze, praying Finn wouldn't turn around to investigate the noise. "I don't think he heard you, Ruth Ann," Inga said. "He's shoving the gun in your chief's back, telling him to hurry. Why do they have to hurry?"

We soon found out. John or Judy must've spotted us hiding there because Judy's voice bellowed, *"We need to run! That bomb's going to blow in three minutes according to my count-down."*

It took a few seconds for us to process what we just heard. There was a bomb on the boat and we had to get off, NOW! I pulled Prunella up and she grabbed Inga's arm, and we ran down the pier without caring who saw us. Finn, Judy, John, and George were almost at the end. They were way ahead of us when Prunella tripped over a raised piece of wood in the pier and wiped out. "Inga, help her up!" I yelled, grabbing one arm and Inga the other.

"No, I think I twisted my ankle," Prunella exclaimed. "I can't walk."

Prunella threw her arms around Inga's neck, and she picked her up as if she was a bag of feathers. We went as fast as we could when John spotted us. He shoved Finn off the pier into the freezing water and came running back toward us. Finn didn't have time to react before he landed in the water, and by the time he pulled himself back up onto the pier his gun wasn't in his hand.

"John," I said, out of breath. "Prunella twisted her ankle and we're almost out of time."

He scooped her out of Inga's arms and told us to run. Finn was at the end of the pier waiting for us. John thrust Prunella back into Inga's arms and ran directly at Finn. Finn was waiting with a huge grin on his face. "Move, Finn," John demanded. "It's you against me," John said, as George and Judy made their way to him to lend a hand.

"I can take all of you," he declared, crossing his arms across his chest. "I don't need a weapon, just my hands."

"The bomb's gonna blow in a few seconds, let's get off this pier!" Judy insisted.

"Get past me first," Finn said with a horrible grin on his face.

John didn't care what Finn said; he bulldozed his way up to Finn slamming him to the ground with one blow. Finn fell instantly and held his hands to his stomach.

"Forget about him now," John yelled. "Get off the pier and run as far from it as you can."

We abandoned Finn and ran into the grass toward the street where the trucks used to be. I glanced over at the car where Axel and Bertha were and it was still parked there. I couldn't tell if anyone was in there, but where would they go?

Within seconds a massive explosion went off and the entire pier and ship were blown to smithereens. We barely made it off and far enough away to avoid the pieces of debris that were flying everywhere. "That was too close for me," I shouted over the loud noise.

John ran over to me and I assured him I was okay. "I think Finn met an ugly, but quick, death."

"There's no way he escaped that one," George stated.

Judy grabbed John's arm and exclaimed, "We need to get to Eklund and that Bertha woman before they take off."

"Wait," I said. "Where are her brothers? Did anyone see where they went, too?"

"Maybe they're in the car, too?" Inga asked, finally setting Prunella back on her feet after she insisted her ankle was better.

"With Eklund?" John asked. "That would make no sense from everything you told me. Eklund and Bertha's brothers are on opposite sides."

"You're right, John," I answered. "They can't be with Axel and Bertha. But why did Axel go to Bertha in the first place?"

"Look," Inga shouted. "They started the car, hurry, we need to follow them."

"We're on foot, Inga. We can't possibly catch up with them," Prunella said.

"Unless they're only going as far as his building," George added. "That's where we parked our car."

"Hey, so did we," Judy stated. "Knowing the way this case is going, we're probably parked next to each other!"

"Let's go," John said, grabbing my arm and running toward the street. "We don't have any time to waste."

The six of us took off down the block and passed Bertha and her brothers" leased apartment. I glanced in the direction of the apartment and couldn't see any lights. John was dragging me so fast I didn't have a choice but to keep up. Good thing it was only a short distance to Eklund Industries.

We made it to the parking lot and saw our cars. They weren't next to each other, but only a few spots apart. John went into the trunk of their rented car and pulled out three guns. He handed one to Judy and George, and kept the last one for himself.

"We all should have a gun," Inga demanded. "I'm a good shooter."

"It's all we have and we have no time to argue." John looked at Prunella and asked her if there was anywhere she thought Axel and Bertha may have escaped to.

"His office," she answered. "He's got the whole top floor of the building for his personal use. There's an office for him, a gym, a small kitchen, a bathroom and even a huge conference room. I know the way." She took the lead and we headed for the front door.

Inga reached for the glass door and it wouldn't open. "It's locked. Now what do we do?"

"This," Prunella replied, pulling out a key from her dress pocket. "I brought it just in case."

"You have a key?" Judy asked suspiciously.

"I use to spend a lot of time here when I worked for him. I had a couple copies made months ago."

"Great, open it, Prunella," John said, reaching for the handle.

Once inside, Prunella took over. She led us to a private set of elevators that only went to the sixth floor. We piled in and she pressed the up button.

"What if he hears us coming?" Inga asked.

"We don't even know if they're there yet, Inga," Judy said, loading her gun with the extra bullets. "Did any of you see Bertha's car?"

"They probably parked out back," Prunella answered. "He always parks back there. It's closer to his private elevator."

Once the elevator stopped, the doors opened without a sound. I was thankful, just in case Axel, Bertha or her brothers were waiting there. We exited the elevator and stepped into a lobby area with a large, modern, glass desk opposite the elevator. There was no one at the desk.

"Where do we go from here, Prunella?" asked John.

"His private office. Follow me," she answered. We followed Prunella to the left and headed down a wide hallway. We passed by the kitchen, workout area, and a luxurious bathroom from what

I could see. Finally, at the very end, we reached a large set of wooden, double doors that were closed. "Here we are."

The three with the guns aimed them directly at the door. "We're going to go in on the count of three," John ordered. "You ready?"

Judy and George nodded. I noticed George's hand was trembling a bit and wondered if John should've given the gun to Inga. She was rocking back and forth ready to jump. John told the rest of us to stay back and wait until he gave us a sign to enter.

John whispered, "One...two...three." John kicked the door to the right and it flew open. The three of them rushed in and I lost sight of them. I didn't follow John's orders. Once I couldn't see them and didn't hear any noise, I ran toward the door. Inga and Prunella followed me and we stopped at the doorway.

"Where'd they go?" Inga asked, gazing in the large office.

"I know," Prunella said, grabbing both my arm and Inga's. We ran through Axel's office toward a door at the opposite side of the room.

"Where does this go to?" I asked, looking around the office. All I could see was a desk, some red leather couches, a round table with four chairs, and floor to ceiling windows that overlooked the burning pier and ship.

"He has more rooms back in here," Prunella said, stepping through the door into another dark hallway. "I forgot about this area. He's got a bedroom back here with another bathroom. But I don't think they went there."

"Where then?" I asked, frustrated. How big was this office?

"He's got another room that contains his safe."

"That has to be where they went," Inga shouted.

We rushed down the hall past the rooms and stopped dead at the end of the hallway. "Wait, we must have passed it," I said. "There's nowhere else to go."

"Ah, but there is, Ruth Ann," Prunella said, feeling the back wall with her hands. "I believe the button is...here!" A door slid open, and before we had time to think clearly, the three of us dashed in. Well, that was a bit of a mistake!

"Hands up, Ruth Ann," Axel said immediately, pointing a gun at me. I immediately did what he asked and so did Inga and Prunella. Axel motioned us to a round, wooden table where we found

John, Judy, and George sitting. They were quietly sitting, watching as Axel escorted the three of us toward the table.

"Where's Bertha?" I asked, wondering if Axel would tell me.

"In there," he said, pointing to a large, safe room. "She's finally putting my possession safely away."

"The necklace?" Prunella asked, knowing the answer.

"Yes, Prunella," Axel said, walking over to the chair Prunella was sitting in. "I knew you weren't sick after I found you all missing. I figured George was pulling a fast one on me."

"You've been horrible to me, Axel," Prunella said, crying. "I loved you and you treated me like I was your servant!"

"I loved you too, at first," he said, putting his hands on her shoulders. "But you didn't understand everything. This necklace is the one thing I had to get back."

"Why, Axel?" she asked, brushing his hands away.

Axel walked over toward the safe and glanced in. "I needed the necklace to save my company."

"What?" I asked. "You only cared about your business? What about Prunella, your marriage, and me? You were willing to kill people to save your company?"

Axel glared over at me and said, "This company is my legacy. I would never be able to live with myself if I let the company go under. My father and grandfather built this company, and I helped it grow into a colossal, money making regime. I will not let it go down because of me!"

"You can't be financially down, Axel," Prunella said. "You make ship after ship and they cost hundreds of thousands of dollars. What have you done to ruin your business?"

Bertha stepped out of the safe and answered that question for him. "He became greedy and started dealing in stolen jewelry. That's why my brothers hated him so much. Axel stole from them and forced them to commit murder in order to keep their own business."

"So that's why they went to Deer Creek?" I asked. "To steal back the necklace and screw over Axel?"

"Yes," Bertha answered. "They were contacted by the lawyer, Svenson, to retrieve it for him. They never intended on giving it to him. My brothers used Svenson for money to get themselves to your stupid little town and back here so they could sell it and make money to reopen their failing business."

"All they had to do was give it to me, Bertha, and I would've opened their business for them. None of this would've happened," Axel said.

"You mean your precious ship and pier wouldn't have been blown up?" Bertha said sarcastically. "I didn't know they were planning on doing that. They were furious with you and it was the only thing they could think of to destroy you."

"But that didn't happen, did it Bertha?"

"What do you mean?" I asked curiously.

"Bertha just now put the necklace into a secure box in my safe. Her brothers watched her do it, didn't they?"

"Andy and David are in the safe room?" I asked.

"Yep," Axel replied. "They're tied up and not going anywhere. They'll die watching the box where the necklace now rests, safe and sound."

"What are your plans for the rest of us?" I asked.

"That's a problem, Ruth Ann," he stated. "I can handle disposing of those two idiots and Bertha, but you all are another situation."

"Just let us go," Prunella said hopefully.

"Now you know I can't do that either, Prunella," Axel replied. "You know what I've done to get this necklace and where it is." He stopped talking and I could tell he was deep in thought. Finally, he said, "I can't put you in the room with Bertha's brothers. There's not enough room in there. However, there are many other places in this building I could hold you in until I come up with a plan."

"You're going to kill us, aren't you?" Prunella asked. "What other option do you have, right?"

"Really, Prunella," George interrupted. "Don't give him any ideas."

Prunella glared at George and replied, "He doesn't have a choice, George. The only reason he's not doing it here is because he doesn't have his goons to clean up the mess. Isn't that right, Axel?"

Axel laughed out loud and said, "So true, Prunella. I'll need to make a few calls before I finish the lot of you off."

"This is ridiculous," John said, jumping in on this conversation.

"Do you think that you can get away with seven more murders if you kill all of us?"

"He won't kill me, will you Axel?" Bertha asked intently.

"Why not?" he replied with an evil smirk on his face. "Now that I have my necklace I have no use for you either. Best to start a fresh new life with none of you in it!"

"But you told me we could be together?" she pleaded.

"Bertha!" I cried out. "You're a fool to believe he would want you. He used you just to get the necklace."

"That's not true," Bertha replied. Her eyes filled with tears as she begged Axel to tell the truth. "No, you wouldn't."

"Sorry, Bertha," he started to say. "Ruth Ann's correct. I never wanted you, and I did use you."

Bertha's face turned a deep shade of purple, and out of the blue she lunged at Axel, giving John and Judy their moment to end the matter once and for all. But before they could get to Axel, Bertha landed on Axel's chest, and as her arm rose to slap him, Axel's gun fired and Bertha fell to the ground. He shot her right in the middle of her chest.

Before Axel could recover, John grabbed Axel's arms and put them behind his back and seized the gun. Once Bertha attacked Axel it was over in ten seconds.

Axel knew it was over. I ran to Bertha to see if she was still alive, but it was too late. She died with so much rage and hatred. I hoped she was in peace now.

"Judy, cuff him and call this in. We need to check on her brothers."

Once Axel was securely cuffed, Judy went into the safe room and came back immediately. "They're dead," she declared.

"What?" asked John. "How?"

"I would guess a murder-suicide. The big guy was stabbed in the heart and the smaller one slit his own throat."

I was about to go in there when John took my arm and shook his head. "It's not a pretty sight, Ruth Ann" Judy said. "I'm going to call it in from his office. I'll be right back." Judy left the room and the rest of us stood, wondering what to do.

"What about our necklace?" Prunella questioned. "Can't we get it out of the safe since it isn't Axel's?"

"It is mine!" Axel demanded.

"You won't need it where you're going," John said, shoving him against the wall so he had nowhere to go. "We're going to stay right where we are until the local police show up."

We remained in Axel's building for another couple hours. We were exhausted and John suggested we go back to Eklund's house and get some sleep. Axel was taken into custody and Judy and John followed him to the police station. John promised he would come to the house once the paperwork was finished.

Prunella, George, Inga, and myself went out to our car in the parking lot in silence. "What now?" Inga inquired.

"I'm not sure, Inga," Prunella replied. "I guess we go back get some sleep and see what the police and your friends tell us."

It was the middle of the night by the time we arrived back at Axel's estate. Sherman was frantically waiting for us. The front door flew open as the headlights pulled up to the front of the house. He ran over to our car and opened up the passenger door where Prunella was sitting. "Thank God, you're all here. What happened?"

None of us wanted to relive the experience, but felt it was only right to fill Sherman in on the whole night. We ended up in the kitchen and Inga fixed us a feast. I didn't realize how hungry I was. We each spoke as eggs, bacon, and toast were being shoved into our mouths.

"I really missed it," Sherman said angrily. "I could've helped you all."

"Sherman, if it wasn't for Chief John and Detective Judy, none of us might've survived," I said.

Once Sherman was satisfied with each of our versions, we headed to our rooms to sleep. I didn't even change my clothes. I fell into my bed and before I knew it, I woke to John's face staring back at me. "Ah, you're finally awake," he said, smiling.

I sat upright and noticed the sun creeping in through the heavy, red velvet curtains. "What time is it?" I asked, stretching.

"It's noon, Ruth Ann," he replied. "You were exhausted, rightfully so."

"Oh, no," I said, hopping out of bed. "Where's everybody else?"

"They're all in the dining room eating a late breakfast. Why don't you freshen up and meet me down there?"

"Give me five minutes and I'll be down," I said, running into the bathroom.

I arrived in the dining room to find Prunella and George sitting next to each other at the table. Inga and Sherman had reprised their positions as butler and housekeeper and were serving them. John was on his cell phone standing in the corner.

"Where's Judy?" I asked.

"She's here somewhere," John answered, finishing his call.

"Who were you talking to, John?"

"Your daughters," he said hesitantly. "Don't be mad at me, you can speak with them soon. I thought it best to fill them in myself. They needed to hear you were safe."

"But I need to…" but John cut me off. "Eat. Then you can call them. They've been reassured about your safety and are eager to speak with you."

I knew I wouldn't win this argument, so I sat on the opposite side of the table from Prunella and George. "I'm glad you were able to get some sleep, Ruth Ann," Prunella said, smiling across the table at me.

"I slept from the minute my head hit the pillow. That never happens."

"You've been through a huge ordeal, Ruth Ann," George said to me. "I'm surprised you're here now. Many people in your situation would sleep through the entire day."

"So, George, you really are a doctor?" I asked him.

"Yes, Ruth Ann, I really am a doctor."

John waited until I had finished a pile of chocolate chip pancakes before he spoke to me. "It's all settled here in Stockholm. We can leave on a flight tomorrow morning and have you back at your house soon after we land."

"That's great, John," I said, realizing I wasn't as happy as it sounded. I looked across the table at Prunella and George smiling at me and said, "What about you two? And Inga and Sherman? What will happen with all of you?"

"Actually, Ruth Ann, I have to tell you all one more thing." John hesitated for a moment to make sure we all were paying attention, and then he told us the most shocking news. "Axel Eklund was stabbed in his cell. He's dead and none of you have to worry about him ever again about him," John added, "Since he's dead,

Prunella is Eklund's legal heir. She'll inherit the house and all that's left of his estate. It's quite a large amount if you ask me."

"Really?" I said happily. "You deserve it, Prunella."

Prunella smiled sweetly and said, "Thanks, Ruth Ann, but it's not all going to be mine, I decided."

"What do you mean?" I inquired.

"Well, once all the legal matters are settled I'd like to share it with you and your family."

"Me, why?" I asked, shocked by her announcement.

"Because you and I are the only family left outside of your sister and daughters. It's more than I need. I want to do it."

"Please, Prunella, start a fresh life and be happy. I don't need your money." But then a thought popped into my head. "I do have one request, though."

"What?" Prunella asked curiously.

"I'd like to see the necklace."

John interrupted our conversation and said, "That'll be possible soon. Once the police have closed the books on Eklund's case the necklace gets returned to the rightful owner. I'm not sure if that's Prunella or Ruth Ann, though."

At the same time, Prunella said me and I said Prunella. "We can share it," Prunella laughed. "I'll keep it half the year and you get it the other half."

"You think that's wise?" George asked. "From what I've learned that necklace has been nothing but a curse to whoever possesses it."

"Not anymore," I said. "The curse has been officially broken!"

"I agree, Ruth Ann," Prunella said. "But it may be difficult sending it all the way from here to Colorado. Maybe it would be easier to send it only twenty minutes."

John laughed and said it was a little longer of a flight from Stockholm to Colorado than twenty minutes. Prunella clarified her words and said, "Not if I move to Axel's house in the Colorado mountains. Isn't that only about twenty minutes from your town, Ruth Ann?" She quickly added, "I own that house, too, correct?"

I was so stunned from her announcement I forgot to speak. "Ruth Ann?" Prunella asked. "That is if it's okay with you?"

"I couldn't be happier!" I exclaimed. "You're willing to give up your life here and move all the way to Deer Creek? What about

George, Inga, and Sherman? What will happen to them?"

"Well," Prunella began to say, looking at the three of them. "I'm hoping they'll join me and move, too?"

Inga looked so happy I thought she was going to burst. "Oh, Miss Prunella, do you mean it?"

"Of course I do! I want all of you to come and live with us." Prunella turned to George and grabbed his hand. "George, I know it's a lot to ask, but would you be willing to practice medicine there so we can be together?"

George gazed deeply into Prunella's eyes and I suddenly felt uncomfortable about intruding on a very personal moment. But I wasn't going to excuse myself now, so I might as well hear it out. "Prunella, I would go anywhere you did. You must know how I feel by now. You mean everything to me!"

They embraced and I felt a few, warm tears stream down my face. It was such a happy, touching moment that I didn't want it to end. Well, yes I did. It was time to go home!

The next morning we all flew out of Stockholm's airport, and a short eighteen hours later, after a connection in Chicago, we were in Grand Junction, Colorado. Prunella, Inga, and Sherman were with us and George was to follow as soon as he wrapped up his practice back in Stockholm.

A white stretch limo awaited us and we piled in and popped a bottle of champagne. I couldn't wait to get home, Halloween was a few weeks away and I couldn't wait to get back to my store and decorate for the holidays.

"It's your turn, Prunella," I said, grabbing my shirt collar and opening it just enough to unclasp the necklace from my neck.

Prunella laughed and reached her hand out and took the famous blue gem from my hands and put it around her neck. "Are we going to do this all the time, Ruth Ann?"

"Yep, at least in the beginning," I said, chuckling. "You get to wear it for an hour, then it's my turn. That way we'll have to see each other all the time!" We laughed and drank our champagne all the way back to Deer Creek.

"Home," I said. "Finally!

The End

About the Author

Karin Richardson graduated from The University of Iowa with a communications degree. She currently resides in a suburb of Chicago with her family. Richardson's aspiration has always been to complete a series of mystery novels for readers of all ages. *BLUE ICE* is the first book in this series.

Watch for book two!

If you enjoyed this book, please go to amazon.com and leave a review. Every review counts! And please tell your friends about BLUE ICE! Nothing spreads the word better than a happy reader.

www.ingramcontent.com/pod-product-compliance
Lightning Source LLC
Chambersburg PA
CBHW061308170626
46817CB00001B/107